FIRE
SALE

ALSO BY SARA PARETSKY

FIRE SALE

SARA PARETSKY

G. P. PUTNAM'S SONS | NEW YORK

||P

G. P. PUTNAM'S SONS
Publishers Since 1838
Published by the Penguin Group
Penguin Group (USA) Inc., 375 Hudson Street, New York, New York 10014,
USA · Penguin Group (Canada), 90 Eglinton Avenue East, Suite 700, Toronto,
Ontario M4P 2Y3, Canada (a division of Pearson Penguin Canada Inc.) ·
Penguin Books Ltd, 80 Strand, London WC2R 0RL, England · Penguin Ireland,
25 St Stephen's Green, Dublin 2, Ireland (a division of Penguin Books Ltd) ·
Penguin Group (Australia), 250 Camberwell Road, Camberwell, Victoria 3124,
Australia (a division of Pearson Australia Group Pty Ltd) · Penguin Books India
Pvt Ltd, 11 Community Centre, Panchsheel Park, New Delhi–110 017,
India · Penguin Group (NZ), Cnr Airborne and Rosedale Roads, Albany, Auck-
land 1310, New Zealand (a division of Pearson New Zealand Ltd.) · Penguin
Books (South Africa) (Pty) Ltd, 24 Sturdee Avenue, Rosebank, Johannesburg
2196, South Africa

Penguin Books Ltd, Registered Offices:
80 Strand, London WC2R 0RL, England

ISBN 0-399-15279-2

Printed in the United States of America

BOOK DESIGN BY MEIGHAN CAVANAUGH

This is a work of fiction. Names, characters, places, and incidents either are
the product of the author's imagination or are used fictitiously, and any
resemblance to actual persons, living or dead, businesses, companies,
events, or locales is entirely coincidental.

For Rachel, Phoebe, Eva, Samantha, and Maia

—my own hope for change in the world

THANKS

Helen Martin, M.D., was most helpful in coming up with Long QT Syndrome, the heart condition afflicting one of V.I.'s basketball team. I'm grateful for her advice on the condition, its symptoms, and how to treat it. Thanks to Dr. Susan Riter for introducing us.

Mr. Kurt Nebel, the district manager at the CID Recycling and Disposal Facility on 138th Street, was quite generous with his time and expertise in explaining how and where the City of Chicago disposes of its garbage. Dave Sullivan made that important introduction, and also helped me spend time in the churches of South Chicago; I am grateful for all my experiences in that beleaguered community.

The City of Chicago produces over ten thousand tons of garbage a day; keeping up with it is a daunting task. Although the city's landfills have been topped off in the last year or two, and Chicago sends most residential garbage out of town, I have kept the landfill at 122nd Street active for the purposes of this book.

Thanks to Janice Christiansen, president of FlagSource, for letting me visit their factory, and thanks to Beth Parmley for her informed and lively tour. She also suggested the accident described in chapter 44, "The Recording Angel . . . or Devil?" Sandy Weiss, of Packer Engineering, made this connection for me, and provided invaluable technical advice, including photographs of the accident. Fly the Flag does not resemble FlagSource in any way, shape, or form.

Judi Phillips helped with the plant life in V.I.'s childhood garden.

Kathy Lyndes gave generously of her time and experience in many ways, including the painstaking work of finishing the draft. Jolynn Parker and the Fact Factory were most helpful as well. Calliope kept me from withering away in front of the computer by stealing my shoes at appropriate moments. The Senior C-Dog did his usual kneecap-endangering job as first reader, copy editor, and creator of chapter titles.

I owe special thanks to Constantine Argyropoulos for the CDs he created of V.I.'s music, which include all the pieces she's sung or heard over the years. Nick Rudall provided Coach McFarlane's Latin.

This is a work of fiction. Nothing in it is intended to reflect the reality of modern American life. For NFL purists, I moved the 2004 Kansas City–New England game from November 22 to November 15. For readers who fear that V.I. does not sufficiently adulate multinational conglomerates, please remember that she is a fictional character, and her views are not necessarily those of the management.

CHAPTERS

PROLOGUE

I was halfway down the embankment when I saw the red-orange flash. I dropped to the ground and covered my head with my arms. And felt a pain in my shoulder so intense I couldn't even cry out.

Lying facedown in bracken and trash, I breathed in shallow panting breaths, a dog, eyes glazed, until the pain receded enough that I could move. I edged away from the flames on my hands and knees, then drew myself up on my knees and sat very still. I willed my breaths to come slow and deep, pushing the pain far enough away to manage it. Finally, I put a gingerly hand to my left shoulder. A stick. Metal or glass, some piece of the window that had shot out like an arrow from a crossbow. I tugged on the stick, but that sent such a river of agony flowing through me that I started to black out. I curled over, cradling my head on my knees.

When the wave subsided, I looked across at the factory. The back window that had blown apart was awash with fire, blue-red now, a mass so thick I couldn't make out flames, just the blur of hot color. Bolts of fabric were stored there, fueling the blaze.

And Frank Zamar. I remembered him with a sudden appalled jolt.

Where had he been when that fireball blew up? I pushed myself to my feet as best I could and stumbled forward.

Weeping with pain, I pulled out my picklocks and tried to scrabble my way into the lock. It wasn't until my third futile attempt that I remembered my cell phone. I fumbled it out of my pocket and called 911.

While I waited on the fire trucks, I kept trying the lock. The stabbing in my left shoulder made it hard for me to maneuver the thin wards. I tried to brace them with my left hand, but my whole left side was shaking; I couldn't hold the picklocks steady.

I hadn't expected the fire—I hadn't expected anything when I came here. It was only some pricking of unease—dis-ease—that sent me back to Fly the Flag on my way home. I'd actually made the turn onto Route 41 when I decided to check on the factory. I'd made a U-turn onto Escanaba and zigzagged across the broken streets to South Chicago Avenue. It was six o'clock then, already dark, but I could see a handful of cars in Fly the Flag's yard when I drove by. There weren't any pedestrians out, not that there are ever many down here; only a few cars straggled past, beaters, people leaving the few standing factories to head for bars or even home.

I left my Mustang on one of the side streets, hoping it wouldn't attract any roving punk's attention. I tucked my cell phone and wallet into my coat pockets, took my picklocks from the glove compartment, and locked my bag in the trunk.

Under cover of the cold November night, I scrambled up the embankment behind the plant, the steep hill that lifts the toll road over the top of the old neighborhood. The roar of traffic on the Skyway above me blocked any sounds I made—including my own squawk when I caught my foot in a discarded tire and tumbled hard to the ground.

From my perch under the expressway I could see the back entrance and the side yard, but not the front of the plant. When the shift ended at seven, I could just make out the shapes of people plodding to the bus stop. A few cars bumped behind them down the potholed drive to the road.

Lights were still on at the north end of the plant. One of the basement windows facing me also showed a pale fluorescent glow. If Frank Zamar were still on the premises, he could be doing something—anything— from checking inventory to planting dead rats in the vents. I wondered if I could find a crate in the rubble that would get me high enough to see into the back. I was halfway down the hillside, searching through the debris, when the window went briefly dark, then burst into fiery life.

I was still struggling to undo the front lock when sirens keened up South Chicago Avenue. Two trucks, a command car, and a phalanx of blue-and-whites screamed into the yard.

Men in black slickers surrounded me. Easy there, miss, move away, we've got it covered, the ka-chung of axes breaking metal, my God— look at that thing in her shoulder, get her an ambulance, a giant gloved hand scooping me up as easily as if I were an infant, not a 140-pound detective, and then, as I sat sideways on the command car's passenger seat, feet on the ground, panting again, a familiar voice:

"Ms. W., what in Jesus' name are you doing here?"

I looked up, startled, and felt giddy with relief. "Conrad! Where'd you come from? How did you know I was here?"

"I didn't, but I might have guessed if buildings were blowing up on my turf that you'd be close by. What happened?"

"I don't know." The current of pain was sweeping through me again, tugging me loose from my moorings. "Zamar. Where is he?"

"Who's Zamar—your newest victim?"

"Plant owner, commander," a man outside my narrow field of vision said. "Trapped in there."

A walkie-talkie squawked, cell phones rang, men talked, engines clanged, soot-grimed faces carried a charred body. I shut my eyes and let the current pull me away.

I came to briefly when the ambulance arrived. I stumbled to the rear doors on my own, but the EMT crew had to lift me into the back. When they had me strapped in, awkwardly, on my side, the jolting of the ambulance drew me down to a tiny point of pain. If I shut my eyes I felt sick to my stomach, but the light stabbed through me when I opened them.

As we swooped in through the ambulance entrance, I vaguely noticed the hospital's name, but it was all I could do to mutter answers to the questions the triage nurse was asking. I somehow got my insurance card out of my wallet, signed forms, put down Lotty Herschel as my doctor, told them to notify Mr. Contreras if anything happened to me. I tried to call Morrell, but they wouldn't let me use my cell phone, and, anyway, they had me on a gurney. Someone stuck a needle into the back of my hand, other someones stood over me saying they'd have to cut away my clothes.

I tried to protest: I was wearing a good suit under my navy peacoat, but by then the drug was taking hold and my words came out in a senseless gabble. I was never completely anesthetized, but they must have given me an amnesia drug: I couldn't remember them cutting off my clothes or taking out the piece of window frame from my back.

I was conscious by the time I was wheeled to a bed. The drugs and a throb in my shoulder both kept jerking me awake whenever I dozed off. When the resident came in at six, I was awake in that dull, grinding way that comes from a sleepless night and puts a layer of gauze between you and the world.

She'd been up all night herself, handling surgical emergencies like mine; even though her eyes were puffy from lack of sleep, she was young enough to perch on the chair by my bed and talk in a bright, almost perky voice.

"When the window blew apart, a fragment of the frame shot into your shoulder. You were lucky it was cold last night—your coat stopped the bolt from going deep enough to do real damage." She held out an eight-inch piece of twisted metal—mine to keep, if I wanted it.

"We're going to send you home now," she added, after checking my heart and head and the reflexes in my left hand. "It's the new medicine, you know. Out of the operating room, into a cab. Your wound is going to heal nicely. Just don't let the dressing get wet for a week, so no showers. Come back next Friday to the outpatient clinic; we'll change the dressing and see how you're doing. What kind of work do you do?"

"I'm an investigator. Detective."

"So can you stop investigating for a day or two, detective? Get some rest, let the anesthesia work itself out of your system and you'll be fine. Is there anyone you can call to drive you home, or should we get you into a cab?"

"I asked them to call a friend last night," I said. "I don't know if they did." I also didn't know if Morrell could manage the trip down here. He was recovering from bullet wounds that almost killed him in Afghanistan this past summer; I wasn't sure he had the stamina to drive forty miles.

"I'll take her." Conrad Rawlings had materialized in the doorway.

I was too sluggish to feel surprised or pleased or even flustered at seeing him. "Sergeant—or, no, you've been promoted, haven't you? Is it lieutenant now? You out checking on all the victims of last night's accident?"

"Just the ones who raise a red flag when they're within fifty miles of the crime scene." I couldn't see much emotion in his square copper face—not the concern of an old lover, not even the anger of an old lover who'd been angry when he left me. "And, yeah, I've been promoted: watch commander now down at 103rd and Oglesby. I'll be outside the lobby when the doc here pronounces you fit to tear up the South Side again."

The resident signed my discharge papers, wrote me prescriptions for Vicodin and Cipro, and turned me over to the nursing staff. A nurse's aide handed me the remnants of my clothes. I could wear the trousers, although they smelled sooty and had bits of the hillside embedded in them, but my coat, jacket, and rose silk blouse had all been slit across the shoulders. Even my bra strap had been cut. It was the silk shirt that made me start to cry, that and the jacket. They were part of a cherished outfit; I'd worn them in the morning—yesterday morning—to make a presentation to a downtown client before heading to the South Side.

The nurse's aide didn't care about my grief one way or another, but she did agree I couldn't go out in public without any clothes. She went to the charge nurse, who scrounged an old sweatshirt for me from someplace. By the time we'd done all that, and found an orderly to wheel me to the lobby, it was almost nine.

Conrad had used police privilege to park right in front of the entrance. He was asleep when the orderly wheeled me out, but he came to when I opened the passenger door.

"Woof. Long night, Ms. W., long night." He knuckled sleep from his eyes and put the car into gear. "You still in the old crib up by Wrigley? I heard you mention a boyfriend to the doc."

"Yes." To my annoyance, my mouth was dry and the word came out as a squawk.

"Not that Ryerson guy, I trust."

"Not the Ryerson guy. Morrell. A writer. He got shot to pieces last summer covering the Afghanistan war."

Conrad grunted in a way that managed to heap contempt on mere writers who get shot to pieces: he himself had been hit by machine-gun fire in Vietnam.

"Anyway, your sister tells me you haven't taken monastic vows, either." Conrad's sister Camilla sits on the board of the same women's shelter I do.

"You always did have a way with a phrase, Ms. W. Monastic vows. Nope, none of them."

Neither of us spoke again. Conrad turned his police-issue Buick into Jackson Park. We joined a heavy stream of cars, the tag end of the morning rush, filing through the Jackson Park construction zone onto Lake Shore Drive. A feeble autumn sun was trying to break through the cloud cover, and the air had a sickly light that hurt my eyes.

"You called it a crime scene," I finally said, just to break the silence. "Was it arson? Was that Frank Zamar the firemen carried out?"

He grunted again. "No way of knowing till we hear from the medical examiner, but we're assuming it was—talked to the foreman, who said Zamar was the only person left in the building when the shift ended. As far as arson goes—can't tell that, either, not until the arson squad goes through there, but I don't think the guy died from neglect."

Conrad switched the conversation, asking me about my old friend Lotty Herschel—he'd been surprised not to see her down at the hospital with me, her being a doctor and my big protector and all.

I explained I hadn't had time to make any calls. I kept wondering about Morrell, but I wasn't going to share that with Conrad. Probably the hospital hadn't bothered to call him—otherwise, surely, he would've phoned me, even if he couldn't make the drive. I tried not to think of

Marcena Love, sleeping in Morrell's guest room. Anyway, she was frying other fish these days. These nights. I abruptly asked Conrad how he liked being so far from the center of action.

"South Chicago is the center of action, if you're a cop," he said. "Homicide, gangs, drugs—we got it all. And arson, plenty of that, lots of old factories and what-do being sold to the insurance companies."

He pulled up in front of my building. "The old guy, Contreras, he still living on the ground floor? We going to have to spend an hour with him before we go upstairs?"

"Probably. And there's no 'we' about it, Conrad: I can manage the stairs on my own."

"I know you got the strength, Ms. W., but you don't think it was nostalgia for your beautiful gray eyes that brought me to the hospital this morning, do you? We're going to talk, you and I. You're going to tell me the whole story of what you were doing down at Fly the Flag last night. How did you know the place was going to blow up?"

"I didn't," I snapped. I was tired, my wound was aching, the anesthesia was dragging me down.

"Yeah, and I'm the Ayatollah of Detroit. Wherever you are, people get shot, maimed, killed, so either you knew it was going to happen or you made it happen. What got you so interested in that factory?"

There was bitterness in his voice, but the accusation stung me to an anger that roused me from my torpor. "You got shot four years ago because you wouldn't listen to me when I knew something. Now you won't listen to me when I don't know anything. I am exhausted from you not listening to me."

He gave a nasty police smile, the pale sunlight glinting on his gold front tooth. "Then your wish is granted. I am going to listen to every word you say. Once we finish running the gauntlet."

The end of the sentence came out under his breath: Mr. Contreras and the two dogs I share with him had apparently been watching for me, because all three came bounding down the front walk as soon as I got out of the car. Mr. Contreras checked his step when he saw Conrad. Although he had never approved of my dating a black man, he had helped me nurse my broken heart when Conrad left me, and was clearly staggered to see us arrive together. The dogs showed no such restraint. Whether they remembered Conrad or not I didn't know: Peppy is a golden retriever and her son Mitch is half Lab—they give everyone from the meter reader to the Grim Reaper the same high-energy salute.

Mr. Contreras followed them slowly down the walk, but when he realized I'd been injured he became both solicitous and annoyed because I hadn't told him at once. "I would've come got you, Cookie, if you'd a only let me know, no need for a police escort."

"It was late at night when it all happened and they released me first thing this morning," I said gently. "Conrad's a commander now, anyway, at the Fourth District. This factory that burned last night is in his territory, so he wants to find out what I know about it—he won't believe it's sweet nothing at all."

In the end, we all went up to my apartment together, the dogs, the old man, Conrad. My neighbor bustled around in my kitchen and produced a bowl of yogurt with sliced apples and brown sugar. He even coaxed a double espresso out of my battered stove-top machine.

I stretched out on the couch, the dogs on the floor next to me. Mr. Contreras took the armchair, while Conrad pulled up the piano bench so he could watch my face while I talked. He pulled a cassette recorder from his pocket and recorded the date and place we were talking.

"Okay, Ms. W., this is on the record. You tell me the whole story of what you were doing in South Chicago."

"It's my home," I said. "I belong there more than you do."

"Forget that: you haven't lived there for twenty-five years or more."

"Doesn't matter. You know as well as me that in this town, your childhood home dogs you your whole life."

# REMEMBRANCES OF
THINGS PAST

Going back to South Chicago has always felt to me like a return to death. The people I loved most, those fierce first attachments of childhood, had all died in this abandoned neighborhood on the city's southeast edge. It's true my mother's body, my father's ashes, lie elsewhere, but I had tended both through painful illnesses down here. My cousin Boom-Boom, close as a brother—closer than a brother—had been murdered here fifteen years ago. In my nightmares, yellow smoke from the steel mills still clouds my eyes, but the giant smokestacks that towered over my childhood landscape are now only ghosts themselves.

After Boom-Boom's funeral, I'd vowed never to return, but such vows are grandiose; you can't keep them. Still, I try. When my old basketball coach called to beg, or maybe command me to fill in for her while she dealt with cancer surgery, I said "No," reflexively.

"Victoria, basketball got you out of this neighborhood. You owe something to the girls who've come behind you to give them the chance you had."

It wasn't basketball but my mother's determination I would have a university education that got me out of South Chicago, I said. And my

ACTs were pretty darn good. But as Coach McFarlane pointed out, the athletic scholarship to the University of Chicago didn't hurt.

"Even so, why doesn't the school hire a substitute for you?" I asked petulantly.

"You think they pay me to coach?" Her voice rose in indignation. "It's Bertha Palmer High, Victoria. It's South Chicago. They don't have any resources and now they're on intervention, which means every available dime goes to preparing kids for standardized tests. It's only because I volunteer that they keep the girls' program alive, and it's on life support as it is: I have to scrounge for money to pay for uniforms and equipment."

Mary Ann McFarlane had taught me Latin as well as basketball; she'd retooled herself to teach geometry when the school stopped offering all languages except Spanish and English. Through all the changes, she'd kept coaching basketball. I hadn't realized any of that until the afternoon she called.

"It's only two hours, two afternoons a week," she added.

"Plus up to an hour's commute each way," I said. "I can't take this on: I have an active detective agency, I'm working without an assistant, I'm taking care of my lover who got shot to bits in Afghanistan. And I still have to look after my own place and my two dogs."

Coach McFarlane wasn't impressed—all this was just so much excuse making. *"Quotidie damnatur qui semper timet,"* she said sharply.

I had to recite the words several times before I could translate them: The person who is always afraid is condemned every day. "Yeah, maybe, but I haven't played competitive basketball for two decades. The younger women who join our pickup games at the Y on Saturdays play a faster, meaner game than I ever did. Maybe one of those twenty-somethings has two afternoons a week to give you—I'll talk to them this weekend."

"There's nothing to make one of those young gals come down to Ninetieth and Houston," she snapped. "This is your neighborhood, these are your neighbors, not that tony Lakeview where you think you're hiding out."

That annoyed me enough that I was ready to end the conversation, until she added, "Just until the school finds someone else, Victoria. Or maybe a miracle will happen and I'll get back there."

That's how I knew she was dying. That's how I knew I was going to have to return once more to South Chicago, to make another journey into pain.

 HOMIE

The noise was overwhelming. Balls pounded on the old yellow floor. They ricocheted from backboards and off the bleachers that crowded the court perimeter, creating a syncopated drumming as loud as a gale-force wind. The girls on the floor were practicing layups and free throws, rebounding, dribbling between their legs and behind their backs. They didn't all have balls—the school budget didn't run to that—but even ten balls make a stunning racket.

The room itself looked as though no one had painted, or even washed it, since I last played here. It smelled of old sweat, and two of the overhead lights were broken, so it seemed as though it was always February inside. The floor was scarred and warped; every now and then one of the girls would forget to watch her step at the three-second lane or the left corner—the two worst spots—and take a spill. Last week, one of our promising guards had sprained an ankle.

I tried not to let the daunting atmosphere get me down. After all, Bertha Palmer had sixteen girls who wanted to play, some even playing their hearts out. It was my job to help them until the school found a permanent coach. And to keep their spirits up after the season started, and they went against teams with better facilities, better depth—and much better coaches.

Those waiting a turn under the baskets were supposed to be running laps or stretching, but they tended to hover over the girls with balls, grabbing for them, or shouting hotly that April Czernin or Celine Jackman was hogging shooting time.

"Your moma didn't spread her legs to pay for that ball—give it over here," was a frequent taunt. I had to stay alert to squabbles that might erupt into full-scale war while correcting faults in shooting form. And not be bothered by the howling of the infant and toddler in the bleachers. The babies belonged to my center, Sancia, a gawky sixteen-year-old who—despite her six-foot-two body—looked practically like a baby herself. The kids were nominally under the care of her boyfriend, but he sat sullenly next to them, Discman in his ears, looking neither at his children nor at the action on the floor.

I was also trying not to let Marcena Love disturb me, although her presence was winding my team up, intensifying the pace of insults as well as of the workout. Not that Marcena was a scout or a coach or even knew very much about the game, but the team was ferociously aware of her.

When she'd arrived with me, impossibly soignée in her black Prada spandex, carrying an outsize leather bag, I'd introduced her briefly: she was English, she was a reporter, she wanted to take some notes, and possibly talk to some of them during the breaks.

The girls would have swooned over her anyway, but when they found she had covered Usher at Wembley Stadium, they'd screamed with excitement.

"Talk to me, miss, talk to me!"

"Don't listen to her, she's the biggest liar on the South Side."

"You wanna photograph me doing my jump shot? I'm gonna be all-state this year."

I'd had to use a crowbar to get them away from Love and onto the court. Even as they fought over equipment and shooting rights, they kept an eye on her.

I shook my head: I was paying too much attention to Love myself. I took a ball from April Czernin, another promising guard, and tried to show her how to back into the three-second lane, turning at the last instant to do that fadeaway jumper Michael Jordan made famous. At least my ball went in, always a plus when you're trying to show off a move. April repeated the shot a few times while another player complained, "How come you let her keep the ball and I don't get no time, coach?"

Being called "coach" still disconcerted me. I didn't want to get used to it—this was a temporary gig. In fact, I was hoping to line up a corporate sponsor this afternoon, someone willing to pay good money to bring in a pro, or at least semipro, to take over the team.

When I blew my whistle to call an end to free-form warm-ups, Theresa Díaz popped up in front of me.

"Coach, I got my period."

"Great," I said. "You're not pregnant."

She blushed and scowled: despite the fact that at any one time at least fifteen percent of their classmates were pregnant, the girls were skittish and easily embarrassed by talk about their bodies "Coach, I gotta use the bathroom."

"One at a time—you know the rule. When Celine gets back, you can go."

"But, coach, my shorts, they'll, you know."

"You can wait on the bench until Celine returns," I said. "The rest of you: get into two lines—we're going to practice layups and rebounds."

Theresa gave an exaggerated sigh and made a show of mincing over to the bench.

"What's the point of that kind of use of power? Will humiliating the girl turn her into a better player?" Marcena Love's high, clear voice was loud enough for the two girls nearest her to stop fighting over a ball to listen.

Josie Dorrado and April Czernin looked from Love to me to see what I would do. I couldn't—mustn't—lose my temper. After all, I might only be imagining that Love was going out of her way to get my goat.

"If I wanted to humiliate her, I'd follow her to the bathroom to see if she really had her period." I also spoke just loudly enough for the team to overhear. "I'm pretending to believe her because it might really be true."

"You suspect she just wants a cigarette?"

I lowered my voice. "Celine, the kid who disappeared for a break five minutes ago, is challenging me. She's a leader in the South Side Pentas, and Theresa's one of her followers. If Celine can get a little gang meeting going in the stalls during practice, she's taken over the team."

I snapped my fingers. "Of course, you could go in with Theresa, take notes of all her and Celine's girlish thoughts and wishes. It would raise their spirits no end, and you could report on how public school toilets on Chicago's South Side compare with what you've seen in Baghdad and Brixton."

Love widened her eyes, then smiled disarmingly. "Sorry. You know your team. But I thought sports were meant to keep girls out of gangs."

"Josie! April! Two lines, one shoots, one rebounds, you know the drill." I watched until the girls formed up and began shooting.

"Basketball is supposed to keep them out of pregnancy, too." I gestured to the bleachers. "We have one teen mom out of sixteen in a school where almost half the girls have babies before they're seniors, so it's working for most of them. And we only have three gang members—that I know of—on the team. The South Side is the city's dumping ground. It's why the gym's a wreck, half the girls don't have uniforms, and we have to beg to get enough basketballs to run a decent drill. It's going to take way more than basketball to keep these kids off drugs, out of childbirth, and in school."

I turned away from Love and set the girls in one line to running into the basket and shooting from underneath, with the ones in the second line following to rebound. We practiced from inside the three-second lane, outside the three-point perimeter, hook shots, jump shots, layups. Halfway through the drill, Celine sauntered back into the gym. I didn't talk to her about her ten minutes out of the room, just put her at the back of one of the lines.

"Your turn, Theresa," I called.

She started toward the door, then muttered, "I think I can make it to the end of practice, coach."

"Don't take any chances," I said. "Better to miss another five minutes of practice than to risk embarrassment."

She blushed again and insisted she was fine. I put her in the lane where Celine wasn't and looked at Marcena Love, to see if she'd heard; the journalist turned her head and seemed intent on the play under the basket in front of her.

I smiled to myself: point to the South Side street fighter. Although street fighting wasn't the most useful tool with Marcena Love: she had too much in her armory that went beyond me. Like the skinny—oh, all right, slim—muscular body her black Prada clung to. Or the fact that she'd known my lover since his Peace Corps days. And had been with Morrell last winter in Afghanistan. And had shown up at his Evanston condo three days ago, when I'd been in South Shore with Coach McFarlane.

When I'd reached his place that night myself, Marcena had been perched on the side of his bed, tawny head bent down as they looked at photographs together. Morrell was recovering from gunshot wounds that still required him to lie down much of the time, so it wasn't surprising he was in bed. But the sight of a strange woman, and one with Marcena's poise and ease, leaning over him—at ten o'clock—had caused hackles to rise from my crown to my toes.

Morrell reached out a hand to pull me down for a kiss before introducing us: Marcena, an old journalist friend, in town to do a series for the *Guardian,* called from the airport, staying in the spare room for a week or so while she gets her bearings. Victoria, private investigator, basketball locum, Chicago native who can show you around. I'd smiled with as much goodwill as I could summon, and had tried not to spend the next three days wondering what they were doing while I was running around town.

Not that I was jealous of Marcena. Certainly not. I was a modern woman, after all, and a feminist, and I didn't compete with other women for any man's affection. But Morrell and Love had the intimacy that comes from a long-shared past. When they started laughing and talking I felt excluded. And, well, okay, jealous.

A fight under one of the baskets reminded me to keep my attention on the court. As usual, it was between April Czernin and Celine Jackman, my gangbanger forward. They were the two best players on the team, but figuring out how to get them to play together was only one of the exhausting challenges the girls presented. At times like this it was just as well I was a street fighter. I separated them and organized squads for scrimmage.

We took a break at three-thirty, by which time everyone was sweating freely, including me. During the break, I was able to serve the team Gatorade, thanks to a donation from one of my corporate clients. While the other girls drank theirs, Sancia Valdéz, my center, climbed up the bleachers to make sure her baby got its bottle and to have some kind of conversation with its father—so far I hadn't heard him do more than mumble incomprehensibly.

Marcena began interviewing a couple of the girls, choosing them at random, or maybe by color—one blonde, one Latina, one African-American. The rest clamored around her, jealous for attention.

I saw that Marcena was recording them, using a neat little red device, about the size and shape of a fountain pen. I'd admired it the first time I saw it—it was a digital gizmo, of course, and could hold eight hours of talk in its tiny head. And unless Marcena told people, they didn't know they were being recorded. She hadn't told the girls she was taping them, but I decided not to make an issue of it—chances were, they'd be flattered, not offended.

I let it go on for fifteen minutes, then brought over the board and began drawing play routes on it. Marcena was a good sport—when she saw the team would rather talk to her than listen to me she put her recorder away and said she'd finish after practice.

I sent two squads to the floor for an actual scrimmage. Marcena watched for a few minutes, then climbed up the rickety bleachers to my center's boyfriend. He sat up straighter and at one point actually seemed to speak with real animation. This distracted Sancia so much that she muffed a routine pass and let the second team get an easy score.

"Head in the game, Sancia," I barked in my best Coach McFarlane imitation, but I was still relieved when the reporter climbed down from the bleachers and ambled out of the gym: everyone got more focused on what was happening on the court.

Last night at dinner, when Marcena proposed coming with me this afternoon, I'd tried to talk her out of it. South Chicago is a long way from anywhere, and I warned her I couldn't take a break to drive her downtown if she got bored.

Love had laughed. "I have a high boredom threshold. You know the series I'm doing for the *Guardian* on the America that Europeans don't see? I have to start somewhere, and who could be more invisible than the girls you're coaching? By your account, they're never going to be Olympic stars or Nobel Prize winners, they come from rough neighborhoods, they have babies—"

"In other words, just like the girls in South London," Morrell had interrupted. "I don't think you've got a world-beating story there, Love."

"But going down there might suggest a story," she said. "Maybe a profile of an American detective returning to her roots. Everyone likes detective stories."

"You could follow the team," I agreed with fake enthusiasm. "It could be one of those tearjerkers where this bunch of girls who don't have enough balls or uniforms comes together under my inspired leadership to be state champs. But, you know, practice goes on for two hours, and I have an appointment with a local business leader afterward. We'll be in the armpit of the city—if you do get bored, there won't be a lot for you to do."

"I can always leave," Love said.

"Onto the street with the highest murder rate in the city."

She laughed again. "I've just come from Baghdad. I've covered Sarajevo, Rwanda, and Ramallah. I can't imagine Chicago is more terrifying than any of those places."

I'd agreed, of course: I had to. It was only because Love rubbed me the wrong way—because I was jealous, or insecure, or just a South Side street fighter with a chip on her shoulder—that I hadn't wanted to bring her. If the team could get some print space, even overseas, maybe someone would pay attention to them and help in my quest to find a corporate sponsor.

Despite her airy assurance that she had taken care of herself in Kabul and the West Bank, Love had wilted a little when we reached the school. The neighborhood itself is enough to make anyone weep—at least, it makes me want to weep. When I first drove past my old home two weeks ago, I really did break down in tears. The windows were boarded over, and weeds choked the yard where my mother had patiently tended a *bocca di leone gigante* and a Japanese camellia.

The school building, with its garbage and graffiti, broken windows, and two-inch case-hardened chains shutting all but one entrance, daunts everyone. Even when you get used to the chains and garbage and think you're not noticing them, they weigh on you. Kids and staff alike get depressed and pugnacious after enough time in such a setting.

Marcena had been unusually quiet while we produced our IDs for the guard, only murmuring that this was what she was used to from Iraq and the West Bank, but she hadn't realized Americans knew how it felt to have an occupying power in their midst.

"The cops aren't an occupying power," I snapped. "That role belongs to the relentless poverty around here."

"Cops are on power trips no matter what force places them in charge of a community," she responded, but she'd still been subdued until she met the team.

After she left the gym, I stepped up the tempo of the practice, even though several of the players were sullenly refusing to respond, complaining they were worn out and Coach McFarlane didn't make them do this.

"Forget about it," I barked. "I trained with Coach McFarlane: that's how I learned these drills."

I had them working on passes and rebounds, their biggest weaknesses. I forced the laggards under the boards, letting balls bounce off them because they wouldn't go through the motions of trying to grab them. Celine, my gangbanger, knocked over one straggler. Even though I secretly wanted to do it myself, I had to bench Celine and threaten her with suspension from the team if she kept on fighting. I hated doing it, since she and April, along with Josie Dorrado, were our only hope for building a team that could win a few games. If they picked up their skills. If enough of the others started working harder. If they all kept coming, didn't get pregnant or shot, got the high-tops and weight equipment they needed. And if Celine and April didn't come to blows before the season even got under way.

The energy level in the room suddenly went up, and I knew without looking at the clock that we had fifteen minutes left in practice. This was the time that friends and family showed up to wait for the team. Even though most of the girls went home by themselves, everyone played better with an audience.

Tonight, to my surprise, it was April Czernin who picked up the pace the most—she started knocking down rebounds with the ferocity of Teresa Weatherspoon. I turned to see who she was showing off for, and saw that Marcena Love had returned, along with a man around my own age. His dark good looks were starting to fray a bit around the edges, but he definitely merited a second glance. He and Love were laughing together, and his right hand was about a millimeter from her hip. When April saw his attention was on Marcena, she bounced her ball off the backboard with such savagery that the rebound hit Sancia in the head.

3
ENTER ROMEO
(STAGE LEFT)

The man moved forward with an easy smile. "So it is you, Tori. Thought it had to be when April told us your name."

No one had used that pet name for me since my cousin Boom-Boom died. It had been his private name for me—my mother hated American nicknames, and my father called me Pepperpot—and I didn't like hearing it from this guy, who was a complete stranger.

"You've been away from the hood so long you don't remember your old pals, huh, Warshawski?"

"Romeo Czernin!" I blurted out his own nickname in a jolt of astonished recognition: he'd been in Boom-Boom's class, a year ahead of me, and the girls in my clique had all snickered about him as we watched him put the moves on our classmates.

This afternoon, it was Celine and her sidekicks who laughed raucously, hoping to goad April. They succeeded: April aimed a ball at Celine. I jumped between them, scooping up the ball, trying unsuccessfully to remember Romeo's real name.

Czernin was pleased, perhaps by the juvenile title, or by grabbing the team's attention in front of Marcena. "The one and only." He put an arm around me and bent me backward to kiss me. I turned inside his arm and hooked my left foot around his ankle, sliding away as he stumbled. It wasn't the kind of juke move I wanted to encourage in the team, but unfortunately they all had been watching closely; I had a feeling I'd see Celine using it at the next practice. Marcena Love had also been watching, with an amused smile that made me feel as immature as my own gangbangers.

Romeo dusted himself off. "Same standoffish bitch you always were, huh, Tori? You always were one of McFarlane's pets, weren't you? When I found out she was still coaching basketball, I came over to have a talk with her—I figured she'd dump the same crap on my kid she did on me, and now I suppose I have to make sure you treat April right, too."

"Wrong," I said. "It's a pleasure coaching April; she's shaping into a serious little player."

"I hear any reports that you playing favorites, you letting some of these Mexican scum beat up on her, you answer to me, just remember that."

April was turning red with embarrassment, so I just smiled and said I'd keep it in mind. "Next time, come early enough to watch her scrimmage. You'll be impressed."

He nodded at me, as if to reinforce my acknowledgment of his power, then switched on another smile for Marcena. "Would if I could: it's my hours. I got off early today and thought I'd take my little girl out for a pizza—how about it, sweetheart?"

April, who'd retreated to the background with Josie Dorrado, looked up with the kind of scowl that teenagers use to conceal eagerness.

"And this English lady who's writing about your team and the South Side, she'd like to join us. Met me in the parking lot when I was pulling up in the rig. What do you say? We'll go to Zambrano's, show her the real neighborhood."

April hunched a shoulder. "I guess. If Josie can come, too. And Laetisha."

Romeo agreed with an expansive clap on his daughter's shoulder and told her to hustle; he had to do some driving after pizza.

Zambrano's was just about the only place on the South Side that I remembered from my own youth. Most of the other little joints have been boarded over. Even Sonny's, where you could get a shot and a beer for a dollar—all under the life-sized portrait of the original Richard Daley—isn't open any more.

I sent the girls off to shower, in a locker room whose dank, moldy smell usually kept me in my own sweaty clothes until I got to Morrell's. Marcena followed the team, saying she wanted the whole picture of their experience, and, anyway, she needed to pee. The girls gave gasps of excited shock at hearing her use the word in front of a man, and they clustered around her with renewed eagerness.

I looked up to the stands to see whether Sancia's kids had anyone with them while she showered. Sancia's sister had come in at the end of practice—she and Sancia's mother seemed to alternate in helping out with the babies. Sancia's boyfriend was lounging in the hallway with a couple of other guys who had girlfriends or sisters on the team, waiting for them to finish. After my first practice, when the guys had tested my authority with too much bumping and ball playing, I'd forced them to wait outside the gym until the girls were changed.

Romeo picked up one of the balls and began banging it off the backboard. He was wearing work boots, but I decided we'd had enough friction without me chewing him out for not wearing soft soles on the scarred court.

My cousin Boom-Boom, who'd been a high school star, already recruited by the Black Hawks when he was seventeen, used to make fun of Romeo for trailing after the jocks. I'd joined in, since I wanted my cousin and his cool friends to like me, but I had to admit that even in work boots, Czernin's form was pretty good. He sank five balls in a row from the free throw line, then began moving around the court, trying different, flashier shots, with less success.

He saw me watching him and gave a cocky smile: all was forgiven if I was going to admire him. "Watcha been up to, Tori? Is it true what they say, that you followed your old man into the police?"

"Not really: I'm a private investigator. I do stuff that the cops aren't interested in. You driving a rig like your dad?"

"Not really," he mimicked me. "He worked solo, I work for By-Smart. They're about the only company hiring down here these days."

"They need an eighteen-wheeler down here?"

"Yeah. You know, in and out of their big distribution warehouse, and then over to the stores, not just the one on Ninety-fifth, they've got eleven in my territory—South Side, northwest Indiana, you know."

I passed the giant discount store at Ninety-fifth and Commercial every time I rode the expressway down. As big as the Ford Assembly Plant farther south, the store and parking lot filled in almost half a mile of old swamp.

"I'm going over to the warehouse myself this afternoon," I said. "You know Patrick Grobian?"

Romeo gave the knowing smirk that was starting to get on my nerves. "Oh, yeah. I do a lot with Grobian. He likes to stay on top of dispatch, even though he is the district manager."

"So you going to show Marcena the northwest Indiana stores after you take the girls to Zambrano's?"

"That's the idea. On the outside she looks as stuck up as you, but that's just her accent and her getup; she's a real person, and she's pretty interested in how I do my work."

"She drove down with me. Can you take her as far as the Loop when you're done? She shouldn't ride the train late at night."

He grinned salaciously. "I'll see she gets a good ride, Tori, don't you worry your uptight ass about that."

Resisting an impulse to smack him, I started collecting balls from around the floor. I let him hang on to the one he was playing with, but I put the rest in the equipment room. If I didn't lock them up at once they evaporated, as I'd learned to my cost: we'd lost two when friends and family were milling around the gym after my first practice. I'd scrounged four new ones from friends who belong to tony downtown gyms. Now I keep all ten balls in a padlocked bin, although I've had to share keys with the boys' coach and the PE teachers.

While the girls finished changing, I sat at a tiny table in the equipment room to fill out attendance forms and progress reports for the benefit of the mythical permanent coach. After a moment, a shadow in the doorway made me look up. Josie Dorrado, April's particular friend on the team, was hovering there, twisting her long braid around her fingers, shifting from one skinny leg to the other. A quiet, hardworking kid, she was another of my strong players. I smiled, hoping she wasn't going to bring up a time-consuming problem: I couldn't be late to my meeting with the By-Smart manager.

"Coach, uh, people say, uh, is it true you're with the police?"

"I'm a detective, Josie, but I'm private. I work for myself, not the city. Do you need the police for some reason?" I seemed to have a version of this conversation with someone at every practice, even though I'd told the team when I started coaching what I did for a living.

She shook her head, eyes widening a bit in alarm at the idea that she herself might need a cop. "Ma, my ma, she told me to ask you."

I pictured an abusive husband, restraining orders, a long evening in violence court, and tried not to sigh out loud. "What kind of problem is she having?"

"It's something about her job. Only, her boss, he don't want her talking to no one."

"What—is he harassing her in some way?"

"Can't you just go see her for a minute? Ma can explain it, I don't really know what's going on, only she told me to ask you, because she heard someone at the laundry say how you grew up down here and now you're a cop."

Romeo appeared behind Josie, twirling the ball on his fingertip à la the Harlem Globetrotters. "What does your ma need a cop for, Josie?" he asked.

Josie shook her head. "She don't, Mr. Czernin, she just wants Coach to talk to her about some kind of problem she's got with Mr. Zamar."

"What kind of problem she have with Zamar that she wants a dick on his tail? Or is it the other way around?" He laughed heartily.

Josie looked at him in bewilderment. "You mean does she want him followed? I don't think so, but I don't really know. Please, coach, it'll only take a minute, and every day she keeps bugging me, have you talked to your coach yet? have you talked to your coach yet? so I gotta tell her I asked you."

I looked at my watch. Ten to five. I had to be at the warehouse by five-fifteen, and visit Coach McFarlane before I went to Morrell's. If I went to see Josie's ma in between, it would be ten o'clock again before I made it home.

I looked at Josie's anxious chocolate eyes. "Can it wait until Monday? I could come over after practice to talk to her."

"Yeah, okay." It was only the slight relaxation in her shoulders that told me she was relieved I'd agreed to do it.

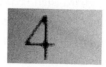 MOUNTAINS OF THINGS

I threaded my way through the trucks in the yard at the warehouse, looking for the parking area. Eighteen-wheelers were backing up to loading bays, smaller trucks were driving up and down a ramp leading to a lower level, a couple of waste haulers were picking up Dumpsters and emptying them, and all around me men in hard hats and beer bellies were shouting at each other to watch where the hell they were going.

Trucks had dug deep grooves in the asphalt and my Mustang bounced unhappily through them, splashing my windows with mud. It had been raining off and on all day and the sky still seemed sullen. A century of dumping everything, from cyanide to cigarette wrappers, into South Chicago's swampy ground had turned the landscape tired and drab. Against this leaden backdrop, the By-Smart warehouse looked ominous, a cavern housing some ravening beast.

The building itself was monstrous. A low-slung brick structure, perhaps originally red, turned grimy black with age, it filled two city blocks. The building and the yard lay behind high wire fencing, with a guard station and everything. When I turned off 103rd Street and pulled in, a man in some kind of uniform demanded to see my pass. I told him I had an appointment with Patrick Grobian; the man phoned into the cavern and confirmed that I was expected. Parking lay straight ahead, I couldn't miss it.

Straight ahead meant something different to the guard than it did to me. After I'd jolted around two sides of the building, I finally came on the parking area. It looked like the lot to a run-down used-car dealer, with hundreds of beaters parked every which way among the ruts. I found a spot that I hoped was out of the way enough that no one would sideswipe my Mustang.

When I opened the door, I looked with dismay at the ground. The warehouse entrance lay several hundred yards away and I was going to have to pick my way through rain-filled potholes in my good shoes. I knelt on the driver's seat and leaned over to paw through the papers and towels in back. Finally, I dug up a pair of flip-flops I'd used at the beach last summer and wiggled my stocking feet around the little toe bars. It made for a slow and embarrassing waddle across the yard to the entrance, but at least I reached it with only my stockings and trouser cuffs spackled in mud. I slipped on my pumps and stuck the muddy flip-flops into a plastic bag before shoving them into my briefcase.

High doors opened onto a consumer nightmare. Shelves stacked with every imaginable product stretched as far as I could see. Directly in front of me dangled brooms, hundreds of them, push brooms, straw brooms, brooms with plastic handles, with wood handles, brooms that swiveled. Next to them were thousands of shovels, ready for every Chicagoan who wanted to clear their walks in the winter ahead. On my right cartons labeled "ice-melt" were stacked halfway to a ceiling that yawned thirty feet overhead.

I started forward, and backed up again as a forklift truck rattled toward me at high speed, its front-loader high with cartons of ice-melt. It stopped on the far side of the shovels; a woman in overalls and a bright red vest began slitting the boxes before they were even off the loader. She pulled smaller boxes of ice-melt out and added them to the mound already there.

Another forklift pulled up in front of me. A man in an identical red vest started loading brooms onto it, checking them against a computer printout.

When I stepped forward again, trying to decide on a route through the shelves, a guard moved to intercept me. A large black woman wearing a vest with safety reflectors, she also had a hard hat labeled "Be Smart, By-Smart," and a belt that seemed to hold everything the complete law officer needed—including a stun gun. Above the racket of the conveyor belts and the trucks, she demanded my business.

Once again, I explained who I was and why I was there. The guard took a cell phone from her belt to call for approval. When she had it, she gave me a badge and directions to Patrick Grobian's office: down Aisle 116S, left at 267W, all the way to the end, where I'd find all of the company offices, toilets, canteen, and so on.

It was then that I saw big red numbers that labeled the entrance to each row. These were so large that I'd missed them at first. I'd also missed a series of conveyor belts high above the aisles; they had chutes that lowered stacks of goods to various loading depots. Signs proclaiming "No Smoking Anywhere, Anytime" were plastered prominently on the walls and shelves, along with exhortations to "Make the Workplace a Safe Place."

We were facing Aisle 122S, so I turned left at the shovels and walked down six aisles, passing a mountain of microwaves, followed by a forest of artificial Christmas trees. When I reached Aisle 116, I moved into Christmas decorations: avalanches of bells, lights, napkins, plastic angels, orange-faced Madonnas holding ice-white baby Jesuses.

Between the mountains of things stretching endlessly away, the conveyor belts ratcheting overhead, and the forklifts rolling around me, I began to feel dizzy. There were people in this warehouse, but they seemed to exist only as extensions of the machines. I clutched a shelf to steady myself. I couldn't show up at Patrick Grobian's office looking woozy: I wanted his support for Bertha Palmer's basketball team. I needed to be upbeat and professional.

Three weeks ago, when I met the assistant principal who oversaw Bertha Palmer's after-school programs, I knew I was going to have to find

Mary Ann's replacement myself if I didn't want to stick around the high school for the rest of my life. Natalie Gault was in her early forties, short, stocky, and very aware of her authority. She was swamped in a flood of paperwork. Girls' basketball ranked in her consciousness somewhere below upgrading the coffeemaker in the faculty lounge.

"I'm only filling in for Mary Ann until the end of the year," I warned her when she thanked me for taking over at short notice. "I won't have time to come down here once the playing season starts in January. I can keep the girls conditioned until then, but I'm not a trained coach, and that's what they need."

"All they really need is for a grown-up to show interest in them, Ms. Sharaski." She flashed a bright meaningless smile at me. "No one expects them to win games."

"Warshawski. And the girls expect to win games—they're not playing to show what good sports they are. Which they're not. Three or four of them could be top-notch players with the right coaching—they deserve more than the short time and mediocre skills I can give them. What is the school doing to find someone?"

"Praying for a miracle with Mary Ann McFarlane's health," she said. "I know you went to school down here, but back then the school could rent an instrument for any child who wanted to play one. We haven't offered music in this school for eighteen years, except for the Band Club, which one of the reading teachers runs. We can't afford an art program, so we tell kids to go to a free downtown program—two hours and two buses away. We don't have an official basketball team—we have a basketball club. We can't afford a coach—we need a volunteer, and we don't have a teacher who has the time, let alone the skills, to take it on. I suppose if we could find a corporate sponsor we could hire an after-school coach."

"Who's down here who could put that kind of money into the basketball program?"

"Some small companies in the neighborhood, places like Fly the Flag, sometimes put up money for uniforms or instruments in the band. But the economy's so bad right now that they aren't doing anything for us this year."

"Who's big down here now that the mills are closed? I know there's the Ford Assembly Plant."

She shook her head. "That's all the way down on 130th, and we're too far away and too small for them, even though some of the parents work down there."

Her phone rang at that point. Someone from the city health department was coming by tomorrow to look for rodent droppings—what should they do about the kitchen? A teacher stopped by to complain about the shortage of social studies texts, and another wanted eight students moved out of his room to a different section.

By the time Ms. Gault got back to me, she couldn't remember whether I was Sharaski or Varnishky, let alone whether the school would help find a coach. I ground my teeth, but when I got back to my own office that afternoon I did a search on companies within a two-mile radius of the school. I'd found three that were big enough to afford serious community service; the first two hadn't even let me make an appointment.

By-Smart had both the discount megastore at Ninety-fifth and Commercial, and their Midwest distribution center at 103rd and Crandon. The store told me they didn't make any community service decisions, that I needed to see Patrick Grobian, the Chicagoland south district manager, whose office was in the warehouse. A kid in Grobian's office who answered the phone said they'd never done anything like this before, but I could come in and explain what I wanted. Which is why I was hiking through mountains of things on my way to Grobian's office.

For some reason, when I was growing up in South Chicago I'd never heard of the By-Smart company. Of course, thirty years ago they had only begun the most phenomenal part of their staggering growth. According to my research, their sales last year had been $183 billion, a number I could hardly comprehend: that many zeroes made my head swim.

I guess when I was a kid, their warehouse had already been here at 103rd and Crandon, but nobody I knew worked here—my dad was a cop, and my uncles worked at the grain elevators or steel mills. Looking around me now, it was hard to believe I hadn't known about this place.

Of course, you'd have to be a Trappist monk not to know about the company today—their TV commercials are ubiquitous, showing their happy, nurturing sales staff in their red "Be Smart, By-Smart" smocks. All over America, they've become the only retail outlet for a lot of small towns.

Old Mr. Bysen had grown up on the South Side, over in Pullman; I knew that from Mary Ann's telling me he'd gone to Bertha Palmer High. His standard bio didn't talk about that, instead dwelling on his heroics as a World War II gunner. When he got back from the war, he'd taken over his father's little convenience store at Ninety-fifth and Exchange. From that tiny seed had sprouted a worldwide empire of discount superstores— to use the overheated imagery of one business writer. Of the sixteen girls I was coaching at Bertha Palmer, four had mothers who worked at the superstore, and now I knew April Czernin's father drove for them, too.

The South Side had been Bysen's base and then became his hub, I'd learned from *Forbes*; he'd bought this warehouse from Ferenzi Tool and Die when they went bankrupt in 1973 and kept it as his Midwest distribution center even after he moved his headquarters out to Rolling Meadows.

William Bysen, known inevitably as Buffalo Bill, was eighty-three now, but he still came into work every day, still controlled everything from the wattage of the lightbulbs in the employee toilets to By-Smart's contracts with major suppliers. His four sons were all active in management, his wife, May Irene, was a pillar of the community, active in charity and in her church. In fact, May Irene and Buffalo Bill were both evangelical Christians; every day at corporate headquarters began with a prayer session, twice a week a minister came in to preach, and the company supported a number of overseas missions.

Several of the girls on my team were also evangelical Christians. I was hoping the company might see this as a faith-based opportunity to serve South Chicago.

By the time I got to Aisle 267W, I was just praying that I'd never have to shop again in my life. The aisle emptied into a drafty corridor that ran the length of the building. At the far end I could see the silhouettes of smokers huddled in a wide doorway, desperate enough to brave the chill and rain.

A series of open doors dotted the corridor. I poked my head into the nearest, which turned out to be a canteen, its walls banked with vending machines. A dozen or so people were slumped at the scarred deal tables. Some were eating machine stew or cookies, but a number were asleep, their red smocks trailing on the grimy floor.

I backed out and started looking into the rooms lining the corridor. The first was a print room, with two large Lexmarks dumping out stacks of inventory. A fax machine in the corner was doing its part in the paperless society. As I stood mesmerized by the flow of paper, a parade of forklifts pulled up to collect output. When they trundled off, I blinked and followed them back into the corridor.

The next two doors opened onto tiny offices, where people were doing such energetic things with computers and binders of paper that they didn't even look at me when I asked for Grobian, just shook their heads and kept typing. I noticed little video cameras mounted in the ceilings: maybe their paychecks were docked if the cameras caught them looking up from their work when they weren't on break.

Five guys were waiting in the hall outside a closed door a little farther down the hall. Some were drinking out of cardboard canteen cups. Despite the pervasive cameras and the big sign ordering "No Smoking Anywhere, Anytime," two were smoking surreptitiously, cupping the cigarettes in their curled fingers, tapping the ash into empty cups. They had the worn jeans and work boots of tired men who worked hard for not very much money. Most had on old bomber or warm-up jackets, whose decals advertised everything from Harley-Davidson to New Mary's Wake-Up Lounge.

Grobian's nameplate was on the door in front of them. I stopped and raised an eyebrow. "The great man at home?"

The Harley jacket laughed. "Great man? That's about right, sis. Too great to sign our slips and get us on our way."

"Because he thinks he's on his way to Rolling Meadows." One of the smokers coughed and spat into his cup.

New Mary's Wake-Up Lounge grinned unpleasantly. "Maybe he is. Isn't the bedsheet queen—what the fuck was that for, man?" Another smoker had kicked him in the shin and jerked his head in my direction.

"It's okay, I'm not the gabby type, and I don't work for the company, anyway," I said. "I have an appointment with the big guy, and ordinarily I would just butt in on him, but since I'm here to ask a favor I'll wait in line like a good kindergartner."

That made them laugh again. They shifted to make room for me against the hall wall. I listened as they talked about their upcoming routes. The guy in the Harley jacket was getting ready to leave for El Paso, but the others were on local runs. They talked about the Bears, who had no offense, reminded them of the team twenty-five years back, right before Ditka and McMahon gave us our one whiff of glory, but was Lovey Smith the man to bring back the McMahon-Payton era. They didn't say anything further about the bedsheet queen or Grobian's ambitions for the home office. Not that I needed to know, but I suppose the main reason I'm a detective is a voyeur's interest in other people's lives.

After a longish wait, Grobian's door opened and a youth emerged. His reddish-brown hair, cut short in a futile effort to control his thick curls, was slicked down hard. His square face was dotted with freckles, and his cheeks still showed the soft down of adolescence, but he surveyed us with an adult seriousness. When he caught sight of the man in the Harley jacket, he smiled with such genuine pleasure that I couldn't help smiling, too.

"Billy the Kid," the Harley said, smacking him on the shoulder. "How's it hanging, kid?"

"Hi, Nolan, I'm good. You heading for Texas tonight?"

"That's right. If the great man ever gets off his duff and signs me out."

"Great man? You mean Pat? Really, he's just been going over the logs and he'll be right out. I'm real sorry you had to wait so long, but, honest, he'll be with you in a second." The youth stepped over to me. "Are you Ms. War-sha-sky?"

He pronounced my name carefully, although not quite successfully. "I'm Billy—I said you could come in today, only Pat, Mr. Grobian, he's not quite a hundred percent, well—he's running late, and, uh, he may take some persuading, but he'll see you, anyway, as soon as he gets these guys on their way."

"Billy?" a man shouted from inside the office. "Send Nolan in—we're ready to roll. And go collect the faxes for me."

My heart sank: a nineteen-year-old gofer with enthusiasm but no authority had organized my meeting with the guy who had authority but no enthusiasm. "Whenever I feel dismayed, I hold my head erect," I sang to myself.

While Billy went up the hall to the print room, the smokers pinched off the ends of their cigarettes and carefully put them in their pockets. Nolan went into Grobian's office and shut the door. When he came out a few minutes later, the other men trouped in in a group. Since they left the door open, I followed them.

IMPERIAL RELATIONS

Offices in industrial spaces aren't designed for the comfort or prestige of the inhabitant. Grobian got a bigger space than the tiny rooms I'd poked into earlier—it even included a closet in the far corner—but it was painted the same dirty yellow, held the same metal desk and chairs as the others, and, like them, even had a video cam in the ceiling. Buffalo Bill didn't trust anyone, apparently.

Grobian himself was an energetic young man, thirty-something, shirt-sleeves rolled up to reveal muscular arms, with a big marine anchor tattooed on the left bicep. He looked like the kind of guy truckers would respect, with a square quarterback jaw jutting beneath a buzz haircut.

He frowned when he saw me behind the men. "You new on the job? You don't belong in here—check in with Edgar Díaz in—"

"I'm V. I. Warshawski. We had an appointment at five-fifteen." I tried to sound upbeat, professional, not annoyed that it was almost six now.

"Oh, yeah. Billy set that up. You'll have to wait. These men are already late getting on the road."

"Of course." Women are supposed to wait on men; it's our appointed role. But I kept the thought to myself: beggars have to have a sunny disposition. I hate being a beggar.

When I looked around for a place to sit, I saw a woman behind me. She was definitely not a typical By-Smart employee, not with a face whose makeup had been as carefully applied as if her skin were a Vermeer canvas. Her clothes, too—a body-hugging jersey top over a lavender kilt artfully arranged to show black lace inserts—hadn't been bought on a By-Smart paycheck, let alone off a By-Smart rack, and none of the exhausted workers I'd seen in the canteen could have the energy to create that toned supple body.

The woman smiled when she saw me staring: she liked attention, or perhaps envy. She was in the only chair, so I went to lean against a metal filing cabinet next to her. She held a binder in her lap, open to an array of numbers that meant nothing to me, but when she realized I was staring down at them she shut the book and crossed her legs. She was wearing knee-high lavender boots with three-inch heels. I wondered if she had a pair of flip-flops to put on before going to her car.

Two more men joined the four lined up at Grobian's desk. When he'd finished with them, another three came in. They were all truckers, getting their loads approved, either for what they'd delivered or what they were getting ready to drive off with.

I was growing bored and even a bit angry, but I'd be even more upset if I blew a chance to get out from under the girls' basketball team. I sucked in a deep breath: keep it perky, Warshawski, and turned to ask the woman if she was part of the warehouse's management team.

She shook her head and smiled a little condescendingly. I would have to play twenty questions to get anything out of her. I didn't care that much, but I needed to do something to pass the time. I remembered the trucker's remark about the bedsheet queen. She either bought them or lay in them—maybe both.

"You the linen expert?" I asked.

She preened slightly: she had a reputation, people talked about her. She ordered all the towels and sheets for By-Smart nationwide, she said.

Before I could continue the game, Billy came back into the room with a thick sheaf of papers. "Oh, Aunt Jacqui, there are faxes for you in this bunch. I don't know why they've sent them here instead of up to Rolling Meadows."

Aunt Jacqui stood up, but dropped her binder in the process. Some of the papers fell out and fluttered to the floor, three landing under Grobian's desk. Billy picked up the binder and put it on her chair.

"Oh, dear," she murmured, her voice languid, almost liquid. "I don't think I can crawl under the desk in these clothes, Billy."

Billy set the faxes on top of her binder and got down on his hands and knees to fetch the scattered pages. Aunt Jacqui picked up the faxes, riffled through them, and extracted a dozen or so pages.

Billy scrambled back to his feet and handed her the sheets from her binder. "Pat, you ought to make sure that floor gets washed more often. It's filthy under there."

Grobian rolled his eyes. "Billy, this ain't your mother's kitchen, it's a working warehouse. As long as the floor doesn't catch on fire I can't be bothered about how dirty it is or isn't."

One of the truckers laughed and cuffed Billy on the shoulder on his way out the door. "Time you went on the road, son. Let you see real dirt and you'll come back and eat off Grobian's linoleum."

"Or let him wash it," the remaining driver suggested. "That always makes dirt look good."

Billy blushed but laughed along with the men. Pat chatted briefly with the last driver about a load he was taking to the Ninety-fifth Street store. When the man left, Pat started to give Billy an order to go down to the loading bays, but Billy shook his head. "We need to talk to Ms. War-sha-sky, Pat." He turned to me, apologizing for my long wait, adding that he'd tried to explain what I wanted, but didn't think he'd done a good job of it.

"Oh, yeah. Community service, we already do plenty of that." Grobian's frown returned. Busy man, no time for social workers, nuns, and other do-gooders.

"Yes, I've studied your numbers, at least the ones you make public." I pulled a sheaf of papers out of my briefcase, spilling the flip-flops in their plastic bag onto the floor.

I handed business cards to Grobian, Billy, and Aunt Jacqui. "I grew up in South Chicago. I'm a lawyer now and an investigator, but I've come back as a volunteer to coach the basketball team at Bertha Palmer High."

Grobian looked ostentatiously at his watch, but young Billy said, "I know some of the girls there, Pat, through our church exchange. They sing in the choir at—"

"I know you want money from us," Jacqui interrupted in her languid voice. "How much and for what?"

I flashed an upbeat, professional smile and handed her a copy of a report I'd created on By-Smart's community actions. I gave another set to Grobian and a third to Billy. "I know that By-Smart encourages grass-roots giving at its local stores, but only for small projects. The Exchange Avenue store gave out three one-thousand-dollar scholarships to college students whose parents work in the store, and the staff are encouraged to serve in local food pantries and homeless shelters, but your manager over on Exchange told me Mr. Grobian was in charge of larger giving for the South Side."

"That's right: I manage the warehouse, and I'm the South Chicago–Northwest Indiana district manager. We already support the Boys and Girls Clubs, the Firemen's Survivor Fund, and several others."

"Which is great," I said enthusiastically. "Profits for the Exchange Avenue store last year were a shade under one-point-five million, a little less than the national average because of the bad economy down here. The store, as far as I could tell, gave away nine thousand dollars. For fifty-five thousand—"

Grobian shoved my report aside. "Who talked to you? Who gave out confidential store information?"

I shook my head. "It's all on the Web, Mr. Grobian. You just have to know how to look. For fifty-five thousand, the store could cover the cost of uniforms, weight equipment, balls, and a part-time coach. You'd be real heroes on the South Side, and, of course, you'd get a substantial tax benefit from it as well. Heck, you might even be able to supply weight equipment out of old inventory."

All I really wanted from By-Smart was a coach, and I figured for about twelve thousand they could get someone to commit to the job. She (or he) wouldn't have to be a teacher, just someone who understood the game and knew how to work with young people. A graduate student who had played college ball would be good; someone who was doing a degree in sports management and training even better. I was hoping if I started with four or five times what I wanted, I might at least get a coach.

Grobian was still mad, though. He tossed my proposal into his wastebasket. Jacqui, with another of her languid movements, slid her papers toward the trash. They fell about a yard short.

"We never give that kind of money to an individual store," Grobian said.

"Not to the store, Pat," Billy objected, bending over to retrieve Aunt Jacqui's papers. "To the school. It's just the kind of thing Grandpa loves, helping kids who show enthusiasm for improving their lives."

Ah: he was a Bysen. That was why he could set up meetings with beggars even though he was inexperienced and had a boss who didn't want to hear about the matter. That meant Aunt Jacqui was a Bysen, too, so I didn't have to keep playing twenty questions with her.

I smiled warmly at Billy. "Your grandfather went to this high school seventy years ago. Five of the girls on the team have parents who work for By-Smart, so it would be great synergy for the store and the community." I winced at hearing corpu-speak fall so effortlessly from my lips.

"Your grandfather doesn't believe in giving that kind of money to charity, Billy. If you don't know that by now, you haven't been listening to him very hard," Jacqui said.

"That's not fair, Aunt Jacqui. What about the wing he and Grandma built on the hospital in Rolling Meadows, and the mission school they started in Mozambique?"

"Those were big buildings that have his name on them," Jacqui said. "A little program down here that he won't get any glory for—"

"I'll talk to him myself," Billy said hotly. "I've met some of these girls, like I said, and when he hears their stories—"

"Large tears will fill his eyes," Jacqui interrupted. "He'll go, 'Hnnh, hnnh, if they want to succeed they need to work hard, like I did. No one gave me any handouts, and I started out the same place they did, hnnh, hnnh.'"

Patrick Grobian laughed, but Billy looked flushed and hurt. He believed in his grandfather. To cover his confusion, Billy started sorting out the papers that Aunt Jacqui had dropped, separating my proposal from several sheets of fax paper.

"Here's something from Adolpho in Matagalpa," he said. "I thought we agreed not to work with him, but he's quoting you—"

Jacqui took the papers back from him. "I wrote him last week, Billy, but maybe he didn't get the letter. You're right to point it out."

"But it looks like he has a whole production schedule."

Jacqui produced another dazzling smile. "I think you misread it, Billy, but I'll make extra sure we're all clear on this."

Pat pulled my report out of his trash. "I moved too fast on this one, Billy; I'll take a closer look at my numbers and get back to your friend. In the meantime, why don't you go out to the loading bays, make sure that Bron at bay thirty-two has taken off—he has a tendency to linger, wasting time with the girls on the shift. And you, Ms.—uh, we'll call you in a couple of days."

Billy looked again at Aunt Jacqui, a troubled frown creasing his smooth young face, but he obediently got up to go. I followed him from the room.

"I'd be glad to get you any other information you want that might help your grandfather make a decision about the team. Maybe you'd like to bring him to one of our practices."

His face lit up. "I don't think he'd come, but I could, that is, if I could take off from here, maybe if I came in early, aren't Mondays and Thursdays your practice days?"

I was surprised and asked how he knew.

He flushed. "I'm in the choir and the youth group at my church, our church, I mean, the one my family goes to, and we do these exchanges with inner-city churches sometimes, like, where we trade ministers, and our choirs sing together and stuff, and my youth group has adopted Mount Ararat down on Ninety-first Street, and some of the kids at the church, they go to Bertha Palmer. Two of them play on the basketball team. Josie Dorrado and Sancia Valdéz. Do you know them?"

"Oh, yes: there are only sixteen girls on the team, I know them all. So how come you're working here at the warehouse? Shouldn't you be in college or high school or something yourself?"

"I wanted to do a year of service, something like the Peace Corps, after I finished high school, but Grandpa persuaded me to spend a year on the South Side. It's not like he's sick or dying or anything, but he wanted me to work for a year in the company while he was still around to, like, answer my questions, and meantime I can do service through the church and stuff. That's why I know Aunt Jacqui is just being, well, cynical. She is sometimes. A lot of the time. Sometimes I think she only married Uncle Gary because she wanted—" He broke off, blushing even more darkly.

"I forgot what I was going to say. She is really committed to the company. Grandpa, he doesn't really like the ladies in the family to work in the store, not even my sister Candace, when she was running—but, anyway, Aunt Jacqui, she has a degree in design, I think it is, or fabric, something like that, and she persuaded Grandpa that she would go crazy staying at home. We beat Wal-Mart in towels and sheets every quarter since she took over the buying for those things, and even Grandpa is impressed with how thorough she is."

Aunt Jacqui only married Uncle Gary because she wanted a piece of the Bysen family fortune. I could hear the accusations flying around the Bysen dinner table: Buffalo Bill was a tightwad, Aunt Jacqui was a gold digger. But the kid was a hardworking idealist. As I followed him along the corridors to the loading bays, I hoped I could get him to blurt out more indiscretions, like where or what Candace had been running, but he only explained how he came to have his nickname. His father was the oldest son—William the Second.

"It's sort of a family joke, not that I'm crazy about it. Everyone calls Dad 'Young Mister William,' even though he's fifty-two now. So I got nicknamed Billy the Kid. They think I shoot from the hip, see, and I know that's what Pat is going to tell Dad about me bringing you in here, but don't give up, Ms. War-sha-sky, I think it would be really great to help the basketball program. I promise you I'll talk to Grandpa about it."

 ## GIRLS WILL BE GIRLS

As nearly as I could figure it out, the fight Monday afternoon began over religion and spread to sex, although it might have been the other way around. When I reached the gym, Josie Dorrado and Sancia Valdéz, the center, were sitting on the bleachers with their Bibles. Sancia's two babies were on the bench, along with a kid of ten or so—Sancia's younger sister, who was babysitting today. April Czernin stood in front of them, bouncing a ball that some gym teacher had left on the floor. April was a Catholic, but Josie was her best friend; she usually hovered around while Josie did Bible study.

Celine Jackman came in a minute after me and cast a scornful look at her teammates. "You two be praying for a new baby in your families, or what?"

"At least we praying," Sancia said. "All that Catholic mumbo jumbo ain't going to save you none after you been hanging with the Pentas. The truth is in the Bible." She thumped the book for emphasis.

Celine put her hands on her hips. "You think Catholic girls like me are too ignorant to know the Bible, because we go to mass, but you still hang out with April, and last I saw, she was in the same church as me, Saint Michael and All Angels."

April bounced the ball hard and told Celine to shut up.

Celine went on unchecked. "It's you good girls who read your Bibles every day, you the ones who know right from wrong, like you with your two babies. So me, I'm too damned to know stuff in the Bible, like do it say anything about adultery, for instance."

"Ten Commandments," Josie said. "And if you don't know that, Celine, you are dumber than you're trying to pretend."

Celine swung her long auburn braid over her shoulder. "You learned that at Mount Ararat on Ninety-first, huh, Josie? You should take April with you some Sunday."

I grabbed Celine by the shoulders and pointed her toward the locker room. "Drills start in four minutes. Hustle your heinie straight in there and change. Sancia, Josie, April, you start loosening your hamstrings, not your lips."

I made sure Celine had left the gym floor before going into the equipment room to unlock the rest of the balls. When I started the warm-up a little later, I was shy only four players, a sign we were all getting to know each other: my first day, over half the team arrived late. But my rule was that you kept doing floor exercises for the number of minutes you'd missed, even when the rest of the team was running drills with balls. That brought most of the team in on time.

"Where's that English lady, the one who's writing us up?" Laetisha Vettel asked as the girls lay on the floor stretching their hamstrings.

"Ask April." Celine snickered.

"Ask me," I said at once, but April, who was bending over her left leg, had already sat up straight.

"Ask me what?" she demanded.

"Where the English lady be at," Celine said. "Or you don't know, ask your daddy."

"Least I got a daddy to ask," April fired back. "Ask your moma does she even know who your daddy is."

I blew my whistle. "Only one question you two girls need to answer: how many push-ups will I be doing if I don't shut up right now and start stretching."

I spoke with enough menace in my tone to send the two back to pulling their toes toward their chins, left leg, hold eight, right leg, hold eight. I was tired, and not interested in thinking of empathic ways to reach the adolescent psyche. The ride from South Chicago to Morrell's home in Evanston was about thirty miles, an hour on those rare days when the traffic gods were kind, ninety minutes when they more frequently weren't. My own office and apartment lay somewhere near the middle. Keeping on top of my detective agency, running the dogs I share with my downstairs neighbor, doing a little caretaking for Coach McFarlane were all taking a toll on me.

I'd been handling everything okay until Marcena Love arrived; until then, Morrell's place had been a haven where I could unwind at day's end. Even though he was still weak, he was an alert and nurturing presence in my life. Now, though, I felt so jolted by Marcena's presence there that going to see him had turned into the final tension of the day.

Morrell keeps open house in Chicago most of the time—in any given month, everyone from fellow journalists to refugees to artists passes through his spare room. Usually, I enjoy meeting his friends—I get a view of the larger world I don't normally see—but last Friday I'd told him bluntly that I found Marcena Love hard to take.

"It's only for another week or two," he'd said. "I know you two rub each other the wrong way, but honestly, Vic, you shouldn't worry about her. I'm in love with you. But Marcena and I have known each other twenty years, we've been in tight holes together, and when she's in my city she stays with me."

I'm too old to have the kind of fight where you give your lover an ultimatum and break up, but I was glad we'd postponed any decision on living together.

Marcena had stayed away on Saturday night, but returned the day after, sleek as a well-fed tabby, exuberant about her twenty-four hours with Romeo Czernin. She'd arrived at Morrell's just as I was putting a bowl of pasta on table, burbling about what she'd seen and learned on the South Side. When she exclaimed how super it was to drive such an enormous truck, Morrell asked how it compared with the time she managed to get a tank through Vukovar to Cerska in Bosnia.

"Oh, my God, what a time we had that night, didn't we?" she laughed, turning to me. "It would have been right up your alley, Vic. We stayed long past our welcome and our driver had disappeared. We thought it might be our last night on Earth until we found one of Milosevic's tanks, abandoned but still running—fortunately, since I don't know how you turn one of those things on—and I somehow managed to drive the bloody thing all the way to the border."

I smiled back at her—it was indeed the kind of thing I'd have done, with her enthusiasm, too. I felt that twinge of envy, country mouse with city mouse. My home adventures weren't tame, exactly, but nothing I'd done compared to driving a tank through a war zone.

Morrell gave an almost invisible sigh of relief at seeing Marcena and me in tune for a change. "So how did the semi compare with the tank?"

"Oh, an eighteen-wheeler wasn't nearly as exciting—no one was shooting at us—although Bron tells me it has happened. But it's tricky to drive; he wouldn't let me take it out of the parking lot, and, after I'd almost demolished some kind of hut, I had to agree he was right."

Bron. That was his real name; I hadn't been able to come up with it. I asked if the Czernins had put her up for the night; I was wondering how April Czernin's hero worship of the English journalist would survive if she knew her father were sleeping with Marcena.

"In a manner of speaking," she said airily.

"You spend the night in the semi's cab?" I asked. "These modern trucks sometimes almost have little apartments built into them."

She flashed a provocative smile. "As you guessed, Vic, as you guessed."

"You think you have a story there?" Morrell interposed quickly.

"My God, yes." She ran her fingers through her thick hair, exclaiming that Bron was the key to an authentic American experience. "I mean, everything comes together, not exactly through him, but around him, anyway: the squalor, the heartache of these girls imagining that their basketball may get them out of the neighborhood, the school itself, and then Bron Czernin's story—truck driver trying to support a family on those wages. His wife works, too; she's a clerk of some kind at By-Smart. My next step is his firm, By-Smart, I mean, the firm he drives for. One knows about them in a vague way, of course: they've been making European retailers shake in their boots since they launched their transatlantic offensive three years ago. But I didn't realize the head office was right here in Chicago, or at least in one of the suburbs. Rolling-something. Fields, I think."

"Rolling Meadows," I said.

"That's right. Bron tells me old Mr. Bysen is incredibly pious, and that at headquarters the day starts with a prayer service. Can you imagine? It's utterly Victorian. I'm dying to see it, so I'm trying to organize an interview up there."

"Maybe I should come with you." I explained my efforts to enlist the company as a sponsor for the team. "Billy the Kid might get us in to meet his grampa."

She flashed her enthusiastic smile at me. "Oh, Vic, super if you can manage it."

We'd ended the evening still in relative harmony, which was a mercy, but I still didn't sleep well. I slipped out of Morrell's place early this morning, while he was still asleep, so I could drive to my own home and give the dogs a long run before my day started: today would take me down to coach again at Bertha Palmer, and I had promised Josie Dorrado to talk to her mother after practice.

The dogs and I ran all the way down to Oak Street and back, about seven miles. All of us needed the workout, and I thought I was feeling a lot better until Mr. Contreras, my downstairs neighbor, told me I was looking seedy.

"Thought with Morrell coming home, you'd perk up, doll, but you're looking worse than ever. Don't go tearing off to your office now without eating a proper breakfast."

I assured him I was fine, truly fine, now that Morrell was home and mending well, that my current overload was temporary until I found a real coach for the girls at Bertha Palmer.

"And whatcha doing about that, doll? You got anyone lined up?"

"I've put out a few feelers," I said defensively. Besides meeting with Patrick Grobian at By-Smart, I had talked to the women I play Saturday pickup games with and to someone I know who runs a volunteer program for girls at the park district. So far, I'd come up empty, but if Billy the Kid could pry some bucks loose from Grampa one of my contacts might become more enthusiastic.

I fled the apartment before Mr. Contreras got himself revved into a high enough gear to keep me for another hour, promising over my shoulder that I'd eat breakfast, really. After all, my family motto is never skip a meal. Right underneath the Warshawski coat of arms—a knife and fork crossed over a dinner plate.

Privately, I was affronted at being told I looked bad. When I got into my car, I studied my face in the rearview mirror. Seedy, indeed: I was merely interestingly haggard, my lack of sleep making my cheekbones jut out like an anorexic runway model's. In lieu of eight hours in bed, all I needed was a good concealer and some foundation, although not when I was going to spend two hours with sixteen teenagers on a basketball court.

"Morrell thinks I'm beautiful," I grumbled out loud, even if Marcena Love is there in front of him right now, suave and perfectly groomed, probably had her makeup on just so when she commandeered the tank and headed for the border. I snapped my seat belt in hard enough to pinch my thumb, and made a rough U-turn into traffic. When I get my turn to hijack a tank, I'll put on fresh lipstick, too.

I stopped at a diner for scrambled eggs, stopped at a coffee bar for a double espresso, and reached my office by ten. I concentrated on SEC filings and checked arrest records around the country for a man one of my clients was looking to hire. For the first time in a week, I actually managed to stay focused on my real work, completing three projects and even sending out the invoices.

I ruined my better mood by trying to phone Morrell while I waited at a light on Eighty-seventh Street and only reaching his answering machine. He had probably gone to the botanic gardens in Glencoe with Marcena; they'd talked about it last night. I had no problem with that whatsoever. It was great that he was feeling well enough to be up and about. But the idea added to the ferocity with which I stomped on Celine and April at the start of practice.

The team kept quiet for about five minutes, barring the usual jostling and the mutterings that they couldn't do it, the exercises were too hard, Coach McFarlane never made them do this.

Celine, who seemed primed for mischief today, broke the silence by asking if I knew *Romeo and Juliet*. She was standing on her left leg and pulled her right leg straight over her head by the heel. She had extraordinary flexibility; even when she was driving me to the brink of pounding her, she could transfix me by the fluid beauty of her movements.

"You mean, the civil war that makes two star-crossed lovers take their life?" I said cautiously, wondering where this was going. "Not by heart."

Celine momentarily lost her balance. "Huh?"

"Shakespeare. It's how he describes Romeo and Juliet."

"Yeah, it's like a play, Celine," Laetisha Vettel said. "If you ever came to English class, you'd a heard about it. Shakespeare, he lived like a thousand years ago, and wrote Romeo and Juliet up in a play before there was a movie. Before they even knew how to make movies."

Josie Dorrado repeated the line. " 'Star-crossed lovers.' That means even the stars in heaven wouldn't help them."

To my astonishment, April kicked her warningly in the leg. Josie blushed and started touching her toes with a ferocious energy.

"That what 'star-crossed lovers' means?" Theresa Díaz said. "That's me and Cleon, on account of my mama won't let me see him after supper, even for a study break."

"That's because he in the Pentas," Laetisha said. "Your mama is smarter than you, you listen to her. Get clear of the Pentas yourself, girl, you want to live to your next birthday."

Celine pulled her left leg up, her long braid swaying. "You and Cleon should do like April's daddy. I hear everyone do like coach did on Thursday, call him Romeo. Romeo the Roamer, he got the English lady in his—"

April jumped her before she finished the sentence, but Celine had been ready for it—she swung her left leg like a weight, knocking April to the floor. Josie jumped in on April's side, and Theresa Díaz hustled in to help Celine.

I grabbed Laetisha and Sancia as they were about to pitch in and marched them to the bench. "You sit there, you stay there."

I ran to the equipment room and picked up a janitor's bucket. It was full of nasty water, which suited me just fine: I rolled it out to the gym and poured it over the girls.

The cold foul water brought them up from the floor, sputtering and swearing. I seized Celine and April by their long braids and pulled hard. Celine started to throw another punch. I let go of the braids and grabbed Celine's arm, bringing it up behind her back while pinning her right shoulder against me. I got my right arm under her chin and held her close while I gripped April's hair again with my left. Celine cried out, but the sound was covered by the larger yells from Sancia's babies and her sister, who were all screaming.

"Celine, April, I am going to let go of you, but if either of you makes a move I am going to knock you out. Got it?" I moved my forearm tighter under Celine's chin to let her know how serious I was and tugged sharply on April's braid.

The two stood mutely for a long moment, but finally both gave a sullen assent. I let them go and sent them over to the bench.

"Sancia, tell your sister to take your children into the hall: we're going to talk as a team and I won't have the three of them howling during our meeting. All of you girls, sit down. Now. Move it."

They scuttled to the bench, frightened by my show of strength. I didn't want to manage through fear. While they settled themselves I stood quietly, trying to get centered, to focus on them, not on my own frustrations. They watched me wide-eyed, for once completely silent.

Finally, I said, "You all know that if I report this fight to your principal,

Theresa, Josie, Celine, and April will be suspended not just from the team but from school. All four were fighting, and"—I held up a hand as Celine started to protest that April jumped her—"I do not give a rat's tailbone about who started it. We're not here to talk about blame, but about responsibility. Do any of you want to play basketball? Or do you want me to tell the school that I'm too busy to coach a bunch of girls who only want to fight?"

That started an uproar; they wanted to play; if Celine and April were going to fight, they shouldn't be on the team. Someone else pointed out that if Celine and April were thrown out, they wouldn't have much of a team.

"Then they just be selfish," another girl shouted. "If all they care about is their head games, they should stay out of the gym."

One of the girls who usually never spoke up suggested I punish the two for fighting, but not take them off the team. That idea brought a wide murmur of support.

"And what do you suggest by way of punishment?" I asked.

There was a lot of bickering and snickering over possible penalties, until Laetisha said the two should wash the floor. "We can't play today until that floor get mopped up, anyway. They clean the floor today, then we have practice tomorrow."

"What's been going on here?"

I turned, as startled as my team to see an adult standing behind me. It was Natalie Gault, the assistant principal who couldn't remember my name.

"Oh, Ms. Gault, these two—"

"Delia, did I ask you to report?" I cut off the tattletale. "The team has had a little friction, but we've sorted it out. They're going home now, except for four who are staying to wash the floor. Which, although there is a mop and a bucket in the equipment room, and a janitor drawing a paycheck, seems to have been building up dirt since my graduation back in the Stone Age. April, Celine, Josie, and Theresa here are going to build team skills by cleaning off the grime. We'd like to use the gym tomorrow for a makeup practice."

Ms. Gault measured me with the same look the principal's staff used to give me when I was a student all those years back. I felt myself wilting as I used to back then; it was all I could do to keep my glib patter going to the end.

Gault waited long enough to let me know she knew I was covering up a serious problem—which the blood trickling down Celine's leg and on April's face testified to, anyway—but finally said she would sort things out with the boys' coach: if we were going to clean the gym, we should have the right to use it first. She said she'd get the janitor to bring in additional mops and a new box of cleaning solution.

Building teamwork through scrubbing floors turned out to be a successful exercise: by the end of the afternoon, the four malefactors were united in their anger against me. It was after six when I finally let them go. Their uniforms were soaked and they were limp with fatigue, but the floor gleamed as it hadn't since—well, a day twenty-seven years ago when my own teammates and I had scrubbed it. After a far worse episode than a mere gang fight. It wasn't an episode in my life I liked to dwell on, and even now—even now I wouldn't think about it.

I followed them into the locker room while they changed. Mold made little furry patches along the showers and the lockers, some of the toilet seats were missing, some of the toilets were filled with used napkins and other bloody detritus. Maybe I could get Ms. Gault to pressure the janitor into scrubbing this now that the team had cleaned the gym. I held my nose and called to Josie that I would wait for her in the equipment room.

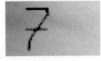 **CLOSE QUARTERS**

Josie lived with her mother—and her older sister and her sister's baby, and her two young brothers—in an old building on Escanaba. As we drove over, Josie implored me not to tell her mother she'd been punished. "Ma, she thinks I should go to college and all, and if she knows I been in trouble over basketball maybe she'll say I can't play no more."

"Do you want to go to college, Josie?"

I pulled up behind a late-model pickup parked outside her building. Four speakers stood in the bed, with the volume cranked so high that the truck itself was vibrating. I had to lean over to hear Josie's response.

"I guess I want to go. Like, I don't want to spend my life working as hard as Ma does, and if I go to college maybe I can be a teacher or coach or something." She picked at a loose cuticle, staring at her knees, then burst out, "I don't know what college is, what it's like, I mean. Like, would they be all stuck up, not liking me because I'm Latina, you know, and growing up down here. I met some rich kids at church, and it's, like, their families don't want them to know me, on account of where I live. So I'm worrying college would be like that."

I remembered the church exchange program that Billy the Kid had mentioned. His choir had been singing with Josie's Pentecostal church choir. I could well imagine families as rich as the Bysens not wanting their children getting too friendly with girls from South Chicago.

"I grew up down here, Josie," I said. "My mother was a poor immigrant, but I still went to college up at the University of Chicago. Of course, there were morons there who thought they were better than me because they grew up with a lot of money and I didn't. But most of the people I met, students and professors, all they cared about was what I was like as a person. If you want to go to college, though, you're going to have to work hard on your studies as well as your basketball. You know that, right?"

She hunched a shoulder and nodded, but the confidence was over; she undid her seat belt and got out of the car. As I followed her up the walk to the front door, I saw five youths lounging around the truck, smoking reefer. One of them was the guy who sat morosely in the bleachers with his and Sancia's children during practice. The other four I hadn't seen before, but Josie clearly knew them. They called out to her, something taunting that I couldn't hear over the booming speakers.

Josie yelled back, "You better hope Pastor Andrés don't come round—he totally fix that truck for you like he did before."

The youths shouted something else at her. When it looked as though she was going to stay to fight, I pushed her up the front walk. The noise followed us up the stairs to the second floor; even though the Dorrados lived in the back of the building, I could still feel the bass rocketing inside my stomach as Josie unlocked her front door.

The door led directly into a living room. A girl was sitting on the couch, dressed only in a baby-doll T-shirt and underpants. She was watching television with a ferocious intensity, her hand moving from an open chip bag in her lap to her mouth. An infant lay next to her on the plastic-coated cushion, staring vacantly at the ceiling. The only decorations in the room were a large, plain cross on one wall and a picture of Jesus blessing some children.

"Julia! Coach is here to see Ma. Put some clothes on," Josie cried. "What you thinking, sitting around naked in the middle of the afternoon?"

When her sister didn't move, Josie walked over and yanked the potato chip bag from her lap. "Get up. Get out of this dreamworld and into the daylight. Is Ma home?"

Julia hunched over, so that her face was only a yard from the screen, where a woman in red was leaving a hospital room; a man accosted her. The conversation, in Spanish, had something to do with the woman in the room behind them.

Josie stood between the set and her sister. "You can see *Mujer* again tomorrow, and the day after and the day after that. Now, go put on your clothes. Is Ma home?"

Julia got sullenly to her feet. "She's in the kitchen. Mixing María Inés's formula. Take María Inés out with you while I put on my jeans."

"I gotta meet April. We have a science project together, so don't expect me to stay home looking after your own baby," Josie warned, scooping up the infant. "Sorry, coach," she added over her shoulder to me. "Julia lives inside that telenovela. She even named the baby for one of the people in it."

I followed her through a doorway into a room that doubled as a dining and bedroom: bed linens were folded neatly at one end of an old wood table; plates and silver were stacked at the other. Two air mattresses lay under the table; next to them, a box held Power Rangers and other action toys that must have belonged to Josie's brothers.

Julia shoved her way past Josie into a small room on our left. Twin beds were neatly made. The linens were startling, bright replicas of the Stars-and-Stripes. I hadn't realized patriotism was so important to the Dorrados.

A rope slung above the two twin beds was festooned with baby clothes. On the wall above one bed, I glimpsed a poster for the University of Illinois women's basketball team: Josie's side of the room. Like most of the girls on the team, the U. of I. women were her heroines, because that's where Coach McFarlane had gone to school. Despite the clutter in the cramped quarters, everything was neatly organized.

We passed on to the kitchen, a room just big enough for one person to stand in easily. Even back here, the thud from the giant speakers outside still carried faintly.

Josie's mother was warming a bottle in a pan of hot water. When Josie explained who I was, her mother wiped her hands on her baggy black pants and apologized repeatedly for not being in the living room to greet me. She was short, with bright red hair, so unlike her tall, skinny daughters that I blinked at her rudely.

When I shook hands and called her "Ms. Dorrado," she said, "No, no, my name is Rose. Josie, she didn't say you was coming over today," she explained.

Josie ignored the implied criticism and handed the baby to her mother. "I ain't staying around to babysit. April and me, we had to stay late at practice, and now we need to work on our science project."

"Science project?" Rose Dorrado repeated. "You know I don't want you doing anything like cutting up frogs."

"No, Ma, we ain't doing nothing like that. It's on public health, like, how do you keep from catching the flu in school. We have to set up the study, uh, pamters." She cast a cautious look at me.

"Parameters," I corrected.

"Yeah, we're gonna do that."

"You get back here by nine o'clock," her mother warned. "You don't and you know I'm sending your brother to look for you."

"But, Ma, we're late starting on account of coach kept us late," Josie protested.

"Then you work that much harder," her mother said firmly. "And what about your supper? You can't ask Mrs. Czernin to feed you."

"April brought an extra pizza home with her Thursday, when Mr. Czernin took us out with the lady reporter. She said she saved that for her and me to eat tonight." She didn't wait for further reaction but bolted back through the apartment. We heard an extra jolt on top of the bass as Josie slammed the door.

"Who is this lady reporter?" her mother asked, testing some formula on her wrist. "Josie said something about her on Thursday, but I didn't follow it."

I explained who Marcena Love was, and what she was doing with the team.

"Josie's a good girl, she helps me a lot, like with little María Inés, she should have a treat now and then," her mother sighed. "She doing okay with the basketball team? You think maybe basketball can get her a scholarship for college? She needs an education. I won't have her end up like her sister . . ." her voice trailed away, and she patted the baby reassuringly, as if trying to say she wasn't blaming it for her worries.

"Josie works hard and she looks good on the court," I said, not adding that the odds of making a college team from a program like Bertha Palmer's were pretty abysmal. "She said you want to talk to me about a problem of some kind?"

"Please, let me give you something to drink; then we can talk more easily."

Given a choice of instant coffee or orange Kool-Aid I started to refuse anything, but remembered in the nick of time the important hospitality rituals in South Chicago. Romeo Czernin was right: I had been away from the 'hood too long if I was going to turn up my nose at instant coffee. Not that my mother ever served it—she'd do without other things before giving up her Italian coffee, bought at a market on Taylor Street— but instant was certainly a staple on Houston Street when I was growing up.

Baby propped on her shoulder, Rose Dorrado poured some of the water she'd been boiling to heat the bottle into two plastic mugs. I carried those into the living room, where Julia, in jeans, had reestablished herself in front of her telenovela. Josie's two young brothers had come home, too, and were fighting their sister over the channel she was tuned to, but their mother told them if they wanted to watch soccer they had to mind the baby. The boys quickly fled back down to the street.

I sipped the thin, bitter coffee while Rose fretted out loud about the future of her boys without a father; her brother tried to help out, playing with them on Sundays, but he had his own family to look after, too.

I looked at my watch and tried to push Rose Dorrado to the point. The story, when it came out, wasn't the tale of personal violence I'd been imagining. Rose worked for Fly the Flag, a little company on Eighty-eighth Street that made banners and flags.

"You know, your church, your school, they want a big banner for parades or to hang in the gym, that's what we do. And we iron them if you need that done. Like, you keep it rolled up all year and you want it for your graduation march, only our shop has the machines big enough to press one of those banners. I been there nine years. I started even before my husband left me with all these children, and now I'm like a supervisor, although, of course, I still sew, too."

I nodded politely and congratulated her, but she brushed that aside and went on with her tale. Although Fly the Flag made American flags, those had just been a sideline to their main business until September 11. They'd always produced the outsize flags that schools and other institutions liked to spread across an upper balcony or wall, but before September 11 such enormous flags had had a limited market.

"After the Trade Center went down, there was a very big demand for them, you understand, everyone wanted a flag for their business, even some rich apartment buildings wanted to hang them from the roofs, and suddenly we had a lot of orders, almost too much, we couldn't even keep up with it. Everything we do is by hand, you know, for this kind of banner, but for the flags we use machines, and so we even had to buy a second machine."

"Sounds great," I said. "South Chicago needs more business success stories."

"We do need these businesses. I need this job: I got four children to feed, plus now Julia's baby. If this business don't stay in business, I don't know what I can do."

And now she came to the crux of the matter. Since the summer, work had fallen off. Fly the Flag was still running two shifts, but Mr. Zamar had laid off eleven people. Josie's mom had a lot of seniority but she was afraid for the future.

"It sounds very worrying," I agreed, "but I'm not sure what you want me to do about it."

She laughed nervously. "Probably it's all my imagination. I worry too much because of having so many children to feed. I make good money at the plant, thirteen dollars an hour. If they close, if they go to Nicaragua or China, like some people think, or if Mr. Zamar—if some accident happens to the building—where else can I work? Only at By-Smart, and there you start at seven dollars. Who can feed six people on seven dollars an hour? And the rent. And we're still paying for María Inés, for her birth, I mean. The hospital, they charge so much interest, and then she needs her shots, all the children, they all need shoes . . ." Her voice trailed off into a sigh.

All during Rose Dorrado's rambling remarks, Julia continued to watch the television as if her whole life depended on it, but the tension in her thin shoulders showed she was acutely aware of her mother's words. I drank my coffee down to the last undissolved crystal: I couldn't waste anything here.

"So what's happening at the plant?" I tried to bring her back to her problem.

"Probably it's nothing," she said. "Maybe it's nothing; Josie kept saying not to bother you with it."

When I pressed her harder, though, she finally blurted out that last month, when she arrived at work—and she always got there early, always anxious that she be thought a good employee—if there were going to be more layoffs she couldn't let anyone say she had a bad attitude—anyway, she arrived to find she couldn't get her key in the lock. Someone had filled the keyholes with Krazy Glue, and they lost a whole day's work while they waited for a locksmith to come and drill them out. Then another time she opened the factory and found it full of a really bad smell, which turned out to be dead rats in the heating ducts.

"Because I'm there early I got all the windows open, and we could still do some work, it wasn't too bad, but you can imagine! We were lucky the weather was not so bad—in November, you know, it could be a blizzard, or rain or something."

"What does Mr. Zamar say?"

She bent over the baby. "Nothing. He tells me accidents happen at plants all the time."

"Where was he when the locks were glued shut?"

"What do you mean?" Rose asked.

"I mean, wasn't it surprising that you discovered they were glued shut? Why wasn't he there?"

"He don't come in early because he stays late, until seven or eight at night, so he don't come in usually till eight-thirty in the morning, sometimes even nine."

"So he could have glued the doors shut himself when he left the night before," I said bluntly.

She looked up startled. "Why would he do that?"

"To force the plant out of business in a way that let him collect the insurance."

"He wouldn't do that," she cried, too quickly. "That would be wicked, and, really, he is a good man, he tries hard . . ."

"You think maybe one of the people he laid off could be doing it for revenge?"

"Anything is possible," she said. "That's why—I'm wondering—when Josie told me a lady cop is coaching now instead of Mrs. McFarlane—can't you go in there and find out?"

"It would be much better if you'd call the police, the real police. They can ask—"

"No!" the word came out so loudly that the baby hiccupped and began to cry.

"No," she said more quietly, rocking the infant against her shoulder. "Mr. Zamar, he told me no police, he won't let me call. But you, you grew up here, you could ask some questions, no one would mind questions from the lady who helps the girls play basketball."

I shook my head. "I'm just one person working alone, and an investigation like this, it's time-consuming, it's expensive."

"How much money?" she asked. "I can pay you something, maybe when I finish paying the hospital for Julia."

I couldn't bring myself to tell her my usual fee was $125 an hour, not to someone who thought she was lucky to feed five children on thirteen dollars an hour. Even though I often do pro bono work—too often, my accountant keeps telling me—I didn't see how I could conduct an investigation at a shop where the owner didn't want me.

"But don't you see, if you don't find out, if we don't stop this, the plant will close, and what will happen to me, to my children?" she cried out, tears in her eyes.

Julia hunched deeper inside her T-shirt at her outburst and the baby squalled more loudly. I rubbed my head. The idea of one more obligation, one more rope tying me to my old neighborhood, made me want to join Julia on the couch with my head buried in an imaginary world.

With a leaden hand, I pulled my pocket diary out of my bag and looked at my commitments. "I can come down early tomorrow, I guess, but you know I'm going to have to talk to Mr. Zamar, and if he orders me off the premises I won't be able to do anything else but leave."

Rose Dorrado beamed at me in relief. She probably figured once I took the first step, I'd be committed to the whole journey. I hoped very much she was wrong.

8 PLANT LIFE

I hugged my windbreaker close to my chest and slipped through a loose piece of the chain-link fence. The pale steel of a late-fall dawn was just beginning to lighten the sky, and the air was cold.

When I told Rose Dorrado I'd come by Fly the Flag this morning, I'd originally planned to arrive around eight-thirty to question the crew. Last night, though, when I was talking to Morrell about the situation, I realized I should come early: if someone was sabotaging the plant before the morning shift arrived, I might catch them in the act.

I'd had another late night last night, between staying at the school with my warring players, calling on Rose, and then, finally, stopping to check on Mary Ann McFarlane on my way north. Although a home care provider came in four times a week and did laundry and other difficult jobs, I'd gotten in the habit of bringing her food, sometimes dinner, sometimes just extra treats she enjoyed that no one else thought worth shopping for.

Mary Ann lived just north of my old neighborhood in an apartment like my own, four rooms built railway style in an old brick eight-flat. She had been in bed when I reached her last night, but she called out to me in a voice still strong enough to reach the hall. I shouted back a greeting as I bent to pet Scurry, her dachshund, who was turning inside out in his eagerness at seeing me.

What I would do with the dog when—if—he needed a new home was one of my ongoing concerns. I already had a golden retriever and her gigantic half-Lab son. A third dog would bring the health department down on me—not on account of the dogs, but to put me into a locked ward.

By the time I got to the bedroom, my old coach had hoisted herself out of bed and made it to the doorway. She was clutching the edge of the dresser, but she waved off my offered arm and stood panting until she got her breath back. In the bedroom's dim light she looked ghastly, her cheeks sunken, the skin around her neck hanging in folds. She used to be a stocky woman; now cancer and chemicals had sucked the life out from under her flesh. The chemo had also turned her bald. The hair was growing back, covering her head with a coarse, gray-streaked red stubble, but even when she was as bald as Michael Jordan she had refused to wear a wig.

When I first saw her like this, it had been a shock: I was so used to her muscular energy that I couldn't think of her as ill, or old. Not that she was old—she was only sixty-six, I'd learned to my surprise. Somehow, when she was coaching me, and teaching me Latin, she'd looked as formidably ancient as her bust of Caesar Augustus.

She waited to talk until she'd walked to the kitchen and was sitting at the old enamel table there. Scurry jumped up onto her lap. I put the kettle on for tea and unpacked the groceries I'd picked up for her.

"How did practice go today?" she asked.

I told her about the fight; she nodded approvingly of the way I'd handled it. "The school doesn't care if those girls play or not. Or even if they attend—under No Child Left Behind, Celine Jackman is dragging the test scores down, so they'd have been just as happy if you kicked her out, but basketball's her lifeline. Don't let her get suspended if you can help it."

She stopped to catch her breath, then added, "You're not making any of that tofu slop, are you?"

"No, ma'am." When I first started cooking for her, I'd tried making her miso soup with tofu, thinking it would be easier for her to digest, and maybe help her get some strength back, but she'd hated it. She was a meat-and-potatoes woman through and through, and if she couldn't eat much of her pot roast these days she still enjoyed it more than tofu slop.

While she slowly ate as much of the meal as she could manage, I went to the bedroom to change her sheets. She hated my seeing the blood and pus in her bed, so we both pretended I didn't know it was there. On days when she was too weak to get out of bed, her embarrassment at the condition of the linens was more painful than the tumors themselves.

While I bundled everything into a bag for the laundry service, I glanced at the books she'd been reading. One of Lindsay Davis's Roman mysteries. The most recent volume of LBJ's biography. A collection of Latin crossword puzzles—all the clues were in Latin, no English hints at all. It was only her body that was failing.

When I got back to the kitchen, I told her Rose Dorrado's story. "You know everyone in South Chicago. You know Zamar? Is he likely to sabotage his own factory?"

"Frank Zamar?" She shook her head. "I don't know that kind of thing about anyone, Victoria. People down here get desperate, and they do the things desperate people do. I don't think he'd hurt anyone, though: if he's trying to destroy his own plant, he won't do it while any of his employees are on the premises."

"He have kids in the school?"

"He doesn't have a family, as far as I know. Lives on the East Side, used to be with his mother, but she's been gone three, four years now. Quiet man, fifty-something. Last year he donated uniforms to our program. Josie's mom probably put him up to it. That's how I met him at all— Rose Dorrado got him to come watch Julia play. That's Josie's sister, you know. She was my best player, maybe since you were in school, until she had the kid. Now her life's unraveled, she doesn't even come to school."

I slapped the sponge against the counter hard enough to bounce it across the room. "These girls and their babies! I grew up in that neighborhood, I went to that high school. There were always some girls who got pregnant, but nothing like what I'm seeing down here now."

Mary Ann sighed. "I know. If I knew how to stop them I would. Girls in your generation weren't so sexually active so young, for one thing, and you had more possibilities in front of you."

"I don't remember too many kids in my class going to college," I said.

She paused, catching her breath. "Not what I mean. Even the ones who only wanted to get married and raise a family down there, they knew their husbands would work, there were good jobs. Heck, there were jobs. Now no one feels they have a future. Men who used to make thirty dollars an hour at U.S. Steel are lucky to work for a quarter of that at By-Smart."

"I tried to talk to your center, Sancia, about birth control—I mean, she already has the two babies. Her boyfriend hangs around during practice; he looks like he's at least twenty-five, but if the word *work* has ever crossed his mind he's dismissed it as something in a foreign language, probably obsolete. Anyway, I suggested if Sancia was going to stay sexually active it would help her chances in school and in life if she didn't have any more children, but her mother came over to me the next day and told me she would yank her daughter out of basketball if I talked any more about birth control to the team, but—I can't leave them lurching around in ignorance, can I?"

"I'd be glad if every kid in that school practiced abstinence, believe me," Mary Ann said bluntly, "but since that's as likely as the dinosaurs reviving, they should have reliable information about contraception. But you can't go giving it to them unsolicited. Trouble is, Sancia's mother goes to a Pentecostal church that believes if you use birth control you go to hell."

"But—"

"Don't argue with me about it, and don't, for heaven's sake, argue with the kids. They take their faith very seriously in those storefront churches. You see them reading their Bibles before practice?"

"Another change from my youth," I said wryly, "the mass defection of Latinos from mass. I've read about it, of course, but hadn't experienced it before. And they don't seem to have a problem proselytizing among some of the other girls on the team—I've had to break that up once or twice."

Mary Ann showed her strong teeth in a grin. "It's hard work being a teacher these days—what you can talk about, what you can't, what can get you and the school sucked into a lawsuit. Still, Rose Dorrado is a more practical mom than Sancia's mother. Since Julia's baby, she's been on Josie like a hawk, checking who she sees after school, not letting her go out alone with any of the boys. Rose wants that kid in college. April's folks are pushing her, too."

"Come on!" I protested. "If Romeo—Bron—Czernin has one thought above his zipper, it's about himself."

"Her mother, then," Mary Ann conceded. "She's determined that her kid is going to get out of South Chicago. She tolerates the basketball in case it gets April a scholarship, but she's probably one of a dozen parents in that school sitting on the kid's head and making her do homework every night."

The long conversation had worn out my coach. I helped her back into bed, took Scurry for a walk around the block, and then went north to deal with my own dogs. My downstairs neighbor had let them out, but I drove to the lake so they could run. I took Mitch and Peppy up with me to Morrell's, where I left them when I got up the next morning at five to return to the South Side.

Even though the city was still shrouded in the mantle of night, the expressway was already busy—although, when is it ever not? Trucks, anxious people getting to the early shift, detectives looking for who knows what, filled the ten lanes. It was only when I exited at Eighty-seventh Street and headed east that the streets became quiet.

Fly the Flag stood against the embankment of the Skyway on South Chicago Avenue. I suppose there was a time when the avenue was full of active, prospering factories and shops, but I couldn't remember it. Unlike the Skyway overhead, where traffic was thick with commuters from northwest Indiana, the avenue was deserted. A few cars were not so much parked as abandoned along the curbs, hoods sprung or axles reeling at odd angles. I left my Mustang on a side street so it wouldn't stand out among the wrecks, and walked two blocks south to Fly the Flag. Only a CTA bus, grinding slowly north like a bear lumbering into the wind, passed me.

Except for an iron works, whose locked yard protected a modern sprawling plant, most of the buildings I passed looked as though only some defiant opposition to gravity kept them upright. Windows were missing or were boarded over; strips of aluminum waved in the wind. It's a sign of the neighborhood's desperate job shortage that people will work in these collapsing structures.

To my surprise, Fly the Flag didn't share the general decay along the avenue. Rose Dorrado's story had half persuaded me that Frank Zamar was engineering his company's demise himself, but, if he was, I'd have expected him to let the plant itself run down: a lot of arson is caused by malign neglect—letting buildings carry more power than their wiring can stand, not repairing frayed wires, letting garbage accumulate in strategic corners—rather than outright torching. At least from the outside, Fly the Flag looked in good shape.

Flashlight in hand, I made my way around the exterior. The yard was small, big enough for an eighteen-wheeler to maneuver in if necessary, but not for much more than that. A drive led down to a basement-level loading dock; there were two ground-level entrances.

I walked all the way around the building, looking for holes in the foundation, looking for cuts in the electric cable and gas line leading into the plant, or for footprints in the damp ground, but didn't see anything unusual. All of the entrances were locked; when I probed with my picklocks, I didn't feel any obstructions.

I looked at my watch: six-oh-seven. Flashlight trained on the lock, I used my picks to open the rear door. Someone from the Skyway might see me, but I doubted anyone up there cared enough about life down here to call the cops.

Inside the plant, the layout was pretty simple: a large open floor where the giant cutting and pressing machines stood, long tables where people sewed, all dominated by the biggest American flag I'd ever seen. When I shone my flashlight up on it, the stripes looked so soft and rich I wanted to touch them. By climbing up on a tabletop and stretching up a hand, I could just reach the bottom stripe. It felt like a silken velvet, so voluptuous that I wanted to hug it to myself. The careful stitching along the stripes showed the workers believed in the slogan they'd posted above it: "We Fly the Flag Proudly."

I jumped down and wiped my footprints from the table before continuing to explore. In one corner, space had grudgingly been given over to a tiny canteen, a dirty toilet, and a minute office where Frank Zamar did his paperwork. In an alcove next to the canteen stood a row of beat-up metal lockers, enough that I guessed they must be for employees to store their personal things in during the day.

On the other side of the room, an open-sided service elevator went down to the basement. I used its hand crank to lower myself. The front opened onto the dock; the rear to the storeroom where bolts of fabric were kept. There were hundreds of bolts of all different colors and long spools of braid, even a wire cage holding flagpoles of different lengths. Everything the compleat flag producer required.

It was after six-thirty now, not enough time to check Zamar's office before Rose Dorrado showed up to prove her zeal as an employee. I wondered idly if she had glued the locks herself: she could be trying to prove she was indispensable by protecting the plant from saboteurs. Collecting enough dead rats to stink up the heating vents seemed like a horrible job, but I supposed it all depended on how determined you were.

I saw a set of iron stairs leading to the main floor and was starting up them when I heard a noise above me, a thud of the kind a door makes when it closes. If it was Rose Dorrado, I was okay, but if not—I turned off the flashlight, sticking it in my pack, and crept upward by feel. I could hear footsteps; when my eyes were level with the floor, my view was blocked by a giant sewing machine, but I could see a cone of light wobbling around the worktables—someone picking their way. If it was someone with a legitimate reason to be there, they would have switched on the fluorescent overheads.

A pair of high-tops appeared around the edge of the sewing machine, laces slapping against the floor. An amateur: a pro would have tied his shoes. I ducked down. My picklocks jangled against the iron banister. The feet above me froze, turned, and started running.

I jumped up the stairs and reached the intruder just as he was opening the door. He flung his flashlight at me. I ducked a second too late and reeled as it hit the top of my head. By the time I regained my balance and got out the fire exit after him, he had cleared the fence and was scrambling up the embankment toward the Skyway. I followed him, but I was too far behind to bother trying to climb the fence; he was already hoisting himself over the concrete barricade next to the road.

I heard horns blaring, and the raw screech of skidding tires, and then the roar of engines as the traffic came back to life.

If he hadn't cleared all six lanes, I'd hear sirens soon. When a couple of minutes passed without them, I turned and went back down the hill. It was close to seven now; the morning shift should be arriving. I trudged across the muddy ground, reflexively rubbing the sore spot where the flashlight had hit my head.

As I turned around the corner of the building, heading toward the front, I could see Rose Dorrado crossing the yard, her red hair standing out like a flare in the dull day. By the time I got to the main entrance, Rose had the front unlocked and was already inside. A few other people were coming through the gate into the yard, talking quietly to each other. They looked at me without much curiosity as they passed.

I found Rose at the metal lockers, pulling out a blue smock and hanging up her coat. The inside of her locker was pasted with Bible verses. Her lips were moving, perhaps in prayer, and I waited for her to finish before tapping her shoulder.

She looked at me, surprised and pleased. "You got here early! You can talk to people before Mr. Zamar shows up."

"Someone else was here early, a youngish man. I didn't get a good look, but maybe in his early twenties. Tall, but his cap was pulled down too low for me to see his face. He had a thin mustache."

Rose frowned in worry. "Some man was here trying to do something? It's what I said, it's what I tried to warn Mr. Zamar about. Why didn't you stop him?"

"I tried, but he was too fast for me. We could call the police, see if he left fingerprints—"

"Only if Mr. Zamar says it's all right. What was he trying to do, this man?"

I shook my head. "I don't know that, either. He heard me and ran off, but I think he was heading for the stairs down to the basement. What's there, besides all the fabric?"

She was too upset to wonder how I knew about the fabric in the basement, or to question where I had been when the intruder heard me. "Everything. You know, the boiler, the drying room, the dry-cleaning room, everything for running the factory, it's all down there. *Dios*, we can't be safe now? We have to keep worrying is someone in here planting a bomb in the morning?"

 **THE FOG OF . . . WHAT?**

B usiness is full of risks. I can handle this fine without you butting in."
Frank Zamar's stubby hands moved restlessly over his desk, like birds
uneasy about landing on a branch.

"According to Rose, you've had quite a history of sabotage in the last
few weeks: rats in the heating ducts, Krazy Glue in the door locks, and
now someone breaking in at six this morning. Aren't you worried about
what's going on?"

"Rose means well, I know she does, but she had no right to call you in."

I looked at him in exasperation. "So you'd rather let your plant go up
in smoke than figure out who is doing this, or why?"

"No one's going to burn up my plant." His square face sagged around
the corners; the bravado of his words wasn't matched by the worry in
his eyes.

"Do you have the local gangbangers so pissed off at you that you're
scared to report them? Is this about 'protection' payoffs, Zamar?"

"No, it damn well isn't about paying protection." He slapped the desk
for emphasis, but I wasn't convinced.

"I'd like to talk to your crew, to see if anyone seems to be hiding something. Or maybe they have an idea about the guy who broke into the plant this morning."

"No way do you talk to any of my workers! Who told you to mind my business, anyway? You think I'm going to pay you for lurking around my factory?"

He was muttering his complaints, not shouting, which seemed ominous to me: a man afraid of what I would learn. I nodded, though, at his words: no one was going to pay me for spending my time at Fly the Flag.

As I stood to leave, I said casually, "You wouldn't be doing this yourself, would you?"

"Doing what—you mean, putting dead rats in my own heating system? You are crazy, you, you—nosy bitch! Why would I do such an insane thing?"

"You laid off eleven people this fall. Your business is in trouble. You wouldn't be the first person to try to sell your plant to the insurance company—solve a lot of problems, wouldn't it, if sabotage forced you out of business."

"I laid people off because of the economy. As soon as the economy improves, I'll hire them back. Now get out of here."

I took a card out of my bag and laid it on his desk. "Call me when you decide you can tell me who has you so scared you won't even protect your own business."

I left the office and walked across the floor to where Rose was stitching an intricate gold logo onto an outsize navy banner. She looked up at me but didn't stop moving the heavy fabric through the machine. The racket on the floor was intense, what with the sewing machines, the giant electric shears, and the industrial steam pressers; I squatted so I could yell directly into her ear.

"He claims nothing's going on, despite the evidence. He's scared of someone or something, too scared to talk about it, in my opinion. Do you have any idea what that could be?"

She shook her head, her eyes on the work in front of her.

"He says it's not gang protection. Do you believe that?"

She hunched a shoulder, not breaking the quick movement of her hands as they guided the needle through the appliqué. "You know this neighborhood. You know there are a lot of street gangs down here. The Pentas, the Latin Kings, the Lions, any of them could do anything bad. But usually they're more—more violent than this—they would break the windows, something like that, not put glue in the locks."

"And how did the guy get in this morning?" Maybe I'd left the back door open when I undid the lock this morning: I didn't think so, but I couldn't swear to it a hundred percent, either. "Who has keys besides Zamar?"

"The foremen—Larry Ballatra, he's the day man, and Joey Husack, he's the second shift."

"And you, right, since you often come in early?"

Her lips moved in a nervous smile. "Yes, but me, I'm not trying to hurt the plant, I'm trying to keep it open."

"Or trying to get Zamar to think you're indispensable, so he doesn't let you go in the next round of job cuts."

For the first time her hands slowed and she didn't feed the fabric through fast enough. She hissed a curse at me as it bunched up under the needle. "Now look what you've made me do. And how can you say such things? You're Josie's coach! She trusts you. I trusted you."

A hand suddenly gripped my shoulder and yanked me to my feet. The noise from the machines had been so loud I hadn't heard the foreman come up behind me.

Although he was holding me, he spoke to Rose Dorrado. "Rose, since when do you have the right to have guests at your workstation? You better not be short when the day ends."

"I won't be," Rose said, her face still red with anger. "And she's not a guest, she's a detective."

"Who you invited into the plant! She doesn't belong in here. The boss told her to get out, so what business you got talking to her?" He shook my shoulder. "The boss told you to leave, now you're going to leave."

He frog-marched me to the door and pushed me outside so hard that I stumbled against a man who was crossing the apron to the front door.

"Steady there, steady there." He caught me and held me upright. "You're not drinking on the job, are you, my sister?"

"No, my brother, not today, although, at the moment, it doesn't sound like a bad idea." I backed away from him and dusted my shoulders where the foreman had gripped them.

He looked startled, then concerned. "You have been fired, perhaps?"

He had a slight Hispanic accent, whether Mexican, Puerto Rican, or even Spanish, I was too ignorant to know. Like much of the work crew, he was a swarthy, thickset man, but his somber suit and tie didn't belong in a factory.

"I'm an investigator, whom Mr. Zamar doesn't want to hire, or even talk to. Do you know about the attempts to sabotage the plant?" When the man nodded, I asked what he knew about it.

"Only that some members of the community are concerned. Has there been another episode today?"

I looked at him narrowly, wondering how trustable he was—but, after all, if he knew anything about this morning's intruder I wasn't going to give him news by discussing it. When I told him what I'd seen, he only said that Mr. Zamar had many problems, that he couldn't afford to lose the factory.

"Why won't he call in the cops?" I demanded.

"If I knew that, I would be a wise man. But I will ask him."

"And if he answers, do me a favor and let me in on the secret." I pulled one of my cards from my case and handed it to him.

"V. I. Warshawski." He read my name carefully. "And I am Robert Andrés. Good day, Sister Warshawski."

We shook hands on his odd and formal greeting. Even though I spent the rest of the day on work for my paying clients, my mind kept wandering back to Frank Zamar and Fly the Flag. I worried that I had needlessly alienated Rose by suggesting she could be the saboteur. Before I met Zamar it had seemed possible to me, because she was so worried about her job that she might want to prove she was indispensable: there she was, arriving early, finding rats in the air ducts, summoning help—even hiring a detective! Who could fire such a zealous employee?

Now that I'd seen Zamar, I didn't really believe Rose was involved. Something was worrying him too badly about all these episodes. The man I'd stumbled into at the entrance, Robert Andrés, he might know; I should have gotten his phone number. I'd been too busy feeling angry and humiliated by the foreman tossing me out to take care of fundamentals.

Maybe Zamar was in love with Rose and worried because he thought she was responsible. Or Rose's daughter with the baby, Julia—he'd donated warm-up jackets, he used to watch her play. Could he be the baby's father? Was Rose going to destroy Fly the Flag to punish him for that?

"Give it up, Warshawski," I said out loud. "Any more like that and you'll be writing scripts for Jerry Springer."

I was in the western suburbs, looking for a woman who had abandoned a safe-deposit box holding eight million dollars in bearer bonds, and I needed to put all my attention on that project. I located her daughter and son-in-law, who seemed to me to know more than they wanted to say. My client managed the little deli belonging to the woman—she'd gotten worried when the owner suddenly disappeared. A little before three, I finally found the woman in a nursing home where she'd been involuntarily committed. I talked to my client, who rushed out west with a lawyer. I was tired but triumphant as I raced back to South Chicago for my team's makeup practice.

The girls played well, pleased with their clean gym. For the first time, they actually looked like a team—maybe the fight really had brought them together. We did a short workout, and they left with their heads up, triumphant from my praise—and their pleasure in their own ability.

On my way home, while I sat motionless in the rush hour traffic, I called my answering service to pick up my messages. To my astonishment, I had one from Billy the Kid. When I reached him on his own mobile phone, he stammered that he'd told his grandfather about me and the Bertha Palmer basketball program. If I wanted, I could go to corporate headquarters in the morning to sit in on the prayer meeting that would start the day. "If Grandpa has time, he'll talk to you afterward. He couldn't promise me he'd see you, or do anything for you, but he did say you could come out there. The only thing is, you have to be there by around seven-fifteen."

"Great," I said with a heartiness I was far from feeling. Even though

I'm often up early, I've never been as big a cheerleader for mornings as Benjamin Franklin was. I asked young Billy for directions to the Rolling Meadows office.

He spelled these out for me. "I'm actually going to be there myself, Ms. War-sha-sky, because I'm helping a little with the service. The pastor is coming up from Mount Ararat Church of Holiness, you know, the one where my home church is doing the exchange, to preach the morning service. Aunt Jacqui will probably be there, too, so it's not like everyone will be a stranger. Anyway, I'll call Herman, he's the guard on the morning shift, he'll know to let you in. And Grandpa's secretary, I'll let her know, just in case, you know, in case Grandpa has time to talk to you. How's the basketball team doing?"

"They're working hard, Billy, but of course they don't start playing other teams until New Year's."

"What about, uh, Sancia, and, uh, Josie?"

"What about them?" I asked.

"Well, you know, they go to Mount Ararat, and, well, how are they doing?"

"Okay, I guess," I said slowly, wondering if I could enlist Billy's help in tutoring Josie: if she was going to go to college, she'd need extra help. But I didn't know what kind of a student he'd been himself, and I didn't want to start a conversation like that in the middle of the expressway.

"So can I come over sometime and watch them practice? Josie said you're real strict about not letting boys in the gym."

I told him we might find a way to make an exception if he could get off work early some afternoon, and ended the conversation with a warm thanks for getting me into his grandfather's office. Even if it did mean getting up again at five so I could trek across Chicagoland.

When he'd hung up, I thought again about my time with Rose Dorrado this morning. I had handled the whole situation badly, and I needed to apologize to her.

It was Josie who answered the phone. I could hear Baby María Inés squalling close at hand, and before she answered she yelled at her sister to take the child.

"It's your baby, Julia, you do some of the work for a change . . . Hello? Oh, coach, oh!"

"Josie, hi. Is your mom there? I'd like to talk to her."

She was silent for a moment. "She hasn't come home yet."

I eyed a beat-up Chevy that wanted to muscle in front of me, and eased up to make room for it. "I went to the factory this morning; did she tell you that?"

"I haven't seen her since breakfast, coach, and now I got to figure out how to make dinner for my brothers, and everything."

The worried undertone in her voice got through to me. "Are you worried that something's happened to her?"

"No-o, I guess not. She called and all, she say she going—I mean, she said she had something else to do, maybe extra work, I guess, but she don't say what, just help out with the boys' supper, and, you know. But I already get their breakfast, 'cause Ma leaves for work before we get up, and now the baby is crying, Julia won't help, and I got my science project."

I could picture the crowded apartment. "Josie, put the baby to bed. She can cry for a while without it doing her any harm. Unplug the TV and do your science project in the living room. Your brothers are big enough they can open a can of something, and they can play with their Power Rangers in the dining room. You got a microwave? No? Well, you got a can of soup? Heat it up on the stove and let them eat. Your education comes first. Okay?"

"Uh, okay, I guess. But what am I going to do if this keeps on?"

"Will it?" A semi honked at me; I'd lost track of the traffic, and a big gap had opened in front of me.

"If she got another job, it will."

"I'll talk to your mom about it. I need to, anyway. Can you write down my number? Tell her to call me when she gets in."

When she'd repeated my cell phone number, I reiterated my message. Before I hung up, I heard her yelling at her sister that she could look after María Inés or Josie was going to put her to bed. I guess I'd done one good deed for the day—two, if I counted finding my client's missing employer.

When I reached Morrell's, the dogs danced around me, as ecstatic as if it had been twelve months, not twelve hours, since we last met. Morrell told me proudly that he had taken them over to the lake—a real feat: he hadn't been able to walk up the single flight of stairs to his condo when I brought him back from Zurich seven weeks ago. He still needed a cane to walk, and Mitch had challenged Morrell's balance several times; he'd had to lie down for an hour after the exertion, but he'd managed the four blocks there and back without mishap, and didn't seem any worse for the outing.

"We'll celebrate," I said enthusiastically. "I outdid Sherlock Holmes today, at least this afternoon, and you outdid Hillary on Everest. Are you up to another excursion, or shall I go get something?"

He was not only fit enough to go out but eager: we hadn't had an evening together for a long time.

While I was in showering and changing, Marcena returned. When I got out, she was sitting on a couch with a bottle of beer, fondling Mitch's ears. He thumped his tail gently when I came into the room, to acknowledge that he knew me, but he was looking at Marcena with an expression of idiotic bliss. I should have realized she'd be as good with dogs as with everything else.

She lifted her beer bottle to me in a toast. "How are the budding athletes?"

"Coming along. Actually, they were fighting over you on Monday: they missed you. You coming back any time soon?"

"I'll try to get over to the school one of these afternoons. The last few days, I've been doing research in the community." She grinned provocatively.

"Thus intensifying the conflict on the court," I said drily. "Just so you know, South Chicago is the kind of small community where everyone minds their neighbors' business."

She gave me a mocking bow of thanks.

"Really, Marci," Morrell said, "you want to write about these people. You can't stir them up and create the story just so you have something dramatic to cover."

"Of course not, darling, but is it my fault if they pay too much attention to me? I'm trying to see the nuts and bolts of the community. I'm doing other things, though: I'm trying to get the head office to let me interview old Mr. Bysen. He never talks to the press, his secretary told me, so I'm trying to find a different angle. I thought about pitching your basketball program as an entrée, Vic."

"Actually, my basketball program has gained me an entrée of my own," I said airily. "I'm going out to morning prayers tomorrow."

Her eyes widened. "Do you think—oh, help, wait a second."

Her cell phone had started to ring. She fished it out of the cushions. Mitch pawed her leg, annoyed that she'd abandoned him, but she ignored him.

"Yes? . . . Yes . . . She did? Really, how funny! What did he do? . . . Oh, bad luck. What do you do now? . . . You are? Are you sure that's a good idea? . . . What, now? . . . Oh, all right, why not. In forty-five minutes, then."

She hung up, her eyes sparkling. "Speaking of South Chicago, that was one of my community contacts. There's a meeting I want to sit in on, so I'll leave you two for an evening of private bliss. But, Vic, I want to go with you in the morning."

"I suppose," I said doubtfully, "but I'm going to take off at six-thirty—I was told to be there by seven-fifteen, and I don't want to blow a chance to talk to Buffalo Bill."

"Buffalo Bill? Is that what they call him? Oh, of course, because he's a bison. No problem. What time will you be getting up? That early? If I'm not out here by six, come get me, okay?"

"There is an alarm next to the bed," I said, annoyed.

She flashed a wide smile. "But I may not hear it if I get in too late."

Five minutes later, she was gone. Morrell and I went down to Devon Avenue for samosas and curry, but I found it hard to recapture my earlier celebratory mood.

10 UNIONS? NOT A PRAYER!

"Heavenly Father, Your power fills us with awe, and yet You conde-scend to love us. Your love pours down on us constantly and as its proof, You sent us Your darling Son as a precious gift to bring us close to You." Pastor Andrés's public voice was deep and rumbly; with the mike overamplifying him, and the faint Hispanic accent, he was hard to understand. At first I strained to follow him, but now my attention wandered.

When Andrés first came into the meeting room with Billy the Kid, I'd been startled enough to wake up for a moment: the pastor was the man I'd bumped into yesterday morning at Fly the Flag—the one who won-dered if I were drunk at nine in the morning. His church, Mt. Ararat Church of Holiness in Zion, was where Rose Dorrado and her children worshiped. I knew the ministers at these fundamentalist churches wielded tremendous authority in the lives of their congregations; maybe Rose had confided her fears about sabotage to Andrés. And maybe, in turn, Andrés had persuaded the plant owner to explain why he wouldn't bring in the cops to investigate the sabotage.

It wasn't possible to squeeze past all the people between me and the front of the room to talk to him before the service; I'd intercept him on his way out at the end. If the service ever did end. Every now and then, what seemed to be an approaching climax jerked me briefly awake, but the pastor's deep voice and accent were a perfect lullaby, and I would drift off again.

"With Your Son, You show us the way and the truth and the light, with Him at our head we will move through all life's obstacles to that glorious place where we will know no obstacles, no grief, where You will wipe away all our tears."

Nearby, other heads were nodding, or eyes shifting to wristwatches, the way we used surreptitiously to peek at each other's test papers in high school, all the time imagining no one could tell our eyes weren't glued to our own desktops.

In the front row, Aunt Jacqui had her hands folded piously in prayer, but I caught a glimpse of her thumbs moving on some handheld device. Today, she was wearing a severe black dress that didn't quite match the evangelical mood of the meeting, despite its color: it was cinched tightly to show off her slim waist, and the buttons down the front ended around her thighs, allowing me to see that the design on her panty hose went all the way up her legs.

Next to me Marcena was sleeping in earnest, her breath coming in quiet little puffs, but her head bobbed forward as if she were nodding in prayer—no doubt a skill she'd learned at her fancy girls' school in England.

When we'd left Morrell's condo at six-thirty, her face was gray and drawn; she'd slumped in the passenger seat, groaning. "I can't believe I'm going to chapel at dawn after three hours' sleep. This is like being back at Queen Margaret's, trying to make the headmistress believe I hadn't crept into hall after hours. Wake me when we're ten minutes from By-Smart so I can put on my face."

I knew how little sleep she'd had, because I knew what time she'd gotten in last night: three-fifteen. And I knew that because Mitch had announced her arrival with considerable vigor. As soon as he started barking, Peppy joined in. Morrell and I lay in bed, arguing over who had to get out of bed to deal with them.

"They're your dogs," Morrell said.

"She's your friend."

"Yeah, but she isn't barking."

"Only in the sense of barking mad, and, anyway, she provoked them," I grumbled, but it was still me who stumbled down the hall to quiet them.

Marcena was in the kitchen, drinking another beer, and letting Mitch play tug-of-war with her gloves. Peppy was on the perimeter, dancing and snarling because she wasn't included in the game. Marcena apologized for waking the house.

"Stop playing with Mitch so I can get them to lie down and shut up." I snapped. "What kind of meeting went on this late?" I took the gloves away from Mitch, and forced both dogs to lie down and stay.

"Oh, we were inspecting community sites," Marcena said, wiggling her eyebrows. "What time do we need to set out? It really takes almost an hour? If I'm not up by six, knock on the door, will you?"

"If I remember." I shuffled back to bed, where Morrell was already sound asleep again. I rolled over, hard, against him, but he only grunted and put an arm around me without waking up.

I assumed from Marcena's suggestive grin that site inspections meant she'd been out with Romeo Czernin in his big truck, having sex at the CID landfill golf course, or maybe the high school parking lot. What point was there in acting so cute about it? Because he was married, or because he was a blue-collar guy? It was as though she thought I was a prude whom this kind of teasing would both offend and titillate. Maybe because I'd told her the kids were talking about their affair, or whatever it should be called.

"Let it go," I whispered to myself in the dark. "Relax and let it go." After a while I managed to doze off again.

Morrell was still asleep when I got up at five-thirty to give the dogs a short run. When we got back from our dash to the lake, I opened the door to the spare room so Mitch and Peppy could wake Marcena while I showered. I put on the one business outfit I'd left at Morrell's. It was a perfectly nice suit in an umber wool, but when Marcena appeared in a red-checked swing jacket I did look like a prude next to her.

There's no easy way to get from Morrell's place by the lake to the vast sprawl beyond O'Hare where By-Smart had its headquarters. My own eyes sandy with fatigue, I threaded my way along the side streets, which were already full, even at this hour. I had the radio on, keeping awake to Scarlatti and Copeland, mixed in with ads and dire warnings about traffic mishaps. Marcena slept through it all, through the radio, through the woman in the Explorer who almost creamed us as she pulled out of her driveway without looking, the man in the Beemer who ran the red light at Golf Road, and then gave me the finger for honking.

She even slept, or skillfully feigned sleep, when Rose Dorrado called me back around a quarter to seven.

"Rose! I owe you an apology. I'm sorry I suggested you could be involved in sabotaging the plant; that was wrong of me."

"I don't mind, you don't need to mind." She was mumbling, hard to hear over the traffic sounds. "I think—I think I worry for nothing about what is happening—a few accidents and I am imagining the worst."

I was so startled I let my attention slip from the road. A loud honking from the car to my left brought me back in a hurry.

I pulled over to the curb. "What do you mean? Glue doesn't fall accidentally into locks, and a sackful of rats doesn't just drop into a ventilation system."

"I can't explain how these things happen, but I can't worry about them no more, so thanks for your trouble, but you need to leave the factory alone."

That sounded like a rehearsed script if ever I heard one, but she hung up before I could press her further. Anyway, I couldn't afford to be late out here; I'd have to worry about Rose and Fly the Flag later.

I gave Marcena's shoulder a tap. She groaned again, but sat up and began putting herself together, putting on makeup, including mascara, and fishing her trademark red silk scarf out of her bag to knot under her collar. By the time we turned onto By-Smart Corporate Way, she looked as elegant as ever. I glanced at myself in the rearview mirror. Maybe mascara would further enhance the red in my eyes.

By-Smart's headquarters had been designed along the utilitarian lines of one of their own megastores and appeared as big, a huge box that overwhelmed a minute park around it. Like so many corporate parks, this one looked tawdry. The prairie had been stripped from the rolling hills, covered with concrete, and then a tiny bit of grass Scotch-taped in as an afterthought. By-Smart's landscaper also included a little pond as a reminder of the wetlands that used to lie out here. Beyond the wedge of brown grass, the parking lot seemed to stretch for miles, its gray surface fading into the bleak fall sky.

When we'd tapped our high-heeled way across the lot to the entrance, it was clear that the building's utility stopped at its shape. It was constructed from some kind of pale gold stone, perhaps even marble, since that seemed to be what covered the lobby floor. The lobby walls were paneled in a rich red-gold wood, with amber blocks set into them here and there. I thought of the endless rows of snow shovels, flags, towels, ice-melt in the warehouse on Crandon, and Patrick Grobian, hoping to make the move out here from his dirty little office. Who could blame him, even if it meant sleeping with Aunt Jacqui?

This early in the day, no receptionist sat behind the giant teak console, but a sullen-faced guard got up and demanded our business.

"Are you Herman?" I asked. "Billy the Ki—young Billy Bysen invited me up for the morning prayer meeting."

"Oh, yes." Herman's face relaxed into a fatherly smile. "Yes, he told me a friend of his would be stopping by for the prayer meeting. He said you should go straight to the meeting room. This lady with you? Here, these passes are good for the day."

He handed over a couple of large pink badges labeled "Visitor," with the day's date stamped on them, without even asking for photo IDs. I didn't think Herman's sudden friendliness was because we knew a member of the family, but because Billy the Kid made the people around him happy and protective—I'd seen the same reaction in the truck drivers who'd been teasing him on Thursday night.

Herman also handed us a map, marking the route to the meeting room for us. The building was constructed like the Merchandise Mart, or the Pentagon, with concentric corridors leading to labyrinths of cubicles.

Although each corner had a black plastic tag identifying its location, we kept getting turned around and needing to retrace our steps. Or I kept getting turned around; Marcena stumbled blindly in my wake.

"You going to pull yourself together before we meet Buffalo Bill?" I snarled.

She smiled seraphically. "I always rise to the occasion. This one just doesn't seem to need my best effort yet."

I bit back a retort: I couldn't win at any sniping interchange.

I knew I was on the right trail, or corridor, when we started meeting other people heading the same way we were. We got a lot of stares—strangers in the midst, women, to boot, in the midst of a sea of gray- and brown-suited men. When I double-checked that we were going the right direction, I found people assumed we were vendors from outside the company. I wondered if morning church was a required ritual for doing business with By-Smart.

As we looked around for seats together, a woman whispered to me that the front row was reserved for the family and for senior officers of the company. Marcena said that was fine, the farther from the center of the action the better. We found two chairs together about ten rows back.

When Billy the Kid had invited me to the prayer meeting, I'd pictured something like the Lady Chapel at a church where a friend of mine is in charge—statues of Mary, candles, crucifixes, an altar. Instead, we were in a nondescript room in the interior of the fourth floor, windowless except for the skylights. I saw later it was a kind of multipurpose room, smaller and less formal than the auditorium, where employees could hold exercise classes or other activities that weren't exactly work related.

This morning it was set up with chairs fanning out in concentric half circles from a blond wood table in the middle. Old Mr. Bysen arrived just before the session got under way, when everyone else was seated. A thickset man whose midsection had expanded in old age, he wasn't fat, but certainly substantial. He carried a cane, but he still walked briskly, using the cane almost like a ski pole to propel himself along. An entourage, chiefly of men in the ubiquitous gray or brown, clustered in his wake. Billy the Kid, in jeans and a clean white shirt, entered with Andrés at the tail of the parade. His reddish brown curls were slicked down heavily. In this room of gray-and-white men, Andrés's dark skin stood out like a rose in a bowl of onions.

There were a few women besides Marcena and me; one of them arrived in Bysen's entourage. She appeared both deferential and self-assured—the perfect personal assistant. Her face was flat, like a skillet, and covered in heavy pancake. She was carrying a slim gold portfolio that she unzipped and left on the desktop, open so that both she and Bysen could see it. It was she who sat at Bysen's right hand as the inner circle fanned out in the padded chairs; Aunt Jacqui, who arrived a few minutes later, only rated the front row.

Morning service seemed to be where Bysen held court. Before the prayers started, a number of people came up to hold low-voiced conversations with him. The skillet-faced woman paid careful attention to them all, jotting notes into the gold portfolio.

Besides the pastor and Billy the Kid, there were four other men at the table; people waiting for their moment with Bysen would engage with one or another of those four, but everyone, I noticed, had a smile and a quick word with Billy. At one point, he happened to catch sight of me in the audience; he gave his sweet shy smile and a little wave, and I felt momentarily cheerier.

After about fifteen minutes of attending his vassals, Bysen nodded at the woman, who put away her portfolio. This was the signal for everyone to get back to their chairs. Billy, blushing with importance, got up to introduce the pastor from Mt. Ararat, with a few words about his own involvement in South Chicago, and how important church life, and Pastor Andrés's work, were for that community. Andrés gave an invocation, and Billy read a passage from the Bible, the bit about the rich man with the unfaithful steward. When he'd finished, he took a seat near his grandfather.

We started with prayers for everyone involved in By-Smart's far-flung enterprises, petitions for the wisdom of management to make good decisions, petitions for the workers here and abroad, for the strength to do what was required of them. As Pastor Andrés moved into his address and the rest of us dozed, Bysen kept his attention fixed on the minister, his heavy brows twitching.

I was dozing myself when the tempo of Andrés's voice picked up. His voice became louder, more declamatory. I sat up to pay attention to his conclusion.

"When Jesus talks about the steward who has misused his master's gifts, He is talking to us all. We are all His stewards, and to those whom the most is given, from them is the most expected. Heavenly Father, You have bestowed on this company, on the family who owns it, very great gifts indeed. We beseech You in Your Son's name to help them remember they are Your stewards only. Help everyone in this vast company to remember that. Help them to use Your gifts wisely, for the betterment of all who work for them. Your Son taught us to pray 'Lead us not into temptation, but deliver us from evil.' The success of By-Smart leaves much temptation in its path, the temptation to forget that many who labor are heavy-laden, that they will present themselves to Your Son with many, many tears for Him to wipe away. Help everyone who works here in this great company to remember the lowest in our midst, to remember they have the same divine spark, the same right to life, the same right to a just return for the fruits of their labor—"

A loud clatter startled me. Mr. Bysen had pushed himself out of his chair, shoving his walking stick so that it had bounced on the floor. One of the gray men at the table jumped to his feet and took the old man's arm, but Bysen shook him off angrily and pointed to the stick. The man stooped for it and handed it to Bysen, who stumped toward the exit. The skillet-faced woman quickly slid the gold portfolio under her arm and followed him, catching up with him before he reached the door.

In the audience, everyone had woken up and was sitting straighter in the uncomfortable chairs. A buzz went through the room, like wind through prairie grasses. Marcena, who'd jerked awake at the commotion, nudged me and demanded to know what was going on.

I shrugged in incomprehension, watching the man who'd retrieved Bysen's stick: he was having an angry conversation with Billy the Kid. Pastor Andrés stood with his arms crossed, looking nervous but belligerent. Billy, scarlet-faced, said something that made the older man fling his arms up in exasperation. He turned his back on Billy and told the rest of us that the service had been going on longer than usual.

"We all have meetings and other important projects to attend to, so let's end by bowing our heads for a minute, and asking God's blessing on us as we try to face the many challenges we encounter. As Pastor Andrés reminds us, we are all only stewards of God's great gifts, we all carry heavy burdens, we all can use divine help on every step of our journey. Let us pray."

I bowed my head dutifully with the rest of the room, but glanced at Aunt Jacqui from under my eyelashes. Her head was lowered, her hands were still, but she was smiling in a secretive, gloating way. Because she wanted Billy to be on the hot seat with his grandfather? Or because she enjoyed turmoil for its own sake?

We sat silently for about twenty seconds, until the gray-haired man announced "Amen," and strode to the exit. As soon as he was gone, the rest of us burst into excited conversation.

"Who was that?" I asked the woman on my left, who was checking her cell phone as she got up to leave.

"Mr. Bysen." She was so astonished I didn't know that she sat back down.

"Not him. The man who finished the service just now, the one arguing with Billy the—with young Billy Bysen."

"Oh—that's young Mr. William. Billy's father. I guess he wasn't too pleased with the minister Billy brought up from the South Side. I see you're a visitor—are you one of our suppliers?"

I smiled and shook my head. "Just an acquaintance of young Billy from South Chicago. He invited me here today. Why was Mr. Bysen so upset by Pastor Andrés's remarks?"

She looked at me suspiciously. "Are you a journalist?"

"Nope. I coach basketball at a high school on the South Side."

Marcena was leaning across me to listen in on the conversation, her nifty little fountain-pen recorder in her hand; at the journalism question, she gave a wolfish smile and said, "I'm just a visitor from England, so the whole thing was confusing to me. And I had trouble understanding the pastor's accent."

The woman nodded condescendingly. "You probably don't get too many undocumented Mexicans in England, but we see a lot of them here. Anyone could have told young Billy that his grandfather wouldn't enjoy hearing that kind of message, even if the pastor had delivered it in plain English."

"Is he Mexican?" I asked. "I wasn't sure from the accent."

Marcena kicked my shin, meaning, they're giving us information, don't get their backs up.

Our informant gave a meaningless laugh. "Mexico, El Salvador, it's all the same thing; they all come to this country thinking they have a right to a free lunch."

A man in front of us turned around. "Oh, Buffalo Bill will get that nonsense out of Billy's system fast enough. It's why he sent the Kid down to South Chicago."

"But what nonsense?" Marcena looked and sounded hopelessly ignorant; she was almost batting her eyelashes. What a pro.

"Didn't you hear him talking about workers and the fruits of their labors?" the man said. "Sounded a lot like union organizing, and we won't stand for that at By-Smart. Billy knows that as well as the rest of us."

I looked to the front of the room, where Andrés was still talking to Billy. With his short, square body, he did look more like a construction worker than a minister. I suppose he could have been a union organizer: a lot of the little churches on the South Side can't support a pastor, and the staff have to work regular jobs during the week.

But would Billy have really tried to bring an organizer into Buffalo Bill's prayer service? The impression I'd gotten last Thursday had been that Billy loved his grandfather, that he thought only the best of him.

Billy clearly also was attached to Andrés; as the room cleared, he'd stayed next to Andrés, and his posture suggested embarrassment and apology. As I watched, the pastor put a hand on the young man's shoulder, and the two of them made their way out.

I suddenly remembered my own mission with Andrés. Calling out that I'd be back in a minute, I threaded my way through the chairs and sprinted after them, but by the time I got to the far exit they had disappeared into the maze. I ran down the hall, checking different turns, but I'd lost them.

When I got back to the meeting room, a couple of janitors were folding up the chairs, stacking them on pallets along the wall. When they'd finished with that, they opened a door and began pulling out exercise mats. A woman in leotard and tights carried in a large boom box; Aunt Jacqui, who'd disappeared when I was trying to find Andrés, came back into the room in her own exercise gear and began doing stretches that emphasized the smooth curve of her buttocks.

The man who'd told us By-Smart wouldn't allow unions followed my amazed gaze, his own resting on Jacqui's rear end as she bent to the floor. "Aerobics meet here next. If you and your friend want to work out, you'd be welcome to stay."

"So By-Smart does it all," Marcena laughed. "Prayers, push-ups, whatever employees need. How about physical sustenance? Can I get breakfast? I'm famished."

The man put his hand in the small of her back. "Come to the cafeteria with me. We all get a little hungry on church mornings."

As we followed our guide back through the maze, we could hear the boom box begin an insistent beat.

 **HOME ON THE RANGE**

"B ut, Grandpa, I wasn't trying—"

"In front of the entire workforce. I never thought you would have so little respect. Your sister, yes, but you, William, you I thought appreciated what I've spent my life building up here. I won't have it torn down by some welfare cheat who doesn't have the backbone to support himself and his family, so he needs to steal from me and mine."

"Grandpa, he's not a welfare—"

"I understand how it happened: like everyone else in the world, he saw how good-natured you are and took advantage of it. If that's what goes on at that church, that Mount Ararat, it should change its name to Mount Error-rat, and you, my boy, should stay as far away from them as possible."

"But, Grandpa, it really isn't like that. It's about the community—"

I was in the antechamber to Bysen's office, the room where the secretaries guarded the great man's gate. One of the inner doors wasn't completely shut; Buffalo Bill's bellow carried easily through the crack, as easily as it rode over young Billy's efforts to explain himself.

The big desk in the middle of the room was empty and I was heading toward the sound of battle when someone called to me from the corner. It was a thin, colorless woman at a small metal desk, doing things on a computer, demanding my name and business in the pinched nasal of the city's old South Side. When I said that Billy had arranged a meeting for me with his grandfather, she flicked a nervous glance from the inner office to her computer screen, but answered the phone before responding to me.

"I don't see you in the book, miss, for having an appointment with Mr. Bysen."

"Billy probably thought he could take me directly to his grandfather after the service." I smiled easily: I'm not threatening, I'm a team player.

"Just a second." She answered the phone again, putting her hand over the mouthpiece to speak to me. "You'll have to talk to Mildred; I can't authorize you to see Mr. Bysen without her say-so. You can sit down; she'll be back in a minute."

The phone kept ringing. Her eye on me, the assistant said in her prim nasal voice, "Mr. Bysen's office . . . It really was not a big serious event, but if you need to talk to Mr. Bysen, Mildred will get back to you to set up a phone meeting."

I strolled around the room, looking at the pictures on the wall. Unlike most corporate offices, there wasn't any art to speak of, just photographs of Bysen. He was greeting the president of the United States, he was laying a cornerstone for the thousandth By-Smart emporium, he was standing next to a World War II–vintage plane. At least, I guess it was Bysen—it was some young man in a leather helmet and goggles with his hand resting on one of the engines. I gazed at him intently, straining to hear the argument in the inner office.

"Billy, there are a million sob stories and a million swindlers out there. If you're going to take your place in this company, you're going to have to learn how to recognize them and deal with them."

This time the speaker was the reedy, petulant baritone who'd dismissed us from the prayer service: Mr. William, dealing sternly with his impulsive son. I looked longingly at the crack in the door, but the woman in the corner appeared primed to leap up and tackle me if I made a false move.

I wanted to go in before Marcena finished breakfast and joined me—I didn't want her urge for an interview with Bysen to get in the way of my own agenda. And she was too skillful at getting people to notice her for me to have much hope of keeping Bysen's attention once she'd joined us. She'd shown that again, when I left her in the cafeteria a few minutes ago—she'd persuaded the guy we'd been talking to to join her for a full cooked breakfast. Just as she had with the girls on the basketball team, Marcena understood how to make the guy (just call me Pete; I'm in procurement and whatever you want I can get it for you, hah, hah, hah) feel she was the perfect empathic listener. As they stood in front of the scrambled eggs, she had already gotten him to start talking about By-Smart's history with union organizers. I could learn something from her about how to conduct interrogations.

I'd looked wistfully at the eggs, but picked up a carton of yogurt to eat as I hunted for Buffalo Bill's office: not only did I want to see him alone, I also wanted to get to him while young Billy was still on the premises. I was hoping that Grandpa would have enough tenderness for his grandson to overlook the regrettable lapse made by the preacher, and I knew I'd do better with the old man if the Kid were with me.

From the sound of things, today was not going to be a good day for putting the bite on Grandpa. If a pastor preaching about fair labor practices was a welfare cheat, I hated to think what a bunch of girls who couldn't afford their own coach would be called. However, the reedy baritone's attack on Billy seemed to calm down the old man; I heard him rumble, "Grobian can put some backbone into Billy; that's why he's down in the warehouse."

"That doesn't make it any better, Father. If he's so naïve that some preacher can take advantage of him, he shouldn't be out on his own in the field," Mr. William said.

At that point, so many voices jumped in at once that I couldn't make out any individual sentences. Behind me, the phone kept ringing; the fracas at the service was apparently setting off seismic shocks around the company. As the assistant repeated her insistence that the sermon hadn't been a big deal, a couple of men strode into the office.

"Mildred?" the taller, older one called.

"She's in with Mr. Bysen, Mr. Rankin. Good morning, Mr. Roger. Do you want some coffee?"

"We'll go on in." The shorter, younger one, Mr. Roger, was clearly another Bysen—unlike Mr. William, he looked strikingly like Buffalo Bill: the same stocky body, the same thick eyebrows and pincer-shaped nose.

When the pair pushed open the door to the inner office, I followed them, ignoring a flustered protest from the corner. Bysen was standing in front of his desk with Billy, young Mr. William, and Mildred, the skillet-faced woman from the meeting. Another man, tall and thin like Mr. William, was with them, but the two I'd followed ignored everyone but Bysen and Billy.

"Good morning, Father. Billy, what in hell were you thinking, bringing a rabble-rouser into the prayer meeting?"

Again an attack on Billy by one of his grown sons made Bysen rise to the Kid's defense. "It's not as bad as all that, Roger. We'll have to spend the morning putting out fires, is all—half the board has heard about it already. Bunch of silly old women: the stock dropped two-fifty on the rumor that we're letting in the union." He cuffed his grandson on the head. "Just a couple of guys with more zeal than forethought, that's all. Billy says this spi—Mexican preacher isn't a labor leader."

Billy was bright-eyed with emotion. "Pastor Andrés only cares about the welfare of the community, Uncle Roger. They have forty percent unemployment down there, so people have to take jobs—"

"That's neither here nor there," William said. "Really, Father, you let Billy get away with murder. If Roger or Gary or I did something that drove the stock down that far, you'd be—"

"Oh, it will come back up, it will come back up. Linus, you get onto the corporate communications staff? They good to go? Who is this? One of the speechwriters?"

Everyone turned to look at me: the skillet-faced woman, who was standing next to Bysen's desk with a laptop open in front of her, the two sons, the man named Linus.

I smiled sunnily. "I'm V. I. Warshawski. Morning, Billy."

Billy's face relaxed for the first time since his grandfather had stormed from the meeting. "Ms. War-sha-sky, I'm sorry I forgot about you. I should have waited for you after the meeting, but I wanted to escort Pastor Andrés to the parking lot. Grandpa, Father, this here is the lady I told you about."

"So you're the social worker down at the high school, hnnh?" Buffalo Bill lowered his head at me like a bull about to charge.

"I'm like you, Mr. Bysen: I grew up on the old South Side, but I haven't lived there for a long time," I said easily. "When I agreed to fill in as a basketball coach for the girls' team, I was truly dismayed by the terrible changes in the neighborhood and at Bertha Palmer. When were you last in the school?"

"Recently enough to know that those kids expect the government to hand them everything. When I was in school, we worked for—"

"I know you did, sir: your work ethic is extraordinary, and your energy is an international byword." He was so surprised at my riding over his harangue that he stared at me, openmouthed. "When I played on the Bertha Palmer team, the school could afford to pay a coach, it could afford to pay for our uniforms, it had a music program where my own mother taught, and boys like you got to go to college on the GI bill."

I paused, hoping he'd make a tiny connection between his own government-funded education and the kids on the South Side, but I didn't see a dawning light of empathy in his face. "Now the school can't afford any of these things. Basketball is one of the things—"

"I don't need a lecture from you or anyone, young woman, on what kids need or don't need. I raised six of my own without any government help, hnnh, hnnh, and without any charity, hnnh, and if these kids had any spine, they'd do just like I did. Instead of littering the South Side with a bunch of babies they can't feed, and then expecting me to buy them basketball shoes."

I felt such an impulse to slap his face that I turned my back on him and jammed my hands into my suit jacket pocket.

"They're really not like that, Grandpa," Billy said behind me. "These girls work hard, they do the jobs they can get down there, at McDonald's, or even at our store on Ninety-fifth, a lot of them work thirty hours a week to help their families besides trying to stay in school. I know if you saw them, you'd be really impressed. And they're crazy about Ms. War-sha-sky, but she can't stay on coaching down there."

Crazy about me? Was that what the girls at Mt. Ararat were saying, or was this Billy's interpretation? I turned back around.

"Billy, you keep sticking your naive nose into things you don't know jack shit about." The man who'd been in the room with Mr. William spoke for the first time. "Jacqui told me you had this insane idea that Father would bankroll your pet project; she says she warned you that he wouldn't be the least bit interested, and now, on today of all days, when you've done your best to destroy our good name with our shareholders, you waste more valuable time by encouraging this social worker to come up here."

"Aunt Jacqui wouldn't even listen to Ms. War-sha-sky, Uncle Gary, so I don't know how she can figure out whether it's a good proposal or not. She threw her copy out without even taking one look at it."

"It's okay, Billy," I said. "Do your folks understand I'm not a social worker? I'm doing volunteer work that I don't have the skills for. Or the time. Since the government in the form of the Board of Education can't hand the girls at Bertha Palmer the help they need, I'm hoping the private sector will pick up the slack. By-Smart is the biggest employer in the community, you have a history of helping out down there, and I'd like to encourage you to make the girls' basketball team one of your programs. I'll be glad to bring you down to one of our practices."

"My own girls do volunteer work," Bysen observed. "Good for them, good for the community. I'm sure it's good for you, hnnh?"

"What about your sons?" I couldn't resist asking.

"They're too busy helping run this business."

I smiled brightly. "My problem in a nutshell, Mr. Bysen. I own my own business, and I'm too busy running it to be an effective volunteer. Let me bring you down and show you the program. I know the high school would be thrilled if their most famous graduate came back for a visit."

"Yes, Grandpa, you should come with me. When you meet the girls—"

"It would only encourage them to expect handouts," Uncle Gary said. "And frankly, while we're putting out the fire Billy created, we don't have time for community work."

"Can't you shut up about that for two minutes?" Billy cried out, his eyes bright with unshed tears. "Pastor Andrés is not a labor organizer. He only worries about all the people in his congregation who can't do stuff we take for granted, like buy shoes for their children. And they work hard, I know they do, I see them at the warehouse every day. Aunt Jacqui and Pat sit in that back room calling them names, but these people are working fifty and sixty hours a week, and we could do better by them."

"It was a mistake to let you get so involved in that church down there, Billy," Bysen said. "They see how good-hearted you are, so they're playing on that, they're telling you things about us, about the company, and about their own lives that are distortions. These people aren't like us, they don't believe in hard work the way we do, that's why they depend on us for jobs. If we weren't down in that community seeing they got a paycheck, they'd be loafing around on welfare, or gambling."

"Which they probably do, anyway," Mr. Roger added. "Maybe we should take Billy out of the warehouse, send him to the Westchester or Northlake store."

"I'm not leaving South Chicago," Billy said. "You all stand around acting like I'm nine, not nineteen, and you're not even polite enough to talk to my guest, or offer her a chair or a cup of coffee. I don't know what Grandma would say about that, but it's not what she taught me all these years. All you care about is the stock price, not about the people who keep our company going. When we're standing in front of the Judgment Seat, God won't care about the stock price, you can count on that."

He shoved past his grandfather and uncles and stopped briefly to shake my hand, and assure me that he would talk to me in person. "I do have a trust fund, Ms. War-sha-sky, and I really care what happens to that program."

"You have a trust that doesn't mature until you're twenty-seven, and if this is how you behave we'll make it thirty-five," his father shouted.

"Fine. Do you think I care? I can live on my paycheck like everyone else on the South Side." Billy stormed from the office.

"What'd you and Annie Lisa feed your kids, William?" Uncle Gary asked. "Candace is a junkie and Billy is an overwrought baby."

"Yeah, well, at least Annie Lisa raised a family. She doesn't spend her life in front of a mirror trying on five-thousand-dollar outfits."

"Save it for the competition, boys," Buffalo Bill grunted. "Billy's an idealist. Just got to channel that energy in the right direction. But don't go threatening him like that over his trust fund, William. While I'm still on the planet, I'll see the boy gets his share of his inheritance. When I'm in front of the Judgment Seat, God will surely want to know about how I treated my own grandson, hnnh, hnnh, hnnh."

"Yes, whatever I say or do I can be sure you'll undercut it," William said coldly. He turned to me. "And you, whoever you are, I think you've hung around our offices long enough."

"If she's one of the people influencing Billy down there, I think we'd better find out who she is and what she's telling him," Mr. Roger said.

"Mildred? We got time for this?"

His assistant looked at the laptop and tapped a couple of keys. "You really don't have time, Mr. B., especially if you have to take phone calls from the board."

"Ten minutes, then, we can take ten minutes. William can call back the board, doesn't take any great genius to tell them they're letting the rumor mills grind 'em down."

Pink stained William's cheeks. "If it's that trivial a problem, let Mildred handle it. I have a full day scheduled without Billy's setting the house on fire."

"Oh, don't take these things so personally, William. You're too thin-skinned, always have been. Now, what's your name again, young woman?"

I repeated my name and handed cards around the room.

"Investigator? Investigator? How in hell did Billy get involved with a detective? You and Annie Lisa ever talk to the boy?" Roger demanded.

William ignored him, and said to me, "What are you doing with my son? And don't try shuffling around with lies about girls' basketball."

"I have only the truth to tell about girls' basketball," I said. "I met your son for the first time last Thursday, when I went to the warehouse to talk to Pat Grobian about getting By-Smart to back the team. Billy was enthusiastic, as you know, and sent me up here."

Buffalo Bill stared at me under his heavy brows, then turned to the man he'd called Linus. "Get someone on this, see who she is and what she's doing there. And while you're calling around, we'll all just go into the conference room and talk this over. Mildred, put through those calls to Birmingham for me, I'll take 'em in there."

12   COMPANY PRACTICE

In the conference room, the party was essentially configured the way it had been for prayers, with Bysen at the head of the table and Mildred on his right. The sons and Linus Rankin sat along the sides. Mildred's assistant, the nervous woman in the corner of the front room, came in with a stack of phone messages, which Mildred distributed to the men.

I handed Mildred the report I'd created for my meeting at the warehouse; when I told her I'd only brought two copies, she sent her assistant scurrying to photocopy it. The assistant came back in short order, somehow juggling a stack of copies and a tray holding coffee, soda cans, and water.

While we'd been waiting, the men had all whipped out cell phones. Linus was asking someone to find out about me, and William was working his way through his share of the messages, calling board members to reassure them that By-Smart was not budging on unions. Roger was dealing with a vendor who didn't think he could meet By-Smart's price demands. Gary held an animated conversation about a problem with a store where the overnight crew had been locked in: someone had had an epileptic seizure, as nearly as I could gather from my frank eavesdropping, and bitten off her tongue because no one could get the door open to admit the EMTs.

"Locked in?" I blurted out, when he hung up, forgetting I was trying to be supersaccharine to all these Bysen men.

"None of your business, young woman," Buffalo Bill snapped. "But when a store is in a dangerous neighborhood, I won't risk our employees' lives by leaving them exposed to every drug addict walking the streets. Gary, get onto the local manager: he has to have a backup available to let people out in case of emergencies. Linus, we got a legal exposure here?"

I bit my own tongue to keep from saying anything else, while Rankin made a note. He was apparently the corporate counsel.

Roger flung his own cell phone down in disgust and turned to William. "Now, thanks to your idiot son, we have three vendors who think they can back out of their contracts because our labor costs are going to be going up, if you please, and they know we'll understand that unless they shut down and move to Burma or Nicaragua, they can't meet our price standards."

"Nonsense," the old man interjected. "Nothing to do with Billy, just the usual whiny weaseling. It's a game with some people, to see whether we have the guts God gave a goose. You boys are all too thin-skinned. I don't know what will happen to this company when I can't be here in the kitchen every day, taking the heat."

Mildred murmured something in Bysen's ear; he gave his "hnnh, hnnh" snort and looked at me. "Okay, young woman, come to the point, come to the point."

I folded my hands on the table and looked him in the eye, or as much of the eye as I could see below his overhanging brows. "As I said, Mr. Bysen, I grew up in South Chicago and attended Bertha Palmer High. From there, I went to the University of Chicago, having played in high school on a championship team; that earned me the athletic scholarship that made my university education possible. When you were at Bertha Palmer, and some years later when I was a student, the school provided programs in—"

"We all know the sad story of the neighborhood's decline," William snapped. "And we all know you've come here expecting us to give a handout to people who won't work for a living."

I felt blood rushing to my cheeks and forgot my need to stay on my best behavior. "I don't know if you really believe that, or if you keep saying it so you don't have to think about the reality of what it's like to support a family on seven dollars an hour. It might do for everyone at this table to try to do that for a month before being so quick to jump to judgment on South Chicago.

"A lot of the girls on my team live in families where mothers are working sixty hours a week without overtime pay on just that wage. They may be in your warehouse, or your store on Ninety-fifth, Mr. Bysen, or at the McDonald's, but, I assure you, they are working hard, harder than me, harder than you. They aren't on street corners looking for a handout."

William tried to interrupt me, but I glared at him at least as fiercely as his father ever did. "Let me finish, and then I'll listen to your objections. These women want their kids to have a decent shot at a better life. A good education is the best chance these young women will have for that kind of shot, and athletics are a key factor in keeping them in school, maybe even giving some of them a chance at college. For you to fund a program that would give my sixteen teenagers access to proper equipment, proper coaching, and a facility where they didn't risk a broken leg every time they tried a fast break, would be a great act of charity. Its cost would be down in the noise even for your South Chicago store; for the company as a whole, you'd never notice it, but the PR opportunity would be enormous.

"I just heard Mr. Roger Bysen—persuade—some manufacturer or other to supply you with something at six cents a piece less than they wanted to. Mr. Gary Bysen is annoyed that an employee bit her tongue off because she was locked in overnight. When these things are reported, they make you seem like the Scrooge of North America, but if you rolled out an important program in Mr. Bysen's own neighborhood, his own high school, you could look like heroes."

"You've got ten kinds of nerve, I'll hand you that," William said in his weedy baritone.

Bysen's thick eyebrows met across his nose, so deeply was he frowning. "And you think fifty-five thousand dollars is 'down in the noise,' hnnh, young woman? Your own business must be very successful indeed if that sum seems trivial to you."

I scribbled some calculations on the paper in front of me. "Your guy Linus will get my numbers for you, I'm sure, so I won't detail them for you, but if there were a way to cut a dollar into forty thousand pieces, one of those forty thousand pieces would be the equivalent in my operation to fifty-five thousand dollars in yours. I think that's trivial. And that doesn't even include the tax benefits. Nor the intangibles, the PR benefits."

Gary and William both tried to speak at once; Linus Rankin's cell phone rang at the same time, and Bysen himself was starting to roar when Marcena pushed open the conference room door and danced in.

She gave me a quick wink, meant to be too subtle for the men to notice, and turned to Bysen. "I'm with Ms. Warshawski—Marcena Love—your Pete Boyland was talking to me about procurement and I got held up. Is that you next to the Thunderbolt on the wall out there? My father flew Hurricanes out of Wattisham."

Buffalo Bill broke off midsnort. "Wattisham? I spent eighteen months there. Hurricane was a good ship, good ship, doesn't get the respect it deserves. What was your father's name?"

"Julian Love. Seventy Tiger Squadron."

"Hnnh, hnnh, you and I will have to have a talk, young lady. You work with this basketball gal?"

"No, sir. I'm just visiting from London. I've been touring South Chicago, actually with one of your lorry drivers, I mean, truck drivers. Sorry, I can't get the American lingo quite right."

Marcena's accent had become more pronounced the longer she spoke. Bysen was bathing in it, but his sons weren't as enthusiastic.

"Who is letting you in the cab of one of our trucks?" William demanded. "That is against the law, as well as against corporate policy."

Marcena held up a hand in a fencer's stop. "I'm sorry, are you in charge of the trucks? I didn't know I was breaking any laws."

"I still want his name," William said.

She made a rueful face. "I have put my foot in it, haven't I? I don't want to get some bloke in trouble, so let's just say I won't do it again. Mr. Bysen, is there any chance I could meet with you before I go back to England? I grew up on my father's aerial battles; I'd love to hear your version of those years; my father would be thrilled to know I met up with one of his old war buddies."

Bysen preened and snorted a little and told Mildred to figure out a free time slot some time in the next week, before turning to glower at me. "And you, young woman, with your fancy cutting dollar bills into forty thousand pieces, we'll get back to you."

Linus had been talking on his cell phone during Marcena's performance; he got up now to hand a piece of paper to Bysen. The old man scanned it, and scowled at me even more fiercely.

"I see you've destroyed a number of important businesses, young woman, and you've meddled in affairs that were none of your business. Do you always butt in where no one wants you, hnnh?"

"Young Billy wants me meddling in girls' basketball, Mr. Bysen— that's good enough for me. I know he'll be eager to hear how our conversation went."

Bysen stared at me for a long moment, as if weighing Billy's needs against my meddlesomeness. "We're through here, young woman. William, Roger, see she gets out the door."

William told his brother he'd take care of me. When we'd left the conference room, his hand on the small of my back, he said, "My son is basically a good kid."

"I believe you. I saw him at the warehouse and was impressed with how the men responded to him."

"The problem is, he's too trusting; people take advantage of him. Added to that, my father has always been so indulgent with him that he doesn't have a good sense of how the world really works."

I couldn't see where this was going, so I said cautiously, "It's a common problem with self-made men like your dad: they're overly strict with their own offspring, but the third generation doesn't get those same restrictions."

He looked startled, as if I'd uncovered a subtle truth about his life. "So you noticed how the old man treats him? It's been the same story since Billy was born: every time I try to set—not even the same limits Dad gave us, just some kind of parental guidance—Dad undercuts me, then blames me for—well, that's neither here nor there. I am the company's chief financial officer."

"And obviously very good at it, to turn in the numbers you do." We were being so lovey-dovey, I thought I'd try molasses.

"If I had real authority, we could pass Wal-Mart, I know we could, but my company decisions are just like my parental—anyway, I want to know when you're planning on seeing Billy, and what you're planning to say to him."

"I'm going to tell him exactly what got said in our meeting and ask him to interpret it for me: you're all strangers to me, so I don't understand what you mean when you say things."

"That's just it," William said. "We all say things, but we work together as a family. My brothers and I, I mean: we grew up fighting, the old man thought it made us tougher, but we run this company as a family. And we present a family front to competitors."

So I wasn't supposed to take dissension among the brothers to a bigger public. I had destroyed some important businesses with my meddling; I needed to know that By-Smart would fight me hard if I tried to do anything to them.

"Is Billy living in South Chicago?"

"Of course not. He may be infatuated with that storefront preacher, but he comes home to his mother at the end of the day. Just watch what you say and do with him, Ms.—uh—because we'll be watching you."

Our moment of palliness was apparently at an end. "Warshawski. I believe you will—I saw all the spy cams in the warehouse. I'll be real careful what I say just in case you've put one in my car."

He forced a laugh. So we still were pals after all? I waited for him to come to the point, schooling my face into the bland mask that makes people think you're a discreet listener—not the woman who destroyed Gustav Humboldt.

"I need to know who this English woman is riding with in South Chicago. It could be bad for us, from a liability standpoint, I mean, if she got injured."

I shook my head regretfully. "She hasn't told me who she's met down there, or how she's met them. She has a lot of friends, and she makes friends easily, as you saw with your dad just now. I'd think it could be almost anybody, maybe even Patrick Grobian, since she likes to make sure the top man is in her court."

The mention of Grobian's name seemed to bother him, or at least put him off balance. He drummed his fingers on the doorjamb, wanting to ask something else, but unsure how to phrase it. Before he figured it out, Mildred's nervous assistant claimed his attention: one of his directors was returning his call.

He went to Mildred's desk to answer the phone. I walked over to the picture of Buffalo Bill and the airplane. If I stood on tiptoe and squinted down, I could see the name of a photographer's studio with an address in Wattisham at the bottom of the matting. Marcena was not only a more skilled interrogator than I, but a cleverer investigator. It was depressing.

William was still on the phone when Buffalo Bill escorted Marcena out of the conference room, his hand on her waist. He frowned when he saw I was still there, but he spoke to Marcena. "You don't come without those photographs of your father, young woman, you hear?"

"Absolutely not; he'll be thrilled to know I've met you."

While they did an intricate separation dance, William put a hand over the mouthpiece and beckoned me to his side. "Find out who this gal is riding with, okay, and give me a call."

"In exchange for funding for my program?" I said brightly.

He stiffened. "In exchange for keeping it under discussion, certainly."

I looked mournful. "That offer won't really make me summon my best effort, Mr. William."

Bysens weren't used to beggars trying to be choosers. "And that kind of attitude definitely won't bring forth any effort on my part, young—"

"The name is Warshawski. You can call me that."

Marcena had finished with Buffalo Bill; I turned my back on young

William and headed down the hall with her. Once we were clear of the office, her shoulders sagged and she dropped her perky grin.

"I am *so* fagged!" she said.

"You should be; you've done a full day's work this last hour, what with Pete, and Buffalo Bill. I'm a little beat, myself. Is there really a Julian Love who flew Hurricanes in the war?"

She smiled mischievously. "Not exactly. But my father's tutor at Cambridge did, and when I was up, I used to have tea with him once or twice a term. I heard all the stories; I think I can fake it."

"I don't suppose he flew out of Wattisham, either."

"It was Nacton, but Buffalo Bill won't remember after all these years what one airfield or another looked like. I mean—he thinks I'm old enough to have a father who flew in the war!"

"And the photographs of your father, I suppose, will get lost in the mail. Sad, really, because they were taken before digital photography, and now they can't be replaced."

She gave a loud shout of laughter that made several people stare at us. "Something like that, Vic, something very like that, hnnh, hnnh."

 HIRED GUN

Thursday started early, with a call from my answering service. I was luxuriating in a private morning with Morrell—I hadn't seen Marcena since dropping her off after yesterday's prayer service. I'd gotten up to turn on Morrell's fancy espresso machine. I was turning pirouettes in the hall, happy to be able to prance around naked, when I heard my cell phone ringing in my briefcase.

I don't know why I didn't just let it go—that Pavlovian response to the bell, I suppose. Christie Weddington, the operator with my answering service who's known me longest, felt entitled to be severe.

"It's someone from the Bysen family, Vic: he's already called three times."

I stopped dancing. "It's seven fifty-eight, Christie. Which one of the great men?"

It was William Bysen, whom I thought of as "Mama Bear," sandwiched between Buffalo Bill and Billy the Kid. I resented the interruption, but I hoped it might mean good news: Ms. Warshawski, your fearless disposition and your brilliant proposal have caused us to shred one of our billions into forty thousand small pieces for the Bertha Palmer school.

Christie gave me William's office number. His secretary was, of course, already at her post: when the big gun starts firing early, the subalterns are there ready to load.

"Is this Ms. Warshawski? It is? Do you normally make people wait this long before you get back to them?"

That didn't sound exactly like the harbinger of glad tidings. "Actually, Mr. Bysen, I'm usually too busy to return calls this fast. What's up?"

"My son didn't come home last night."

Heart-stopping—kid was nineteen, after all, but I gave a noncommittal "oh" and waited.

"I want to know where he is."

"Do you want to hire me to find him? If so, I'll fax a contract for your signature, after which I'll need to ask a bunch of questions, which will have to be done over the phone, since I have a full calendar today and tomorrow."

He sputtered, taken aback, then asked where Billy was.

I was getting cold, standing naked in the living room. I picked the afghan up from Morrell's couch and draped it over my shoulders. "I don't know, Mr. Bysen. If that's all, I'm in the middle of a meeting."

"Is he with the preacher?"

"Mr. Bysen, if you want me to look for him I'll fax you a contract and call you later with a list of questions. If you want to know whether he's with Pastor Andrés, then I suggest you call the pastor."

He hemmed and hawed, and finally demanded my rates.

"One-twenty-five an hour, with a four-hour minimum, plus expenses."

"If you want to do business with By-Smart, you'd better rethink that rate structure."

"Am I talking to a canned recording? The worried father wants me to negotiate my fee?" I burst out laughing, then suddenly thought maybe he was making me a subtle offer. "Are you saying that By-Smart will fund my basketball program if I'll lower my fee for asking about your kid?"

"It's possible that if you can locate Billy, we'll discuss your proposal."

"Not good enough, Mr. Bysen. Give me your fax number; I'll send you a copy of the contract; when I get back a signed copy, we'll talk."

He wasn't sure he was ready to go that far. I hung up and went into the kitchen to flip on the espresso machine. My cell phone started ringing as I was going back up the hall: my answering service, with Bysen's fax number. Hey-ho. I stopped in the small bedroom Morrell uses as a home office and sent through a contract. This time, I turned my phone off before going back to bed.

"Who was that so early? You spent a lot of time with him—should I be worried?" Morrell demanded, pulling me down next to him.

"Yep. I've met his papa and his kid already—I've never even laid eyes on your family and we've been knowing each other for almost three years now."

He bit my earlobe. "Oh, yes, my kid, a little something I've been meaning to tell you about. Anyway, you get to meet my friends. Have you met this guy's friends?"

"Don't think he has any, at least, not any as cool as Marcena."

When I finally got to my office, a little before ten, I had a fax from William waiting for me: he had signed the contract, but had exxed out several provisions, including the four-hour minimum, and the paragraph on expenses.

Whistling between my teeth, I sent an e-mail: I regret not being able to do business with you but will be glad to talk to you in the future about your needs for an investigator. Not that I never negotiate my fees—but never with a company that has annual sales of over two hundred billion.

While I was online, I checked By-Smart's stock. It had dropped ten points by the end of the trading day yesterday and was down another point this morning. The question about whether By-Smart was going to open its doors to unions had made CNN's breaking news banner on my home page. No wonder they were gnashing their teeth over Billy up in Rolling Meadows.

By eleven, Mama Bear had decided he could meet my terms. He then wanted me to drop everything to dash out to Rolling Meadows. By-Smart was so used to a parade of vendors, offering everything, including their firstborn offspring, for the chance to do business with the Behemoth, that young Mr. William actually couldn't grasp that someone might not want to jump through his hoops. In the end, after a time-wasting argument, when I'd hung up once and threatened to twice more, he answered my questions.

They hadn't seen Billy since he left the meeting yesterday. According to Grobian, Billy had gone to the warehouse, put in eight hours, and then disappeared. He usually returned to the Bysen complex in Barrington Hills by seven at the latest, but last night he hadn't shown up, hadn't answered his cell phone, hadn't called his mother. When they got up at six, they found he'd never returned. That was when Mama Bear had made his first call to me. Thank goodness, I had left my own phone in the living room.

"He's nineteen, Mr. Bysen. Most kids that age are in college, if they're not working, and even if they live at home they have their own lives, their own friends. Their own girlfriends."

"Billy isn't that kind of boy," his father said. "He's part of True Love Waits, and his mother gave him her own Bible and engagement ring to seal his vows. He would never go out with a girl if he didn't intend to marry her."

I forbore to mention that teens who take pledges of chastity have the same rate of sexually transmitted diseases as nonpledgers. Instead, I asked if Billy had ever spent a night away from home in the past.

"Of course, when he's gone to camp or to visit his aunt in California or—"

"No, Mr. Bysen, I mean, like this, without telling you. Or his mother."

"No, of course not. Billy is very responsible. But we're concerned that he's too much under the thumb of that Mexican preacher who came up here yesterday, and since you spend a lot of time down in South Chicago we decided you were the best person to make inquiries for us."

" 'We,' " I repeated. "Is that you and your wife? You and your brothers? You and your dad?"

"I—you ask too many questions. I want you to get to work finding him."

"I'll want to talk to your wife," I said, "so I need her phone number, home, office, cell, I don't care which."

This caused more spluttering: I was working for him, his wife was worried enough.

"You don't need me, you need a tame cop," I snapped. "You must have fifty or sixty of 'em scattered around the city and suburbs. I'll tear up the contract and messenger it out to you."

He gave me his home phone number and told me to report back by noon.

"I have other clients, Mr. Bysen, who've been waiting a lot longer than you have for help. If you think your son's life is in imminent danger, then you need the FBI or the police. Otherwise, I'll report when I know something." I really, really hate working for the powerful: they think they're the boss of the whole world, as we used to say in South Chicago, and that includes being the boss of you.

While I was on the phone with Bysen, Morrell had made me a cappuccino and a pita with hummus and olives. I sat at his desk, eating, while I talked to Bysen's wife. In a quiet, almost little-girl voice, Annie Lisa Bysen told me nothing: oh, yes, Billy had friends, they were all in the church youth group together, they sometimes went camping together, but never without him talking to her first. No, he didn't have a girlfriend; she repeated his participation in True Love Waits, and how proud they were of Billy after their experience with their daughter. No, she didn't know why he hadn't come home, he hadn't talked to her, but "my husband" was sure he was with that preacher in South Chicago. They had asked their own pastor, Pastor Larchmont, to call down to the South Side church, but Larchmont hadn't been able to reach anyone yet.

"It was probably a mistake, that exchange program with the inner-city churches, they have so many bad kids who can influence Billy. He's so impressionable, so idealistic, but Daddy Bysen wanted Billy to go work in the warehouse. It was where he started his business, and all the men in the family have to go. I tried to tell William we should just let Billy go to college, like he wanted, but you might as well talk to Niagara Falls as get Daddy Bysen to change his mind, so William didn't even try, just sent Billy down there, and ever since it's been Pastor Andrés, Pastor Andrés, as if Billy was quoting the Bible itself."

"What about your daughter, Billy's sister—does she know where he is?"

A long pause at the other end. "Candace—Candace is in Korea. Even if it wasn't so hard to get to her, Billy wouldn't do that; he knows how much William—how much we—would hate it."

I wished I did have time to drive up to South Barrington to the Bysen enclave. There's so much that you get from body language that you can't see over the phone. Did she really believe her son would avoid his sister on his parents' say-so—especially if he was running away from home? Did Annie Lisa do everything Daddy Bysen said? Or did she resist passively?

I tried to get Candace's e-mail address, or a phone number, but Annie Lisa refused even to acknowledge the question. "What about your sister-in-law, Jacqui Bysen. Did Billy talk to her at the warehouse yesterday?"

"Jacqui?" Annie Lisa repeated the name doubtfully, as if it were in a strange language, maybe Albanian, that she'd never heard of. "I guess it never occurred to me to ask her."

"I'll do that, Ms. Bysen." I took the names of the two youths she thought her son might be closest to, but I expected the Bysens were right: Papa and Mama Bear had insulted a man Billy looked up to, and Baby Bear had probably fled to him for cover. If he hadn't, I suppose I could begin the unenviable job of trying to find Candace Bysen. I would also check area hospitals, because you never know—accidents happen even to the children of America's richest men. I scribbled all this down in a set of notes, since I've learned the hard way that I can't keep track of so many details in my head.

I had business in the Loop for a couple of significant clients, but I finished before one and drove early to the South Side. I stopped by the warehouse to talk to Patrick Grobian first. He and Aunt Jacqui were deep in a discussion of linens; neither had seen Billy today.

"If he wasn't a Bysen, he'd be out on his can, believe me," Grobian snapped. "No one who wants a job with By-Smart comes and goes as they please."

Aunt Jacqui stretched, catlike, with the same look of mischief around her mouth I'd seen yesterday during the uproar at the prayer meeting. "Billy is a saint. You'll probably find him eating honey and locusts in a cave someplace, maybe even under the boxes in the basement—he's always preaching to Pat and me about work conditions here."

"Why?" I widened my eyes, innocence personified. "Is there something wrong with work conditions here?"

"It's a warehouse," Grobian said, "not a convent. Billy can't tell the difference. Our work conditions comply with every OSHA standard ever written."

I let that lie. "Would he go to his sister, do you think?"

"To Candace?" Jacqui's carefully waxed brows rose to her hairline. "No one would go to Candace for anything except a trick or a nickel bag."

I left while she and Grobian enjoyed a complicit laugh over that witticism. I had to be at the school for basketball practice at three, which is when Rose's shift also ended. I couldn't keep the girls waiting for me, so that meant if I wanted to talk to Rose I had to go back to the factory.

 (RE)TIRED GUN

The yard in the middle of the afternoon looked different than at six in the morning. A half-dozen cars were parked on the weedy verge, a panel truck stood in the drive, partly blocking my way, while several men were hauling fabric, shouting to each other in Spanish. I drove the Mustang onto the weeds, next to a late-model Saturn.

The factory's front doors stood open, but I went down to the loading bay, where a second truck was docked, motor running. I went over next to it and pulled myself up onto the lip of the dock, hoping to avoid both the foreman and Zamar. I sketched a grin and a wave at the men, who had stopped to stare at me. They had driven a forklift up to the back of the truck and were loading boxes, which they hurriedly covered with a tarp when they saw me watching. I pursed my lips, wondering what they were hiding. Maybe they were even smuggling some kind of contraband. Maybe this somehow lay behind the sabotage attempts, but they were staring at me with so much hostility that I went on in to the main part of the factory.

On one side of the floor, a team of women were folding banners into packing crates. As luck had it, Larry Ballatra, the foreman, was right in front of me, barking orders to the crew. I passed him without pausing, going straight to the iron stairs. He glanced at me but didn't seem to really notice me, and I ran up to the work floor.

Rose was at her station, working this time on an American flag, outsize, like the one hanging over the shop floor. The soft fabric was falling from her machine into a wooden box: the U.S. flag must not touch the ground. I squatted next to her so that she could see my face.

She gasped and turned pale. "You, what are you doing here?"

"I'm worried, Rose. Worried about you, and about Josie. She said you had to take a second job, and you left her in charge of the boys and the baby."

"Someone has to help out. You think Julia can do it? She won't."

"You said you want Josie to go to college. It's too much responsibility for her, at fifteen, and, besides, it makes it hard for her to study."

Her lips tightened in anger. "You think you mean well, but you know nothing about life down here. And don't tell me a story about growing up here, because you still know nothing, anyway."

"Maybe not, Rose, but I know something about what it takes to leave here to go to college. If you can't be with Josie, making sure she gets her homework done, what's she going to do? If she gets frustrated with the responsibility, she could start cruising the streets, she could come home with another baby for you to look after. What job is important enough for that?"

Anger and anguish chased each other across her face. "You think I don't know that? You think I don't have a mother's heart? I have to take this other job. I have to. And if Mr. Zamar, if he sees you here, he will fire me anyway from this job, then I have nothing for my children, so leave before you destroy my whole life."

"Rose, what changed overnight? Monday, you needed me to find the plant saboteurs; today, you're scared of me."

Her face was contracted in torment, but her hands kept steadily feeding fabric through the machine. "Go, now! Or I will yell for help."

I didn't have any choice except to leave. Back in my car, I didn't go anywhere for a while. What had changed in three days? Me offending her wouldn't have caused this agonized outburst. It had to be something else, some threat Zamar or the foreman had used against her.

What were they making her do? I couldn't imagine, or I could imagine lurid things, but not likely things—you know, prostitution rings, that kind of misery. But what hold could they have on Rose Dorrado? Her need to keep working, I suppose. Perhaps there was some connection to the boxes going into the panel truck, but the truck had left while I was in the plant, and I had no idea how to track it.

Finally, I put the car into gear and drove slowly down the avenue to Mt. Ararat Church of Holiness, at Ninety-first and Houston—just a block south of the house where I grew up. I came at the church from Ninety-first—I didn't want to see the wrecked tree in my mother's front garden again.

In a neighborhood where twenty people with Bibles and an empty storefront constitute a church, I hadn't known what to expect, but Mt. Ararat was big enough to have an actual building, with a steeple and a few stained-glass windows. The church was locked, but a sign on the door listed the hours for services (Wednesday choir practice, Thursday evening Bible study, Friday AA meetings, and on Sundays, Sunday school and church) along with Pastor Robert Andrés's phone numbers.

The first number turned out to be his home, where I got an answering machine. The second number, to my surprise, connected me to a construction company. I asked for Andrés, somewhat uncertainly, and was told he was out on a job.

"A funeral, you mean?"

"A construction job. He works for us three days a week. If you need to reach him, I can give the foreman your phone number."

The woman wouldn't direct me to the jobsite, so I gave her my cell phone number. A few minutes later, Andrés called back. Construction noise at his end made conversation difficult; he had trouble understanding who I was or what I wanted, but "Billy the Kid," "Josie Dorrado," and "girls' basketball" seemed to get through, and he gave me the address where he was working, over at Eighty-ninth and Buffalo.

Four town houses were going up in the middle of a long, empty block.

The little boxes, rising out of the rubble of the neighborhood, had a kind of gallant optimism about them, splashes of hope against the general gray of the area.

One house seemed close to completion: someone was painting trim, a couple of guys were on the roof. I took a hard hat from my trunk—I keep one handy because of all the industrial sites I visit—and walked over to the trim painter. He didn't look up from his work until I called out to him; when I asked for Robert Andrés, he pointed his brush at the next building over and went back to work without speaking.

No one was outside the second house, but I could hear a power saw and loud shouting from within. I picked my way around rusted pipe and wedges of concrete, the crumbling remains of whatever had stood here before, and climbed over the ledge through the open hole where the front door would be.

A stairwell rose in front of me, the risers fresh sawn, the nailheads new and shiny. I could hear desultory hammering from the room beyond me, but I followed the sound of shouting up the stairs. All around me were open joists, the skeleton of the house. In front of me, three men were about to lift a piece of drywall into place. They bent and chanted a countdown in unison in Spanish. On *"cero"* they started lifting and walking the wallboard into place. It was heavy work; I could see trapeziuses quivering even on this muscular crew. As soon as the wallboard was up, two more men jumped to either end and began hammering it home. Only then did I step forward to ask for Pastor Andrés.

"Roberto," one of the guys bellowed, "lady here asking for you."

Andrés stepped through the open area that would eventually be another wall. I wouldn't have known him in his hard hat and equipment apron, but he apparently recognized me from our encounter on Tuesday outside Fly the Flag—as soon as he saw me, he turned and went back to the other room. At first, I thought he was running away from me, but apparently he was merely telling the foreman that he'd be taking a break, because he came back a minute later without the apron and gestured to me to go back down the stairs.

Buffalo Avenue was relatively quiet in the middle of the afternoon. A woman with a pair of toddlers was heading toward us, pushing a shopping cart full of laundry, and on the far corner two men were having a heated exchange. They were listing so precariously I didn't think they'd be able to connect if they came to blows. The real action in South Chicago heats up as the sun goes down.

"You are the detective, I think, but I've forgotten your name." One on one, Andrés's voice was soft, his accent barely noticeable.

"V. I. Warshawski. Do you do counseling at jobsites in the neighborhood, pastor?"

He shrugged. "A small church like mine, it cannot pay my full wage as a pastor, so I do a little electrical work to make ends meet. Jesus was a carpenter; I am content in His footsteps."

"I was at By-Smart yesterday morning and attended the service. Your sermon certainly electrified the congregation. Were you trying to give Billy's grandfather a lecture on unions?"

Andrés smiled. "If I start preaching about unions, the next thing I know I've invited pickets to jobsites like this one. But I know that's what the old one believes, and that poor Billy, who wants only to do good in the world, had a fight with his family because of what I said. I tried to call the grandfather, but he wouldn't speak to me."

"What were you preaching about, then?" I asked.

He spread his hands. "Only what I said—the need for all people to be treated with respect. I thought that was a safe and simple message for such men, but apparently it was not. This neighborhood is in pain, Sister Warshawski; it is like the valley of dry bones. We need the Spirit to rain down on us and clothe our bones with flesh and animate them with spirit, but the sons of men must do their part."

The words were spoken in a conversational tone; this wasn't prayer or preaching or public show, just the facts as he saw them.

"Agreed. What concrete things should the sons and daughters of women and men do?"

He pursed his lips, considering. "Provide jobs for those who need work. Treat workers with respect. Pay them a living wage. It is a simple thing, really. Is that why you came to find me today? Because Billy's father and grandfather are searching for hidden meanings? I am not educated enough to speak in codes or riddles."

"Billy was very upset yesterday morning because of the way his father and grandfather reacted to you. He chose not to go home last night. His father wanted to know if Billy is staying with you."

"So you are working for the family now, for the Bysen family?"

I started to deny it, reflexively, and then realized that, of course, yes, I was working for the Bysen family. Why should that make me feel ashamed? If things kept on at the current rate, the whole country would be working for By-Smart within the decade.

"I told Billy's father I'd try to locate him down here, yes."

Andrés shook his head. "I think if Billy does not want to talk to his father right now, that is his right. He is trying to grow up, to think of himself as a man, not a boy. It will do his parents no harm if he stays away from home for a few nights."

"Is he staying with you?" I asked bluntly.

When Andrés turned as if to walk back into the house, I quickly added, "I won't tell the family, if he really doesn't want them to know, but I'd like to hear it from him in person first. The other thing is, they think he has come to you. Whether I tell them I can't find him, or that he's safe but wants to be left alone, they have the resources to make your life difficult."

He looked over his shoulder at me. "Jesus did not count any difficulties as a reason to turn back from the way to the Cross, and I pledged myself long ago to follow in His steps."

"That's admirable, but if they send the Chicago police, or the FBI, or a private security firm, to break down your door, will that be the best thing for Billy, or for the members of your church, who count on you?"

That made him turn back to me, with a glimmer of a smile. "Sister Warshawski, you are a good debater, you make a good point. Perhaps I do know now where is Billy, but perhaps I do not, and if I do know I can't tell someone who works for his father because my duty is to Billy. But—by five o'clock, if the FBI breaks down my door, they will find only my cat Lazarus."

"I'm certainly plenty busy between now and five; I won't have time to call the family before then."

He bowed his head in a courtly fashion and started back to the house. I walked with him. "Before you go back inside, can you tell me anything about Fly the Flag? Did Frank Zamar explain to you why he wouldn't call the police about the sabotage in his plant?"

Andrés shook his head again. "It will be a good thing for you to work with the girls on their basketball, instead of all these other matters."

It was a pretty stinging slap in the face. "All these other matters are directly connected to the girls and their basketball, pastor. Rose Dorrado is a member of your church, so you must know how worried she is about losing her job. Her kid Josie plays on my team—she took me home to her mother, who asked me to investigate the sabotage. It really is a simple story, pastor."

"South Chicago is full of simple stories, isn't it, each beginning in poverty and ending in death."

This time he sounded pompous, not poetic or natural; I ignored the comment. "And now something has gone even more amiss. Rose has taken a second job, one that keeps her away from her children in the evening. It's not just that her children need her, but I have the feeling she was coerced into taking this job, whatever it is. You're her pastor; can't you find out what the problem is?"

"I cannot force anyone to confide in me against their wishes. And she has two daughters who are old enough to look after the house. I know in the ideal world that you live in, girls of fifteen and sixteen should have a mother's supervision, but down here girls that age are considered grown up."

I was getting extremely tired of people acting like South Chicago was a different planet, one that I couldn't possibly comprehend. "Girls of fifteen should not become mothers, whether they are in South Chicago or Barrington Hills. Do you know that every baby a teenage girl has chops her lifetime earning potential by fifty percent? Julia already has a baby. I don't think it will help her or Rose or even Josie, if Josie starts running around the streets and has one of her own."

"It is necessary for these girls to put their trust in Jesus, and to keep their lives pure for their husbands."

"It would be lovely if they did, but they don't. And since you know that as well as I do, it would be really great if you stopped telling them not to use contraceptives."

His mouth tightened. "Children are a gift of the Lord. You may think you mean well, but your ideas come from a bad way of thinking. You are a woman, and unmarried, so you don't know about these matters. You concentrate on teaching these girls to play basketball and do not injure their immortal souls. I think it is better—"

He broke off to look over my shoulder at someone behind me. I turned to see a young man ambling toward us along Ninety-first Street. I didn't recognize his sullen pretty-boy face, but something about him did seem vaguely familiar. Andrés clearly knew him: the pastor called out something in Spanish, so rapidly I couldn't follow it, although I did hear him asking "why" and tell him not to come here, to leave. The younger man stared sullenly at Andrés, but finally hunched a shoulder and sauntered back the way he'd come.

"*Chavo banda!*" Andrés muttered.

That much I understood from my days with the public defender. "Is he a punk? I've seen him around, but I can't think where. What's his name?"

"His name doesn't matter, because he is only that: a punk one sees around, taking from jobsites, or even doing little jobs for bigger thugs. I don't want him at this jobsite. Which I must return to."

"Tell Billy to call me," I shouted to his back. "Before the end of the day, so I can pass the word on to his parents." Although, frankly, in the mood I was in, I'd be happy to see the cops break down the minister's damn door.

He flung out a hand at me, a wave of some kind—assent, dismissal?—I couldn't tell, because he continued into the house, an effective brush-off. He knew a lot, Pastor Andrés did, about Billy, about the *chavos banda* of the neighborhood, about Fly the Flag, most of all about right and wrong: it was better for me to mind my own business, he'd said, not to meddle with any of it, which meant to me that he knew why Frank Zamar didn't want the police involved in exploring the sabotage at the plant.

I walked back to my own car. Should I leave it alone? I should. I didn't have the time or the desire to look into it. And maybe if Andrés hadn't told me an unmarried woman shouldn't know or talk about sex, I would have left it alone. I tripped on a piece of concrete and did a kind of cartwheel to keep from going over completely.

I wished my Spanish were better. It's similar to Italian, so I can follow it, but I don't speak Italian often enough these days for either language to stay fresh in my mind. I had a feeling Andrés knew this *chavo banda* better than just from seeing him around the neighborhood; I had a feeling Andrés specifically didn't want me to see him with this *chavo*. Next week, I'd make it a little project, to try to find out who this particular punk was.

At practice that afternoon, I couldn't get anyone to pay attention to the game. Josie, in particular, was like a cat on a hot shovel. I figured the load of domestic responsibilities her mother had dumped on her must be getting to her, but it didn't make working with her easier. I called a halt to scrimmage twenty minutes early and could hardly wait for them to get out of the showers before taking off myself.

Billy the Kid phoned me as I was leaving Coach McFarlane's house. He wouldn't tell me where he was; in fact, he would barely talk to me at all.

"I thought I could trust you, Ms. War-sha-sky, but then you go and start working for my father, and on top of that you bothered Pastor Andrés. I'm an adult, I can take care of myself. You have to promise to stop looking for me."

"I can't make such a sweeping promise, Billy. If you don't want your dad to know where you are, I guess that's a reasonable request, as long as I can assure him you're not being held somewhere against your will."

His breath came heavily over the phone to me. "I haven't been kidnapped or anything like that. Now promise me."

"I'm tired enough of all the Bysens to be willing to run an ad in the *Herald-Star* promising never to talk to any of you again about each other or anything else."

"Is that supposed to be a joke? I don't think this is very funny. I just want you to tell my dad that I'm staying with friends, and if he sends anyone else looking for me I'm going to start calling shareholders."

"Calling shareholders?" I repeated blankly. "What's that supposed to mean?"

"That's my whole message."

"Before you hang up, you ought to remember something about your cell phone: it puts out a GPS signal. A bigger, richer detective agency than mine would have equipment to track you. As would the FBI."

He was silent for a moment. In the background, I could hear sirens, and a baby crying: the sounds of the South Side.

"Thank you for the tip, Ms. War-sha-sky," he finally said in a careful voice. "Maybe I misjudged you."

"Maybe," I said. "Do you want—" but he hung up before I could finish asking him if he wanted to see me.

I pulled over to the curb to relay Billy's message to his father. Naturally enough, Mr. William wasn't pleased, but his response took the form of petulant bullying ("That's all? You think I'm paying your fee for sending me a disrespectful message? I want my son *now.*") But when I told him I was going to have to quit the assignment, he stopped complaining about the message and demanded that I get back to work.

"I can't, Mr. William, not when I promised Billy to stop looking for him."

"What's that got to do with it?" He was astonished. "It was a good ploy—he won't be suspecting you."

"It's my word, Mr. William—I don't have three thousand stores to carry me through lean times. My good word is my only asset. If I lose that, well, it would be a bigger disaster for me than losing all those stores would be for you, because I wouldn't have any capital to start over again."

He still didn't seem to understand: he was willing to overlook my insolence, but he wanted his son without delay.

"Fee, fie, foe, fum," I muttered, slamming the car into gear. Halfway up Lake Shore Drive to Morrell's place, I decided to put everything behind me, the Bysens, the South Side, even my important paying clients and my tangled love life. I needed time alone, just for myself. I went to my own apartment and collected the dogs. When Morrell didn't answer the phone, I left a message on his voice mail, told a startled Mr. Contreras I'd be back late on Sunday, and took off for the country. I ended up in a B and B in Michigan, took the dogs for ten-mile rambles along the lakeshore, read one of Paula Sharpe's quirky novels. Every now and then, I wondered about Morrell, with Marcena down the hall, but not even those thoughts undid my essential pleasure in my private weekend.

 **HEART-STOPPER**

My peaceful mood held until Monday afternoon, when April Czernin collapsed in the middle of practice. At first, I thought Celine Jackman had taken her out in an escalation of their ongoing feud, but Celine was in the backcourt; April had been driving under the basket when she fell all in a heap, as if she'd been shot.

I blew my whistle to stop practice and ran to her side. Her skin was blue around the mouth, and I couldn't feel a pulse. I started CPR on her, trying to keep my own panic at bay so my horrified team wouldn't disintegrate completely.

The girls crowded around us.

"Coach, what happened?"

"Coach, is she dead?"

"Did someone shoot her?"

Josie's face loomed next to mine. "Coach, what's wrong?"

"I don't know," I panted. "Do—you—know of any health problems, problems April has?"

"No, nothing, this never happened before." Josie's cheeks were white with fear; she could hardly get the words out.

"Josie," I kept pushing on April's diaphragm, "my cell phone is locked in the equipment room, inside my bag in the desk."

I took my hands away from April for a brief second and handed the keys to her. "Go get it, call 911, tell them exactly where we are. Repeat for me!"

When she parroted back my instructions, I told her to move. She ran, stumbling, to the equipment room. Sancia went with her, murmuring petitions to Jesus.

Celine I sent to the principal's office: gangbanger she might be, but she had the coolest head on the team. Maybe the school nurse was still here, maybe she knew something about April's history. Josie came back with the phone, her face pinched and white: she was so nervous, she couldn't figure out how to use the phone. I stepped her through it, not pausing in my work on April's chest, and had her put the phone to my head so I could talk to the dispatcher myself. I waited long enough for an acknowledgment of our location, then told Josie to take the phone and try to reach April's folks.

"They're both at work, coach, and I don't know how to get them. April's mom, she's a cashier over at the By-Smart on Ninety-fifth and, well, you know, her dad, he drives that truck, I don't know where he is." Her voice cracked.

"Okay, girl, it's okay. You call . . . this number, and hit the send key." I squinted, trying to calm down enough to remember Morrell's number. When I finally came up with it, I had Josie type it in and then hold the little phone up to my head.

"V.I.," I said, continuing my work on April's chest. "Emergency, with Romeo's kid . . . need to find Romeo. Ask . . . Marcena, okay? If she can . . . track him down . . . have him . . . call my cell."

Years in battle zones made Morrell accept what I said without wasting time on useless questions. He simply said he was on it and let me get back to the task at hand. I didn't know what else to do while I waited for the ambulance, so I kept pushing on April's chest and blowing into her mouth.

Natalie Gault, the assistant principal, sailed into the room. The girls reluctantly pulled back to let her in next to me.

"What's happened here? Another team fight?"

"No. April . . . Czernin . . . collapsed. You got anything . . . in her file . . . on medical history?" Sweat was running down my neck, and my back was wet with it.

"I didn't check for that—I thought this was more of your gang warfare."

I didn't have energy to waste on anger. "Nope. Nature's doing. Worried . . . about her heart. Check her file, call . . . her mother."

Gault looked down at me, as if deciding whether she could take an order from me. Fortunately, at that moment, we had one of the South Side's major miracles: an ambulance crew actually arrived, in under four minutes. I got gratefully to my feet and wiped sweat from my eyes.

While I gave the techs a sketch of what had happened, they moved in next to April with a portable defibrillator. They slid her onto a stretcher and pulled up her damp T-shirt to attach the pads, one below her left breast, the other on her right shoulder. The girls crowded in, anxious and titillated at the same time. As if we were in a movie, the techs told us to stand clear; I pulled the girls away while the techs administered a shock. Just as in a movie, April's body jerked. They watched their monitor anxiously; no heartbeat. They had to shock her twice more before the muscle came back to life and began a sluggish beat, like an engine slowly turning over on a cold day. As soon as they were sure she was breathing, the techs packed up their equipment and began running across the gym with the stretcher.

I trotted along next to them. "Where are you taking her?"

"University of Chicago—it's the closest pediatric trauma center. They'll need an adult to admit her."

"The school is trying to find the parents," I said.

"You in a position to okay medical treatment?"

"I don't know. I'm the basketball coach; she collapsed during practice, but I don't think that gives me legal rights."

"Up to you, but the kid needs an adult and an advocate."

We were outside now. The ambulance had drawn a crowd, but the students stood back respectfully as the techs opened the door and slid April inside. I couldn't let her go alone; I could see that.

I scrambled into the back and took her hand. "It's okay, baby, you'll be okay, you'll see," I kept murmuring, squeezing her hand while she lay semiconscious, her eyes blunking back in her head.

The heart monitor was the loudest sound in the world, louder than the siren, louder than my cell phone, which rang without my hearing it until the EMT crew told me to turn it off because it could interfere with their instruments. The irregular beeping bounced in my head like a basketball. *A-pril's still alive but isn't stable, A-pril's still alive but isn't stable.* It drowned any other thoughts, about By-Smart, or Andrés, or where Romeo Czernin might be. The sound seemed to go on forever, so when we arrived at the hospital I was startled to see we'd covered seven city miles in twelve minutes.

As soon as we pulled into the ambulance bay, the EMTs whisked April into the emergency room and left me to grapple with her paperwork, a frustrating bureaucratic battle, since I had no idea what kind of insurance her parents had. The school had a little policy on the athletes, but only for injuries sustained while playing; if this was a preexisting condition, the policy wouldn't cover it.

When the ER staff saw I didn't know enough to fill out the forms, they sent me off to a tiny cubicle to wrestle with an admissions official. After forty minutes, I felt like a boxer who'd been punched for thirteen rounds but couldn't quite fall over. Because April had come in as a pediatric emergency, they were treating her, but they needed parental consent, and they needed to be paid—not, I need hardly add, in that order.

I couldn't guarantee the payment, and I wasn't legally able to give consent, so I tried to track down April's mom at work, which was in itself a bureaucratic nightmare; it took me nine minutes to find someone with the authority to deliver a message to an employee working the floor, but that someone said Mrs. Czernin's shift had ended at four and she wasn't in the store any longer. She wasn't at home, either, but the Czernins did have an answering machine, with a message delivered in the hesitant voice of someone uncomfortable with technology.

I tried Morrell again. He hadn't been able to track down Marcena. Only because I'd run out of other ideas, I called Mary Ann McFarlane.

My old coach was alarmed when she heard what had happened—she didn't know about any health problems April had, certainly she had never collapsed before. Several times last year, she'd suddenly run out of steam during drills, but Mary Ann had put that down to lack of conditioning. The coach knew nothing about health insurance, either: she assumed most of the girls on the team had green cards, entitling them to Medicaid, but she'd never needed to check. And, of course, both April's parents worked, so the Czernins probably didn't qualify for public assistance.

When I hung up, the admissions official told me if I couldn't get April's care sorted out they'd have to move her to County. We argued over it for a few minutes, and I was demanding to see a supervisor, when a woman burst in on us.

"Tori Warshawski, I might have known. What did you do to my girl? Where's my April?"

Her use of Boom-Boom's old name didn't register with me at first. "Did you get the message I left on your machine? I'm sorry I had to notify you that way, Mrs. Czernin. April collapsed during practice. We were able to revive her, but no one knows what's wrong. And they need her insurance information here, I'm afraid."

"Don't 'Mrs. Czernin' me, Tori Warshawski. If you hurt my girl, you are going to pay for it with the last drop of blood in your body."

I stared at her blankly. She was a thin woman, not thin like Aunt Jacqui or Marcena, with the carefully tended slimness of the wealthy; she had tendons in her neck like steel cables, and deep grooves around her mouth, from smoking or worry or both. Her hair was bleached and scraped back from her head in waves as hard as coiled wire. She looked old enough to be April's grandmother, not her mother, and I wracked my tired brain for where we might have met.

"You don't know me?" she spat. "I used to be Sandra Zoltak."

Against my will, a wave of crimson flooded my cheeks. Sandy Zoltak. When I last knew her, she'd had soft blond ringlets, a plump soft body, like a Persian cat, but a sly smile, and a way of turning up when you didn't expect or even want her. She'd been in Boom-Boom's class in high school, a year ahead of me, but I'd known her. Oh yes indeed, I'd known her.

"I'm sorry, Sandy, sorry I didn't recognize you. Sorry, too, about April. She collapsed suddenly in practice. Does she have anything wrong with her heart?" My voice came out more roughly than I'd meant, but Sandra didn't seem to notice that.

"Not unless you did something to her. When Bron told me you was filling in for McFarlane, I told April she had to be careful, you could be mean, but I never expected—"

"Sandy, she was going in for a basket and her heart stopped beating."

I talked slowly and loudly, forcing her to pay attention. Sandy had been riding with demons all the way to the hospital, worrying about her child; she needed someone to take it out on, and I wasn't just convenient, I was an old enemy, from a neighborhood that stored grudges as carefully as if they were food in a bomb shelter.

I tried telling her what we'd done to help April, and what the impasse was here at the hospital, but she poured furious accusations over me: my negligence, my bullying, my desire to get back at her through her daughter.

"Sandy, no, Sandy, please, that's all dead and gone. April's a great kid, she's about the best athlete on the team, I want her to be healthy and happy. I need to know, the hospital needs to know, does she have some kind of heart problem?"

"Ladies," the woman at the admissions cubicle interrupted us in magisterial tones, "save your fight for the home, please. All I want to hear right now is billing information for this child."

"Naturally," I snapped. "Money comes way ahead of health care in American hospitals. Why don't you tell Mrs. Czernin what's happening with her daughter? I don't think she can answer any billing questions until she knows how April's doing."

The administrator pursed her lips, but turned to her phone and made a call. Sandy stopped shouting and strained to listen, but the woman was speaking so quietly we couldn't make out what she was saying. Still, within a few minutes a nurse from the emergency room appeared. April was stable; she seemed to have good reflexes, good recall of events: although she couldn't name the mayor or the governor, she probably hadn't known those facts this morning. She could name her teammates and recite her parents' phone number, but the hospital wanted to keep her overnight, and maybe for a few days, for tests, and to make sure she was stable.

"I need to see her. I need to be with her." Sandra's voice was a harsh caw.

"I'll take you back as soon as you finish with the paperwork here," the nurse promised. "We told her you'd arrived, and she's eager to see you."

When I was fifteen, I would have wanted my mother, too, but it was hard to picture Sandy Zoltak thinking about another person with the passion and care my mother had felt for me. I found myself blinking back tears—of frustration, fatigue, longing for my mother—I didn't know what.

I abruptly left the area, prowling around the hall until I saw Sandra return from the emergency room to the admissions desk. When I went over, she was fishing an insurance card out of her wallet. By-Smart was written on it in big letters; I was relieved but surprised—from what I'd read, the company didn't provide insurance to their cashiers. Of course, Romeo drove for them; maybe he had real benefits. When Sandra had finished filling out forms, I asked if she wanted me to wait for her.

Her mouth twisted. "You? I don't need your help for anything, Victoria Iffy-genius Warshawski. You couldn't get a husband, you couldn't have a kid, now you're trying to muscle into my family? Just go the hell away."

I'd forgotten that tired old insult the kids used to use. My middle name, Iphigenia, the bane of my life—who had let it out on the playground to begin with? And then my mother's ambitions for me to go to college, the support of teachers like Mary Ann McFarlane, my own drive, some of the kids thought I was a snot, an egghead, an iffy genius. Being Boom-Boom's cousin, and his sidekick, had been a help in high school, but all those taunts, maybe that's why I'd done some of the things I'd done, trying to prove to the rest of the school that I wasn't just a brain, that I could be as big an idiot as any other adolescent.

Despite her spitefulness, I handed Sandra a business card. "My cell phone's on here. If you change your mind, give me a call."

It was only six o'clock when I walked out of the hospital. I couldn't believe it was that early—I thought I must have been working all night, I felt so beat. I looked aimlessly around Cottage Grove Avenue for my car, wondering if I'd forgotten to set the alarm, when I remembered it was still down at the high school—I'd ridden to Hyde Park in the ambulance.

I picked up a taxi at the stand across the street and bullied the driver into going south. All the way down Route 41, the cabbie kept hectoring me on how dangerous it was, and who was going to pay his fare back north?

I refused to take part in one more fight, leaning back in the seat with my eyes shut, hoping that would make the driver close his mouth. He may have kept up his complaint, but I did fall into a sound sleep that lasted all the way to the high school parking lot.

I made my way home more by luck than skill, and fell back down into the well of sleep as soon as I got home. My dreams weren't restful. I was back in the gym, fifteen years old. It was dark, but I knew I was there with Sylvia, Jennie, and the rest of my old basketball team. We'd run the length of the room so many times, we automatically avoided the sharp edges of the bleachers, and the horse and hurdles leaning against the wall. We knew where the ladders were, and which one had the climbing ropes looped around it.

I was the strongest: I clambered up the narrow steel ladder and unhooked the climbing ropes. Sylvia was like a squirrel on the ropes. She clung with her thighs, hauling up the underpants and the sign. Jennie, keeping watch at the gym doors, was sweating.

Homecoming was the next night, and the dream switched to that. Even in my dream, I felt thick with grievance against Boom-Boom—

he'd promised to take me and now he wouldn't. What did he see in Sandy, anyway?

It was the exposure waiting round the bend in my mind that woke me. I wasn't going to let myself dream to the end, to Boom-Boom's anger and my own mortification. I sat in bed, sweating, panting, seeing Sandy Zoltak again as she'd been then, soft, plump, with a sly smile for the girls, a foxy one for the guys, her shimmery satin dress a blue that matched her eyes, going into the gym on Boom-Boom's arm— I pushed aside the memory and thought instead how I wouldn't have known Sandy on the street today—I certainly hadn't known her in the hospital.

It must have been that random thought that brought the punk I'd seen on the street when I was talking to Pastor Andrés back into mind, the *"chavo banda"* Andrés chewed out for showing up at his construction site.

Of course I'd seen him before: he'd been in Fly the Flag last Tuesday morning. "A punk one sees around, taking from jobsites, or even doing little jobs," Andrés had said.

Someone had hired him to vandalize Fly the Flag. Was it Andrés, or Zamar, or someone Andrés knew? It was four in the morning. I wasn't going to go all the way down to South Chicago to see if the *chavo* was trying for a repeat attack against Fly the Flag. But the thought stayed with me through the rest of my uneasy sleep. All day Tuesday, when I had a heavy schedule at my agency, I kept wondering about this *chavo* and the flag factory, about the cartons they'd been taking out of the plant that they hadn't wanted me to see the last time I was there.

In the evening, when I'd finished my real work, I couldn't resist going back down to Fly the Flag to see for myself what was going on. And while I was creeping around the plant in the dark, I watched it blow up.

16 COMMAND PERFORMANCE

That was the tale I told Conrad, mostly warts, mostly all. When I finished talking, it was late afternoon. The anesthesia in my system kept pulling me under, and I drifted off to sleep from time to time. Once when I woke up, Conrad was stretched out asleep on the floor. Mr. Contreras had been compassionate enough to put a pillow under his head, I saw with some amusement; my neighbor had left while we were both asleep, but came back half an hour or so later with a big bowl of spaghetti.

At first, Conrad kept challenging me; interviewing me had him off balance, and he was jumpy, aggressive, interrupting every few sentences. I was too tired and too sore to fight. Whenever he broke in, I would only wait for him to finish, and then just start the previous sentence again from the beginning. Finally, he settled down, not even barking at me when I took phone calls—although my long conversation with Morrell made him leave the room. Of course, Conrad had calls of his own, from the medical examiner's office, from his secretary, from the Tenth Ward alderman, and a couple of newspaper and TV stations.

While he was dealing with the media, I bathed and put on clean clothes, a tough job with the pain stabbing from my shoulder down my left arm. I risked wetting the dressing by washing my hair, which stank of smoke, and felt better for getting all the grime off my body.

I talked until I was hoarse. Not that I told Conrad every detail; he didn't need to know about my private life, or my complicated reaction to Marcena Love. He didn't need to know my ancient history with Bron Czernin and Sandy Zoltak, and I didn't hand him Billy the Kid or Pastor Andrés on a platter. Still, I covered all the essentials, including a lot more detail than he wanted on the Bertha Palmer basketball program—especially when I suggested that the Fourth Police District might adopt the team as part of their community outreach.

I didn't hide anything that I'd learned at Fly the Flag, not even my own break-in at the premises the week before, or the *chavo banda* I'd intercepted or Frank Zamar's refusal to let me call the cops then. I told Conrad how Rose Dorrado had brought me into the flag factory to begin with, and then ordered me to stay away. And I told him that Andrés knew this *chavo* by sight.

"And that's the whole truth, Ms. W., so help you God?" Rawlings said when I'd finished.

"Too many people doing weird things in God's name these days," I grumbled. "Let's just say I've given you an honest factual narrative."

"Where does this Marcena Love fit into the picture?"

"Don't think she does," I said. "I've never seen her near the factory, for one thing, and there's nothing connecting Czernin to it, either. She might have heard something, roaming around the South Side, that's all. I'm guessing a look at Zamar's books will tell you what you need to know."

"Meaning?"

"Meaning, I'm wondering if the guy was in a hole and was being squeezed. Rose Dorrado said he'd bought a fancy new machine he was having trouble paying for. Say Zamar didn't, or couldn't, respond when his creditors put dead rats in his ventilator shaft. This annoyed them enough that they made the biggest statement possible, took out his factory and him at the same time."

Conrad nodded and switched off his recorder. "It's a good theory. It might even be right—it's worth looking into. But I want you to do me a favor. No, take that back: I want a promise out of you."

My brows jumped up to my hairline. "And that would be?"

"Not to do any more investigating on my turf. I'll get our forensic accountants to check into Zamar's finances, and I don't want to find that you've been there ahead of them, helping yourself to his files."

"I promise you that I will not help myself to any of Zamar's files. Which, I have a feeling, are charcoal now, anyway."

"I want more than that, Vic. I don't want you investigating crimes in my district, period."

"If someone in South Chicago hires me, Conrad, I will investigate to the best of my ability." Despite the spurt of anger I felt, I almost laughed—I hadn't wanted to be sucked back into South Chicago, but as soon as someone told me to stay away my hackles went up and I dug in my heels.

"That's right, cookie," Mr. Contreras put in. "You can't be letting people tell you what you can and can't do for a living."

Conrad glared at the old man but spoke to me. "Your investigations are like Sherman's march through Georgia: you get where you're going, but God help anyone within five miles of your path. South Chicago has enough death and destruction without you adding your investigative skills to my war zone."

"That badge and gun don't make you owner of the South Side," I began, my eyes hot. "It's just that you cannot bear the memory—"

The doorbell rang before I could finish my own offensive retort. Peppy and Mitch began a deafening barking, whirling around me in circles to let me know someone was approaching. Mr. Contreras, in his element when I'm on the disabled list, bustled out, the dogs clattering behind him.

The interruption gave me time to take a breath. "Conrad, you're too good a cop to be threatened by anything I do. I know you're not afraid I'll steal glory you have coming to you if I turn up something that helps you solve a case. And you're a generous coworker with women. So your reaction is totally about you and me. Do you think I—"

I broke off as I heard the expedition to the third floor making its way up the stairs: the dogs racing up and down as Mr. Contreras slowly puffed his way upward, and the hollow thump of a cane against the hard stairwell carpet.

Morrell was coming to visit me. It was his first time moving this far from his own place since he'd come home, and I was touched, and delighted—so why was I feeling embarrassed? Surely not because Morrell would see me with Conrad—and absolutely not because Conrad would see me with Morrell. Which meant I was blushing for no good reason.

Then, over the sound of the cane and Mr. Contreras's heavy tread, I heard Marcena's light high voice and my embarrassment receded into annoyance. Why was she raining on my parade once again? Didn't she have to get back to England, or Fallujah?

I turned my back on the door and doggedly continued my speech to Conrad. "If you've been holding a grudge against me for four years, that makes me feel sad. But, even so, you're asking something that you have no right to, under law, something you must know I wouldn't agree to, even if it would end your bitter feelings against me."

Conrad looked at me, lips compressed, trying to make up his mind how to answer. The dogs raced in before he decided, dancing around me with their tails waving like banners: they'd brought me company, and they wanted petting and cheers for being so clever.

Behind them, I could hear Marcena saying to Mr. Contreras, "I adore horse racing; I had no idea you could see it in Chicago. Before I go home, you must take me to the track. Are you a lucky punter? No? No more am I, but I never can resist."

So now she was charming the socks off my neighbor, too. I got to my feet again as she and Mr. Contreras came through my little vestibule.

"Marcena! What a pleasure. And horse racing, of course, another passion of yours that I never knew about, like World War Two fighter planes! Come meet Commander Rawlings, and tell him how much you adore model trains, and how your Uncle Julian—or was it your Uncle Sacheverel?—used to let you play with his H.O. layout at Christmas." Conrad had an unexpected passion for model railroads; his living room held an intricate setup that he turned to when he needed to unwind, and he had a small shop in his garage where he built houses and molded miniature scenery.

Conrad shook his head several times, just a reflex, startled by my sudden chirpy outburst, while Marcena looked at me through narrowed eyes. I introduced them, and went out to the landing to find Morrell. He had reached the top of the stairs, but was getting his breath back before coming in to face a crowd. Peppy came out to see what we were doing, but Mitch had also fallen for Marcena and was staying close to her.

"So you've been back in the wars, my mighty Amazon?" Morrell pulled me close and kissed me. "I thought the house rule was only one of us could be injured at a time."

"Just a flesh wound," I said gruffly. "It hurts horribly right now, but it's not serious. Thanks for coming. I'm just finishing with the cops; Commander Rawlings wanted complete chapter and verse."

"I would have been here sooner, but Marcena didn't get in until noon, and she needed to rest before setting out again. Sorry to bring her, darling, but I don't trust myself driving in city traffic yet."

One of the bullets had nicked Morrell's right hip where the sciatic nerve comes out. The nerve had been damaged, and it wasn't clear how completely it would recover. His occupational therapist had urged him to learn to use hand controls to drive, but he was resisting, not wanting to acknowledge that he might not regain full use of his leg. I put my arm around him, and we went back into my apartment, where Marcena was petting Mitch and asking Conrad about his work.

Conrad was answering her tersely. His jaw was rigid, and when he saw me come in with Morrell he broke off midsentence. I introduced the two men before sitting heavily down again—all this commotion was wearing me out.

"You been shot, huh?" Conrad said to Morrell. "Not running in front of a bullet meant for Vic, were you?"

"No, these were all meant for me," Morrell said. "Or, at least, for anyone trying to get into Mazar-e-Sharif that day. Or that's what the army told me—I don't remember it myself."

"Sorry, man, tough. I took a few at Hill 882."

Conrad was embarrassed at letting his feelings about me goad him into plain bald rudeness. For several minutes, he and Morrell and Mr. Contreras traded war stories—my neighbor had somehow survived one of World War II's bloodiest battles without being hurt, but he had seen plenty of other dead and wounded men. Marcena had her own store of war zone anecdotes to contribute. South Side street fighter that I am, I've seen my share of ugly fights, but these were small and personal, so I kept them to myself.

" 'War is sweet to those who never saw one,' " Morrell said, adding to me, "Erasmus, I think—you'll have to ask Coach McFarlane how he said it in Latin."

His words broke the chain of reminiscences; Conrad turned to Marcena. "Vic was telling me you've been riding around the South Side, Ms. Love. Have you been on your own?"

Marcena looked at me reproachfully; I hadn't been a good chum, telling on her to the cops.

"You've spent a lot of time down there lately, you've seen a lot of the community, and people talk to you frankly," I said. "I told Commander Rawlings, because you might have seen or heard something that would be useful to him."

"I can ask my own questions, Vic, thanks, and don't go tipping off witnesses again, okay? Maybe Ms. Love and I will go out for coffee and let you two be alone."

"Absolutely," Marcena said. "Morrell, when you're ready for me to drive you back to Evanston, ring me on my mobile. This will be great, commander: I've needed to talk to someone in the police to round out my picture of South Chicago. So much of it seems to be under permanent surveillance."

Conrad ignored her to stand over me. "Vic, I meant what I said about you messing up my turf. Take care of the basketball program. Deal with the financial crooks on La Salle Street. Leave the Fourth District to me."

A FROG IN MY JEANS

W hat'd you do to get a police commander so annoyed with you,
Pepperpot?" Morrell asked.

"Nothing he won't get over in another decade or two." I leaned against
him and shut my eyes.

"He thinks Cookie here got him shot four years ago," Mr. Contreras
put in, "when it was his own darn fault for not listening to her to begin
with. Good thing, if you ask me, 'cause it made him—"

"It's never a good thing to get shot." I couldn't bear to hear Mr. Contreras celebrate Conrad's and my breakup, especially not in front of Morrell. "And maybe I should have had that bullet instead of him. Anyway,
Marcena will charm him out of his bad mood."

"Probably will," my Job's comforter agreed. "She's perky enough for a
whole squad of cheerleaders."

Morrell laughed. "She's a prizewinning journalist—I don't think she'd
appreciate being compared to a cheerleader."

"But she is full of zip," I murmured, "and she knows how to home in
on everyone's wavelength."

"Except yours," Morrell said.

"But I'm a pepperpot, not a cheerleader."

He pulled me closer. "I like pepper better than cheers, okay?"

"Yeah, but, cookie, you could learn something from her," Mr. Contreras said, his brown eyes full of concern. "Look how she got Conrad Rawlings eating out of her hand, after he'd been threatening you."

I stiffened but didn't say anything; the old man had been so supportive all day it would be mean to turn on him, and, anyway, it would just prove his point. I looked up to see Morrell grinning at me, as if reading my mind. I punched him in the ribs, but settled back against his shoulder.

Finally, after fidgeting around the living room for several minutes, my neighbor announced he was taking the dogs out. "You two ain't fit for anything but sleep right now," he said, then turned brick red at the innuendo.

"Don't worry; sleep is *all* I'm fit for." I thanked him for all his help during the day. "Especially the spaghetti—a real corpse reviver."

"Clara's old meatball recipe," he beamed.

It took another ten minutes for him to finish his strictures on Conrad, his advice for my recovery, his promise to intercept Marcena so she wouldn't wake us when she came back.

"That's right," I said. "You two figure out a strategy for the Arlington track that'll set you up for the rest of your life. Morrell and I will design a strategy for healing our torn-up bodies."

We did pretty well sleep the clock around, at least in shifts. I got up briefly to talk to Marcena, who came up the stairs, despite Mr. Contreras's efforts to hold her at bay, so she could fetch Morrell. Morrell hobbled out in his jeans to say he'd stay with me until I could drive him home myself.

Marcena lingered in the doorway to report on the super time she'd had with Conrad; he'd promised her a ride-along next week to round out her picture of the South Side—she'd get a Kevlar vest and everything, just like being back in Kosovo.

I felt as though my skin might ignite from the force of the energy she was putting out, or maybe from my jealousy. "You able to tell him anything useful out of your nocturnal junkets?"

She grinned. "My eyes haven't been scanning the streets that closely, Vic, but I did want to thank you for not ratting out Bron to him—if word gets back to By-Smart about him having me in his truck, it could cost him his job."

I felt a sudden jolt: I couldn't believe I had forgotten about April Czernin so completely. "When did you last talk to Bron? Since yesterday? Does he know about April?"

"Oh, his daughter, right, Morrell told me. He can't take personal calls on his cell phone: it belongs to the company, and they monitor every call he makes and gets, so I didn't try to reach him. Anyway, he was headed for home, so I'm sure his wife told him."

"You didn't try to reach him yourself?" I couldn't keep the scorn out of my voice. "Even when you found out his kid was close to dying?"

"I don't think it would have been helpful for him to hear it fourth-hand from the hospital via you to Morrell to me. Or for his wife to talk to me if I reached her." She sounded disdainful, like the headmistress annoyed with the poor work of an unpromising student, but at least she'd stopped bubbling over like the La Brea tar pits.

"No wonder Sandra Czernin thinks my name is mud down there. I'm the person who introduced him to the woman he's been seeing the sights with."

I shut the door on her, but had to open it a second later—Peppy and Mitch had followed Marcena upstairs, and while Mitch, like every other male I knew, was clinging to Marcena, Peppy wanted to be let in with me. I glared at Mitch's retreating tail and stumped over to the phone.

Once again I got Sandra's stilted voice on her answering machine; I figured she, at least, was at the hospital—who knew where Bron was. I left a message, explaining that I'd been hit in the explosion at Fly the Flag, and asking Sandra to call me with news about April.

I was still groggy from anesthesia and my long day with Conrad, but Morrell said he'd slept enough for the time being. He settled himself on the couch with Peppy and his new laptop. He was working on the book he'd been researching when he got shot. His original laptop had been stolen while he lay bleeding on a mud track in Afghanistan; he'd backed up most of his files onto a portable key, but there was material he was trying to reconstruct, notes he'd been taking shortly before he was hit that he hadn't had time to organize or copy.

I went back to bed but slept fitfully, the pain in my shoulder jerking me awake whenever I turned in my sleep. At one-thirty, I woke to an empty bed; Morrell was still working. I got out two of my mother's red Venetian glasses and poured Armagnac for us. Morrell thanked me, but didn't look up long from his screen—his reconstruction had him totally absorbed. While he wrote, I watched William Powell and Myrna Loy dash around San Francisco, solving crimes with their faithful terrier, Asta.

"Myrna Loy solved crimes in evening gowns and high heels; maybe that's my problem—I spend too much time in blue jeans and sneakers."

Morrell smiled at me absently. "You'd look wonderful in one of those old forties dresses, Vic, but you'd probably trip a lot chasing people down alleys."

"And Asta," I went on. "How come Mitch and Peppy don't cleverly retrieve clues as people hurl them in through the windows?"

"You shouldn't encourage them," he murmured, frowning over his computer.

I finished my Armagnac and went back to bed. When I woke again, it was nine and Morrell was sleeping soundly next to me. He'd flung his left arm clear of the bedclothes, and I sat for a while, looking at the jagged raw scar along his shoulder where one of the bullets had gone in. Conrad had scars like that, older, less angry, one underneath his rib cage, one in his abdomen. I used to look at those while he slept, too.

I got up abruptly, staggering slightly as the pain hit me, but made it the bathroom without falling. Disregarding the young surgeon's instructions, I stood under a hot shower, protecting the wound by wrapping a dry-cleaning bag over my shoulder. Come to think of it, I'd have my own jagged little scar, discreetly concealed on my back. A dainty, ladylike scar, the kind that Myrna Loy could have sported and still looked sexy in her backless gowns.

Peppy tapped after me while I struggled into a bra and a blouse. I let her out the back door before trying to make my breakfast. I had planned to go to the store this morning. No bread. No fruit, not even an old apple. No yogurt. A little milk that smelled as if it should have been drunk yesterday. I poured it down the sink, and made myself a cup of stove-top espresso, which I drank out on the back porch, hugging my arms against the thin gray air, eating some rye crackers to keep my stomach company.

I lounged around most of the day, calling clients, doing what I could at home from my laptop, finally venturing out in the late afternoon to get some food. I had hoped to get down to Bertha Palmer for basketball, but I had to call the school to cancel. Friday, to my annoyance, I still had enough anesthesia in me that I continued to be too groggy to do much, but Saturday I woke early. The thought of lounging around the house for one more day made me feel like nails on a blackboard.

Morrell was still asleep. I finished dressing, including putting on a sling that the hospital had given me with my discharge papers, then scribbled a note that I propped on Morrell's laptop.

When I got downstairs, Mr. Contreras was glad to see me, but not happy when I announced I was going out for a while with Peppy. Even though she's so well trained she'll heel without straining on her leash, he thought I should spend the weekend in bed.

"I'm not going to do anything stupid, but I'll go nuts if I lie around the house. I've already spent almost three days in bed—way beyond my lounging limit."

"Yeah, you never yet listened to nothing I had to say, why should you start today? Whatcha gonna do when you're out on the Tollway and that shoulder of yours won't let you turn the steering wheel fast enough to get out of the way of some crackpot?"

I put my good arm around his shoulders. "I'm not going on the Tollway. Just down to the University of Chicago, okay? I won't go over forty-five, and I'll stay in the right lane all the way there and back."

He was only mildly mollified by my sharing my plans, but he knew I was going to go whether he grumped or not; he muttered that he'd walk Mitch and slammed his door on me.

I was halfway down the walk when I remembered that my car was still in South Chicago. I almost rang the bell to get Mr. Contreras to take Peppy, but didn't think I could face him again today. No dogs on the CTA; I went down to Belmont to try my luck with cabs. The fourth one I flagged was willing to drive to the far South Side with a dog. The driver was from Senegal, he explained during the long ride, and had a Rottweiler for companionship, so he didn't mind Peppy's golden hairs all over his upholstery. He asked about the sling and tutted solicitously when I explained what had happened. In turn, I asked him how he came to be in Chicago, and heard a long story about his family and their optimistic hopes that his being here would make their fortune.

My Mustang was still on Yates, where I'd parked it Tuesday evening. My lucky break for the week: it had all four tires, and all the doors and windows were intact. The cabdriver kindly waited until I had Peppy inside and the engine going before he left us.

I drove over to South Chicago Avenue to look at the remains of Fly the Flag. The front was still more or less intact, but a big chunk of the back wall was missing. Pieces of cinder block were strewn around, as if some drunk giant had stuffed a hand through the window and pulled off bits of the building. I slipped on long feathers of ash, the residue of the rayons and canvas that had gone up in Tuesday's fireball. With my arm in a sling, keeping my balance was tricky, and I ended up tripping on a piece of rebar, landing smartly on my good shoulder. The pain made my eyes tear up. If I injured my right arm I wouldn't be able to drive, and Mr. Contreras would have a field day, probably field month, full of "I told you so"s.

I lay in the detritus, looking at the low gray sky overhead, flexing my right arm and shoulder. Just a bruise, nothing I couldn't ignore if I put my mind to it. I twisted around and sat on one of the pieces of cinder block, absently picking through the remains around me. Fragments of windowpane, a whole roll of marigold braid miraculously intact, warped shards of metal that might once have been spools, an aluminum soap dish in the shape of a frog.

Now that was a strange thing to find in a place like this, unless the bathroom had been blown to bits and this had fallen through to the fabric storage area. But the bathroom had been a nasty utilitarian hole: I didn't remember seeing anything as whimsical as a frog in it. I tucked it into my peacoat pocket and pushed myself back to my feet. Just as well I was in jeans and sneaks for this particular adventure, instead of a backless evening gown: the jeans could go through the washer.

I went as far as the back wall, but the ruin inside looked too unstable to risk going inside for further exploration. The front was intact, but the fire had started in the back, on the building's Skyway side—out of sight of the street. I could have gone in through the loading dock, but that meant hoisting myself up, and my shoulder gave an almighty jolt when I tried it.

I returned to my car, frustrated by my limited mobility, and headed north, keeping the pace sedate so I could steer one-handed. When we got to Hyde Park, I parked outside the University of Chicago campus, and let Peppy chase squirrels for a while. Despite the cold weather, a number of students were sitting outside with coffee and textbooks. Peppy made the rounds, giving people that soulful look that says, you can feed this dog or you can turn the page. She managed to cadge half a peanut butter sandwich before I called her sharply to heel.

When I had bundled her back into the Mustang, I went into the old social sciences building to scrub the worst of the ash off my clothes and hands: I couldn't visit April looking like a Halloween ghoul. As I turned to go, I saw the gash in my coat's shoulder, where they'd cut it away from me in the emergency room. I didn't look like a ghoul, but a bag lady.

 **VISITING HOURS**

Balloons and stuffed animals lined the scuffed corridors of the children's hospital, looking like desperate offerings to the arbitrary gods who play with human happiness. As I wound my way along halls and up stairwells, I passed little alcoves where adults sat waiting, silent, unmoving. Passing the patient rooms, I heard snatches of overly bright talk, moms using sheer energy to coax their children to health.

When I got to the fourth floor, I didn't have any trouble finding April's room: Bron and Sandra Zoltak Czernin were fighting in a nearby alcove.

"You were out screwing some bitch and your kid was dying. Don't tell me you love her!" Sandra was trying to whisper, but her voice carried beyond me; a woman walking the hall with a small child attached to an IV looked at them nervously and tried to shepherd her toddler out of earshot. "You didn't even get to the hospital until almost midnight."

"I came here as soon as I heard. Have I left the hospital for one second since? You know damned well I can't take calls on the truck phone, and I get home to find you gone, the kid gone, no message from you. I figured you and April were out, you're always taking her off someplace, buying her crap we don't have money for.

"As far as you're concerned, I don't exist. I'm just the paycheck to cover the bills you can't pay on your own. You didn't even have the sense or decency to call me, the kid's own father. I had to get the news off the answering machine, and it wasn't you who called but that goddamn Warshawski bitch. That's how I find out my own kid is sick, not from my own wife, Mrs. High-and-Mighty, Virgin Mary had nothing on you for purity, and you wonder why I look for human flesh and blood someplace else."

"At least you can be sure April is your daughter, which is more than Jesse Navarro or Lech Bukowski can say about their own kids, all the time you spent with their wives, and now, now they're saying April has this thing with her heart, this thing, she can't play basketball anymore." Sandra's thin aging face was twisted in pain.

"Basketball? She's sick as a horse, and you're upset she can't play a stupid goddamn ball game? What's with you?" Bron smashed the wall with the palm of his hand.

A nurse making rounds paused next to me, gauging the level of anger in the alcove, then shook her head and moved on.

"I don't care about the stupid goddamn ball game!" Sandra's voice rose. "It's April's ticket to college, you—you loser. You know damned well she can't go on your paycheck. I'm not having her do like me, spend her life married to some creep who can't keep his pants zipped, working her life away at By-Smart because she can't do any better. Look at me, I look as old as your mother, and talk about the High-and-Mighty Mother of God, that's how she looks on you, and me, I'm supposed to get down on my knees and slobber thanks because I married you, and you can't even support your own kid."

"What do you mean, I can't support her? Fuck you, bitch! Did she ever go to school hungry or—"

"Did you even listen to the doctor? It will cost a hundred thousand dollars to fix her heart, and then the drugs, and the insurance pays ten thousand dollars of it? Where are you going to find the money, tell me that? The money we could've been saving if you hadn't spent it on drinks for the boys, and the whores you screw around with, and—"

Bron's head seemed to swell with anger. "I will find the money it takes to look after April! You cannot stand there telling me I don't love my own daughter."

The woman with the small child approached them timidly. "Can you be a little quieter, please? You're making my baby cry, shouting like that."

Sandra and Bron looked at her; the little girl on the IV was crying, silent hiccupping sobs that were more unnerving than a loud howl. Bron and Sandra looked away, which is how Bron caught sight of me.

"It's goddamn Tori Warshawski. What the fuck were you doing, pushing my girl so hard she went and collapsed?" His voice rose to a roar that brought aides and parents scurrying to the hall.

"Hi, Bron, hi, Sandra, how's she doing?" I asked.

Sandra turned away from me, but Bron erupted from the alcove, pushing me so hard he flung me against a wall. "You hurt my girl! I warned you, Warshawski, I warned you if you messed with April you'd answer to me!"

People watched in horror as I carefully righted myself. The pain coursing down my left arm brought tears to my eyes, but I blinked them back. I wasn't going to get into a fight with him, not in a hospital, not with my left arm in a sling, and, anyway, not with a guy so worried and helpless that he had to pick a fight with anyone who looked at him crossways. But I wasn't going to let him see me cry, either.

"Yes, I heard you. I can't remember what you said you'd do if I saved her life."

Bron pounded a fist against his palm. "If you saved her life. If you saved her life, you can kiss my ass."

I turned to Sandra. "I heard you say it was her heart. What happened? I never saw her weak or short of breath at practice."

"You'd say that, wouldn't you?" Sandra said. "You'd say anything to protect your butt. She has something wrong with her heart, it's something she was born with, but you ran her too hard, that's why she collapsed."

I felt cold with a fear that Bron hadn't inspired in me: these words sounded like a prelude to a lawsuit. April's treatment would cost more than a hundred thousand dollars; they needed money; they could sue me. My pockets weren't deep, but they sure hung lower than the Czernins'.

"If she was born with the condition, it could have happened anytime, anywhere, Sandra," I said, trying to keep my voice level. "What do the doctors say they can do to treat her?"

"Nothing. Nothing but rest unless we can come up with the money to pay their bills. All the blacks, they have it easy, just show their welfare cards and their kids get whatever they need, but people like us, people who work hard all the time, what do we have to show for it?"

Sandra glared up the hall at the woman with the small child, who happened to be black, as if the four-year-old had designed the managed care companies that decreed what medical care Americans could get. A nurse who'd come out of one of the patient rooms stepped forward, trying to intervene, but the Czernins were in their own private universe, the world of anger, and no one else could get into it with them. The nurse went back to whatever she'd been doing, but I stayed on the battlefield.

"And I'm married to Mr. Wonderful here, who hasn't been home one night all week and then acts like he's Saint Joseph, the greatest father of all time." Sandra turned her bitter face back to Bron. "I'm surprised you even know your own daughter's name, you sure as hell forgot her birthday this year, out with that English bitch, or was it Danuta Tomzak from Lazinski's bar?"

Bron grabbed Sandra's thin shoulders and started shaking her. "I do love my daughter, you damn cunt, you will not say different, not here, not anywhere. And I can get the fucking money to pay for her heart. You tell that SOB doctor not to move her, not to check her out of the hospital, I'll have the money for him by Tuesday, easy."

He stormed down the corridor and slammed his way through a swinging door that led to a stairwell. Sandra's mouth was a thin bitter line.

"Mary had the Prince of Peace, I get the Prince of Pricks." She turned her scowl on me. "Is he going to ask that English woman he's been screwing for money?"

I shook my head. "I don't know. I don't know if she has any."

And who forks over a hundred grand to the daughter of a man she cares about only as a good story to tell her friends back home? I didn't say it—Sandra was only clutching at straws; she didn't have any sense right now, no sense of what was possible and what wasn't.

"You said the insurance would cover only ten thousand dollars. Is that your insurance?"

She shook her head and said through tight thin lips, "I can't get coverage because I only work thirty-four hours a week. By-Smart says that isn't full-time work, it has to be forty hours a week. So Bron buys the insurance, for him and April, we decided we couldn't afford to cover me, and when the hospital, when they called the company yesterday, it turns out that that's all the coverage she gets for being sick and we pay, Mother of God, we pay two thousand six hundred dollars a year. If I'd known, I'd've been putting all that money in a savings account for April."

"What is it that's really wrong with April?" I asked.

Sandra twisted her hands together. "I don't know, the doctors use fancy language so you won't know if they're doing the right thing for your kid or not. Were you working her too hard because she's mine?"

I wished I'd listened to Mr. Contreras and stayed home. All I wanted right now was to crawl into a cave and sleep until spring.

"Can we talk to a doctor? If I understand what the diagnosis is, maybe I can help find treatment." I was thinking of my friend Lotty Herschel, who's a surgeon at Beth Israel Hospital on Chicago's far North Side. Lotty treats her share of indigent patients; she might know how to help the Czernins dance around the insurance system.

"She fainted once, last summer, when she'd been at a basketball camp, but I didn't think anything of it, girls faint all the time, I know I did when I was her age. I wanted her to have every opportunity, I wasn't going to have you lord it over my kid the way you do over me."

I blinked, reeling under the flow of words and the contradictory ideas jostling for airspace. I was about to utter a reflexive protest, that I didn't lord it over her, but when I remembered our history together I felt myself blushing. That night just before the homecoming dance, if I could call up one evening of my life to do differently that would be the one, unless it was the time I'd snuck a pint of whiskey from Lazinski's the night my mother died—enough. I had enough bad memories to make me squirm all day if I dwelt on them.

The nurse who'd tried to intervene in Sandra and Bron's fight was still lingering nearby. She agreed to page a doctor to come to April's room to talk to the family. While we waited, I crossed the hall to April's room. Sandra followed me without protest.

April was in a room with three other kids. When we came in, she was watching television, her face puffy from the drugs she was taking. A giant teddy bear was propped up next to her in bed, brand new, holding a balloon that read, "Get Well Soon."

April shifted her groggy gaze from *Soul Train* to her mother, but her face brightened when she saw me. "Coach! This is so cool, you coming to see me. You gonna let me come back to the team, even if I miss next week?"

"You can rejoin the team as soon as the docs and your mom say you're ready to play. Great bear—where'd he come from?"

"Daddy." She flicked a wary glance at her mother: the bear had probably already been the focus of a quarrel, but I found it heartbreaking, Bron wanting to do something for his daughter and coming up with this outsize toy.

We talked a little about basketball, about school, what she was missing in her biology class, while Sandra fussed with her pillows, straightened the sheets, pushed April to drink some juice ("You know the doctor said you have to have lots of fluids with this drug you're taking.")

By and by, a young resident came in. He had a chubby, cherubic face, complete with a circlet of soft dark curls, but he had an easy way about him, bantering lightly with April while he checked her pulse and asked her how much she was drinking and eating.

"You got that big bear there to try to scare me off, huh, but I don't scare that easy. Keep him away from your boyfriend, though, boys your age can't stand up to bears."

After a few minutes, he left her with a nod and a wink, and ushered Sandra and me down the hall, out of April's earshot. I introduced myself and explained my role in April's life.

"Oh, you're the heroine who saved her life. That how you got your arm in a sling?"

I hoped hearing the doctor call me a heroine would soften Sandra's views of me. I explained briefly about my injury and asked what the story was on April.

"She has something we call Long QT Syndrome. I could show you the EKG and explain how we know and why we call it that, but what it really means is a kind of arrhythmia in the heart. With proper treatment, she can certainly lead a normal, productive life, but she absolutely has to give up basketball. If she keeps playing, I'm sorry to put it bluntly, Ms. Czernin, but the outcome could be very bad."

Sandra nodded bleakly. She'd gone back to twisting her fingers together, thumbs pushing so hard that the backs of her hands were covered in purplish red welts. I asked the resident what the proper treatment was.

"We've started her on a course of beta-blockers to stabilize her heart." He went into a long explanation about the buildup of sodium ions in the chamber, and the function of beta-blockers in stabilizing the ion exchange, then added, "She should go to a pacemaker, to an implanted cardioverter defibrillator. Otherwise, I'm afraid, well, it's a question of time before there's another serious episode."

His pager sounded. "If there's anything else, please page me. I'll be glad to talk to you at any time. We're going to discharge April Monday if her heart is stable, and we'll keep her on the beta-blockers for the time being."

"Like I can afford those," Sandra muttered. "Even with my employee discount, it's going to be fifty bucks a week for her medication. What do they think, that only rich people get sick in this country?"

I tried to say something commiserating, but she turned on me again; our brief moment of rapport was gone. There was a limit to how much time as a punching bag I felt I owed her; I'd passed it some time back. I told her I'd keep in touch and headed down the hall to the stairwell.

On my way out the hospital's front door, I almost collided with a tall teenager, who was entering from Maryland Avenue. I was intent on my own thoughts, and didn't look at her until she gasped, "Coach."

I stopped. "Josie Dorrado! This is great that you came to see April. She's going to need lots of support in the weeks ahead."

To my astonishment, instead of answering she turned crimson and dropped the pot of daisies she was holding. She half opened the door and made a flapping gesture with her right arm, signaling to someone outside to take off. I stepped over the plants and dirt and pushed open the door.

Josie clutched my left, my sore arm, trying to pull me back inside. I gave a squawk loud enough that she let go of me and muscled my way past her roughly to look at the street. A midnight blue Miata was heading up Maryland, but a group of heavyset women, slowly making their way across the street, blocked the license plate.

I turned back to Josie. "Who brought you here? Who do you know who can afford a sports car like that?"

"I came on the bus," she said quickly.

"Oh? Which one?"

"The, uh, the, I didn't notice the number, I just asked the driver—"

"To drop you at the hospital entrance. Josie, I'm ashamed of you for lying to me. You're on my team; I need to be able to trust you."

"Oh, coach, you don't understand. It's not what you're thinking, honest!"

"Excuse us." The trio of heavyset women who'd been on the street were frowning magisterially at us. "Can you clean up your mess? We'd like to get into this hospital."

We knelt down to clean up the flowers. The pot was plastic and had survived the fall. With a little help from the guard at the reception desk, who found me a brush, we got most of the dirt back in the pot and reorganized the flowers; they looked half dead, but I saw from the price sticker that Josie had got them at By-Smart for a dollar ninety-nine: you don't get fresh, lively flowers for two bucks.

When we'd finished, I stared up at her thin face. "Josie, I can't promise not to tell your mother if you're going out with some older guy she doesn't know or doesn't approve of."

"She knows him, she likes him, but she can't—I can't tell—you gotta promise—"

"Are you having sex with him?" I asked bluntly, as she floundered through unfinished sentences.

Red streaked her cheeks again. "No way!"

I pressed my lips together, thinking about her home, her mother's second job, which would have to support the family now that Fly the Flag was gone, her sister's baby, about Pastor Andrés and his strictures against birth control. "Josie, I will promise not to say anything to your mother for the time being if you make a promise to me."

"What's that?" she demanded, suspicious.

"Before you sleep with him, or with any boy, you must make him wear a condom."

She turned an even darker shade of red. "But, coach, I can't—how can you—and the abstinence lady, she say they don't even work."

"She gave you bad advice, Josie. They aren't a hundred percent effective, but they work most of the time. Do you want to end up like your sister Julia, watching telenovelas all day long? Or do you want to try for a life beyond babies, and clerking at By-Smart?"

Her eyes were wide and frightened, as if I'd offered her the choice between cutting off her head or talking to her mother. She had probably imagined passionate embraces, a wedding, anything but what it meant to lie with a boy. She looked at the door, at the floor, then suddenly bolted up the stairs into the interior of the hospital. I watched as a guard at the entrance stopped her, but when she looked back down at me I couldn't bear the fear in her face. I turned on my heel and walked into the cold afternoon.

19

THE HOSPITABLE
MR. CONTRERAS

I let Peppy back out of the car to chase squirrels around the campus again while I sat on the Bond chapel steps, knees up to my chin, sore back resting against the red doors. A few snowflakes were drifting out of the leaden sky; the students had abandoned the quads. I pulled the collar of my navy peacoat up around my ears, but cold seeped in through the gash in the shoulder.

What warning signs should I have noticed in April before Monday? Was anyone else on my team at risk? I didn't even know if the school performed physicals on its athletes before letting them compete, although a program too poor to pay for a coach and balls probably didn't have a budget for group EKGs and X rays.

If Sandra decided to sue me—I'd cross that bridge, but I should get a few things on paper now, while they were fresh in my mind—April fainting last summer, Sandra's own history. "Girls faint all the time," she'd said; she had herself, although I never remembered her doing so. Maybe she'd swooned in Boom-Boom's arms . . . Surely he hadn't slept with her. The idea of it infuriated me. But what was I doing, turning him into a saint? All these years I'd assumed he took her to the dance just to punish me, but that was because I hadn't ever wanted to think of him having a life apart from mine. Sandra slept around, we all knew that, so why not with Boom-Boom? And he was a sports hero, not exactly leading a celibate life.

Peppy came up to nuzzle me, worried by my stupor. I stood up and tossed a stick for her as best I could. She was satisfied; she took the stick over to the grass to chew.

I realized I felt as battered by Bron and Sandra's furies as by my physical ills. Had there ever been a time when they twined their arms around each other, looked soulfully into each other's eyes? Sandra had been thirty when April was born, so a high school pregnancy hadn't forced them to the altar. Something else had, but I didn't have friends in the neighborhood who could tell me. Did he sleep around because she looked down on him? Did she despise him because he slept around? What was the chicken and what the egg behind such intense hostility?

I got slowly to my feet and called to Peppy. She came running up, pink tongue hanging, grinning with pleasure. I ran my fingers through her silky gold hair, trying to absorb some of her pure joy in the world before putting my weary body into motion again.

At my office, I went through my log of calls from yesterday. A couple of clients I should have been attending to. Three messages from Mr. William, wanting his son, two from Murray Ryerson at the *Herald-Star* wanting to know if there was an important story about Fly the Flag. Fires in South Chicago are a dime a dozen; the story had rated only a paragraph in the metro sections of the city newspapers, and Murray was the only reporter I knew who'd caught my name in the small print (misspelled and misidentified as "Chicago police sergeant I. V. Warshacky," but Murray had seen through that easily enough.)

I called Morrell first. He and Mr. Contreras had sent out for Thai food for lunch, and had played a little gin. My neighbor had left, but Morrell couldn't settle down to his writing; maybe he'd done too much the last few days. When I explained that I was going to do a little work at the office, then try to see Lotty, Morrell said he'd be glad to come with me if she was home; he was going a little stir-crazy.

Lotty was in. Unlike Murray, she didn't scan crime news in the papers, so she was surprised and concerned to hear I'd been injured on the job. "Of course you can come by, my dear. I'm going to the store, but I plan to be home this afternoon. Around three-thirty, then?"

After dictating my notes on my encounter with Sandra and Bron, I talked briefly with Murray: there was no big story down at Fly the Flag, unless you counted the disaster in lives like Rose Dorrado's. He listened to my passionate description of her life for a few minutes, before interrupting me to say he'd see if he could interest the ChicagoBeat editor in a human interest story down there.

"What about the dead man in the building?" I asked. "Has the ME identified him? Was it Frank Zamar?"

I heard the click of Murray's fingers on his keyboard. "Yeah, uh, Zamar, that's right. He had an alarm and a sprinkler system down there. The bomb and arson people are guessing the alarm sounded and he went down to see what the problem was. There's a big drying room at the back of the plant, big propane-fueled blower. The fabric must have been smoldering and set off the propane just as he got down there—it looked as though he was trying to run away but the fire swallowed him."

I dropped the phone. I'd been on the outside, playing spy, while Frank Zamar walked into an inferno. I became aware of Murray's voice coming tinnily from near my right knee. I picked up the receiver.

"Sorry, Murray. I was there, you know. I should have been inside, checking the place over. I'd seen someone there a few days earlier, I should have been inside." My voice was rising in panic, and I kept repeating the same sentence: "I should have been inside."

"Hey, Warshawski, easy does it, easy does it. Would the guy have let you in? You said he stiffed you when you were there last week. Where are you? Your office? Need me to come by?"

I gulped back my hysteria and said shakily, "I think I just need to eat. It's been a while."

When he'd reiterated his offer of help, and urged me on to food and rest, he hung up on the promise of trying to do a story on Rose and some of the other people who'd worked at Fly the Flag.

I walked down to La Llorona, a Mexican diner that's hanging on to its lease by its fingernails—my office is in a neighborhood that's gentrifying so fast rents seem to double every day. After two bowls of Mrs. Aguilar's chicken-tortilla soup, and a short nap on the cot in my office's back room, I finished my phone calls.

I left voice messages with my impatient clients. I didn't tell them I was late because I'd been injured—it makes you seem unreliable if you go and get shot or stabbed when they're expecting you to be thinking about their problems. I just said I had preliminary reports for them, which would be true by the end of the day tomorrow, if my shoulder would let me type all afternoon. I didn't even try to reach Mr. William: whatever was yanking his chain, I couldn't deal with the Bysen family today.

Mitch barked from behind Mr. Contreras's door when I came in, but either my neighbor was busy or he was still miffed with me for disregarding his advice this morning. When he didn't come out to greet me, I took Peppy up to my place.

Morrell greeted me with relief—he was sick of his book, sick of my small space, tired of being up three flights that were so hard for him to negotiate that he felt almost like a prisoner. He limped slowly down the stairs with me for the drive over to Lotty's.

Lotty used to live in a two-flat near her clinic, but a few years ago she'd moved to one of the tony old buildings on Lake Shore Drive. In the summer, it's impossible to park near her place, but on a cold November afternoon, with the gray day fading to the black of early night, we found a space without too much trouble.

She greeted us warmly, but didn't spend time on chitchat. In a back room overlooking Lake Michigan, she stripped off my bandages with quick skilled fingers. She clicked her teeth in annoyance, partly with me, for getting it wet in the shower, partly with the surgeon who'd stitched me up. A sloppy job, she announced, adding that we were going to go over to her clinic where she would put me together properly; otherwise, I'd have adhesions that would be hard to work out once the wound healed.

We had a little argument over who would drive: Lotty didn't think I could be trusted with only one good arm, and I didn't think she could be trusted, period. She thinks she's Stirling Moss, driving the Grand Prix, but the only similarities I can see are the speed she travels, and her belief that no one should be in front of her on the track. Morrell laughed as we argued but voted for Lotty: if I didn't feel like driving when she finished, we'd be stuck at the clinic without a car.

In the end, neither the drive nor the restitching was as big an ordeal as I'd feared—the former because the main streets were so thick with Saturday shoppers that even Lotty had to go slowly. At her clinic, a storefront about a mile west of my apartment, in a polyglot neighborhood on the fringes of the North Side's new construction, she shot Novocain into my shoulder. I felt a faint tugging as she cut the old stitches and put new ones in, but either because of her skill or the anesthetic I could actually move my arm pretty easily when she finished.

With Lotty lying back in an easy chair in her office, we finally got to April Czernin's woes. Lotty listened intently, but shook her head with genuine sorrow over the limited help the Czernins could get.

"The insurance really only covers ten thousand dollars of her care? That's shocking. But it's so typical of the problems our patients face these days, being forced to make these choices of life and death because of what the insurance does or doesn't pay.

"But as for your girl, we can't take her on as a Medicaid patient, because she's not indigent; as soon as the billing department finds out she has insurance, they'll do exactly what the university did, call the company and be told the policy won't cover the defibrillator. The only thing I can suggest is that they try to get her involved in an experimental trial, although the treatment for Long QT is pretty standard at this point, and it may be hard to find a trial group anywhere they can afford to travel to."

"I think Sandra Czernin would go anywhere if she thought it gave April a fighting chance. Lotty, I keep worrying that I should have noticed something before she collapsed."

She shook her head. "Sometimes there may be a fainting spell—you say the mother reports one last summer—but often these collapses come out of the blue, with no warning."

"I'm afraid to go to school Monday," I confessed. "I'm afraid to ask any of these girls to run up and down the court for me. What if there's another one with some time bomb ticking in her chest or brain?"

Morrell squeezed my hand. "Tell the school they have to test the girls before you'll continue the program. I'm sure the moms would agree, at least enough of them to force the school to take action."

"Bring them up to the clinic and I'll do EKGs on them, or Lucy will," Lotty offered.

She was meeting Max Loewenthal for dinner; she invited Morrell and me to join her, which seemed like a welcome change of pace to both of us. We went to one of the little bistros that have sprung up on the North Side, one that had a wine list Max likes, and lingered late over a bottle of Côte du Rhône. Despite my worries and injuries, it was the most pleasant evening I'd spent since Marcena's arrival.

In the cab home, I fell asleep against Morrell's shoulder. When we got to my place, I stood drowsily on the curb, holding his walking stick while he paid off the driver. In the way you don't really notice things when you're half asleep, I saw a Bentley across the street, a man in a chauffeur's uniform at the wheel. I saw the lights in my living room, without thinking about it, but when we'd made our slow way up the stairs, and I saw my apartment door ajar, I woke up in a hurry.

"I'm going inside," I muttered to Morrell. "If I'm not out in two minutes, call 911."

He wanted to argue about which of us got to be the hero, or the fool, but he had to agree that between my injuries and his, I was the one in better shape—and I was the one with street-fighting smarts.

Before either of us could do anything, heroic or foolhardy, Peppy and Mitch started barking and whining from the far side of my door. I kicked the door all the way open, then flattened myself against the wall. The two dogs bounded out to greet us. My lips compressed now more with annoyance than fear, I followed them in.

 BUFFALO—AND GAL—
WON'T YOU COME
OUT TONIGHT?

Mr. Contreras was sitting in the easy chair in my living room. Facing him, on the couch, were Buffalo Bill Bysen and his personal assistant, Mildred. Even at ten o'clock on a Saturday night, she wore heavy makeup. Mr. Contreras looked up at me with the same guilt-filled defiance that the dogs use when they've been digging up the yard.

"So that's why there's a Bentley out there on Belmont: waiting for the head of one of the biggest companies in the world, and he came to visit me." I rubbed my hands together in a display of fake heartiness. "It's delightful that you were able to drop in, but I'm afraid I'm going to bed. Help yourself to the liquor cabinet, and keep the music down—the neighbors are picky."

I went to the front door to tell Morrell that the coast wasn't exactly clear but it was okay to come in.

"I'm sorry, doll," Mr. Contreras followed me out. "When they showed up and said they needed to see you, well, you're always telling me not to butt in, so I didn't like to tell them 'no,' case you'd arranged it; you didn't want me knowing your plans or nothing today."

I bared my teeth at him in an evil grin. "How thoughtful of you. How long have they been here?"

"About an hour, maybe a little longer."

"I have a cell phone, you know, and I've given you the number."

"Do you mind?" Mildred came out to the hall to join us. "Mr. Bysen's day starts early tomorrow. We need to get this over with so we can return to Barrington."

"Of course you do. Morrell, this is Mildred—I'm afraid I don't know her last name—she's Buffalo Bill Bysen's factotum. Mildred, this is Morrell. He doesn't like to use his first name."

Morrell held out a hand, but Mildred only nodded perfunctorily and turned to lead us back into my apartment.

"Mildred and Buffalo Bill have been sitting in the living room for an hour," I said to Morrell. "Mr. Contreras let them in, thinking it was an emergency when they showed up uninvited, and now they're very cross that we didn't use ESP to drop everything and rush home to look after them."

"His name to you is Mr. Bysen," Mildred said through tight lips. "If you treat all your clients this rudely, I'm surprised you have any."

I looked at her thoughtfully. "Are you a client, Mildred? Or is Buffalo Bill? I don't remember you hiring me. I don't remember giving you my home address, either."

Mister Bysen," she said with heavy emphasis, "will explain what he needs you to do."

When we were all back inside, I introduced Bysen to Morrell, and offered refreshments.

"This isn't a social visit, young woman," Bysen said. "I want to know where my grandson is."

I shook my head. "I don't know. If that's all you wanted, you could have saved yourself the drive from Barrington by letting your fingers do the walking."

Mildred sat herself back on the couch next to Bysen and opened her gold leather portfolio, pen poised, ready to take a note or order an execution at a second's notice.

"He talked to you on Thursday. You called him, and he talked to you. Now you tell me where he is."

"Billy called me, not the other way around. I don't know where he is, and I don't have his cell phone number. And I promised him I wouldn't look for him as long as I believed he was safe and not being held against his will."

"Well, that's just fine, you talk to the boy on the phone, and you know he's safe and sound, hnnh? You met him two times, and you know him so well you can tell from his voice on the phone that he's safe? Do you know how much a kidnapper would like to get hold of one of my grandchildren? Do you know what he's worth? Hnnh? Hnnh?"

I pressed my right fingers against the bridge of my nose, as if that would push thoughts into my brain. "I don't know. I'm guessing the company's worth around four hundred billion, and if you've divvied it up evenly—you have six children? So sixty-seven billion a head, and then if young Mr. William is being fair with his own kids, I suppose—"

"This isn't a joke," Buffalo Bill roared, pushing himself standing. "If you don't produce him for me by this time tomorrow, I'll—"

"You'll what? Cut off my allowance? It may not be a joke, but you're turning it into a farce. Your son hired me to look for Billy, and in a thoughtless moment I agreed. When Billy learned about it from someone on the South Side, he called and told me to tell Mr. William to lay off or he, Billy, would start calling shareholders."

Buffalo Bill scowled and sat back down. "Hnnh. What did he mean by that?"

My lips moved into an unpleasant smile. "It seemed to mean something to your son, so I presume it means something to you."

"It could mean any of a dozen things. What did it mean to you? Hnnh? You didn't ask him what he was going to tell the shareholders?"

Was this the real reason for this absurd trip from the gated splendors of Barrington Hills to my four-room apartment? "If you wanted to discuss this with me, why not just phone me, or ask me to come out to your office? I don't know about you, but I've had a really, really long day and I'd like to go to bed."

Bysen's scowl deepened and his heavy brow contracted so tightly that I couldn't see his eyes at all. "Grobian called from the warehouse yesterday. He said he'd seen Billy on the street, over on Ninety-second Street, his arm around some Mexican girl."

"Then you know he's safe."

"I don't know that at all. I want to know who that Mexican is. I won't have my boy taken in by some wetback's hard-luck story, marrying her, promising her diamonds or whatever she thinks she can squeeze out of his granddaddy's fortune. You've met Billy, you see what he's like, he's a sucker for other people's troubles. Boy even hands out dollar bills to panhandlers with their *Streetwise* papers. Can't do a real job, and they cadge dollar bills from naive boys like Billy."

I sucked in a deep breath. Out of the corner of my eye, I saw Morrell give his head a tiny shake—a little warning—go easy, V.I., don't go straight for the guy's jugular.

"Unwise marriages are such a regular feature of daily life, if Billy's taken up with someone unsuitable I don't think I can stop him, Mr. Bysen. But he seems to share his grandmother's religious values; if he gets involved with someone, my guess is it will be a churchgoing young woman. Even if she's poor, she probably won't be a gold digger."

"Don't you believe that for one second. Look at that creature Gary brought home, claimed to be a Christian. We should never have let him go so far away to school, but Duke seemed like a place with lots of good Christian boys and girls, and she was part of the Campus Fellowship."

Mildred murmured something in his ear and he broke off, turning to glare at me again. "I want to know who that girl is, that girl who's attached herself to Billy."

I fought off a yawn. "You have so many resources, you don't need my help. Look at how easily you tracked me down. My phone's unlisted; I have all my bills sent to my office so my home address doesn't show up on Lexis, but here you are. Someone on your payroll knows someone in the phone company, or in the Secretary of State's Office, who's willing to violate the law to help you out. Get them to find out who Billy's dating."

"But he knows you, he trusts you, you're at home down there. I send one of our own security people down to look for him, he'll know they came from me, and then he'll, well, it'll upset him. Whatever terms William agreed to with you, I'll match them."

"I'm sorry, Mr. Bysen. I told your son I was quitting, I explained the reason, I sent him a certified letter spelling it out. I promised Billy I'd lay off, and I'm laying off."

Bysen stood again, leaning on his walking stick. "You're making a serious mistake, young woman. I offered you a fair arrangement, very fair, William's terms sight unseen, no bargaining.

"You don't want to help me, I can make life difficult for you, very difficult. You think I don't know how much your mortgage is worth? What would you do if I got all your clients to leave you for a different investigator, hnnh? What if I made things so difficult for you, you had to come crawling to me, begging me to hire you on any terms, hnnh?"

Mr. Contreras sprang to his feet, and Mitch, alarmed by the tone in Bysen's voice, began to growl, low and deep in the throat, the one dogs make when they're serious. I jumped up to put a hand on his collar.

"Don't you go threatening her," Mr. Contreras cried. "She said she don't want to work for you, take it like a man. It ain't the end of the world. You don't need to own her along with everything else in creation."

"But he does, he does. It's the only thing that keeps him going, gobbling all of us up like so many shrimps on the buffet table." The image made me laugh with genuine amusement, but I looked wonderingly at Bysen. "What is it like to have an appetite like that, so ravenous that nothing will satiate it? Do your sons share it? Will William have the same naked neediness to make your empire grow when you're dead and gone?"

"William!" Bysen spat out his son's name. "Whiny old woman. Why, that sharp little operator Jacqui would do a better—"

Once again, Mildred cut him off, with a deferential murmur in his ear, adding to me, "Mrs. Bysen is sick with worry over Billy. She's eighty-two; she doesn't need this. If you know where Billy is and won't tell us, it might kill her. We might even be able to charge you as an accessory in kidnapping him."

"Oh, go home," I said. "You're used to people needing you so desperately that they'll put up with anything to stay on your good side, what-ever that might be. When you meet someone who doesn't need or want your business, you don't know how to act: should you cajole me, tell me his granny's heart is breaking, or threaten to have me up on federal charges? Go back to the suburbs and think of a serious approach before you talk to me again."

I didn't wait for a reaction from my visitors, but pulled on Mitch's collar to get him to turn around. Calling to Peppy, I led them through my apartment to the kitchen and sent them down the back stairs to the yard to relieve themselves.

I leaned on the porch railing, eyes shut, trying to relax the tension in my neck and shoulders. My wound was throbbing, but Lotty's work had lowered the level of pain to something I could live with. The dogs clambered up the stairs to me, making sure I was okay after Bysen's threats. I ran my fingers through their fur, but stayed on the porch, listening to the faint sounds of the city around me: the rumbling of the El a few blocks away, a distant siren, laughter from a neighboring apartment—my own lullaby.

By and by, Morrell hobbled out to join me. I leaned against his chest and pulled his arms around me. "Are they gone?"

He laughed softly. "Your neighbor got into a fight with Buffalo Bill. I think Contreras was so guilt stricken about letting them in, he had to take it out on Bysen. Mildred kept trying to break it up, but when Contreras said Bysen was a coward, picking on a lone young woman like you, Bysen got furious and trotted out his war record, and Contreras had to top it off with his Anzio reminiscences, so I figured the time had come to move everyone out."

"Even Mr. Contreras?"

"He wanted to stay to make sure you weren't still mad at him, but I promised him you weren't, only tired, and that you'd talk to him in the morning."

"Yessir," I said meekly.

We turned and went back inside. As I was undressing, I found the frog-shaped soap dish in my coat pocket. I took it out and looked at it again. "Who are you? What were you doing down there?" I demanded of it.

Morrell came over to see what it was. He hummed a line or two from *Doctor Dolittle*, "She walks with the animals, talks with the animals," but when I explained what it was, and where I'd found it, he suggested I put it in a baggie.

"It might be evidence. In which case, fondling it might delete any other prints on it."

"I should have thought of that. Dang—I've had it in my coat all day." I should give it to Conrad, for his bomb and arson team. But Conrad had been rude to me. On Monday, I'd send it to a private forensic lab I work with.

As we lay in the dark, Morrell asked if I really knew where Billy was.

"No-o, but Grobian—he's the manager at the By-Smart warehouse down on 103rd—if Grobian really saw him with a Mexican girl, I figure it's someone Billy met at Mount Ararat—he sings in the choir there. So maybe I'll go down to church in the morning."

21

LOOSE BUFFALO IN CHURCH

A dozen children in white and navy—skirts for the girls, trousers for the boys—were doing a synchronized dance in the aisle when I slipped into Mt. Ararat the next morning. According to the notice board out front, church started officially at ten. It was about eleven now. I'd come late on purpose, hoping things would be nearing an end; instead, the service seemed to be barely under way.

I'd driven Morrell back to his own place in Evanston before coming down—he said he'd stayed in Chicago with me because he thought I was going to be laid up with my wounded shoulder, not for the pleasure of holing up with Mr. Contreras and the dogs. I understood his point, but I still felt forlorn; I dropped him at his door without going inside. If Marcena was curled up in front of the television, so be it.

As I drove south, it began to snow. By the time I reached the church, a thin dusting covered the ground. Thanksgiving was two weeks away. The year was drawing to a close, the sky pressing down as if urging me to lie flat and sleep the winter away. I parked on Ninety-first Street and hurried into the church—I'd decided Mt. Ararat deserved a skirt, or expected a skirt, and the cold air whipped through my panty hose and up my thighs.

I stopped inside the front door to get my bearings. The building was hot, with a bewildering barrage of sound and motion. The dancing children weren't the only people in the aisles, just the only ones doing something organized—as I watched, people would jump up into the aisles with a hand held up in the air, and stand for a time before returning to the pew.

The children were wearing long-sleeved T-shirts with red tongues of fire on the fronts, and the legend "Mt. Ararat Troop Marching for Jesus" on the backs. They were doing a routine involving kicking, clapping, and stomping, with more spirit than skill, but the congregation was applauding them and shouting encouragement. An electric band accompanied them, harmonium and guitar with drums.

The choir director, an imposing woman in a scarlet robe, was singing, moving with an electric energy of her own. She moved between the congregation and the front lip of a raised platform where the choir and the ministers shared space with the band. Both she and the band were miked up so high I couldn't make out any of her words, let alone what language she was singing in.

Behind her, wood armchairs were arranged in two semicircles. In the middle one sat Pastor Andrés, wearing navy robes with a pale blue stole. Five other men were ranged around him, including one very old man whose bald head bobbed uncertainly on a thin neck, like a large sunflower on a stalk too thin to support it.

The choir stood behind the men in two densely packed rows, singing along with the choir director, slapping tambourines and twirling around as the spirit moved them. There was so much twirling and arm waving, it was hard to pick out individual faces.

I finally spotted Billy in the back row. He was mostly blocked from view, partly by a tangle of electric cable that snaked between the mikes in front of the minister and the band, partly by a massive woman in front of him who moved with such fervor that he only appeared at intervals—

kind of like the moon popping out from behind a heavy cloud. What made him most noticeable was that he was the one chorister to stand still.

Josie I recognized more easily, since she was at the far end of the front row of the choir. Her thin face was alight, and she shook her tambourine with an abandon she never showed on the basketball court.

I scanned the choir, and then the congregation, looking for other members of my team. The only one I saw was Sancia, my center, near the back of the church, with her two babies, her mother, and her sisters. Sancia was staring vacantly in front of her—I didn't think she'd noticed me.

When I took a seat in a pew partway up the right side, a trim woman in a black suit turned to clasp my hand and welcome me. Another woman bustled up from the back to hand me a program and an offering envelope, and also to say how welcome I was.

"Your first time here, sister?" she asked in a heavy Spanish accent.

I nodded, adding my name. "I coach basketball at Bertha Palmer. Some of the girls on the team come here."

"Oh, wonderful, wonderful, Sister Warshawski, you are really helping these girls. We are grateful."

In a few minutes, a wave ran through the congregation. You couldn't hear the murmur above the music, but people poked each other, heads turned: *"el coche"* cared enough about the children to attend their church. Sancia and her family caught the whisper and turned, stunned to see me here, out of context. Sancia managed a weak smile when she saw me looking at her.

I also caught sight of Rose Dorrado twisting around in a pew on the other side of the aisle to look at me. I smiled and waved; she pressed her lips together and turned to face the front again, hugging her two little boys close to her.

I was shocked at the change in Rose's appearance. She had always been tidily groomed, holding herself well, and even when she was angry with me her face had been full of vivacity. Today, she'd barely troubled to comb her hair, and her head was hunched turtlelike down in her shoulders. The loss of Fly the Flag had devastated her.

The children marching, or stomping, for Jesus finished their routine and sat down in a row of folding chairs in front of the choir. The man with the bald bobbing head stood next, offering a long tremulous prayer in Spanish, punctuated by emphatic chords from the harmonium and "Amens" from the congregation. Even though he used a mike, his voice was so quavery I could only catch a word here or there.

When he finally sat down, we had another hymn, and two women passed through the congregation with offertory baskets. I put in a twenty, and the women looked at me in consternation.

"We can't make change right now," one of them said, worried. "Will you trust us to the end of the service?"

"Change?" I was astonished. "I don't need change."

They thanked me over and over; the woman in front of me who'd welcomed me had turned to watch, and she once again whispered news about me to the people around her. My cheeks turned red. I hadn't meant to show off; it was one of those moments of blind ignorance where I hadn't realized how really poor everyone in the church must be. Maybe everyone who said I didn't understand the South Side anymore was right.

After the collection, and another hymn, Andrés began his sermon. He spoke in Spanish, but so slowly and so simply I could follow a lot of it. He read from the Bible, a passage about the laborer deserving his salary—I caught the words *"digno"* and *"su salario,"* and guessed that *"obrero"* must be a worker; I didn't know the word. After that he started talking about criminals in our midst, criminals stealing jobs from us and destroying our factories. I assumed he was talking about the fire at Fly the Flag. The harmonium began playing an insistent backbeat to the sermon, which made it harder for me to understand, but I thought Andrés was urging a message of courage onto people whose lives were hurt by the criminals *"en nuestro medio."*

Courage, yes, I suppose one needed courage not to be rolled under by the wheels of misery that ran through the neighborhood, but Rose Dorrado had plenty of courage; what she needed was a job. When I thought about the load she was carrying, all those children, and now the factory gone, my own shoulders slumped.

People engaged actively in the sermon, shouting "Amen" at frequent intervals, or *"Sí, señor,"* which I first thought was an assent to Andrés, before realizing they were calling on God. Some stood in the pews or jumped into the aisles, pointing a hand heavenward; others shouted out Bible verses.

After the sermon had gone on for twenty minutes or so, my attention began to wander badly. The wood pew was pressing through my coat and my knit top into my shoulder, and my pelvic bones began to ache. I began hoping the spirit would make me spring to my feet.

It was close to noon; I was wishing I'd brought a novel when I realized people were shifting and turning in their pews to look at another new arrival. I craned my head as well.

To my astonishment, I saw Buffalo Bill stumping his way up the aisle, walking stick in hand. Mr. William was behind him, his arm supporting an old woman in a fur coat. Despite the coat, and the diamond drops in her ears, she had the round amiable face of a Hallmark card grandmother. This must be May Irene Bysen, the grandma who taught Billy his manners and his faith. Right now, she looked a little frightened, a little bewildered by the noise and the strange setting: her soft chin was thrust out, and she clung to her son, but she was looking around, as I had, trying to spot her grandchild.

Completing the parade was Aunt Jacqui, her gloved hand on Uncle Gary's arm. Instead of a coat, Jacqui wore a thigh-length cardigan with bat-wing sleeves. Perhaps she'd chosen thigh-high boots and thick tights to close a gap between her miniskirt and Buffalo Bill or her mother-in-law's outrage. The effect was eye-catching enough to briefly break the electric current running through the congregation as Andrés's delivery approached a climax.

A fourth man, with the bulky build of an off-duty cop, brought up the rear of the entourage. Buffalo Bill's bodyguard, presumably. I wondered if they'd driven themselves, or if they'd left someone in the Bentley.

Maybe they had a different vehicle for the South Side, an armor-plated Hummer or something.

Bysen didn't notice me as he muscled his way past the people in the aisles. He found a partly empty pew near the front; without turning his head to see if his wife and children were following, he sat down, hands on his knees, glowering at Andrés. Jacqui and Gary found seats in the pew behind Buffalo Bill, but Mr. William handed his mother in next to his father. The bodyguard took up a position against the wall at the far side of the pew, where he could survey, or try to survey, the crowd.

The minister didn't falter in his delivery. In fact, with all the commotion in the aisles, people standing or sitting down, dancing, calling out to Jesus, he might not even have noticed the Bysen party's arrival. His sermon was building in fervor.

"Si hay un criminal entre nosotros, si él es suficientemente fuerte para dar un paso adelante y confesar sus pecados a Jesús, los brazos de Jesús, lo sacarán adelante . . ."

Andrés stood like the Prophet Isaiah, his voice loud, his eyes blazing. The congregation responded with a surge of ecstasy so strong it carried me along with it. He repeated his call, in such a loud exultant voice that even I could follow it:

"If there is a criminal among us, if he is strong enough to come forward and confess his sins to Jesus, Jesus' arms are strong enough to hold him up. Jesus will carry him forward. Come unto me, all you who labor and are heavy-laden, those are the words our Savior spoke. All you who labor and are heavy-laden, put down those burdens—*entréguenselas a Jesús, dénselas a Jesús, vengan a Jesús*—give them to Jesus, bring them to Jesus, come to Jesus!"

"Vengan a Jesús!" the congregation cried. *"Vengan a Jesús!"*

The harmonium played louder, insistent, urgent chords, and a woman stumbled forward. She flung herself at Andrés's feet, sobbing. The men sitting with him got up and stood with their hands held out over her head, praying loudly. Another woman staggered up the aisle and collapsed next to her, and, after a few minutes, a man joined them. The electric band was pounding out something with a disco beat, and the choir singing, swaying, shouting. Even Billy was finally in motion. And the congregation kept calling, *"Vengan a Jesús! Vengan a Jesús!"*

The intense emotion hammered against my chest. I was sweating and could hardly breathe. Just when I thought I couldn't take it any more, a woman in the aisle collapsed. My own head spinning, I half rose to go to her aid, but two women in nurse's uniforms rushed to her side. They had smelling salts, which they held under her nose; when she was able to sit, they escorted her to the rear of the church and laid her on a pew.

When I saw them pour her a glass of water, I went back to ask for a glass for myself. The nurses wanted to use their smelling salts on me, but I told them I only needed water and a little air; they made space for me on the rear pew: my faintness made me welcome as one of the saved. After a bit, when I thought I could stand without falling over, I went outside—I needed cold air and quiet.

I leaned against the church door, gulping in air. Across the street stood a giant Cadillac, the size and shape of a cabin cruiser, its motor running. Bysen's chauffeur was at the wheel, a television screen, or maybe a DVD player, propped up on the dashboard in front of him. In its way, the Caddy was even more conspicuous than the Bentley had been, but I didn't really expect any punks to attack a cabin cruiser outside a church on Sunday afternoon.

I stayed outside until the cold seeped through my coat and stockings and my teeth were chattering. When I got back inside, I thought the level of passion in the room was finally dropping. The people at the altar were calming down, and no one else seemed willing to come forward. The harmonium played a few expectant chords, Andrés held his arms out to the congregation, but no one moved. Andrés was returning to his chair when Buffalo Bill got to his feet. Mrs. Bysen grabbed his arm but he shook her off.

The organist played a few hopeful chords as Bysen charged up the aisle. The choir director, who had sat down and was fanning herself, quickly swallowed some water and returned to her place on the lip of the dais. The congregation began clapping again, ready to stay all afternoon if another sinner was coming to God.

Bysen didn't kneel on the platform. He was yelling at Andrés, as far as anyone could see, but of course it was impossible to hear anything over the music. In the second row of the choir, Billy stood stock-still, his face white.

I pushed through the mob packing the center aisle to the far left side, which was empty, and trotted to the front of the church. The band was also on this side. The choir director and the musicians seemed to know that something was amiss: the organist stopped the insistent disco beat of the call to salvation in favor of something more brooding, and the woman began humming in harmony, fumbling her way toward a song. What hymn was appropriate for tycoons haranguing ministers during the service?

I picked my way through the thicket of electric cords to the choir. The children who'd been marching for Jesus when I arrived were kicking bored heels against their chairs; two boys were surreptitiously pinching each other. The harmonium player frowned at me; the man with the acoustic guitar put his instrument down to come over to me.

"You can't be back here, miss," he said.

"Sorry. Just leaving." I flashed a smile and walked behind the Marching Troop for Jesus, past the massive woman in front of Billy, to the Kid himself.

He was staring at his grandfather, but when I touched his sleeve, he turned to me. "Why did you bring him here?" he demanded. "I thought I could trust you!"

"I didn't bring him. It wasn't too hard to figure out that you might be here—you've been worshiping at Mount Ararat, you admire Andrés, you sing in the choir. And then Grobian told someone he'd seen you on Ninety-second Street with a girl."

"Oh, why can't people just mind their own business? Boys walk down the street with girls all over the world, every day! Does it have to go up on the By-Smart Web site because *I* do it?"

We'd both been hissing at each other to be heard below the electronic music, but his voice rose to a wail now. Josie was eyeing us along with the rest of the choir, but while they were frankly curious she looked nervous.

"And now what's he doing?" Billy demanded.

I looked behind me. Buffalo Bill was trying to get to his grandson, but the five men who'd been helping with the service were blocking his path. Bysen actually tried to strike one of them with his walking stick, but the men made a circle around him and moved him from the dais—even the old one with the bobbing head and quavering voice was shuffling along, one hand on Bysen's coat.

Mrs. Bysen struggled out the far side of the pew, her arms stretched out toward her grandson. I noticed Jacqui stayed in her seat, wearing the catlike smile of malicious pleasure she put on for Bysen family discomfiture. Mr. William and Uncle Gary knew their duty, though, and joined the bodyguard in the aisle. For a moment, it looked as though there was going to be a pitched battle between the Bysen men and the Mt. Ararat ministers. Mrs. Bysen was being buffeted dangerously in the melee; she wanted to reach her grandson, but the ministers and her sons were squeezing her between them.

Billy watched his family, white-faced. He made a helpless gesture toward his grandmother, then jumped down from the riser and disappeared behind a partition. I clambered over the riser to follow him.

The partition blocked the body of the church from a narrow space that led to a robing room. I ran through the room as its second door was swinging shut. When I pushed it open, I found myself in a big hall where women were fussing around with coffeepots and Kool-Aid pitchers. Toddlers crawled unsupervised at their feet, sucking on cookies or plastic toys.

"Where's Billy?" I demanded, and then saw a flash of red and a door closing at the far end of the room.

I sprinted across the room and out the door. I was just in time to see Billy climb into a midnight blue Miata and roar south on Houston Street.

22 POVERTY'S WHIRLPOOL

B illy's been sleeping here." I made it a statement, not a question.
Josie Dorrado was sitting on the couch with her sister and the
baby, María Inés. The television was on. I had muted the sound when I
came in, but, for once, Julia seemed more interested in the drama of her
family's life than in what was happening on the screen.

Josie bit her lips nervously, pulling off a piece of skin. "He wasn't here.
Our ma don't let no boys sleep over."

I had driven straight to the Dorrado apartment from the church, waiting outside in my car until Rose walked up the street with her children,
and then following her to their front door.

"You," Rose said dully when she saw me. "I might have guessed. What
devil was in me the day I asked Josie to bring you home? Ever since that
day it's been nothing but bad luck, bad luck."

It's always good to have an outsider to blame your troubles on. "Yes,
Rose, that's a terrible blow, the destruction of the factory. I wish either
you or Frank Zamar had talked to me frankly about what was going on
there. Do you know who burned down the plant?"

"Why do you care? Will it bring my job back, or return Frank to life,
if you find out?"

I pulled the soap dish out of my shoulder bag. I'd sealed it in a plastic bag, but I handed it to Rose and asked if she recognized it.

She barely gave it a glance before shaking her head.

"It wasn't in the employee bathroom at the factory?"

"What? Something like that? We had a dispenser on the wall."

I turned to Josie, who had peered over her mother's shoulder at the little frog.

"You recognize this, Josie?"

She shifted from foot to foot, looking nervously behind her into the living room, where Julia was sitting on the couch. "No, coach."

One of the little boys was jumping up and down. "Don't you 'member, Josie, we seen them, they was at the store, and—"

"Quiet, Betto, don't be butting in when Coach is talking to me. We seen them—saw them—around, they had them at By-Smart around Christmas last year."

"You buy one?" I prodded, puzzled by her nervousness.

"No, coach, I never."

"Julia did," Betto burst out. "Julia bought it, she wanted to give it—"

"She bought it for Sancia," Josie put in quickly. "Her and Sancia used to hang out, before María Inés came."

"Is that right?" I asked the boy.

He hunched a shoulder. "I dunno. I guess so."

"Betto?" I knelt so my head was at his level. "You thought Julia bought it for a different person, not for Sancia, didn't you?"

"I don't remember," he said, his head down.

"Leave him alone," Rose said. "You went and bothered Frank Zamar and he got burned to death, now you want to bother my children so you can see what bad things happen to them?"

She grabbed his hand and dragged him into the apartment. The other boy followed, casting me a terrified glance. Great. Now the boys would think of me as the bogeywoman, able to get them murdered in a fire if they spoke to me.

I pushed Josie into the apartment. "You and I need to talk."

She sat on the couch, the baby between her and her sister. Julia had clearly been paying attention to our exchange at the door: she sat tense and alert, her eyes on Josie.

In the dining room beyond, I could see the two boys sitting under the table, quietly crying. Rose had disappeared, either into the bedroom or the kitchen. It occurred to me that the couch had to be her bed: when I was here before, I'd seen the twin beds where Josie and Julia slept, and the air mattresses for the boys in the dining room. There wasn't any other place in the apartment for Rose.

"So where did Billy sleep?" I asked. "Out here?"

"He wasn't here," Josie said quickly.

"Don't be ridiculous," I said. "When he left Pastor Andrés's house he had to go somewhere. He drove you to the hospital yesterday. I know you and he are seeing each other. Where did he sleep?"

Julia tossed her long mane of hair. "Me and Josie shared one bed, Billy slept in the other."

"Why you have to go shooting off your mouth?" Josie demanded.

"Why you have to let that rich gringo stay here in your bed when he could buy a whole house if he want a place to sleep?" Julia shot back.

Little María Inés began to fuss on the couch, but neither sister paid any attention to her.

"And your mother was okay with this arrangement?" I was incredulous.

"She don't know, you can't tell her." Josie looked nervously at the dining room, where her brothers were still staring at us. "The first time, she was at work, she was at her second job, and she never even got home until one in the morning, and then, last night and Friday, Billy, he come in—came in through the kitchen door after she was in bed."

"And Betto and your other brother won't tell her, and she won't notice? You two are nuts. How long have you and Billy been dating?"

"We're not dating. Ma won't let me date anyone because of Julia having a baby." Josie scowled at her sister.

"Well, anyway, the Bysens don't want Billy dating no spic girl," Julia flashed at her.

"Billy never called me a spic. You're just jealous because a nice Anglo boy is interested in me, not some *chavo* like you picked up!"

"Yeah, but his grandpapa, he called Pastor Andrés, he told him he'd report Pastor to the Immigration if he hear Billy going around with any Mexican girls in the church," Julia shot back. "Wetbacks, he called us, you just ask anyone, you can ask Freddy, he was there when Billy's grandfather called. And after that, how long was it before he called you?"

"He don't need to call me; he sees me every Wednesday at choir rehearsal."

The baby began crying more loudly. When her mother and her aunt still ignored her, I picked her up and started patting her back.

"How about now?" I asked, "Now that he's not living at home. Does Billy call you now?"

"Yes, once, to say, can he come over here, but then, he give away, gave away, his cell phone, on account of he said there's something in the phone, a detective could find him," Josie muttered, staring at her knees.

So he'd paid attention to my warning about the GPS signal. "Why doesn't he want to go home?"

Julia gave a syrupy smile. "He's in l-o-v-e with the little wetback here."

Josie slapped her sister; Julia started pulling her hair. I put the baby down and yanked the sisters apart. They glared at each other, but when I let them go, they didn't lunge for each other. I picked the baby up again and sat cross-legged on the floor.

"Billy's family, they were rude to Pastor Andrés," Josie added. "Billy, he really cares about this neighborhood, do people have jobs, do they have enough to eat, like that, and his family, they just want to exploit us."

Billy had definitely been preaching to his little wetback, and she was an attentive student. The baby grabbed at my earrings. I unclutched her tiny fist and pulled out my car keys for her to play with. She threw them on the floor with an excited crow of laughter.

"Who's Freddy?" I asked.

The sisters looked at each other, but Julia said, "Just a guy who goes to Mount Ararat, it's a small church, we all been knowing each other since we was little."

"Since we *were* little," Josie corrected.

"You want to talk Anglo, be my guest. Me, I'm just a teenage mom, I don't have to know anything."

"Your mom and your aunt are such bad liars. I know, that makes you cry to hear it, but it's true," I spoke to the baby and blew bubbles on her stomach. "Now, who is Freddy really?"

"He's really just a guy who goes to Mount Ararat." Julia stared at me defiantly. "You ask Pastor Andrés, he'll tell you."

I sighed. "Okay, maybe, maybe. There's something about him you don't want me to know, though. It wouldn't be his DNA, would it?"

"His what?" Julia said.

"DNA," Josie said. "We covered that in biology, which you'd know if you ever went to school, it's like how people identify—oh." She looked at me. "Like you think he's María Inés's father or something."

"Or something," I said.

Julia spoke through clenched teeth. "He's just a guy at church, I hardly know him except to talk at church."

"But this casual acquaintance told you he heard old Mr. Bysen call the church and threaten the pastor with deportation?"

"It—he thought we should know," Julia stammered.

Josie was crimson. "Billy been—Billy has been—singing in the church, like, since August, and him and me, we went out for a Coke after rehearsal once, I guess maybe in September, and Mr. Grobian, he's at the warehouse, he's Billy's boss, like, he saw us and he told on us, like, it was a crime, Billy taking me for a Coke, and then Ma, she heard, she said no way can I see him 'less Betto and Sammy are with me. So it's like I have to babysit if I want to see him, which would be horrible if you was on a date, to have your brothers with you, but, see, his ma, his mom, she don't—she doesn't want him going out with me, so we never really was dating. Were dating. Except yesterday, he took me up to the hospital to see April."

So Billy had fallen in love with Josie, so much in love he was teaching her English grammar. And she loved him right back, which is why she was changing her speech. And that was also why Billy was fighting the idea of going back to Barrington. Maybe his ideals played a role, too, but mostly it was those pesky stars, crossing lovers once again. I thought of my own jealous worries about Morrell and Marcena Love—you don't have to be fifteen to live in a soap opera.

"You won't tell Ma, will you, coach?" Josie said.

"I can't believe your ma doesn't already know," I said. "You'd have to be brain-dead not to know when there was an extra person in this apartment. She's probably just too depressed about the fire at Fly the Flag to deal with you and Billy right now. And about that fire—what's the story on this soap dish? Which one of you bought it?"

"I got it at By-Smart," Julia said quickly. "Like Josie said, I bought it for Sancia last Christmas. They're real cute, these frogs, and they don't cost hardly anything. But they had like a hundred of them, so how can I know if it's the one I bought or not? Where you find this, anyway?"

"Outside Fly the Flag. In all the rubble from the building."

"Outside Ma's job? What was it doing there?" Julia's bewilderment seemed genuine—she and her sister looked at each other, as if seeing whether the other knew something she wasn't saying.

"I don't know. Maybe it doesn't mean a thing, but it's my only clue. By the way, Betto thought you got it for someone else, Julia."

"Yeah, well, he was like six years old last Christmas, so I don't know how he knows who I bought presents for." Julia stared at me in hauteur. "All he cared about was, did he get his new Power Ranger?"

"You two make it sound so plausible, but I have to say I don't believe you. I'm going to take this to a forensic lab. They'll test it for fingerprints, they'll test if for chemicals, they'll tell me what it was doing at the plant, and who was doing it."

"So?" the sisters stared at me sullenly, united on this one matter.

"So what?" I said. "So you know there won't be fingerprints, or you don't care who left them, or what?"

"So if Sancia gave it to someone else, I can't help it," Julia said.

"Coach McFarlane said you were the best player she had coached in decades, maybe ever," I said to Julia. "Why don't you go back to school, use your brains for your own future, instead of for spinning up lies for grown-ups like me. You could go back to the game; Sancia does, with her two little ones."

"Yeah, well, her ma and her sisters help her out. Who's going to help me? No one."

"You are so unfair!" Josie cried. "I didn't get you pregnant, but because you went and had a baby now I have to sneak around like a criminal if I want to see a boy! And I help you with María Inés all the time, so there!"

I handed María Inés to Julia. "Play with her, talk to her. Give her a chance, even if you don't want one for yourself. And if you decide, either of you, to start telling the truth, give me a call."

I gave them both business cards and stuck the frog back in my bag. When they stared at me, speechless, I got up and went through the dining room, looking for Rose. Betto and Sammy scuttled deeper under the table at my approach: I was the woman who could get them charcoal roasted if they talked to me.

Rose was lying on Josie's bed in the girls' bedroom. I ducked under the clothesline hung with María Inés's wardrobe and watched her, wondering whether I had anything to ask that justified waking her. Her bright red hair clashed with the red in the American flag pillowcase; the Illinois women's team smiled down at her.

"I know you're standing there," she said dully, without opening her eyes. "What is it you want?"

"I only went to Fly the Flag in the first place because you wanted me to look into the sabotage going on there. Then you told me to back off. What made you change your mind?" I kept my voice gentle.

"It's all about the job," she said. "I thought—what I thought, I can't even remember now. Frank—he told me. He asked me to tell you to go away."

"Why?"

"I don't know. I only know he said it could ruin my job, a detective on the premises. But my job is ruined, anyway—I have no job. And Frank, he was a decent man, he paid good, he did what he could for people, he's dead. And I wonder, was it because I brought a detective on the premises?"

"You don't really believe that, do you, Rose? It wasn't because I was there that someone put rats in the heating ducts or glued the doors shut."

I went to sit on Julia's bed. It smelled faintly of María Inés's diapers. Despite the Dorrados' Pentecostal religion, a little Virgin of Guadalupe stood on the pasteboard chest of drawers between the two beds. I suppose no matter what you think of God, everyone needs a mother to look after them.

Rose slowly turned her head on the pillow and looked at me. "But maybe they was scared, I mean, whoever did those things, maybe when they saw a detective asking questions they got scared and burned down the factory."

It was possible, I suppose; the thought made me queasy, but I said, anyway, "And you don't have any idea who this was?"

She shook her head slowly, as if it weighed a great deal and she could barely move it.

"The second job you took—is that enough to support the children?"

"The second job?" she gave a harsh bark that might have been a crow laughing. "That was also for Frank Zamar. His second business that he was starting. Now—oh, *Dios, Dios,* in the morning I will go down to By-Smart and join all the other ladies in my church lifting heavy boxes onto trucks. What difference does it make? The work will wear me out faster, I will die sooner and be at rest."

"Where was the second factory? Why didn't he just run an extra shift at Fly the Flag?" I asked.

"It was there, it was a different kind of job, but he did run an extra shift, in the middle of the night. I got there right before the shift started on Tuesday night. And the plant was in ruins. I couldn't believe my eyes. Me and the other women, we stood there not believing it, until some cop came along and sent us home."

Josie appeared in the doorway. "Ma, Sammy and Betto are hungry. What's for lunch?"

"Nothing," Rose said. "There is no food, and no money to buy food. We are not having lunch today."

Behind their sister, the boys started to cry again, this time out loud. Rose squeezed her eyes shut tightly. She lay still for a moment, seeming not even to breathe, then she pushed herself upright in the bed.

"No, *mis queridos,* of course there is food, of course I will feed you, while I have blood running through my body I will feed you."

 **STAR-CROSSED LOVERS**

The snow had stopped when I got outside. The snows of November are usually light, merely a warning to the city of what lies ahead, and this one had ended with a scant half inch. It was a fine, dry powder, blowing across the walks, disappointing a group of kids in the vacant lot next to me who were trying to turn it into snowballs.

I sat in my car, the engine running and the heater on, and tried to make a few notes while the conversation with the Dorrados was still more or less fresh in my mind, although I was hard put to make sense of anything I'd heard just now.

BILLY, I wrote in block letters in my notebook, and then stared at it, unable to think of anything to add. What was going on with him? When we spoke on Thursday, he told me to tell his father he'd call the company's shareholders if the family didn't leave him alone. Was that why Buffalo Bill had come to see me last night? And, if that was the case, what didn't the Bysens want the shareholders to know? From my perspective, the company did a ton of outrageous things—locking employees in overnight, paying badly, busting unions, leaving families like the Czernins in the lurch when it came to health insurance—but the shareholders must know those things already. What could be so horrible that the shareholders would shy away from it?

I thought back to the prayer meeting out at By-Smart headquarters. The share price had fallen on the rumor that By-Smart was going to allow union organizers. Maybe Billy was just threatening to call and say that was really going to happen. But what would be the "or else"?

Just why had Billy run away from home? Was it because he was in love with Josie, or troubled by his family's business practices, or ardently committed to the South Side? Certainly he admired Pastor Andrés, but what would make him ally himself with the preacher against his family?

Which brought me to the preacher himself, whom Buffalo Bill had threatened with deportation. Of course, the Buffalo dished out threats like hash at a diner—last night, he'd threatened to get the bank to foreclose on my mortgage and to shut down my business if I didn't do what he wanted. Maybe it was a form of verbal incontinence—Mildred had kept shutting him up in a nice, deferential way.

At the same time, the Bysens really did have enormous power, more than I could imagine. If you operated a colossus like By-Smart, with its global reach, with annual sales bigger than the GDP of most of the countries in the world, you could get congressmen and immigration officers to do pretty much anything you wanted. Say, Pastor Andrés was here on a green card—the Bysens could probably get that revoked with one phone call. Who knows—if he was naturalized, they might even be able to get his citizenship stripped from him. Perhaps that would take three calls instead of just the one, but it wouldn't surprise me to hear they'd done it.

I printed ANDRÉS on the next page. I didn't care much about his ties to Billy, but what did he know about the fire at Fly the Flag? He'd met with Frank Zamar ten days ago, the day I'd surprised the punk in the basement.

That punk. Between April's heart stopping and watching the factory go up in flames, I'd forgotten the punk. Andrés knew who he was. A *chavo banda*, whom one saw around stealing from jobsites, Andrés had said, and he'd shooed him away from the street where we'd been talking.

Maybe Andrés was just protecting his jobsite, but maybe he knew something more about that *chavo*.

FIND THE *CHAVO*, I added, followed by FREDDY?? Did he matter in the scheme of things? Seeing his name next to "Find the *chavo*" made me wonder if he was that *chavo*. But a punk, what would he be doing in Andrés's office, able to overhear Buffalo Bill threaten the pastor? Or, or, or. My brain wasn't working. Despite the heater, my feet were starting to freeze, and I was feeling a dull throb in my wound. I stuck the notebook back in my bag.

I was putting the car into gear when a midnight blue Miata, with a license plate that read "The Kid 1," pulled up in front of the Dorrado building. I hadn't suspected Billy of so much whimsy. I hesitated briefly, then shut off the Mustang's engine and got out to cross the street.

I leaned over the driver's door as Billy was starting to extricate himself. "Your car is about a hundred times easier to trace than your phone, Billy, especially with that vanity plate. Even I could track you if I wanted to. It will be child's play for the big agencies that your dad and your grandfather use. You want them charging in on Josie and her family?"

He turned white. "Are you following me? For them?"

"Nope. I came to see Josie and her mom. And realized you've been sleeping here. It's not a great idea, for lots of reasons, one of which is I don't want Josie having a baby."

"I—we wouldn't, we don't, I respect her. I belong to True Love Waits."

"Yeah, but teenagers in a bedroom all night, respect only carries you so far for so long. Besides that, they don't have any money. Ms. Dorrado lost her job—it's a burden for her to have an extra person there."

"I wasn't taking food from them. But you're right: I should buy some groceries for them." He flushed. "Only, I've never been grocery shopping, I mean for a family, of course I've been in a store sometimes. I don't know what you buy if you want to cook a meal. There are so many ordinary things that I don't know."

He was touching in his earnestness. "Why don't you want to go home?"

"I need to figure some things out. Some things about my family." He shut his mouth tightly.

"What did you mean by that message to your father, about you calling the shareholders if he kept looking for you? I gather it's upset both him and your grandfather."

"That's one of the things I need to figure out."

"Were you threatening to call your major shareholders to say that By-Smart was going to allow union activity?"

His soft face hardened in indignation. "That would be a lie: I don't tell lies, especially not one like that, that would hurt my grandfather."

"What, then?" I tried to smile engagingly. "I'd be glad to lend an ear, if it would help to have someone to talk them over with."

He shook his head, his mouth shut in a thin line. "You may mean well, Ms. War-sha-sky. But right now, I don't know. I don't know who I can trust, besides Pastor Andrés, and he is really helping me, so thank you, but I think I'll be all right."

"If you change your mind, call me; I'll be glad to talk to you. And I really wouldn't betray you to your family." I handed him a card. "But do Josie a favor: find somewhere else to stay. Even if you don't sleep with her, your grandfather is bound to find you here, especially with a car that stands out like yours. People in this neighborhood notice everything, and plenty of them will be willing to tell your dad or your grandfather they've seen you here. Buffalo Bill's—your grandfather's—angry; I know you know he threatened the pastor with deportation just because you and Josie had a Coke together. He could cause Rose Dorrado a lot of trouble, and she needs a job right now, not more trouble."

"Oh. Now that Fly the Flag is gone—I didn't even think." He sighed. "All I thought was, What difference does it make?, and, of course, it makes a terrible difference to the people who worked there. Thank you for reminding me, Ms. War-sha-sky."

"All you thought was 'What difference does it make?'" I repeated sharply. "What do you mean by that?"

He waved his arms in a vague gesture that seemed to mean the South Side around him, or maybe the world around him, and shook his head unhappily.

I turned on my heel to cross the street, then remembered the frog soap dish. I pulled out the baggie again from my bag and showed the frog to him.

He shook his head again. "What is it?"

"To me, it looks like a soap dish in the shape of a frog. Julia Dorrado says she bought it, or one like it, at By-Smart last Christmas."

"We carry so much stuff, I don't know our whole inventory. And I only met Josie this summer, when my church did the exchange. Where did you find it? I hope you aren't trying to say we sell things that are this dirty."

He was so serious all the time that it took me a moment to realize he was trying to make a joke. The license plate, and now a joke: maybe there were depths in the Kid that I was overlooking. I smiled dutifully, and explained where I'd picked it up.

He hunched a shoulder. "Maybe someone dropped it there. There's always a lot of garbage around these old buildings."

"Maybe," I agreed. "But judging from where it was lying when I picked it up, I think it came shooting out when the windows in the drying room blew. So I think it was inside the factory."

He turned the baggie over in his hands several times. "Maybe someone wanted it, like, as an ornament on a flagpole. Or maybe one of the ladies who worked there used it as a mascot. I see that a lot down here, people have funny things as mascots."

"Don't be a wet blanket," I said. "It's my only clue; I have to pursue it enthusiastically."

"And then what? What if it leads you to some poor person down here who's already spent their whole life being harassed by the police?"

I narrowed my eyes. "Do you know who put this in the factory, or why?"

"No, but you, you're treating it like it was a game, like you're in *Crossing Jordan* or something. And people down here—"

"Don't keep talking to me about 'people down here,'" I snapped. "I grew up in this neighborhood. For you, maybe *this* is a game, living among the natives, but for people like me, who never spent a dime we didn't work like dogs to earn, this is not a romantic neighborhood. Desperation and poverty push people to do mean, spiteful, sordid, and even cruel things. Frank Zamar died in that fire. If someone set it, then I will be happy to lead the police to him. Or her."

His soft young face tightened again. "Well, people who are richer than anyone also do mean and spiteful—and—and cruel things. I am not playing a game down here. This is the most serious thing that has ever happened in my life. And if you tell my grandfather where you saw me, it will be—mean and cruel. And spiteful."

"Relax, Galahad, I'm not ratting you out. But he found you at the church on his own this morning, and it won't take much for him to find you here."

He nodded again, his anger disappearing into his serious good manners. "You are giving me good advice, Ms. War-sha-sky. I do appreciate it. And if they can trace my car as easily as you say, I guess I shouldn't hang around here."

He looked forlornly at the battered building for a long minute, then climbed back into his little sports car and took off. I looked up at the apartment, wondering if Juliet had been on the lookout for Romeo. I was tempted to go back inside and reassure her—he came to see you, but one of the Capulets was lurking. It was a silly fantasy—with Rose's economic woes, the Bysen family, Pastor Andrés, and all those young hormones, I definitely shouldn't meddle.

I was crossing the street back to my own car when the cabin-cruiser Cadillac turned south onto Escanaba. The driver did a laborious U-turn and pulled up in front of the Dorrados' building. Young Montague had escaped in the nick of time.

The chauffeur put on his peaked hat and opened the middle door to help Mr. Bysen from the backseat. Mr. William, who'd been sitting in the third row of seats, climbed down to assist his mother.

I crossed Escanaba back to the boat. "Hi, Mr. Bysen. Great service, wasn't it? Pastor Andrés is a truly inspired preacher."

Buffalo Bill pulled his cane out of the middle seat, made sure he was standing erect, and puffed air out at me. "What are you doing here?"

I smiled. "Sunday after church is when we all pay social calls. Isn't that what you're doing?"

I heard a ripple of malicious laughter and peered inside the Caddy. Jacqui was sitting in the front seat. Her husband, who was in the third bank of seats, called out a sharp reprimand to her, but she just laughed again, and said, "I never knew Christian worship could be so dramatic."

"Will you make your wife behave?" William snarled at Uncle Gary.

"Oh, yes," Jacqui said, " 'as the church is subject to Christ, so let wives also be subject in everything to their husbands.' I have heard that verse quoted once or twice, Willie, once or twice. Just because you and your father want it to be true doesn't make it true."

Buffalo Bill put the crook of his cane over my shoulder and jerked me around to face him. "Never mind all that squabbling. I've come to find my boy. Is he here?"

I took the cane from my shoulder and pulled it out of his hand. "There are easier ways to get both my attention and my goodwill, Mr. Bysen."

He glared at me. "I asked you a question and I expect an answer."

"Oh, Bill, never mind all that." Mrs. Bysen had come around the back of the Caddy to where we were standing; she spoke to her husband but looked at me. "We haven't met, but William told me you were the detective he'd hired to find our Billy. Do you know where he is? Is this where that Mexican girl lives? Jacqui thinks she knows something, so she asked one of our people to find their name and address."

"I'm V. I. Warshawski, Mrs. Bysen. I'm sorry, but I don't know where Billy is. The Dorrado family lives here; one of the girls is on my basketball team. They're in considerable distress right now because the factory where the mother worked burned down last week and she has five children to support. They've got a lot more than Billy on their minds, I'm afraid."

"Billy doesn't have good sense," Bysen growled. "If they're giving him a sob story he'll fall for it, hook, line, and sinker."

"Billy is a good boy," his wife reproved him. "If he is helping people in distress, he's a good Christian, and I'm proud of him."

"Oh, enough of this nonsense. I'm going up to see this girl for myself. If she needs to be bought off, well—"

"We will not be blackmailed by any welfare cheats," Mr. William interrupted his father. "Billy needs to learn a few things about life. If he has to learn them the hard way, the lessons will stick with him longer."

"That's a good paternal attitude," I applauded him. "No wonder both your kids ran away from home."

Jacqui laughed again, delighted with the rancor. Buffalo Bill snatched his cane from me and stomped up the broken walk to the front door. His wife squeezed my hand before following him, with Mr. William taking her arm again. The chauffeur opened the apartment door for them, then leaned against the building to smoke a cigarette.

I climbed into the middle row of seats, behind Jacqui. "So you called Patrick Grobian at the warehouse to track down the Dorrados? How does he know them?"

"Not that it's any of your business, but you ought to realize that anyone who wants to move ahead in the Bysen operation has to keep track of what's important to the big buffalo. Pat saw the girl having a Coke with Billy in September; he knew the old man would want that information. He made it his business to find out who she was. So of course he knows where she lives."

"No one can expect to move too far up the By-Smart ladder if they're not part of the family," I said.

"You don't need to be the CEO to have a lot of power and make a lot of money in a company this big. Pat knows that, and he's a go-getter. If he was a Bysen, he'd be leading the pack. As it is, when the old man goes, he's likely to get a good position at the home office."

"If *you're* in charge," her husband said from the back of the Caddy. "But, my dear Jacqueline, you won't be. William will be, and he doesn't like you."

"This isn't medieval England," Jacqui said. "Just because he's the oldest doesn't mean Willie gets the throne, although he's like poor Prince Charles, isn't he, waiting around for his mum to die, except in this case Willie is waiting for Daddy to die. I'm surprised sometimes he doesn't—"

"Jacqui." Gary's voice sounded a warning. "Not everyone has your sense of humor. If you want to keep doing the work you're doing, you need to learn to get along with William, that's all I'm going to say."

Jacqui turned around in the front seat and fluttered improbably long eyelashes. "Darling, I am doing everything I can to help William. *Everything.* Just ask him how much he owes me these days and you'll be surprised by his change in attitude. He finally sees how incredibly useful I can be."

"Maybe," Gary muttered. "Maybe."

I looked over at the apartment, thinking I should go up to give Rose a helping hand. She didn't have the resources to face the Bysens alone. Before I got to the front door, though, the trio reappeared.

"Did they know anything about Billy?" I asked Mrs. Bysen.

She shook her head unhappily. "I can't be sure. I appealed to the woman as a mother and a grandmother—I can see how much she loves those children, and how hard she works to give them a decent life—but she said she only ever sees him at Mount Ararat, and the girls said the same thing. Do you think they're telling the truth?"

"People like that don't know truth from lies, Mother," Mr. William said. "It's easy to see where Billy got his gullibility."

"You don't talk to your mother that way while I'm alive, Willie. If Billy got your mother's sweet disposition, that isn't a bad thing. The rest of you pack of hyenas, you're all waiting for me to die so you can eat the company I built." He glowered at me. "If I find you know where my boy is and you're not telling me—"

"I know," I said wearily. "You'll break me in your soup like crackers."

I stomped across the street again and turned my car around to head for home.

24 YET ANOTHER MISSING CHILD

In the morning, I went to my office early and put the metal frog into a box, messengering it out to Cheviot, the forensic engineering lab I use. I told Sanford Rieff, the engineer I usually work with, I didn't know what I was looking for, so asked him to do a full report on the dish—who made it, whose prints were on it, any chemical residues, anything. When he phoned to ask how big a rush I was in, I hesitated, looking at my month's accounts. No one was paying me; I didn't even know if the dish was connected to the fire. It was what I'd said to Billy yesterday—my only clue, so I was being enthusiastic about it.

"Not a rush job—I can't afford it."

I spent most of the rest of the morning doing work for people who paid me to ask questions for them, but I did take some time to see what information I could get on the Bysen family. I already knew they were rich, but my eyes widened as I went through their history on my law enforcement database. I didn't have enough fingers and toes to count the zeroes in their holdings. Of course, a lot of it was tied up in various trusts. There was a foundation, which supported a wide array of evangelical programs, gave heavily to antiabortion groups and evangelical missions, but also supported libraries and museums.

Three of Buffalo Bill's four sons and one of the daughters lived with him in a gated estate in Barrington Hills. They had separate houses, but all in the same happy patriarchal enclave. The second daughter was living in Santiago with her husband, who headed South American operations; the fourth son was in Singapore managing the Far East. So no one had run away from Papa. That seemed significant, although I didn't know of what.

Gary and Jacqui didn't have any children of their own, but the other five had produced a total of sixteen. The Bysens' commitment to traditional family values certainly carried through in their distribution of assets: as nearly as I could make out, each of the sons and grandsons had trusts worth about three times what the girls in the family got.

I wondered if this was what had Billy wondering about his family, although I sort of doubted it. No one cares too much about women's issues these days, not even young women; I had a feeling that his sister losing out in the will was something Billy would accept unquestioningly. Jacqui was the one family member I'd met who might feel differently—but she was married to one of the men, one of the jackpot hitters, and I didn't picture her caring about anyone else's inheritance as long as she got hers.

Billy's sister, Candace, was twenty-one now. Whatever she'd done that caused the family to ship her to Korea, she was still in the will, so they were fair up to that point. I searched for more specific news about Candace, but couldn't find anything. I printed out some of the more interesting reports, then closed up my office: I wanted to stop at the hospital on my way down to Bertha Palmer High: I figured the team would like an update on April Czernin.

When I got to the hospital, though, I found April had been discharged early this morning. I called Sandra Czernin from my car, but she treated me like a porcupine treats a dog, shooting quills into its mouth.

She reiterated her accusations that April's collapse was my fault. "You've been waiting all these years to get even with me for Boom-

Boom, so you brought that English bitch down to meet him. If not for you, he'd've been home where he belonged."

"Or out with someone from the neighborhood," I said. I regretted the words as soon as they hopped out, and even apologized, but it wasn't too surprising that she wouldn't let me talk to April.

"Any idea when she can come back to school?" I persisted. "The girls will want to know."

"Then their mothers can call me and ask."

"Even if I did bear a grudge after all these years, I wouldn't take it out on your kid, Sandra," I yelled, but she slammed the phone in my ear.

Oh, to hell with her. I put the car into gear, thinking that jealousy of Marcena could have brought Sandra and me together. The image made me snicker inadvertently, and sent me farther south in a better humor.

I was early enough for practice to stop in the principal's office to talk to Natalie Gault. When I asked her what kind of physicals the girls were given before signing up for basketball, she rolled her eyes as if I were some sort of idiot.

"We don't do health screening here. They have to bring in a parent's signed permission slip. That says the parent knows there are risks in the sport and that their child is healthy enough to play. We do it for basketball, football, baseball, all our sports. That document says the school is not liable for any illness or injury the child contracts from playing."

"Sandra Czernin is angry and scared. She needs a hundred thousand dollars to pay for April's health care, for starters, anyway. If it occurs to her to sue the school, it won't be hard for her to find a lawyer to take you to court—a permission slip like that isn't going to stand up in front of a jury. Why not do EKGs on the rest of the squad, cheer everybody up, act like you're paying attention?'

I didn't mention Lotty's offer to do the EKGs—let the school sweat a little. Besides, I couldn't quite get my mind around the logistics of ferrying fifteen teenagers to the clinic. Gault said she would discuss it with the principal and get back to me.

I went on down to the gym, where I found a skeleton squad. Josie

Dorrado was missing, as was Sancia, my center. Celine Jackman, my young gangbanger, was there with her two sidekicks, but even she seemed subdued.

I told the nine who had shown up what I knew about April. "The hospital sent her home today. She can't play basketball again—there's something wrong with her heart, and the kind of workouts you have to do for team sports are too strenuous for her. But she'll be able to return to school, and you won't know by looking at her that there's anything wrong with her. Where are Josie and Sancia?"

"Josie, she cut school today," Laetisha volunteered. "We thought, maybe she caught whatever April got, on account of them two is always together."

"You can't catch what April has: it's a condition, you're born with it." I got out my coach's erasable board and tried to draw a diagram for them, how you "catch" a disease caused by a virus, like chicken pox or AIDS, versus how you can be born with a condition.

"So one of us could have the same thing and not know it." This was Delia, one of the quieter girls, who never put much effort into the game.

"*You* wouldn't," Celine said. "You so slow, people think you don't got a working heart anyway."

I let the insult go unchecked—I wanted them to feel that life was returning to normal, even if normal included getting slammed. I set them on a short course of stretches, and let them go directly to scrimmage, five on four, with all the weakest players on the smaller squad. I joined the weaker girls at point guard, calling my team up, directing traffic, giving a few tips to the opposition, but putting my all into going one on one with Celine. After a short time, everyone, even Delia, forgot that their hearts might give out and started playing. I was hotdogging, bouncing the ball between my legs to someone in the corner, jumping up to block shots, sticking to Celine like her underwear, and the girls were laughing and cheering, and running harder than I'd ever seen them go. Celine took her play up a level and began feinting and nailing her shots as if she were Tamika Williams.

When I called a halt at four, three of the girls begged to stay to work on their free throws. I told them I could let them have ten minutes, when one of the girls screamed, "Ooh, coach, your back, Celine, what you do to Coach?"

I put a hand behind me and realized I was wet with something warmer than sweat: my wound had come open. "I'm fine," I said. "This is just an injury I got over at the factory, you know, Fly the Flag, when it blew up last week. You guys were great tonight. I have to go to the doctor and get this stitched back together now, but Thursday everyone who played today goes out for pizza with me after practice."

When they'd showered and I got the gym locked, I drove up to Lotty's clinic, feeling a happy glow from the workout—the first time I'd left the high school feeling good since—maybe since ever. Since my team won the state championship all those years ago, although even then—my mother had been dying. I had gotten drunk with Sylvia and the rest of them so I didn't have to think of Gabriella in her hospital bed, draped with tubes and monitors as if she were a mummified fly in the middle of a spiderweb.

The memory damped down my good mood. When I got to the clinic, I checked in soberly with Mrs. Coltrain, Lotty's receptionist. A dozen or so people were in the waiting room; it'd be at least an hour. After I turned around and Mrs. Coltrain saw the blood running down my back, she sent me in ahead of the queue. Lotty was at the hospital, but her assistant, Lucy, who's an advanced practice nurse, stitched me up.

"You shouldn't be jumping with these stitches, V.I.," she said, as severely as Lotty would have done. "The wound has to have time to heal. You stink of sweat, but you cannot get this wound wet again under the shower. A sponge bath. Wash your hair in the kitchen sink. Do you understand?"

"Yes'm," I said meekly.

Back at home, I gave the dogs a sketchy walk, and followed Lucy's orders on how to bathe. This meant doing the dishes first, since they'd been building up again. I hadn't even washed my mother's Venetian wineglasses, which I'd brought out for Morrell last week. I was dismayed by my carelessness: my mother had brought them from Italy with her, her only memento of the home she'd had to flee. I'd broken two several years ago; I couldn't bear it if I lost any more.

I carefully rinsed and dried them, but I kept one out for a glass of Torgiano. Usually, I use something replaceable for day-to-day drinking, but my earlier memory was haunting me, making me need to feel close to Gabriella again.

I called Morrell and explained that I was too tired to make it up to Evanston tonight. "Marcena can entertain you with her elegant banter."

"She could if she was here, darling, but she's vanished again. Someone called her this afternoon with the promise of more adventures on the South Side and she took off again."

I remembered Sandra's bitter remark about Bron going off with the British whore. "Romeo Czernin."

"Could be. I wasn't paying special attention. When will I see you again? Could I take you out to dinner tomorrow? Fill you with organic produce and dazzle you with my own elegant banter? I know you're annoyed that I went home yesterday."

I laughed reluctantly. "Oh, yes, I remember: subtlety isn't my strong suit. Dinner would be great, but only with banter."

We settled on a time, and I went into the kitchen to deal with tonight's meal. I'd finally made it to the grocery to do my own shopping on my way back from Lotty's clinic, stocking up on everything from yogurt to soap, as well as fresh fish and vegetables.

I broiled tuna steaks with garlic and olives for Mr. Contreras and myself. We curled up companionably in the living room to eat and watch *Monday Night Football* together, New England against the Chiefs, me with my wine, my neighbor with a Bud. Mr. Contreras, who bets the games, tried to persuade me to put my money where my mouth is.

"Not on who makes the first first down or the biggest tackle," I protested. "Five bucks on the final score, that's all."

"Come on, doll: a dollar if the Chiefs score first, a dollar if they get the first sack." He enumerated about a dozen things I could bet on, then said scornfully, "I thought you called yourself a risk taker."

"You're a risk taker with a union pension," I grumbled. "I just have a 401(k) that I didn't even manage a contribution to last year." Still, I agreed to his scheme and laid out fifteen singles on the coffee table.

Rose Dorrado called just as the Chiefs were mounting a heroic attack late in the first half, when I'd already lost six dollars. I took the phone into the hall to get away from the television noise.

"Josie didn't come home from school today," Rose said without pre-amble.

"She wasn't at school today at all, according to the girls on the team."

"Not at school? But she left this morning, right on time! Where did she go? Oh, no, oh, *Dios*, did someone steal my baby!" Her voice rose.

Images of the dark alleys and abandoned buildings on the South Side, of the girls in this city who've been molested and killed, flitted around the corners of my mind. It was possible, but I didn't think that was what had happened to Josie.

"Have you checked with Sandra Czernin? She could be visiting April."

"I called Sandra, I thought that, too, but she heard nothing from my baby, nothing since Saturday when Josie went to see April in the hospital. What did you say to her yesterday? Did you upset her so much she ran away from me?"

"I told her I didn't think it was a good idea for her and Billy to spend the night together. Do you know where he is?"

She gasped. "You think he ran off with her? But why? But where?"

"I don't think anything right now, Rose. I'd talk to Billy before I called the cops, though."

"Oh, I thought nothing could be worse than losing my job, but now this, this! How do I find him, this Billy?"

I tried to imagine where he might be. I didn't think he'd gone home, at least not willingly. I suppose his grandfather might have had him picked up—Buffalo Bill was clearly capable of anything. Billy had given his cell phone away, Josie said: obviously, my remark about the GPS chip in it had made him cautious. I wondered if he'd also ditched the Miata.

"Phone Pastor Andrés," I said at last. "He's the one person Billy talks to these days. If you can find Billy, I think you'll find Josie, or, at least, Billy may know where she is."

Ten minutes later, Rose called back. "Pastor Andrés, he says he doesn't know where Billy is. He hasn't seen him since church yesterday. You got to come down here and help me find Josie. Who else can I ask? Who else can I turn to?"

"The police," I suggested. "They know how to hunt missing persons."

"The police," she spat. "If they even answer my call, you think they would care?"

"I know the watch commander down there," I offered. "I could phone him."

"You come, Ms. V. I. War— War—"

I realized she was reading from one of the cards I'd left with her daughters, that she didn't in fact know my name. When I pronounced it for her, she reiterated her demand that I come. The police wouldn't listen to her, she knew all about that; I was a detective, I knew the neighborhood, please, it was all too much for her right now, the factory burning down, being out of work, all those children, and now this?

I was tired, and I'd had two glasses of heavy Italian red. And I'd been in South Chicago once already today, and it was twenty-five miles, and I'd split my shoulder open this afternoon . . . and I told her I'd be there as soon as I could.

 **BEDTIME STORIES**

It was close to eleven when we pulled up in front of the Dorrado apartment on Escanaba. Mr. Contreras was with me, and we'd brought Mitch as well. Who knows—his hunting stock might give him a good tracking nose.

My neighbor had been predictably annoyed that I was going out again, but I shut him up by the simple expedient of inviting him to join me. "I know it's late, and I agree I shouldn't be driving. If you want to ride along and help keep me alert, that'd be great."

"Sure, doll, sure." He was touchingly ecstatic.

I went into my bedroom and dressed in jeans and put on a couple of loose knit tops under my navy peacoat. I got my gun out of the wall safe. I wasn't expecting a battle with Billy, if, in fact, he and Josie had run off together. But drive-by shootings were a dreary commonplace in the old 'hood, and I didn't want to end up lying on the floor of an abandoned warehouse with some stray punk's stray bullet in my back, just because I hadn't come prepared. That was the real reason we were taking Mitch, too—not too many gangbangers dis a big dog.

Before we left Lakeview, I called Billy's mother. Her phone was answered by a man who was some kind of butler or secretary—anyway, a call screener. He was very reluctant to disturb Mrs. William, and when I finally pushed him into bringing her to the phone it was clear why: Annie Lisa was high on something other than life. Whether it was modern and respectable, like Xanax, or old-fashioned and reliable, like Old Overholt, she had a delay, like a satellite echo, in answering anything I said.

I spoke slowly and patiently, as if to a child, reminding her that I was the detective who was looking for Billy. "When did you last hear from him, Ms. Bysen?"

"Hear from him?" she echoed.

"Did Billy call you today?"

"Billy? Billy isn't here. William, William is angry."

"And why is William angry, ma'am?"

"I don't know." She was puzzled and talked about it at some length. "Billy went to work, he went to the warehouse, that's what a good boy does, he works hard for a living, it's what Daddy Bysen always told us, so why does that make William angry? Unless it's because Billy is doing what Daddy Bysen says, William always hates for Billy to follow Daddy Bysen's orders, but William also likes children who work hard. Children who lie around using drugs and getting pregnant, they get sent away, so he should be happy that Billy went to the warehouse again."

"Yes, ma'am," I said. "I'm sure deep down he's ecstatic, just hiding it from you."

Irony was a mistake: she thought I was saying William was hiding Billy from her. I cut her questions off and asked for Billy's sister's phone number.

"Candace is in Korea. She's doing mission work, and we're proud that she's turning her life around." Annie Lisa spoke the sentences like an inexpert news reader looking at a teleprompter.

"That's nice. But in case Billy called his sister to talk over his plans, can you give me her phone number?"

"He wouldn't do that; he knows William would be very angry."

"How about her e-mail address?"

She didn't know it, or wouldn't give it. I pressed her as hard as I could without alienating her, but she wouldn't budge: Candace was off-limits until she'd finished serving her sentence.

"Would Billy have turned to any of his aunts or uncles?" I pictured him confiding in Aunt Jacqui while she smirked and preened.

"No one understands Billy the way I do. He's very sensitive, like me— he isn't like the Bysens. None of them has ever really understood him."

That seemed to be the limit, both of what I could get and what I could take from her. Mr. Contreras, who'd gone to his own place for a parka and a pipe wrench, was waiting at the bottom of the stairs with Mitch. As we left, we could hear Peppy's forlorn whine from behind his front door.

The Dorrados' building was alive in the way urban apartments always seem to be. As we walked up the three flights of stairs, we heard babies squalling, stereos cranked up high enough to send vibrations down the banisters, people shouting in a variety of languages, and even a couple locked in ecstasy. Mitch's hackles were on end; Mr. Contreras kept a tight hold on his leash.

I felt a little foolish arriving with an old man, a dog, and a gun, although the gun at least was neatly tucked inside my down vest. The dog and the man were pretty much just out there where anyone could see them. They certainly knocked Rose off balance.

"A dog? Not a dog, he'll eat the baby. Who is this? Your father? What are they doing here?"

Behind her I could hear María Inés howling. "I'll leave the dog tied up in the hall here. We thought he might help track Josie, if we got enough of a clue on where she's gone to track her."

I added an introduction to Mr. Contreras, without explaining his relationship to me—that was so complicated I didn't think I could do it in one sentence. My neighbor astonished me by bypassing Rose to pick up the wailing infant. Maybe it was his deep, soft voice, or just because he was calm: Rose was so wired she could have powered the whole South Side, with enough to spare for Indiana, but in a matter of minutes Mr. Contreras had the baby quiet, resting against his flannel shirt and blinking sleepily at the room. I knew he'd raised a daughter, and he had two grandsons, but I'd never seen him in action with babies.

The couch, where Julia was usually planted watching television, had been pulled out into Rose's bed. Beyond, in the dining room, I saw Betto and Sammy, lying on their air mattresses under the dining room table. They weren't moving, but, as I looked, I saw the living room lamp glint on their eyes: they were awake and watching. Rose was pacing round and round in the tiny space between the bed and the door, wringing her hands, bleating disjoint, contradictory statements.

I took her arm and led her forcibly to the bed. "Sit down and try to think calmly. When was the last time you saw Josie?"

"This morning. She was dressing for school, and I was leaving, I was going to the alderman's office, he's a good person, I'm thinking maybe he knows of a job, something that pays better than By-Smart, and I went to two places, but they're not hiring, and I came back to make lunch for Betto and Sammy, they come home for lunch, but Josie, she eats at school, and that's it, I never see her since then, since this morning."

"Did you two argue about anything? About Billy, maybe?"

"I was very angry that she had this boy staying here. Any boy, I would be angry, but this boy, with his family so rich, what is she thinking? They could hurt us. Everybody knows how they don't want their son dating no Mexican girl, everybody knows they called down to the church and made threats to Pastor Andrés."

Rose sprang back to her feet in her agitation. The disturbance made the baby start to whimper again; Mr. Contreras interrupted to ask for María Inés's bottle.

Rose fished for it on the floor next to the bed, and went on talking. "I said, how did she think she was raised, to have a boy in the room with her overnight? Does she want a baby, like Julia? To ruin her life for a boy, especially a rich boy who don't need to worry about nothing? He says he's a Christian, but the first sign of trouble they run away fast, those rich Anglo boys. She is supposed to go to college, that's what I tell her, she wants to go, with April. Then she don't have to be like me, going around begging for jobs and not getting hired."

"Did she say anything back, threaten to run away, anything like that?"

She shook her head. "All this, we say all this after that boy's family come here. They accused her, they call her ugly names, and, God forgive me, we all lied, we all say, no, Billy don't come here. The grandfather, he was like the police, he listen to nothing, nothing I say, and he actually go into the bedroom, into the bathroom, checking to see if something is there from Billy. He says, if Billy comes here, if I hide him, he'll deport me. Don't you try, I tell him, because I am a U.S. citizen same as you, I belong in this country same as you.

"And the son, Billy's father, he's even worse, looking in my Bible, looking in the children's books, like we have money we stole from them maybe—he even take my Bible and shake it all over the floor, so all my page markers come loose, but when they leave, *Dios*, what a fight I had with Josie then. How could she put us all at such risk and all for a boy. They're like buses, I tell her, always another one will come along, don't ruin your life, not like Julia here.

"She fights, she argues, she cries, but she don't say she's running away. Then in the afternoon, this boy, this Billy, shows up with a box of groceries, and Josie acts like he's Saint Michael coming down from heaven, only then he left again, without her, and she sat all day like Julia, in front of the television, watching their telenovelas."

I rubbed my head, trying to take in the torrent of information. "What about Julia? What does she say?"

"She says she knows nothing. Those two, they fight day and night now, not like before, before María Inés, then they were so close, you think they were one person sometimes. If Josie has a secret, she don't say nothing to Julia about it."

"I'd like to ask her myself."

Rose protested, halfheartedly: Julia would be asleep, and she was too angry with Josie to know anything.

Mr. Contreras patted her hand. "Victoria here won't say nothing to upset your girl. She's used to talking to young people. You just sit down and tell me about this beautiful little girl here. She's your grandkid, huh? She's got your beautiful eyes, don't she?"

His reassuring rumble followed me as I picked my way through the tightly packed dining room to the girls' bedroom. The skin prickled at the back of my neck, knowing the two boys were lying under the table watching me.

The bedroom overlooked an air shaft, and lights from neighboring apartments came in through the thin curtain. When I ducked under the clothes hanging from the rope, I could see Julia's face, with her long lashes fluttering against her cheeks. I could tell from her squinched eyelids that, like her little brothers, she was only pretending to sleep. I sat on the edge of the bed—the tiny room didn't have space for a chair.

Julia's breath came out in quick shallow gusts, but she lay perfectly still, willing me to believe she was asleep.

"You've been angry with Josie ever since María Inés was born," I said, matter-of-factly. "She's going to school, she's playing basketball, she's doing all the things you used to do, before you had María Inés. It doesn't seem fair, does it?"

She lay rigid, in angry silence, but after several minutes, when I didn't say anything else, she suddenly burst out, "I only did it once, once when Ma was at work, and Josie and the boys were in school. He said a virgin can't get pregnant, I didn't even know until—I thought I was dying, I thought I had cancer inside me. I didn't want a baby, I wanted to get rid of it, only the pastor, he and Ma said that's a sin, you go to hell.

"And then, the day he did it to me, Josie came in, she came home early from school, she saw me, and she was like, how could you?, you're a whore. We used to be best friends, even when Sancia and me was friends, and now, whenever I complain about María Inés, she's, like, you didn't have to be a whore. Her and April, they say they're going to college, they say their basketball take them to college. Well, Coach McFarlane, that's what she used to say to me. So when Billy came over on Thursday and begged for a place to sleep, I invited him in, I thought, you do it to her, to Josie, make her get a baby, see what she says then!"

She was panting, as if waiting for me to criticize her, but the whole story was so sad I only wanted to cry. I reached under the coverlet for one of her clenched hands and squeezed it gently.

"Julia, I would love to watch you play basketball. Whatever your sister says, or your mother, or even your pastor, there's no shame in what you did—in having sex, in getting pregnant. The shame is the boy who did it lying to you and you not knowing any better. And it would be another shame if you let your baby stop you from getting an education. If you keep lying around the house, feeling angry, you'll ruin your life."

"And who look after María Inés? Ma, she got to work, now she saying if I don't go to school I got to get a job."

"I'll make some calls, Julia, and see what kind of help I can find. In the meantime, I want you to come to our practice on Thursday. Bring María Inés. Bring Sammy and Betto: they can watch María Inés in the gym with us while you work out. Will you do that?"

Her eyes were dark pools in the half-light. She clutched my hand tightly and finally mumbled, "Maybe."

"And before you go out with another boy, you need to learn something about your body, about how you get pregnant, and what you can do to keep from getting pregnant. You and I will talk about that, too. Are you still seeing María Inés's—father?" I stumbled on the word—the person who got her pregnant wasn't acting like a father to the baby.

"Sometimes. Just to say, 'Hi, look, this is your baby.' I don't let him do nothing to me, if that's what you mean. One baby is enough for me."

"He doesn't help support María Inés?"

"He got two more children spread around this neighborhood," she cried. "And he don't have no job. I ast him and ast him, and he never do nothing, now he cross the street if he see me coming."

"So is it this Freddy whom you and Josie were mentioning yesterday?"

She nodded again, her silky hair ruffling the nylon pillowcase.

"Who is he?"

"Just a guy. I met him at church, that's all."

I wondered if Pastor Andrés, with his stern lectures on sex, ever talked to Freddy about scattering children he couldn't support around the South Side, but when I put it into words Julia turned away from me. I realized I wasn't just making her uncomfortable, I was getting pretty far afield from Josie's disappearance.

"So when Billy stayed here on Friday and Saturday night, did he and Josie have sex together?"

"No," she said dully. "He said, her and me should sleep together, he didn't want temptation in their path. He quoted a bunch of Bible verses. It was almost as bad as Pastor Andrés being in the room with me."

I couldn't quite stifle a laugh, but I could picture the little room, heavy with religion and hormones. A suffocating combination. "Do you think your sister ran away with Billy?"

She turned back to look at me. "I don't know for sure, but she left for school, then, an hour later, she came back. She put her toothbrush in her backpack, and a few things, you know, her pajamas, stuff like that. When I asked where she was off to, she said, to see April, but, well, you know, after all these years I know pretty much when Josie is lying to me. And besides, April, she was coming home from the hospital today. Mrs. Czernin, she wouldn't have let Josie come over to the house, not with April so sick."

"Any idea where they'd go, Billy and Josie?"

Julia shook her head. "All I know is, he wouldn't take her to his house, you know, the rich place he lives with his ma and his daddy, 'cause, you know, they don't want him dating no Mexican girl."

I talked to her for a few more minutes, but she'd clearly told me all she knew. I squeezed her hand again, firmly, the dismissal squeeze. "I'll see you Thursday at three o'clock, Julia. Got that?"

She whispered something that might have been assent. When I got up to leave, I saw a shadow move across the baby clothes lining the middle of the room: Rose had been listening in. Maybe just as well. Maybe it was the only way she'd learn a few things about her own daughters.

26   ANNIE, GET YOUR GUN

I pushed the heels of my hands into my eyes. "Supposing Billy and Josie are holed up down here, we might find them by finding his little sports car, assuming it's on the street." I did some arithmetic in my head. "There are probably only forty or forty-five miles of streets to drive up and down; we could do that in four hours, less if we skipped the alleys."

Mr. Contreras and I were in the Mustang, where we'd fled from Rose's overheated emotions. Almost before I'd left the room, she'd begun upbraiding Julia for not telling her own mother what she'd reported to me: "Did I raise you to be a liar?" she'd shouted, before whirling around to demand that I lose no time in finding Josie.

"Where do you suggest I look, Rose?" I'd asked tiredly. "It's midnight. You say she isn't at April's. What other friends would she go to?"

"I don't know, I can't think. Sancia, maybe? Only Sancia, she was really Julia's friend, although she and Josie—"

"I'll check on Sancia," I interrupted, "and on the other girls on the team. What about any relatives? Is she in touch with her father?"

"Her father? That *gamberro*? He hasn't seen her since she was two. I don't even know where he's living right now."

"But what's his name? Children sometimes hide meetings with their fathers so that their mothers won't know."

When she'd protested that idea—Josie would never do something behind her back—I pointed out that Josie had disappeared behind her back. Rose reluctantly disgorged the man's name, Benito Dorrado; the last time she'd seen him, eight months ago, he'd been in an Eldorado with some overpainted *puta*. In the bed behind me, I heard Julia gasp at the word.

"Any other relatives? Do you have any brothers or sisters here in Chicago?"

"My brother is in Joliet. I already called him, but he didn't hear from her. My sister, she lives in Waco. You don't think—"

"Rose, you're distraught, you're spinning both of us around in circles. Is Josie especially close to your sister? Do you think she would suggest to Billy that they drive a thousand miles to see her?"

"I don't know, I don't know, I just want my girl back." She started to cry, the loud racking sobs of a person who doesn't often permit herself to break down.

Mr. Contreras soothed her with much the same language he'd used on the baby. "You give us something that belongs to your girl, some T-shirt or something you haven't washed. Mitch here will smell it, he'll track her down, you'll see."

The little boys were sitting up on their air mattresses, staring at Rose with large, frightened eyes. It was one thing for their sister to disappear, quite another to see their mother falling apart. To calm everyone down, I said I'd see what I could find out tonight. I gave Rose my cell phone number and told her to call me if she heard anything.

Now my neighbor and I were sitting in my car, trying to figure out what to do next. Mitch was on the narrow backseat, with Josie's unwashed basketball shirt between his paws. I've never thought of him as a star tracker, but you never know.

"You should start with the girls on the team," Mr. Contreras suggested.

"An address book would help, a phone book, some damn thing."

I didn't want to go back up to the apartment to ask for a Chicago directory. Finally, even though it was so late, I called Morrell to see if he would look up the addresses for me. He was still up; in fact, he was watching the football game.

"Two-minute warning, Chiefs down by five," I reported to Mr. Contreras, who rubbed his hands gleefully, anticipating the pot that waited for him back at my apartment.

I heard Morrell's uneven step as he limped up the hallway to get his laptop and his phone directories. In a couple of minutes, he'd read out addresses to me of all the girls on the team who had phones, including Celine Jackman, although I couldn't imagine Josie going to April's archenemy on the team. I sketched out a map of the neighborhood and jotted the addresses onto the grid of streets. The addresses covered over a mile going north to south, but didn't range more than four blocks east to west, except for April's father. Benito Dorrado had moved out of South Chicago to the East Side, a relatively stable, marginally more prosperous neighborhood nearby.

It took well over an hour to poke around the streets and alleys near the homes of the girls on my squad. I didn't feel like rousing any of them to ask after Josie: a late-night visit from the coach, looking for an errant player, would only get everyone on the team completely freaked out. With Mitch next to me on a short leash, I peered into the garages we found—most of the girls lived in the bungalows that dominate the neighborhood, and these often had garages in the alleys behind the houses. In one of the garages, we'd surprised a gang meeting, eight or ten young men whose flat-eyed menace made my skin crawl. They'd thought about jumping us, but Mitch's low-throated growl made them back away long enough for us to beat a retreat.

At one-thirty, Rose called to see if we'd found any signs of Josie. When I gave her all my negatives, she sighed, but said she guessed she had to go to bed: she had to continue her job search tomorrow, although as heavy as her heart was lying in her chest she knew she wouldn't make a good impression.

Mr. Contreras and I headed on south, under the legs of the Skyway, to

Benito Dorrado's small frame house on Avenue J. There weren't any lights on in the bungalow, which was scarcely surprising since it was now after two, but I didn't feel the same scruples against rousing him as I did for the girls on my team—he was Josie's father, he could pay attention to some of the dramas of her life. I rang the doorbell urgently for several minutes, and then called him on my cell phone. When the phone had rung tinnily a dozen times or so behind the dark front door, we went around to the back. The single-car garage was empty; neither Benito's Eldorado nor Billy's Miata were anywhere in sight. Either he'd moved or he was spending the night with the overpainted *puta*.

"I think this is where we go home to bed." I yawned so widely my jaw cracked. "I'm seeing spots instead of street signs, which is not a good time to be driving."

"You tired this early, doll?" my neighbor grinned. "You often ain't later than this."

"Not that you pay any attention, right?" I grinned back.

"No way, doll: I know you don't like me poking around in your business."

Usually when I'm out this late, I'm at a club with friends, dancing, exhilarated by music and motion. Sitting in a car, peering anxiously through the windshield, was another story. South Chicago was a hard area to drive in, too: streets dead-end into bits of the old swamp that underlies the city, or into a canal or shipping lane; others bump into the Skyway. I thought I remembered that I could cross west to the expressway at 103rd Street, but I ended up at the Calumet River and had to turn around. On the far side of the river lay the By-Smart warehouse. I wondered if Romeo Czernin was driving for them tonight, if he and Marcena were parked in some schoolyard, making love behind the seats in the cab.

The road was rutted here, and the houses were spaced wide apart. The long stretches in between weren't really vacant: old beds, tires, and rusted-out car frames poked out of heaps of rotting marsh grasses and dead trees. A couple of rats crossed the road in front of me and slid into the ditch on my left; Mitch began whimpering and turning in the narrow backseat—he'd seen them, too and was sure he could catch them if I'd just turn him loose.

I flexed my cramped shoulder muscles and opened my window to get some fresh air on my face. Mr. Contreras tutted in concern and turned on the radio, hoping the noise would keep me alert. I turned north again, on a street that should get me to an access road for the expressway.

The temperature was hovering just above freezing, WBBM reported, and the expressways were all moving freely—clearly, two in the morning was the time to drive in Chicago. Stock markets had opened sluggishly in London and Frankfurt. The Chiefs had rallied after the two-minute warning, but still fell short by eight points.

"So you beat the spread, cookie," Mr. Contreras consoled me. "That means you only owe me seven bucks more, two for the third-quarter score, one for the total number of sacks by New England, one for—"

"Hang on a second." I stood on the brakes.

We were underneath the stilts of the Skyway. The endless detritus of the South Side stretched depressingly on either side of the road. I'd been focusing on the potholes in front of me when some motion caught the corner of my eye. A couple of guys, poking through the debris. They stopped when I stopped and turned to glare at me. The lights from the highway overhead leaked through the joins in the road and glinted on their tire irons. I squinted beyond them, trying to make out what they were hacking at: the smooth, round fender of a new car.

I pulled my gun from my holster and grabbed Mitch's leash. "Stay in the car," I barked at Mr. Contreras. I wrenched the door open and was out and in the road before he could object.

I had Mitch's leash in my left hand, the gun in my right. "Drop your weapons! Hands in the air!"

They yelled obscenities at me, but Mitch was growling, lunging against his collar.

"I can't hold him long," I warned, advancing on them.

Headlights from above dipped and slipped along our bodies. Mitch's teeth gleamed in the gliding lights. The two dropped their tire irons and put their hands above their heads, backing away from me. When they'd moved, I could see the car. A Miata, driven so hard into the pile of boards and bedsprings that only its tail was visible, with the trunk pried open, and the license plate: The Kid 1.

"Where did you find this car?" I demanded.

"Fuck off, 'ho. We got here first." The speaker dropped his hands and started toward me.

I fired the gun, wide enough to make sure I didn't hit them but close enough to make them pay attention. Mitch roared with fear: he'd never heard a gun go off. He barked and jumped, trying to get away from me. I burned my fingers on the hot barrel as I fumbled the safety into place while Mitch snarled and bucked. When I had him somewhat under control, I was sweating and panting, and Mitch was shaking, but the two gangbangers had turned to stone, their hands once more behind their heads.

Mr. Contreras appeared next to me and took the leash. I was trembling myself, and grateful to him, but I didn't say anything, just made sure my voice came out steady when I spoke to the guys.

"The only name you two punks call me is 'ma'am.' Not ''ho,' not 'bitch,' not any nasty word that pops into your disgusting heads and out your mouths. Just 'ma'am.' Now. Which one of you drove this car down here?"

They didn't say anything. I made a great show of releasing the safety on the Smith & Wesson.

"We found it here," one of them said. "What's it to you?"

"What's it to you, *ma'am*," I growled. "What it is to me is that I'm a detective, and this car is involved in a kidnapping. If I find a body, you guys will be lucky not to face a death sentence."

"We found the car here, it was just here." They were almost whining; I felt sickened by my own bullying—give a woman a gun and a big dog and she can do anything a man can do to humiliate other people.

"You can't prove anything, we don't know nothing, we—"

"Keep them covered," I said to Mr. Contreras.

I backed around in a circle to the car, keeping the gun on them. My neighbor held Mitch, who still was still moving uneasily. The trunk, which the pair had pried open, held nothing but a towel and a few books of Billy's—*Rich Christians in an Age of Hunger* and *The Violence of Love.*

The two punks were still holding their hands over their heads. I turned around and shoved my way into the bracken to peer into the car. No Josie, no Billy. The windshield had a spiderweb crack in front of the driver's seat, and the driver's window was smashed. The ragtop was torn. Maybe the damage had occurred when the car plunged headlong into the pile of garbage. Maybe someone had attacked the car with tire irons.

The traffic overhead sent a constant, irregular thwacking down the rusted legs of the Skyway. The lights swooped past but couldn't penetrate the bracken well enough for me to see inside the car. Turning on the little flashlight on my cell phone, I stuck my head and shoulders through the hole in the Miata's canvas top and shone the light around. Glass shards lay on the dashboard and the seat. I could smell whiskey, maybe bourbon or rye. I slowly moved the light around. An open thermos lay on the passenger floor, with a little puddle underneath the lip.

It was a titanium model, a Nissan. Morrell had one like it—I'd bought it for him when he left for Afghanistan. It had cost a fortune, but nothing dented it, even when he'd gotten shot, although the *i* in the logo had chipped away, just as it had on this one.

I backed out of the car and jerked open the driver's door. Dumbly, I picked up the thermos and stuck it in the pocket of my peacoat. How had Morrell's thermos ended up in Billy's car? Maybe Billy had one like it, and the *i* in the *Ti* logo was prone to chipping, not that I could picture Billy or Josie drinking, especially not bourbon.

Morrell had been with me on Saturday when Buffalo Bill thumped in, demanding his grandson, but even if Morrell were the kind of guy who would go looking for Billy without telling me, he wasn't physically up to the job. And he wasn't much of a drinker.

I opened my phone and pressed the speed dial key for Morrell, then shut the cover again: it was past two-thirty. I didn't need to wake him up for something I could ask him in the morning. Anyway, I had the two thugs who'd pried open the trunk. They could answer a few questions.

As if on cue, a commotion erupted behind me: Mr. Contreras

shouted, Mitch barked full throttle, and then I heard gravel spitting as our captives started running. I backed out of the bracken as fast as I could, dropping the two books in my haste. The youths were running headlong up Ewing. Mitch broke free of Mr. Contreras and tore after them.

I screamed at Mitch to come, but he didn't even break his stride. I pelted after him. I heard Mr. Contreras's lumbering tread for a few yards, but the traffic overhead soon swallowed the sound. At 100th Street, the youths turned west, toward the river, Mitch hot on their heels. I'd gone a block before admitting I'd lost them. I stood still, trying to hear where they'd gone, but couldn't make out anything except the thunking of trucks on the Skyway and the lapping of the river somewhere on my left.

I turned back to Ewing. If Mitch caught them, I'd hear the uproar. But I would be in way over my head if I left the main road and tried to thread my way on foot through the dead-end streets and marshy lots that these guys called home.

27 DEATH IN THE SWAMP

Behind me, a set of headlights picked me out like a deer on a country road. I ducked behind a Dumpster. The car stopped. I huddled in the dark for a moment until I realized it was my own car, that Mr. Contreras, with more sense than I possessed right now, had brought it up from where I'd abandoned it.

"Where are you, doll?" The old man had climbed out of the driver's seat and was scanning the empty street. "I seen you a minute ago. Oh—where's Mitch? I'm sorry, he just suddenly jumped and took after them punks. They go down the road there?"

"Yeah. But they could be anywhere by now, including the middle of the swamp."

"I'm so sorry, doll, I see why you don't want me butting in when you're working, can't even hold onto the damn dog." He hung his head.

"Easy, easy." I patted his arm. "Mitch is strong, and he wanted those guys. If I hadn't been playing Annie Oakley back there, maybe Mitch wouldn't have gotten so wound up to begin with. And if I'd taken the car, instead of thinking I could catch two twenty-year-olds on foot—" I bit off the words: second-guessing and guilt-tripping are luxuries a good detective should never indulge in.

My neighbor and I called to the dog for a minute or two, straining to hear him. The Skyway is a diagonal road and was to our left here, close enough that the traffic made it hard to hear other sounds.

"This isn't doing any good," I said abruptly. "We'll drive the area. If we don't see him soon, let's come back in daylight with Peppy—she might nose him out."

Mr. Contreras agreed, at least with the first part of my suggestion. When he'd climbed into the passenger seat, he said, "You go on home, get some shut-eye, and bring Peppy back, but I ain't gonna leave Mitch out here. He never spent the night outside by himself before, and I'm not gonna have him start now."

I didn't try to argue with him—I sort of felt the same way myself. We crawled west on 100th Street, Mr. Contreras with his head out the window, giving an ear-piercing whistle every few yards. As we got close to the river, the ramshackle houses gave way to collapsing warehouses and sheds. The two punks could have sought refuge in any of them. Mitch might be lying there—I clipped the thought off.

We made a painstaking circuit of the four blocks that lie between the Skyway and the river. Only once did we pass another car, a one-eyed bandit missing the right headlight. The driver was a skinny, nervous kid who ducked his head when he saw us.

At the river, I got out of the car. I keep a real flashlight, industrial-strength, in my glove compartment. While Mr. Contreras stood behind me and played the light along the bank, I poked around in the dead marsh grasses.

We were lucky that we were on the far edge of fall, when the ranker vegetation has frozen and dissolved, and the marsh grasses no longer provide cover to a million biting insects. Even so, the ground was a clammy mud that sucked at my shoes; I felt the cold brackish water oozing into them.

I heard slithering and rustling in the underbrush and came to a standstill. "Mitch," I called softly.

The rustling stopped briefly, then started again. A kind of rat came out, followed by a little family, and slid into the river. I moved on.

I passed a man lying in the grasses, so still I thought he might be dead. My skin curling with disgust, I went close enough to hear him breathe, a slow, kerchunky sound. Mr. Contreras followed me with the flashlight, and I saw the telltale needle lying across the open lid of a beer can. I left him to such dreams as remained for him and climbed back up the embankment to the bridge.

We crossed the river in a strained silence and tried to repeat the maneuver on the far side, both of us calling to Mitch. It was after five, with the eastern sky turning that lighter shade of gray that presages the dying year's dawn, when we staggered back to the car and collapsed against the seats.

I pulled out my city maps. The marshland was huge on the West Side; a team of trained searchers, with dogs, could spend a week here without covering half of it. Beyond the expanse of marsh, the network of streets started up again, mile upon mile of abandoned houses and junkyards where a dog might be lying. I didn't really believe our two thugs would have gone west of the river: people stay close to the space they know. These guys had found or hijacked or whatever they'd done to the Miata close to their home base.

"I don't know what we do next," I said dully.

My feet were numb from the cold and damp, my eyelids ached with fatigue. Mr. Contreras is eighty-one; I didn't know how he was staying upright.

"Me neither, cookie, me neither. I just should never've—" He broke off his lamentation before I did. "Do you see that?"

He pointed down the road at a dark shape. "Probably just a deer or something, but put on the headlights, doll, put on the headlights."

I put on the headlights and got out to crouch in the road. "Mitch? Mitch? Come here, boy, come here!"

He was caked in mud, his tongue lolling with exhaustion and thirst. When he saw me, he gave a little "whoof" of relief and started licking my face. Mr. Contreras tumbled out of the car and was hugging the dog, calling him names, telling him how he'd skin him alive if he ever pulled a stunt like that again.

A car came up behind us and blared on its horn. The three of us jumped: we'd had the road to ourselves for so long we'd forgotten it was a thoroughfare. Mitch's thick leather leash was still attached to his collar. I tried to drag him back to the car, but he planted his feet and growled.

"What is it, boy? Huh? You got something in your feet?" I felt his paws, but, although the pads were nicked in places, I couldn't find anything lodged in them.

He stood up and picked up something from the road and dropped it at my feet. He turned to look back down the road, back west, the way he'd come from, picked up the thing and dropped it again.

"He wants us to go thataway," Mr. Contreras said. "He's found something, he wants us to go with him."

I held the thing he'd been dropping under the flashlight. It was some kind of fabric, but so caked in mud, I couldn't tell what it was.

"You want to follow us in the car while I see where he wants to get to?" I said dubiously. Maybe he'd killed one of the punks and wanted me to see the body. Maybe he'd found Josie, drawn by the scent from the T-shirt he'd been lying on, although this rag was too small to be a shirt.

I found a bottle of water in my car and poured some into an empty paper cup I found in the grass. Mitch was so urgent to get me going west that I persuaded him to drink only with difficulty. I finished the bottle myself, and gave him his head. He insisted on carrying his filthy piece of fabric.

More cars were passing us now, people heading for work in the dreary predawn. I took the flashlight in my right hand so oncoming cars could see us. With Mr. Contreras crawling in our wake, we padded along 100th Street, Mitch looking anxiously from me to the ground in front of him. At Torrence, about half a mile along, he got confused for a few minutes, darting up and down the ditch along the road before deciding to head south.

We turned west again at 103rd, passing in front of the giant By-Smart warehouse. The endless stream of trucks was coming and going, and a dense parade of people was walking up the drive from the bus stop. The morning shift must be starting. The sky had lightened during our march; it was morning now.

I was moving like a lead statue, one numb, heavy foot in front of the other. We were close to the expressway and the traffic was thick, but everything seemed remote to me, the cars and trucks, the dead marsh grasses on either side of us, even the dog. Mitch was a phantom, a black wraith I was dumbly following. Cars honked at Mr. Contreras, inching behind us, but even that couldn't rouse me from my stupor.

All at once, Mitch gave a short bark and plunged from the side of the road into the swamp. I was so startled that I lost my balance and fell heavily into the cold mud. I lay there dizzily, not wanting to make the effort to get back up, but Mitch nipped at me until I struggled back to my feet. I didn't try to pick up the leash again.

Mr. Contreras was calling down to me from the road, wanting to know what Mitch was doing.

"I don't know," I croaked up at him.

Mr. Contreras shouted out something else, but I shrugged in incomprehension. Mitch was tugging at my sleeve; I turned to see what he wanted. He barked at me and started to cut across the swamp, away from the road.

"Try to follow us overland," I shouted hoarsely, and waved.

After a minute or two, I couldn't see Mr. Contreras. The dead grasses with their gray beards closed over my head. The city was as remote as if it were only a dream itself; the only thing I could see was the mud, the marsh rats that skittered at our approach, the birds that took off with anxious cries. The leaden sky made it impossible to guess what direction we were going. We might be heading in circles, we might die here, but I was so tired that the thought couldn't rouse me to a sense of urgency.

The dog was exhausted, too, which was the only reason I could keep up with him. He stayed a dozen paces ahead of me, his nose to the ground, lifting it only to make sure I was still with him before nosing ahead again. He was following the tracks a truck had laid down in the mud, new tracks made so recently that the plants still lay on their sides.

I wasn't wearing gloves, and my hands were swollen with cold. I studied them as I stumbled along. They were large purple sausages. It would be so nice to have a fried sausage right now, but I couldn't eat my fingers, that was silly. I jammed them into my coat pocket. My left hand bumped into the metal thermos. I thought dreamily of the bourbon inside it. It belonged to someone else, it belonged to Morrell, but he wouldn't mind if I had a little, just to keep me warm. There was a reason I shouldn't drink it, but I couldn't think what it was. Was the bourbon poisoned? A demon snatched it from Morrell's kitchen. He was a funny, heavyset demon with thick, twitching eyebrows, and he carried the thermos to Billy's car, then stood watching while I found it. A cry under my nose made me jump. I had fallen asleep where I stood, but Mitch's hot breath and anxious whimper brought me back to the present, the marsh, the dull autumn sky, the meaningless quest.

I slapped my chest, my sausage fingers bunched together inside the coat sleeves. Yes, pain was a good stimulant. My fingers throbbed and that was good; they were keeping me awake. I wasn't sure I could fire a gun again, but who was I going to shoot in the middle of the swamp?

The grasses thinned, and rusty cans began replacing marsh rats. A real rat moved across the track in front of me. It looked at Mitch as though daring him to fight, but the dog ignored it. He was whining constantly now, worried, and he stepped up the pace, urging me forward with his heavy head when he thought I was lagging.

I didn't notice when we left the marsh, but suddenly we were picking our way through a dump. Cans, plastic bags, the white lips of six-pack holders, raggedy clothes, car seats, things I didn't want to recognize, all mashed underfoot by the truck whose tracks we were following. I tripped on a tire, but kept slogging forward.

The refuse sort of ended at a barbed-wire fence, but the truck had been driven straight at the fence, and an eight-foot section had come loose. Mitch was sniffing at a fragment of crimson stuck to the barbs, whining and barking at me. I went to inspect it. It was new, new to the area, I mean, because the color was still so fresh. Every other piece of cloth had turned a dirty gray. I tried to feel it, but my swollen fingers were too cracked to tell anything.

"It looks like silk," I said to Mitch. "Josie doesn't wear silk, so what is it, boy?"

He picked his way across the sagging piece of fence, and I went after him. When we were clear of the fence, Mitch started to run. When I didn't keep up with him, he came back to nip me in the calf. Dehydrated, hungry, frozen, I ran with him across a paved road, up a steep hill, onto a plateau covered in dead grass that was springy and flat underfoot. Maybe I had fallen asleep again, because it was too much like a fairy tale, where you go through the demon-filled woods and come to a magical castle— at least, the grounds to the magical castle.

I had a stitch in my side and black spots dancing in front of my eyes, which I kept confusing with Mitch. Only his hoarse bark kept me going in the right direction, or, at least, the direction he was headed. I was floating now, the turf a yard or more below my feet. I could fly, it was the magic of the fairy castle, one mud-heavy foot leaving the ground, the other leaping behind it, I only had to move my arms a little, and I catapulted headfirst down the hill, rolling over and over until I was almost lying in a lake.

A giant hound appeared, the familiar of the witch whose castle I'd invaded. He grabbed my coat sleeve and tried to pull me along the ground, but he couldn't move me. He bit my arm and I sat up.

Mitch. Yes, my dog. Leading me on a mission impossible, a mission to nowhere. He bit me again, hard enough to break through my peacoat. I shrieked and pushed myself upright again.

"Jeesh, you a marine sergeant or what?" I croaked at him.

He looked at me balefully: I was the sorriest excuse for a recruit he'd seen in all his years in the corps. He trotted along the edge of the water, stopping briefly for a drink. We went around a bend, and I saw in the distance a small fleet of blue trucks and, in front of me, brown mountains of garbage. The city dump. We were at the city dump? This hound led me through hell to get to the world's biggest supply of garbage?

"When I find someone to drive me home, you are—" I broke off my hoarse and useless threat. Mitch had disappeared over the side of a pit. I walked cautiously to the edge. It had been dug out and abandoned: dead, scrubby weeds were starting to grow along the sides.

Two bodies lay at the bottom. I scrambled down the rocky clay, my exhaustion forgotten. Both bodies had been badly beaten, so beaten they were black and purple, with pieces of skin flayed off. One seemed to be a man, but it was the woman Mitch was pawing at anxiously. She had a mass of tawny hair around her swollen, battered face. I knew that hair, I knew that black leather coat. And the crimson fragment on the fence, that had been her scarf. I'd watched Marcena Love tie that scarf up any number of times. My good-luck scarf, she called it, I always wear it in battle zones.

The man—I looked and looked away. Not Morrell, how could it be? The black spots in front of my eyes grew and danced, blotting out the gray sky and the mangled bodies. My gorge rose and my empty stomach heaved. I turned away and vomited up a trickle of bile.

IT'S A BIRD,
IT'S A PLANE,
NO, IT'S . . .

I pulled myself together by force of will. I desperately needed water; my legs were trembling as much from dehydration as from shock and exhaustion. I was tempted again by the bourbon in my pocket, but if I drank whiskey now, on my empty, dried-out stomach, I'd just get sick.

I crouched next to the bodies. The man was taller and broader than my lover, or than Billy.

Think, Warshawski, save the melodrama for the daytime soaps. Romeo, I supposed. Romeo Czernin. He looked very dead to me, but I tried to find a pulse in the purply pulp that had been his neck. I couldn't feel any movement, but my own fingers were so numb I might be missing it. His skin was still warm; if he was dead, it hadn't been for long.

Mitch was anxiously licking Marcena's face. When I dragged him aside to put a hand against her neck, I did feel a faint, erratic beat. I pulled out my cell phone, but using it as a flashlight must have drained the battery—it was completely dead.

I struggled to my feet. The garbage trucks might be a half mile away, a long trek across this terrain, but I didn't know anyplace closer to go for help—I certainly couldn't make it back the way we'd come in the hopes Mr. Contreras was still there with the car.

"Will you stay with her, old boy?" I said to Mitch. "Maybe if you lie against her, keep her warm, she'll live."

I gave him a hand signal, the command to lie down and then to stay. He whimpered and looked at me uncertainly, but settled down again next to Marcena. I was starting to hoist myself up the side of the pit when I heard a phone ring. It was so unexpected that I thought I was hallucinating again, phones in the middle of nowhere, fried eggs might fall at my feet in a second or two.

"Marcena's cell phone!" I laughed a little hysterically and turned back to her.

The ringing was coming from Romeo's body, not Marcena's. It stopped, message going to voice mail, I guess. I stuck a squeamish hand into his coat pockets and came up with a bunch of keys, a pack of cigarettes, and a fistful of lottery tickets. The phone started ringing again. His jeans pockets. His jeans were torn and plastered to his body by his drying blood. I could hardly bear to touch them, but I held my breath and stuck a hand into the left front pocket to extract the phone.

"Billy?" A sharp male voice spoke.

"No. Who are you? We need help, we need an ambulance."

"Who is this?" The voice was even sharper.

"V. I. Warshawski," I croaked. "Who are you? I need you to call for help."

I tried to describe where I was: close to the CID landfill, close to water, probably Lake Calumet, but the man hung up on me. I called 911 and gave the dispatcher my name and the same vague description of my location. She said she'd do her best to get someone to me, but she didn't know how long it would take.

"The man is dead, I think, but the woman is still breathing. Please hurry." My voice was such a hoarse thread by now that I couldn't sound urgent or pathetic; it was all I could do to get the words out.

When I'd hung up, I took off my coat and laid it across Marcena's head. I didn't want to move her, or even try CPR. I didn't know how bad her internal injuries might be, and I could kill her by pushing broken ribs into her lungs, or something equally horrible. But I felt a stubborn conviction that her head should be warm; we lose most of our body heat through our heads. My own head was cold. I pulled my sweatshirt up over my ears and sat rocking myself.

I had forgotten about Mr. Contreras. I'd abandoned him back on 100th Street two hours ago. He could be resourceful; maybe he'd find me, find us. And Morrell—I should have thought of him sooner.

When he answered the phone, I astonished myself by starting to cry. "I'm out in the middle of nowhere with Marcena, she's almost dead," I choked out.

"Vic, is that you? I can't understand a word you're saying. Where are you? What's going on?"

"Marcena. Mitch found her, he dragged me through the swamp, I can't explain it right now. She's almost dead, and Romeo is lying next to her, he is dead, and if someone doesn't get here soon she will be, and maybe I will be, too. I'm so thirsty and cold I can hardly stand it. You've got to find me, Morrell."

"What happened? How did you end up with Marcena? Were you attacked? Are you all right?"

"I can't explain it, it's too complicated. She's not going to make it if we don't get an ambulance." I repeated what little information I could give on our location.

"I'll climb up to the top of this pit thing where they're lying so someone can spot me, but I don't think there's a road very close to here."

"I'll do my best for you, darling. Hang on, I'll figure out something."

"Oh—I forgot. Mr. Contreras. He dropped us off, and now he's probably half crazy with worry."

I tried to remember my plate number, but I couldn't. Morrell repeated that he'd do his best for me, and hung up.

Mitch was lying next to Marcena, his own eyes glazed with exhaustion. He had stopped licking her, was just lying with his head on her chest. When I started up the side of the pit again, he lifted his head to look at me but didn't try to get up.

"I don't blame you, boy. You stay put. Keep her warm."

It was only an eight-foot climb to the top. I dug my fingers in the cold clay and pushed myself up the side. In my normal state, I could have run up, but now it seemed just about insurmountable. This isn't Everest, I thought grimly, you don't have to be Junko Tabel. Or maybe I did: I'd be the first woman to climb not Everest, but a pit near Lake Calumet. The National Geographic Society would wine and dine me. I got my hands over the lip of the pit and pulled myself onto the springy turf. When I looked back down, Mitch had stood up, and was walking nervously between Marcena and the side I'd just climbed.

I gave him another hand gesture to lie down. He didn't obey me, but when he saw I wasn't moving out of his range of vision he returned to Marcena and curled up next to her.

I stood with my hands in my jeans pockets for a bit, watching the army of blue trucks crawling around the landfill. It was funny that I could hear the engines: the trucks looked so far away. Maybe I was close enough to walk to them, really. Maybe I only thought they were far off because I'd lost my sense of time and space. When people fast for a long time, they start seeing visions. They think angels are coming down from the heavens to them, just like I did now, I could see it dropping from the clouds, a giant shape that was coming toward me, with a horrible racket that blocked out every thought I'd ever had.

I put my hands over my ears. I was losing my mind—this wasn't an angel, it was a helicopter. Someone had taken my SOS seriously. I stumbled toward the machine as a stranger in a leather bomber jacket jumped down, ducking to get clear of the blades.

"What's going on here?" he demanded when he'd run across the turf to me.

"They're down there." I pointed into the pit. "Get your stretcher crew out; I don't know what kind of injuries the woman has."

"I can't hear you," the man said irritably. "Where the hell is Billy?"

"Billy?" I croaked, putting my lips close to his ear. "You mean Billy the Kid? I haven't seen him since church on Sunday. This is Marcena Love. And I think Romeo—Bron Czernin. They need to get to a hospital. Don't you have a stretcher on that thing?"

The words came out agonizingly slowly. The man recoiled as my fetid breath hit him. He belonged to a different species than me: he was alert, he'd breakfasted, I could smell coffee on his breath, and a heavy dollop of aftershave on his skin. He'd had a shower, he'd shaved. I probably smelled like the landfill itself, since I'd spent most of the night walking through the garbage-laden swamp.

"I'm looking for Billy Bysen. I don't know anything about these people. How come you answered his phone?"

"It was in the dead man's pocket."

I turned away from him and stumbled over to the helicopter, remembering only at the last second to stoop under the blade. The motion sent me sprawling, and the clean-shaven man dragged me to my feet, yelling at me to tell him where Billy was. He was getting really annoying, like the boys on the playground chanting "Iffy-genius" at me, and I wanted to take out my Smith & Wesson and shoot him, but that would really get my father mad. "You can't go around telling your schoolmates I'm a cop and I'll arrest them," he'd said. "You can't go trading on my badge. You solve your problems without using a club on people. That's the only way good cops and honest men and women act, you hear me, Pepperpot?"

I twisted out of the shaved man's grip and flung myself into the helicopter's open door. The pilot looked at me without interest and turned back to his instruments. I didn't think I could climb into the helicopter on my own, and I couldn't make myself heard above the racket of the rotors. I clung desperately to the struts while the clean-shaven man grabbed my sore shoulder and tried to pry me loose.

Suddenly, the racket of the engines stopped. The pilot was taking off his headset and getting out of his seat. The world around me was filled with flashing reds and blues. I looked around and blinked at the array of cop cars and ambulances.

The man let go of my shoulder as a familiar voice spoke behind me. "That you, Ms. W.? I thought I told you to stay the hell out of South Chicago. What you been doing down here? Bathing in the landfill?"

29

ON THE DL— ONCE AGAIN

It was only later, after the IVs were pulled out of my arms and County Hospital pronounced me rehydrated and fit to leave, that I was able to make sense of the confusing swarm of cops and stretchers that descended on us, and later still that I found out where the helicopter had come from.

At the moment, though, I didn't try to understand anything—just gave a little squawk of relief at seeing Conrad. I tried to tell him what was happening, but no sound came from my swollen, parched throat. I waved a shaky arm toward the pit. While I collapsed against the chopper's doorway, Conrad walked over to the rim and peered down. When he saw Marcena and Romeo, he sprinted back to the ambulances and summoned a couple of stretcher crews.

I dozed off, but Conrad shook me awake. "You have to get your dog. He won't let the techs take the woman, and we don't want to have to shoot him."

Mitch had been protecting Marcena all night, and he was prepared to bite anyone who tried to move her. I stumbled back down to the bottom, sliding the final four feet on my ass. That was the journey that completely finished me. I did make it to Mitch's side, and I did get a hand on his collar, but the rest of the morning disappeared into a few fragments— Conrad hoisting me over his shoulder and handing me to a couple of uniformed men to carry to the surface—the struggle to keep a grip on Mitch's leash all the time I was dropping down the well of sleep—waking again to hear the clean-shaven man shouting at Conrad about the chopper.

"You can't barge in here and take private property. This helicopter belongs to Scarface."

That couldn't be right, not to Al Capone. I couldn't figure it out, though, and gave up trying, just watched Conrad signal to some uniformed men to hold the guy while the stretchers were loaded. What a good idea; I wished I'd thought of it. I drifted again and lost hold of Mitch, who clambered into the chopper after Marcena.

"Better take her, too." Conrad said to the ambulance crew, pointing at me. "She can take care of the dog, and, besides, she needs a doctor."

He patted my shoulder. "We're going to talk, Ms. W., we're going to talk about how you knew to come to this place, but it'll keep a few hours."

And then the rotors started up, and despite the racket and the lurching, which made Mitch tremble and burrow into my side, I fell asleep again. I woke only when the techs carried me out of the helicopter into the emergency room, but the hospital didn't want Mitch inside. I couldn't leave him. I couldn't talk. I sat on the floor next to him with my arms around his blood-stiffened fur. A security guard was trying to reason with me, and then to shout at me, but I couldn't respond, and then somehow Mr. Contreras was there with Morrell and I was on a gurney, and asleep for good.

When I finally woke up, it was late evening. I blinked sleepily at the hospital room, not remembering how I'd gotten here but feeling too lazy to worry about it. I had that sense of pleasure in my body that comes when a fever breaks. I wasn't sore any more, or thirsty, and while I slept someone had washed me. I was wearing a hospital gown, and I smelled of Jergens.

After a while, a nurse's aid came in. "So you're awake. How you doing?"

She took my blood pressure and temperature, and told me, when I asked, that I was at Cook County Hospital. "You been asleep twelve hours, girl: I don't know what war you were fighting in, but you definitely were going down for the count. Now you drink some juice; the orders are, fluids, fluids, fluids."

I obediently drank the glass of apple juice she held out to me, and then a glass of water. While she bustled about the room, I slowly remembered what had brought me here. I tried out my voice. I could speak again, albeit still rather hoarsely, so I asked after Marcena.

"I don't know, honey, I don't know about anyone you came in with. If she was hurt bad, like you're saying, she'd be in a different unit, you see. You ask the doc when he comes along."

I slept for the rest of the night, although not as soundly as before. Now that the hardest edge was off my exhaustion, I couldn't block out the hospital noise—or the parade of people who came to check on me. Leading the band, naturally, was someone from admissions who wanted my insurance information. My wallet had been in my jeans pocket; when I asked for my clothes, someone dug a nasty bundle out of the locker. By an act of mercy, my wallet was still there, with my credit cards and my insurance card.

When they woke me again for rounds at six Wednesday morning, Morrell was sitting next to me. He gave me a crooked smile.

The team of doctors pronounced me combat ready, or at least fit enough to get up and go. They asked about the hole in my shoulder, which had leaked a little from my travails but was basically healing, wrote up my discharge papers, and, finally, left me alone with my lover.

Morrell said, "So, Hippolyte, Queen of the Amazons. You survived another battle."

"I guess they haven't sent Hercules to fight me yet. How long have you been here?"

"About half an hour. They told me when I called last night they were going to discharge you in the morning, and I figured you might want a change of underwear."

"You're almost as good as a girl, Morrell, figuring that out. You can join my horde of wild women, you can set us an example of breastless-ness."

He leaned over to kiss me. "That's a myth, you know, that they cut off their breasts. And I especially like yours, so don't do anything rash. Although that's the most futile statement ever made, considering the way you've been treating your body the last ten days."

"Spoken by the man who still has a bullet chip near his spine."

He handed me a carry-on bag, packed with his usual precision: tooth-brush, hairbrush, bra, clean jeans, and a cotton sweater. The bra was my favorite rose-and-silver lace, which I'd left at his place several weeks ago, but the clothes were his. We're the same height, and the clothes were a pretty good fit—although I'd never have gotten the jeans buttoned if I hadn't been fasting for thirty-six hours.

We took a cab to my apartment, where Mr. Contreras and the dogs greeted me as a sailor returned from a shipwreck. My neighbor had bathed Mitch and taken him to the vet, who'd put stitches in one of his feet where he'd sliced it on a can or the barbed wire. After his initial ec-stasy, Mitch went back inside my neighbor's apartment and climbed up on the couch to sleep. Mr. Contreras didn't want to leave him, so we set-tled in the old man's kitchen. Mr. Contreras began making pancakes, and we exchanged war stories.

When he'd seen Mitch lead me into the swamp, Mr. Contreras had tried to follow us in the car, but the road went too far to the west of where we were walking, and, anyway, after a couple of minutes he couldn't see us at all through the marsh grasses. He'd gone back to the place where Mitch started into the swamp, but after half an hour a state trooper came along and ordered him to leave.

"I tried to tell the guy you was lost in there, and he says, tell the local cops, not him, it's Chicago's responsibility, so I beg him to call the Chicago cops, and he won't, only tells me he'll impound the car if I don't move it, so I had to go home." The old man's voice was still thick with grievance. "When I got home, I called 911, and they told me to wait until morning, and, if I hadn't heard from you, to file a missing persons.

I should have called Captain Mallory, I guess, didn't think of that, but, anyway, by and by I heard from Morrell here, he told me about Mitch leading you all the way to that Miss Love."

"I don't understand that part," I said. "Not that I understand anything right now, but—whoever attacked Marcena and Romeo must have done it around 100th and the river, because that's where Mitch disappeared. He was following the two thugs who attacked Billy's car, and then, all I can figure is, he somehow caught Marcena's scent and went after her. Has Conrad been looking by the river?"

Morrell shook his head. "I haven't talked to him since we parted company at the hospital yesterday."

"How did you and Conrad hook up, anyway?" I demanded.

"I called him after you phoned me from your pit—do you know where you were, by the way? The edge of the Harborside Golf Course, where it peters out into a no-man's-land leading down to the garbage dump. Anyway, South Chicago is Rawlings's turf; I thought he was the fastest route to finding you and getting Marcena to a hospital."

I hesitated over the question, but finally asked how Marcena was doing.

"Not good, but still on planet Earth." He must have seen the tiny sigh of relief I gave, because he added, "Yes, you're a jealous street-fighting pit dog, but you're not mean-spirited. She wasn't conscious when she got to the hospital, but they put her into a medical coma, anyway, to make sure she didn't wake up. She lost skin over about a quarter of her body, and is going to need massive grafts. If she were alert enough to answer questions, she'd be in so much pain the shock would probably kill her."

We sat in silence for a time. To Mr. Contreras's consternation, I could only manage one pancake after my fast, but I ate it with about a quart of honey and started to feel better.

After a bit, Morrell picked up his part of the story again. "When Rawlings called to tell me they'd found you, I phoned Contreras, here, and got a cab to pick him up on the way to the hospital—which was a mercy, let me tell you, Queen of the Amazons, because your guard dog wasn't going to leave your side."

"Really?" I brightened. "Yesterday, he attached himself so thoroughly to Marcena I thought he didn't love me anymore."

"Maybe he just figured you were his last tie to her." Morrell wiggled his eyebrows provocatively. "Be that as it may, if Contreras hadn't shown up you'd probably be in County Jail right now, not County Hospital, and the dog would be dead. But it all worked out. Contreras here persuaded the Hound of the Baskervilles to let go of the security guard's leg, I saw you into the emergency room, we waited until the charge nurse said you just needed rest and rehydration, and then Rawlings arrived, wondering if he could get a statement from you about Marcena. When he saw that was no go, we found a cabbie who'd take Mitch; Contreras set off with him. Rawlings left to do police stuff, but I went across the street to the morgue and talked to Vish; he was doing the autopsy on Bron Czernin."

Nick Vishnikov was the deputy chief medical examiner at the Cook County Morgue, and an old friend of Morrell's—he did a fair amount of forensic pathology for Humane Medicine, the group that had sent Morrell to Afghanistan. Because of that, he'd given Morrell a number of details he would probably have kept from me if I'd asked.

"They were beaten so badly." I shivered at the memory of that flayed and mottled flesh. "What happened to them?"

Morrell shook his head. "Vish can't figure it out. It's true they were beaten, but he doesn't think with something conventional, like clubs or whips. He says oil was embedded in Czernin's skin. He was hit hard on the head, hard enough to break his spine, but it didn't kill him, at least not right away. He died from asphyxiation, not from spinal injuries. But what has Vish really baffled is that the injuries are uniform across both their bodies. Except for Czernin's broken neck, obviously. Whatever brutal hit he took, Marcena managed to avoid, which is hopeful for her ultimate recovery."

The two men tried to think of things that would cause that kind of injury. Morrell wondered about rollers from a steel mill, but Mr. Contreras objected that those would have crushed the bodies. In his turn, the old man suggested that they'd been dragged along the road from the back of a truck. Morrell thought that sounded plausible and phoned Vishnikov to propose it, but apparently dragging would have left burn marks and distended tendons in the arms or legs.

The images were too graphic for me: I'd seen the bodies, I couldn't deal with them right now as an academic exercise. I abruptly announced I was going upstairs. When I got to my own place, I decided to wash my hair, which the hospital had left alone when they hosed me off. I figured my back had healed enough that I could stand under a shower.

When I was clean, and had my own jeans on, I checked my messages. It was getting hard to remember that I run a business, that life wasn't all coaching basketball and hiking across swamps.

I had the predictable queries from Murray Ryerson at the *Herald-Star* and Beth Blacksin, a television reporter with Global Entertainment. I told them what I knew, which wasn't much, and checked in with clients who were waiting for reports—with ever-decreasing patience.

I had a message from Sanford Rieff, the forensic engineer I'd sent the frog dish to. He had a preliminary report for me that he was faxing to my office. I tried to call him, but got only his voice mail; I'd have to wait until I got to my office and my fax machine to see what he'd found.

Rose Dorrado had phoned, twice, to see if Josie had been in the pit with Bron and Marcena. Julia answered the phone when I called: her ma was out job hunting. No, they hadn't heard anything from Josie.

"I heard how April's dad got killed. You don't think they'll kill Josie, do you?"

"Who, Julia?" I asked gently. "Do you know anything about how Bron got killed?"

"Someone told Ma they found Billy's car all wrecked, and I thought, since him and Josie disappeared the same night Mr. Czernin got killed, some gangbanger could be out there just knocking people off and the police, like they ever care about us, they'll never find them."

Her voice held genuine terror. I did my best to reassure her without offering her cold comfort—I couldn't promise Josie wasn't dead, but it seemed hopeful to me that no one had seen her. If she had been assaulted, and by the same people who went after Marcena and Bron, all their bodies would have been found together.

"I'm going to see you tomorrow at practice, right, Julia?"

"Uh, I guess so, coach."

"And tell your ma I'm coming over after practice to talk to her. I'll give you and María Inés a lift home, just this once."

When I'd hung up, I sat down with a large pad of newsprint and a Magic Marker to write down everything I knew, or thought I knew, about what had been happening in South Chicago.

A lot of lines ran through Rose Dorrado and Billy the Kid. Rose had taken a second job, which upset Josie; the night the plant blew up, the Kid had come to stay at the Dorrados, running away from his family. Because they objected to Josie? Because of something they were doing themselves? Then there was Billy's car, but it had Morrell's flask in it. Somehow, Billy had gotten involved with Bron or Marcena, or both. And Bron had had Billy's phone in his pocket.

I remembered Josie telling me that Billy had given his phone to someone. To Bron? But why? And then had he given the Miata to Bron so that detectives couldn't find him through his car? Had Bron been killed by someone who mistook him for Billy? Had Billy really been running away from danger, danger whose seriousness he was too naive to recognize?

The cell phone. What had I done with it. I had a vague memory of the clean-shaven man from Scarface demanding it from me, but I couldn't remember whether he'd gotten it.

I'd dropped my dirty clothes just inside my door. Billy's cell phone was still in the jacket pocket. As was Morrell's thermos, or the thermos that looked like his. I'd handled it so much by now that I doubted it had much forensic value, but I still put it in a plastic bag, and went back down the stairs on slow, stiff legs. It used to be that I could have gone running after twenty-four hours of rest, but these legs were not going running any time soon that I could imagine.

30 COMRADES IN ARMS

When I returned to Mr. Contreras's kitchen, I found Conrad had arrived. He was sitting next to Morrell at the chipped enamel table while Mr. Contreras finished flipping a stack of fresh flapjacks for him.

"How good and pleasant it is when brothers dwell together in unity," I said.

Conrad grinned at me, his gold tooth glinting. "Don't think of this as a macho meeting, Ms. W.; you are definitely the star attraction. Tell me, what led you to that pit yesterday?"

"The dog," I said promptly, adding, as the good nature faded from his face, "no, really: ask Mr. Contreras."

I explained what had happened, from Rose Dorrado's call to finding Billy's Miata under the Skyway, and Mitch's reappearance west of the river on 100th Street. "Billy knows April Czernin because he knows Josie. And he knows—knew—Bron because Bron drove for the Bysen warehouse on 103rd and Billy knew all the truckers. So I'm wondering if Billy gave Bron his phone, and then his car."

Conrad nodded. "It could be. Ms. Czernin—she's one tormented, twisted-up lady. Her girl is sick, I understand, and now she doesn't know which end is up. I didn't ask her about the phone, because I didn't know about it, but she might not have, either: by what she was saying, he didn't tell her much."

He took out his cell phone and called down to his charge sergeant to send someone over to the underpass for whatever might be left of the Miata. "And get a really good tracking team to scour the area between Ewing and the river at 100th Street. A PI's dog picked up the Love woman's scent down there someplace: it may be where they were attacked."

When he'd hung up, I produced the thermos. "This was in the front seat, spilling out bourbon."

"You took that?" Conrad was annoyed. "What the hell you think you're doing, removing evidence from a crime scene?"

"It looked like the thermos I gave Morrell," I said. "I didn't want the bottom-feeders who were taking the car apart to walk off with it."

Morrell limped over to look at it. "I think it is mine; that's where the *i* came off when I was shot at. I told Marcena she could borrow it while she was doing her late-night jaunts—I assumed, somehow, for coffee, not bourbon. Are you impounding it, Rawlings? I want it back."

"Then you shouldn't have let her take it to begin with," I said, and then I remembered her lying in a coma, a quarter of her skin missing, and felt immediately ashamed.

"We've been in so many war zones together," Morrell said. "She's my comrade-in-arms; you share your stuff with your comrades, Vic. Like it or lump it."

Conrad looked at me, as if daring me to push one more relationship to the limit. I shook my head and changed the subject, asking who the guy at the helicopter had been.

"Colleague of yours, broadly speaking," Conrad said.

My forehead wrinkled while I figured it out. "A private eye, you mean?"

"Yep, with Carnifice Security. That was their chopper."

Not Scarface. Carnifice. The biggest player in the international private security business. They do everything, from kidnap protection in Colombia and Iraq to running private prisons, which is where I first met them—I almost died in their custody a couple of years back.

According to Conrad, someone in the Bysen operation had figured out the same thing I'd told Billy last week—that his cell phone contained a global tracking signal. "The kid's father got fed up with old Mr. Bysen butting in, going down to that church, whatever it was he did. So the father decided to hire Carnifice to use their tracking equipment to find his kid's phone, which they traced to the pit. When the gumshoe didn't find Billy, he wanted to take off again—they hadn't been hired to save extraneous lives."

"Thank you, Conrad," I said awkwardly. "Thank you for showing up, and saving my life, and saving Marcena, too."

He gave a twisted smile. "We serve and protect, Ms. W., even the undeserving."

He took out a tape recorder. "Now, the part I need on the record. What was the Love woman doing down on my turf?"

Morrell and I exchanged uneasy glances, but Morrell said, "She was working on a series for an English newspaper. She met Czernin when he came to pick his daughter up from basketball practice. I don't know what she was doing specifically—she said he was showing her the neighborhood, things behind the scenes she wouldn't have had access to without him."

"Such as what?" Conrad demanded.

"I don't know. She only talked in generalities, about the poverty and housing problems she was learning about."

"She's staying with you, right, Morrell? How often was she meeting Czernin?"

"She made a lot of contacts in Chicago—including you, Rawlings—she said you were going to take her on a ride-along this week. She would take off for a day, sometimes more, and I never knew if it was with Czernin or you or some of the other people she was meeting. I didn't make her sign in and out when she came and went," Morrell added with bleak humor.

"Did she tell you more?" Conrad turned to me. "You spend a lot of time in that apartment, right?"

I smiled. "That's right, commander, but Marcena didn't confide in me. She did say that Bron let her drive his semi the first night they met, and that she almost took out a shed or something in the school parking lot, but I can't remember her talking about him more specifically."

"Ms. Czernin said the Love woman was screwing her husband," Conrad said.

Mr. Contreras made a noise at the vulgarity, which wasn't typical of Conrad—I figured he was trying to get Morrell off balance, to see what indiscretion he might blurt out.

Morrell gave a tight smile. "Marcena didn't confide her private business to me."

"Or to you, Warshawski?" Conrad said. "No? One of the girls on your team said that everyone in the school knew about it."

My face grew hot. "Why are you harassing my team, Conrad? Do you imagine one of them killed Bron Czernin? Do I need to make sure my girls have a lawyer?"

"We're talking to everyone who knew the guy down there. He had a way about him around that neighborhood—a lot of men might have had a reason to kill him over the years."

"Why would the men of South Chicago go for him now if he and Marcena were an item? I'd think they'd be glad he was finding more distant pastures to roam in—except maybe Sandra, and I don't see how she could have beaten up both her husband and Marcena and dragged them to that pit."

"She could have had help." Conrad tipped his head toward Morrell, who looked at him in bewilderment.

"Am I supposed to have been jealous of Czernin?" Morrell said. "Marcena and I are old friends, which is why I'm putting her up, but we're not lovers. She has wide-ranging and eclectic tastes. When we were in Afghanistan last winter, she got involved with one of the orderlies at Humane Medicine, a Pakistani army major, and someone from the Slovenian wire services, and those were the three I knew about. Believe me, if I were a jealous lover who wanted her dead I would have done it up in the Pathan hills where no one would have cared."

Conrad grunted: maybe he believed it, maybe he didn't. "What about her work? What was she writing?"

Morrell shook his head. "The series was on the America Europe doesn't know. After she met Czernin, she decided to focus on South Chicago. She spent time out at By-Smart headquarters—old Mr. Bysen seemed to like her, and she had a couple of private meetings with him. That's all I can tell you: she played her cards close to her chest."

"Not that close, if you knew about her Pakistani major and the orderly and so on," Conrad said. "I want to see her notes."

"You think the attack had to do with the story she was working on? Not someone who was out to get Bron and hit her because she was there?"

"I don't have a theory," Conrad grumbled. "I only have a woman whose daddy is in the British Foreign Office, so the consul has called the super five times and he's called me ten times. Czernin gave horns to any number of guys in South Chicago, and we're looking at that. I don't think it was a routine gangbanging, because whatever happened to them took a lot of work, and even though my punks in South Chicago have way too much time on their hands they don't go in for elaborate murder. So I'm looking at people Czernin pissed off, and I'm looking at what Love was working on. I can get a warrant to search your place, Morrell, easy, because the mayor is yanking the super's chain and the super is yanking mine—any judge will be happy to oblige. But it would be real, real nice if you'd save me the trouble."

Morrell studied him thoughtfully. "Police departments are walking off with people's files these days under cover of the Patriot Act. I don't want to invite police into my home so that they can take my machine or someone else's."

"So you want me to waste time on a warrant."

"I don't think legal protections are a waste of time, Rawlings. But I won't ask you to go to a judge if you'll come with me yourself, and go through Marcena's computer with me file by file. If she has personal material on it, we'll leave it lay. If she has notes that may suggest a perpetrator, you'll copy them and take them with you."

Conrad didn't like it. He is a cop, after all, and cops don't like civilian oversight of their work. But he's a fundamentally decent guy who doesn't want to harass citizens for the pleasure of it.

"I'm a watch commander. I can't take that kind of time, but I can give you a good detective and a uniformed officer. With orders not to take anything you haven't seen."

"With orders to take copies, not originals," Morrell said.

"With orders to take anything that looks relevant to the work the Love woman was doing in South Chicago."

"As long as it's a copy, and her machine isn't impounded."

"This is like watching Lee Van Cleef and Clint Eastwood," I complained. "The standoff could go on all afternoon. I've got to get to my office, so I'm going to leave you two to sort it out; Mr. Contreras will be Eli Wallach. He'll let me know which one of you gets the gold."

Conrad gave a grunting little laugh. "Okay, Ms. W., okay. I'll let your boyfriend monitor the files, but I get to choose what I copy. Or my detective does. Her name is Kathryn Lyndes; she'll be at your home in ninety minutes."

The mayor was riding hard on this case, if Conrad could guarantee a detective running all the way from South Chicago to Evanston at a moment's notice.

"Marcena's father must be something pretty important if the consul is making the mayor care about a South Chicago mugging. Do you think you could spare a resource for someone who isn't connected? I told you I was looking for Josie Dorrado when I found Marcena and Bron. She still hasn't turned up, and I'm out of ideas."

"Tell the mother to go down to the precinct and file a missing persons report."

"And someone will jump right on it and start scouring the abandoned buildings and vacant lots?" I was scornful.

"Don't ride me, Ms. W. You know what resources I have, and how tight I'm stretched."

"Last week, you told me to butt out of South Chicago. This week, you don't have the resources to look after the neighborhood."

"Whenever you and I start to get along, you decide to open a machine gun on me," Conrad said. "If I put you down last week over that fire, can you blame me?"

I took a breath: a who-said-what fight was a losing battle for everyone. "Okay, Conrad, this isn't an attempt to put a machine gun on you, but have you found out anything about the fire? Who set it, or even why they were after Frank Zamar?"

"Nope. We don't even know if Zamar set it and couldn't get out of the building on time, although I don't believe it. If the place had burned down last summer, when his business was slumping, it'd be a different story—he'd done a ton of business with By-Smart when everyone had to have an American flag; he'd even added an owl shift, and taken on a debt load with some fancy new cutting machines. Then that contract stopped abruptly and he had to shut down the owl shift. But not long before the fire, he'd signed a new contract with By-Smart to do a line of flag sheets and towels."

Sleep at night on Old Glory and in the morning dry your bottom with the flag. In its way, it seemed as outrageous as burning, but what did I know? Was that the second job Rose had taken? Running the towel factory for Zamar? Why was she so defensive and secretive about it—it seemed perfectly legitimate.

I shook my head, unable to figure it out, and said to Conrad, "Just so you know, the Carnifice guy looking for Billy the Kid, he does have a lot of resources. I think Josie Dorrado is with Billy. The Bysen family has cast her in the role of blackmailing wetback trying to squeeze money out of Billy. I'd hate for her to get hurt."

"I'll keep that in mind, Ms. W., I'll keep that in mind." Conrad spoke heavily, but he did scrawl something in his pocket notebook. I'd have to be content with that.

Morrell limped out of Mr. Contreras's apartment with me. "I'm going to catch a cab home right now so I can look at some things before Rawlings's detective arrives. You going to be okay?"

I nodded. "Desk work is all I'm good for today. Are Marcena's parents flying in?"

"The Foreign Office is trying to find them—they're inveterate trekkers, and right now they're in a remote part of India." He smoothed the hair out of my eyes and kissed me. "We had a dinner date last night, darling, but you stood me up. Should I trust you with a second chance?"

Conrad came out at that moment, and, against my will, I felt my cheeks grow hot.

 ## THE WALKING
WOUNDED

My office had a forlorn, abandoned feeling to it, as if no one had been inside it for months. My footsteps echoed off the floor and seemed to bounce around the walls and ceilings. Although I'd stopped by two days ago, I wasn't really working here these days—I was just dropping in between treks through swamps.

My lease partner, Tessa, who's a sculptor, was vacationing in Australia. I dropped her mail on her drafting table. Her work space was meticulously tidy, every tool hung on a Peg-Board, drawings put in neatly labeled drawers, her blowtorch and sheets of metal carefully covered with drop cloths. Quite a contrast to my own side of the building, with files on the edges of tables and office supplies that seem to migrate at will.

In a way, my space is too big, the ceilings too high, the way they can be in these old warehouses. I'd had fake ceilings put in in places, but the windows were around the perimeter at the top; I hadn't had the money to tear down a wall to let in outside light. I did put up partitions to make the area more human in scale, with my desk in one, my supplies and printers in another, and a bed for when I needed to crash away from home in a third, but the big room at the west end was where I did most of my actual work.

There's a little alcove with the couch and some armchairs to have casual meetings with clients, a setup with a screen for more formal presentations, a long table where I map out work in progress, a desk for my assistant, if I ever get off my butt and find a full-time person. I looked at the stacks of paper on the long table and decided I wasn't ready to face them yet.

I walked down to the corner to drop my peacoat at the cleaners. Ruby Choi, who has cleaned spaghetti sauce off silk shirts and tar out of wool slacks for me, looked at it dubiously. "This coat has been through too much. I try, I do my best, but I promise nothing. You take better care of your clothes, you make my job much easier, Vic."

"Yeah, that's what the doctor said about my body, which, believe me, looks a lot worse than the coat."

On my way back up Oakton, I stopped for a cappuccino and bought myself a large bunch of flowers, big red spiky things that stood out even in my warehouse. Welcome back, V.I., we missed you!

The fax from Sanford Rieff at Cheviot Labs was waiting for me, as he'd promised. He'd looked at the little froggy soap dish from its bulging eyes to its stubby feet. It had been made in China, surprise, out of a pewter alloy whose rough surface didn't hold fingerprints well. Underneath the smoke stains, Sanford could still detect oil from human fingers; perhaps it would be possible to get a DNA sample, although he wasn't optimistic.

The soap dish part of the frog was the back, which was hollowed out and had a hole in it for drainage. Someone had put a rubber plug in the hole and then poured nitric acid into the dish. The acid had burned out the plug, but traces of it remained, melted into the sides of the drainage hole.

"Nitric acid dissolves soap," Sanford concluded, "so there was no soap residue in the bowl of the dish, but I took some samples from the sides; whoever used it for its intended purpose used a heavy-scented rose soap, probably Adoree, a cheap brand sold in most drugstore chains and discount stores. I have the frog secure in a specimen box. Let me know if you want it returned or if we should store it until it's needed as evidence."

I stared at the fax, willing it to mean something more than it did. What was it doing at Fly the Flag. Why did it have nitric acid in it? Maybe acid was used somehow in the manufacture of flags. Maybe they dissolved glue with it, or something, and tried to use the froggy as a container, but the acid burned out the rubber plug.

My precious clue didn't seem to mean much, but I still went to my desk and typed up labels for a set of files: Fly the Flag, Arson, By-Smart, Billy, and put Rieff's lab report in the Fly the Flag folder. That was productive. Standing at my worktable, I shut my eyes, trying to visualize the back of the plant, where the fire had started. I'd been inside only twice, very briefly both times. The mechanicals were down there, the drying room, the storage area for fabrics. I made a rough sketch; I couldn't remember enough detail, but I was pretty sure the heart of the fire was in the drying room, not the fabric storage area.

R-A-T-S, I slowly wrote. Glue. Everything that had been done to the plant had slowed down production, not put them out of business. Was the arson a final act, because Zamar hadn't heeded the warnings? Or had this been intended as another warning, but one that went out of control? The punk I'd surprised at Fly the Flag two weeks ago, that *chavo banda* Andrés had driven from his construction site, he held the key to this. I needed to find him. And it wouldn't hurt to get some corroboration of what had happened at the fire.

I tried Sanford Rieff again out at Cheviot Labs. This time I reached him at his desk. When I'd thanked him for the report, and told him to log the frog into their safe, I asked if he had an electrical engineer, or arson expert, who could meet me at Fly the Flag sometime soon.

"I'd like an expert to look at the wires with me to see if it's possible to tell where or how the fire started. The police aren't putting real resources into this."

And why should I, for even less money than the cops? I imagined the conversation with my accountant. Because my professional pride was wounded: I'd been watching when the factory went up in flames. What should I have seen if I'd been paying closer attention?

Of course, Cheviot had just the expert I needed; he'd get her to give me a call to set up an appointment. Just so I knew, the company billed her time at two hundred dollars an hour. That was good to know: it was good to know I was sinking thousands of dollars into an investigation I hadn't been hired to take on while I abandoned the business that made money for me.

If I didn't finish three background checks for Darraugh Graham, my most important client, I'd be living on cat food in an alley pretty soon, and not the good stuff, either. I tapped my teeth with my pencil, trying to figure out how to juggle it all, then remembered Amy Blount. She'd earned a Ph.D. in economic history a year or so ago; while she looked for a full-time academic appointment, she sometimes did research projects for me, among other odd jobs she found. Fortunately enough, she was free, and willing, to pull things together in my office for a few days. We agreed to meet at nine in the morning to go over my caseload.

I walked aimlessly around the big room. Who had been gunning for Marcena, and why? Was it because of her that Bron had been killed or because of Bron that she'd been attacked? When we were talking to Conrad, Morrell had said she'd had a couple of meetings with Buffalo Bill Bysen since our initial prayer meeting two weeks ago. She'd presumably used her father's imaginary war experience as her entrée, but maybe they'd touched on something relevant. Buffalo Bill had crashed my apartment, and the Mt. Ararat church service; I could drive out to Rolling Meadows and tackle him unawares.

It was an appealing thought, but I didn't have enough information to put any questions to him. Fly the Flag was connected to By-Smart because they were manufacturing for the behemoth, first flags and now sheets. I wondered if Buffalo Bill paid enough attention to small details to look at sheets or if that was something that Jacqui handled. I could talk to Jacqui, anyway.

Billy the Kid was connected to Bron and Marcena because he had given

Bron his cell phone, and Morrell's flask, which Marcena was using, had been in Billy's car. Billy was connected to Fly the Flag because he was dating Josie. Had run away with Josie. I hoped. I hoped she was with him and not—I shut my mind: I didn't want to imagine the horrible alternatives.

Where were those two kids? Maybe Josie had confided in April. I picked up my phone to call Sandra Czernin and then decided it would be easier to talk to her in person, especially if I wanted to speak to her daughter. I owed her a courtesy visit, anyway, since I'd been the person who found her dead husband. And I wanted to talk to Pastor Andrés. It was time for him to answer a few direct questions. Like, was that *chavo* connected to the fire? And where did he hang out? I'd round out my afternoon in South Chicago with a visit to Patrick Grobian—Billy had had a meeting with the warehouse manager sometime just before he disappeared.

I put my labeled files into a drawer and collected what I needed for an afternoon in the cold. I was wearing a parka, bulkier and much less chic than my navy coat, but maybe better for standing on a street corner on a cold day. This time, I remembered gloves, or, rather, mittens: my fingers were still so sore and swollen from Tuesday night's escapade that I couldn't work my gloves over them. If I needed to use my gun, I'd be in trouble. I took it with me, though: whoever had attacked Bron and Marcena had a scary imagination. Binoculars, phone book, peanut butter sandwiches, a flask of coffee. What else did I need? A new battery for my flashlight, which Mr. Contreras had left in my car, and my picklocks.

I'd told Morrell I'd be doing desk work today; I thought about calling to say I'd changed my mind, but I didn't want to go into a long discussion of what I felt fit enough to do. If I were truthful, I'd have to admit that twenty-four hours in the hospital hadn't been enough for me to feel fully recuperated. And if I were smart, I'd go home and rest until I did feel fit enough again. I hoped this didn't mean I was dishonest and stupid.

"It's a long and dusty road. / It's a hard and heavy load," I sang to myself as I picked up the southbound expressway. I was getting very tired of this route, the leaden sky, the dirty buildings, the endless traffic, and then, after the eastbound cutoff from the Ryan, the ruined neighborhood that used to be my home.

The exit at 103rd goes right by the golf course where Mitch had found Marcena and Bron. I stopped briefly to look at it, wondering why their attackers had chosen this spot. I took a side road south and looked at the entrance to the course. Enormous gates were padlocked for the winter. The gates were pretty solid, attached to a razor-wire fence that wouldn't be easy to scale, or even climb under.

I slowly drove back to 103rd, inspecting the fence for access, but the razor wire had been rolled out with a lavish hand. The side road wound past a police pound, the graveyard for a thousand cars. Many were wrecks, twisted hunks of metal that had been scraped off the Dan Ryan Expressway, although some seemed to be whole cars that had been parked in tow zones. While I watched, a little fleet of the city's blue tow trucks trundled in, pulling cars behind them, like a team of ants carrying food to their queen. Empty trucks were leaving, going off to forage in the countryside. I wondered if Billy's little Miata was in there now or if the family had collected it.

On beyond the pound, razor wire continued to divide road from the marsh. I parked on the verge at the spot where Mitch had left the road for the swamp. The fence was still down there, and you could still see a faint wheel track through the gray-brown grasses.

I didn't understand why their assailants had taken Bron and Marcena through the marsh and then dumped them at the edge of the golf course. If you were going to break down the fence, why not just leave the bodies in the marsh itself, where rats and mud would obliterate the flesh fast enough. Why take them to a pit on the edge of a tony golf course, where someone might stumble on them at any moment? Even at this time of year, there were groundskeepers wandering around. And why go into the marsh at all—it took so much work. Why not just come up Stony Island from the south and drop them in the garbage dump?

I got back in my car, unsatisfied with the whole setup. As I put the car in gear, my cell phone rang. I looked at the readout: Morrell. I felt guilty, being caught out far from my office, and almost let his call go through to voice mail.

"Vic, are you on your way home? I just tried your office."

"I'm in South Chicago," I confessed.

"I thought you were staying close to home today."

He sounded resentful, which is so out of character for him that my own visceral anger at being monitored didn't kick in. I asked what the problem was.

"The most outrageous thing—someone broke into my place and stole Marcena's computer."

"What—when?" A By-Smart eighteen-wheeler honked furiously as I stepped on the brakes and pulled onto the verge.

"Sometime between five this morning, when I left to go down to the hospital, and now, I mean ninety minutes ago, when I got home. I lay down on the couch to rest for half an hour, then went into the back to get things organized for Rawlings's detective. That's when I found someone had been through my papers like a wind machine."

"How do you know they took Marcena's computer? Wouldn't she have had it with her?"

"She'd left it on the kitchen counter. I put it by her bed when I was straightening up Sunday night. It's gone now, along with my jump drives. As far as I can tell, nothing else is missing."

His jump drives, the little key-sized gizmos he uses to back up his data, which he does every night, storing the neatly labeled drives in a box on his desktop.

"They didn't take your computer?"

"I had it with me when I went to the hospital—I thought I might write a little while I was sitting with you—not that I did, but it turned out to be a good thing, since it saved my machine."

I asked about his other electronics. His fancy sound system was intact, along with the TV and DVD player.

He'd called the Evanston police as soon as he discovered the loss, but, from the sound of it, they'd only gone through the motions, figuring drug addicts were responsible. "But my place hadn't been broken into. I mean, whoever did this came in through the front door with a key, and those are very good locks. Which doesn't sound like an addict, and, anyway, an addict would have taken the portables, like the DVD."

"So someone with sophisticated skills wanted Marcena's files, and those only, and doesn't care that you know it," I said slowly.

Morrell said, "I called Rawlings, and he swears it wasn't the Chicago police. Should I believe him?"

"This isn't like him," I said, "and if he swears he didn't do it—I don't know. He's a cop, and we live in such a screwed-up world these days that it's hard to know who to trust. But he's a fundamentally good person; I want to believe he wouldn't do it, or wouldn't lie if he had. Do you want me to come up to canvas the neighbors?"

"I hadn't even thought of doing that, which just shows this has knocked me off balance. No, you go on doing what you're doing; I'll feel less impotent if I talk to my neighbors myself. And then I'm going to buy some new jump drives and work in the university library where no one can mug me for my machine. What did you say you were doing?"

"I'm in South Chicago. I want to talk to the minister again, and also to Sandra Czernin. Maybe Josie Dorrado told April where she and Billy were running to."

"Vic, you'll look after yourself, won't you? You won't take stupid risks? You're not in top physical shape, and—I'm useless right now."

The last sentence came out with unaccustomed bitterness. Morrell had not uttered one complaint about his disability since he'd come home. He worked doggedly on his physical therapy, put as much energy as he had into his book and looking after his contacts, but, for the first time, I saw how hard it was for him to feel unable to help me if I got into trouble.

I promised to call him if I was going to be a minute later than seven-thirty. When I'd hung up, I frowned at the phone. Something had clicked at the back of my mind when I answered Morrell's call. Before I could ferret around for it, the phone rang again.

It was Conrad, wanting to know if Morrell would have ditched Marcena's computer to keep the cops from looking at it. "He says his place was busted, but how can I know he's telling the truth? I sent my detective up just in case, but anyone can throw their papers around."

I burst out laughing, which miffed Conrad. "Morrell just asked me the very same question about you. Now at least I know you're both telling the truth."

Conrad laughed reluctantly, but added what Morrell and I had already been discussing, that someone thought Marcena's notes mattered. Which meant Morrell shouldn't hang out alone anywhere because whoever had come into his place after the computer might think Marcena had confided in him.

A shiver ran through my body. When we'd finished, I called Morrell again and told him if he was home alone, to put on a chain bolt. "And look out where you park; don't come into your condo through the alley for a while, okay?"

"I'm not going to start living in fear, V.I. It's mentally exhausting. I'll take sensible precautions, but I'm not going to find a concrete bunker to hide in."

"Morrell, I saw Marcena and Bron. Whoever attacked them has a very ugly imagination, and a disposition to match. Don't be an idiot!"

"Oh, Christ, Vic, don't you go telling me not to be an idiot when you're down there on the South Side where it all happened. If you're attacked again—"

He broke off, unwilling to complete the sentence. We both hung up without saying anything else.

32

TIME TO NAIL THE
PASTOR TO THE CROSS

The construction crew had made good progress on the four little houses where the pastor was working. One seemed finished, while the second, where I'd found Andrés two weeks ago, now had a bright red front door. The remaining two were still skeletons of poured concrete with a few boards outlining their ultimate shape.

As I'd driven across the South Side, I'd kept worrying about the break-in at Morrell's. I'd tried to imagine what Marcena knew that someone wanted to keep quiet. I had warned Morrell to use caution in case her assailants came after him, but someplace between Torrence, where I'd turned north, and Eighty-ninth, which led me east to the construction area, I'd realized that people might think I knew Marcena's secrets also. After all, both of us were sleeping at Morrell's, I'd introduced her to Bron. I saw again her swollen, bleeding body, and started looking nervously in my rearview mirror every few seconds. My gold Mustang would be very easy to track.

When I got to the jobsite, I drove on without slowing and parked two blocks away. The deserted streets would make tailing hard if someone was tailing me. By the time I got to the little houses, I was confident I was alone.

I put on my hard hat and walked through the red door without knocking. The familiar sounds of saws, hammers, and shouted Spanish echoed around the empty rooms. Drywall was complete in the entryway, but the stairwell was still naked. I asked the first man I saw for Andrés; he jerked a thumb over his shoulder.

I went down a minute hall and found Andrés in what was going to be the kitchen. He was trying to work wires through a large section of flex pipe, shouting in Spanish through an opening in the floor to a man feeding wiring in from below. He didn't look up when I came into the room.

I waited until he was finished wrestling before I spoke. "Pastor Andrés, we need to talk."

"You came to Sunday's service, Miss Detective. Have you come here today to make a commitment to Jesus? I am happy to stop for such an event."

I squatted next to him on the raw floorboards. "Bron Czernin was killed late Monday night."

"I am always sad at the needless death of one of God's children." Andrés's voice was calm, but his eyes were wary. "Especially when he has died without turning to Jesus."

"I don't think his priest will deny him a Christian burial."

"A Catholic burial," Pastor Andrés corrected me. "Not a Christian one: Bron Czernin died in the company of the woman who had been driving a wedge into his marriage."

"Bron was a passive bystander, by-layer, maybe I should say, while Ms. Love drove her wedge into his marriage?"

He frowned. "He was responsible, too, of course, but a woman has greater—"

"Powerlessness, usually," I cut in, "although I grant probably not in this particular instance. But speaking of powerless women, let's talk about Josie Dorrado. She disappeared Monday night, I think with Billy the Kid, Billy Bysen. Where are they?"

"I don't know. And if I did, I do not understand why you are interested."

"Because Rose asked me to find her. And, since you know Bron died in a pit lying next to Marcena Love, you must know that Ms. Love was in Billy's car when it plowed into the undergirders of the Skyway. I'd like to know where Billy and Josie were when that happened."

All the time I was speaking, he was shaking his head. "I do not know. Billy came to me on Sunday night, pleading with me to take him in again. He had gone to stay with Rose but now thought that was unsafe, for him or for Rose, I was not sure, but he wanted me to shelter Josie as well as himself. I said I could not, that his father's detectives would look for him at my home first. They have already been to see me twice, and when I look out my window at night I see a car in the street now, always. I also pointed out that he and Josie must be married, anyway, before I will give them a bed together."

"I don't know a state in the union where it's legal to get married that young," I said sharply. "Fortunately. Where did you send him?"

"If you are going to judge what you have no business judging, we cannot have this conversation."

I could feel hot spots in my eyes. I swallowed my anger as best I could: arguing with Andrés over morality would not get me any of the information I needed.

"Was the car watching your house Sunday night when he came to plead with you?"

He thought about it. "I don't think so. I first became aware only on Monday, when I went home for lunch. But if they were there Sunday night and looking for Billy, they would take him then, and you say he was with Josie on Monday."

"So where did you suggest he go?" I said.

"I suggested he go home to his family and take Josie with him, so that they can see her for themselves, instead of judging her by rumors. But he would not go."

"That's the real question," I said. "What is going on with him that he won't go home? He told me he had questions about his family, and that you were the only person he trusted. What happened to make him so untrusting of his family?"

"Any confidences he made to me were to me alone, not to share with any other person. Which includes you, Miss Detective."

"But the problem is connected to his work at the warehouse, isn't it?"

"That is always possible, since he was working there."

"And to Fly the Flag."

That was a random guess, but Andrés looked nervously over his shoulder. The man he'd been handling pipe with was watching him with a worried expression.

"I will not be tricked into disclosing confidences. What do you know about Fly the Flag?"

"Frank Zamar had just signed a big contract to deliver sheets and towels to By-Smart, not long before his plant burned down. That sounds like good news, not the desperation that would make a man blow up his own plant with himself inside it. So someone was annoyed with him."

I slapped my head, the caricature of someone struck by a hot idea. "Come to think of it, you yourself were at Fly the Flag a couple of days before the fire. You had some kind of issue with Frank Zamar. You're an electrician. You'd know just how to set up something that could start a fire while you were long gone. Maybe you put it in place that Tuesday when I saw you at the factory."

"You should be careful about making such accusations." He tried to speak angrily but his lips were stiff; I had the feeling that if he relaxed they might start trembling. "I would do nothing to risk the life of a man, especially not Frank Zamar, who was not wicked, just troubled."

"But, Roberto," his coworker said, "we all know—"

Andrés interrupted him to tell him in Spanish to be careful with what he said—I was not a friend.

"I'm not your enemy," I said in English. "What do we all know?"

With another reproving look at his coworker, Andrés said stiffly, "As you said, Zamar signed a new deal, to make sheets for the Bysens, sheets and towels with the American flag. Only—he signs in a panic, because he has lost so much business, and the bills for the new machines don't stop just because the machines have stopped. And Zamar says he will make these sheets, but for so little money he cannot pay his workers in Chicago. So he has to do it in Nicaragua, or China, or someplace where people will work for a dollar a day, not thirteen dollars an hour. And I went to warn him, he could lose everything if he takes his jobs out of the neighborhood, and not only takes them out but pays people so bad they are no better than slaves."

"And he wouldn't listen?" I said. "So you put rats in his heating ducts, and he still didn't agree so you torched the factory?"

"No!" Andrés roared, then said in a more level voice, "He promised me he would go back to By-Smart, tell them he changed his mind, and I even told him I would help him if he did go. And young Billy said Frank did go, he did see the woman in charge of sheets, and also Patrick Grobian, whom we all know, but—then I think he changed his mind."

"Did he tell you he had opened his second plant? Did Rose Dorrado tell you she was supervising the night shift for him in it?"

"What?" He was thunderstruck. "She was doing that and she said nothing to me, to her pastor, about this important thing in the life of the neighborhood?"

"But wasn't that good?" I was genuinely bewildered now. "That meant he was keeping jobs in the community."

"He lied to me!" Andrés's color rose. "And so did she. Or worse, she did not look me in the face and tell me the truth!"

"About what?"

"About—Frank Zamar's financial situation."

I didn't think that was what he meant, and from the look on the other electrician's face he didn't think so, either, but I couldn't get Andrés to budge, and I couldn't get his coworker to talk. We'd been at it for about ten minutes when a man came in and spoke to Andrés in Spanish—they needed the work in the kitchen finished so that the floor could be something—closed up, I think. Andrés told me I had to leave, he had nothing further to say to me.

I pushed myself to my feet. My hamstrings were stiff from squatting so long. "Okay. Just so you know, though, this morning people broke into the apartment where Ms. Love has been staying. They took her computer: they don't want whatever she knows about the South Side to be made public. Bron Czernin was killed in a very ugly way. If she survives, Ms. Love will face many surgeries before she recovers. Whoever attacked them is ruthless. If they think you know whatever secrets she and Bron shared, you could be the next target."

Andrés straightened himself; his face took on a rapt expression. "*Jesús se humillo así mismo, haciendose obediente, hasta la muerte.* Jesus became obedient to death upon the cross. I will not show fear to go where my Master went before me."

"And it's okay with you if they attack Billy and Josie as well?"

Andrés frowned. "You have given me no reason to believe that the death of Bron Czernin has anything to do with Billy Bysen and his family. Perhaps even Mrs. Czernin organized this attack herself. Have you spoken with her? A woman who is betrayed, who feels angry, she can well commit murder, especially a woman like Mrs. Czernin, who now has a daughter gravely ill, she will not be the most reasoning person. She can well do something terrible to her husband and his lover in her anger and her grief."

"It's not impossible," I conceded. "It took a lot of strength to heft those bodies around. If Ms. Czernin had knocked them out, she could have moved them with a forklift, if she had one, into whatever truck that took them to the pit. It's all possible, but not very believable."

The man who'd told Andrés to finish the kitchen made a great show of looking at his watch.

"I'm leaving," I said. "But, pastor, if Billy calls you again, tell him to talk to me, or to Conrad Rawlings in the Fourth District, if his worries about his family include knowledge of some kind of crime. There's an awfully big tiger out there for a nineteen-year-old to grab by his tail. Thanks, by the way, for the information about Fly the Flag."

That startled him out of his detached demeanor. "I told you nothing! And if you say otherwise, you are committing a terrible sin by bearing false witness."

"So long." I smiled and turned on my heel.

I left the house slowly, hoping he might change his mind and come after me with more information. A couple of men taking a cigarette break out front gave me a cheerful greeting as I passed, but Andrés remained in the kitchen.

I walked to the Czernin's house from the jobsite, since it was only three blocks away. The day continued cold, the sky filled with clouds that rolled and twisted over the lake. Despite the bitter weather, I went slowly, not eager to face Sandra Czernin and her unpredictable rages. And wondering, too, about Andrés.

I wanted to hang him upside down from the roof joists and shake him until whatever he knew about Billy and his family and Fly the Flag came tumbling out of his head. I found it impossible to believe Andrés had set the fire at the factory, but he was an electrician. He would know where the wiring came into the plant and how to use it to cause maximum devastation. But I didn't think he would engineer a man's death, and I couldn't imagine any reason he'd shut down a business that provided good jobs to the community.

Since I couldn't get Andrés to talk, it was even more important that I find Billy. The Kid had run away right after his grandfather insulted Pastor Andrés at the church service, so it didn't seem as though his quarrel with his family had anything to do with Bron and Marcena. The next day, he'd gone to work in the usual way: it wasn't until he got to work that something happened to make him disappear altogether. That sounded like Billy's problems lay in the warehouse, not around Fly the Flag. That meant, presumably, something his Aunt Jacqui was doing, since she was the one family member who showed up regularly at the warehouse. So the warehouse had to be my next port of call, once I'd gotten past Sandy Zoltak. Sandra Czernin.

Despite my foot-dragging, I'd reached the Czernin house, a bungalow near the corner of Ninety-first and Green Bay Avenue, catty-corner to the six-hundred-acre wasteland that used to be the USX South Works.

I stared at the rubble. When I was a child and we had to wash the windows every day because of the thick smears of smoke that settled on them, I would long for twenty-four hours without the mills, but I could not have imagined them gone, those giant sheds, the miles of conveyor belts ferrying coal and iron ore, the orange sparks filling the night sky that told you they were pouring. How could something so big disappear into a pile of rubble and weeds? I couldn't fathom it.

My mother insisted on facing unpleasant chores head-on, whether washing windows, or talking to people like Sandra Czernin. I always thought it would be better to play first and see whether there was time left in the day to do the dirty work, but I could hear Gabriella's voice: the longer you indulge yourself over that steel mill, the harder it will be in the end to do the job you came here for.

I squared my shoulders and walked up to the front door. On a street of sad and sagging houses, the Czernins' place was neatly painted, all the siding intact, the small yard tidy, with a lawn that had been trimmed for the winter and some chrysanthemums lining the short walk. Sandra's anger at least took a constructive turn, if it drove her to maintain her home like this, or to push Bron into doing it.

Sandra came to the door within seconds of my ringing the bell. She stared as if she didn't recognize me. Her stiff bleached hair hadn't been washed or combed recently and stood out from her head at wild angles. Her blue eyes were bloodshot, and the shape of her face indistinct, as if the bones had dissolved behind the skin.

"Sandra, hi, I'm sorry about Bron."

"Tori Warshawski! You have one hell of a nerve coming around here now, two days late. Your sympathy doesn't mean shit to me. You found him, that's what that cop told me. And you didn't think you owed me even a phone call? I found your husband, Sandra, go order a coffin, because you're a widow now?"

Her anger sounded forced, as though she were trying to whip herself into feeling something, anything, and anger were the only emotion she could come up with when she couldn't muster grief. I almost started justifying myself—my night in the swamp, my day in the hospital—but I swallowed it all.

"You're right. I should have called you right away. If you let me in, I'll tell you what I know." I pushed forward, not waiting for her to decide if she could stand for me to be in her house, and she backed up automatically, the way people do.

"He was with that English whore, wasn't he?" she said when we were in her entryway. "Is she dead, too?"

"No. Very badly injured, too much to talk and tell the cops who attacked them."

"Yeah, dry your eyes while I start playing 'My Heart Cries for You' on the violin." To my dismay, she rubbed the tip of her middle finger against the top of her index finger, the way we did as kids when we were being sarcastic—a flea playing "My Heart Cries for You" on the world's smallest violin, we used to say.

"How's April holding up?" I asked.

"Oh, she was Daddy's little angel, she can't believe he's dead, can't believe he was with this English reporter, even though all the kids at school knew about it and told her."

"Bron thought he'd be able to find money for her defibrillator. Do you know if he'd come up with anything?"

"Bron and his ideas." She contorted her face into a horrible sneer. "He probably thought he could steal a load of TVs from By-Smart. If he ever had a good idea above his waistline, I never heard about it. There's only one thing that could help and that's if he died working for the company."

Her bitterness was so hard to listen to that it took me a minute to understand what she meant. "Oh. So you could collect his workers' comp indemnity. He didn't have life insurance?"

"Ten thousand dollars. By the time I've buried him, there'll be about seven left." Tears spurted from her eyes. "Oh, damn him, what am I going to do without him? He cheated on me every five seconds, but what am I going to do? I can't keep the house, I can't look after April, damn him, damn him, damn him."

She started sobbing in a rasping dry way that shook her thin body so hard she had to lean against the wall. I took her arm and gently moved her into the living room, where the prim furniture was encased in plastic. I took the cover off the couch and sat her down.

HAPPY FAMILIES ARE ALL ALIKE, UNHAPPY FAMILIES . . .

The Czernin house was laid out like every other bungalow on the South Side, including the one where I grew up. I moved by instinct through the dining room to the kitchen. I put water on for tea, but, while waiting for it to boil, I couldn't resist opening the back door to see if they had a little lean-to like ours. My dad had stored his tools there; he could repair most things around the house. He'd even replaced a broken wheel on my roller skates. It seemed satisfying to find an identical one behind Sandra's kitchen, although it wasn't as tidy as my dad's. My dad would never have left cut-up pieces of rubber lying around the work surface like that, or the frayed ends of old lengths of wiring.

I was turning back to the kitchen to hunt for tea when April appeared in the doorway. She was clutching the giant bear Bron had given her in the hospital; her face was still puffy from the heart meds she was taking.

"Coach! I didn't know—didn't expect—"

"Hi, honey. I'm sorry about your dad. You know I'm the person who found him."

She nodded bleakly. "Were you looking at his shop? He taught me how to use a soldering iron. I even worked on a project with him last week, but I don't think Ma will let me use his tools now. Does she know you're here?"

"She's in the living room, pretty upset; I'm trying to find tea."

April opened a canister on the counter and pulled out a tea bag. While she got mugs down from a shelf, I asked how she was feeling.

"Okay, I guess. They're giving me these drugs that make me sleepy, that's all. You know, they're saying I can't play anymore, can't play basketball."

"I know: it's a shame; you're a good player, and we'll miss you, but you can't risk your health running around the court. You can still be part of the team if you want, come to the practices and help chart plays."

Her face brightened a little. "But how am I going to get to college if I can't get a scholarship?"

"Academics," I said dryly. "Not as glamorous as a sports scholarship, but they'll carry you further in the long run. Let's not worry about it today, though—you've got enough going on, and it's a year before you have to start applying."

The kettle started boiling, and I poured water into the mugs. "April, have you talked to Josie since she came to the hospital?"

She turned away from me and became very busy at the counter, moving the tea bag from one cup to the next until all three had turned a pale yellow.

"Josie disappeared the same night your father died, and I'm very worried about her. Did she run away with Billy?"

She scrunched her face unhappily. "I promised not to say anything."

"I found Billy's sports car wrecked under the Skyway around one in the morning. I think the English reporter had been in it, but where were Billy and Josie?"

"Billy gave Daddy his car," she whispered softly. "He said he couldn't use it anymore, and he knew Daddy didn't have a car, if we wanted to go out he had to borrow a car from a buddy, or sometimes he drove us in the semi if he thought Mr. Grobian wouldn't find out, you know, it was By-Smart property."

"When did he give your dad the car?" I tried to keep my voice low and level, not to make her more nervous than she already was.

"Monday. He came to the house Monday morning, after they brought me home from the hospital. Ma had to be at work; they only gave her one hour off to bring me home, but Daddy was working a late shift so he didn't leave until three. And then, then Josie came. I called her and told her to come here before she went to school. She and Billy used to meet here, see, it was a place she could come and be doing her homework so her ma didn't mind, and my ma, she just thought Billy was a boy from school, we didn't tell her he was one of the Bysens, she would, like, totally lose it if she knew that."

Those school projects that Josie was so intent on, her science and health studies homework she had to do with April. Maybe I should have guessed that they were a cover story, but it didn't matter now.

"Why was Billy so angry with his family?" I asked.

"He wasn't angry with them," April said earnestly. "Worried, he was worried by what he saw at the plant."

"And what was that?"

She hunched a shoulder. "You know, everybody works hard for not enough money. Like Ma. Even Daddy, he made more driving a truck, but Billy said it wasn't right, people's lives being so hard."

"Nothing more specific than that?" I was disappointed.

She shook her head. "I never listened that hard, mostly he would be talking to Josie, you know, off in one corner, but Nicaragua came in somehow, and Fly the Flag, I think—"

"What are you doing in here, bothering my girl?" Sandra appeared in the doorway, her tears gone, her face set in its usual hard lines.

"We're making you a cup of tea, Ma. Coach says I can still suit up and be with the team, chart plays maybe." April handed her mother and me each one of the mugs. "And maybe my academics will get me into college."

"But they won't pay your medical bills. You want to do something for April, don't go putting ideas in her head about academics. Prove Bron was driving for the company when he died."

I was startled. "Is By-Smart saying he wasn't? Do they know where he was when he was jumped?"

"They won't tell me anything. I went to see Mr. Grobian this morning over at the warehouse, I told him I was filing a claim, and he said, 'Lots of luck.' He said Bron was violating company rules when he was working, having that bitch in his cab, and they'd fight the claim."

"You need a lawyer," I said. "Someone who can take them to court for you."

"You are so—so ignorant," Sandra shrilled. "If I could afford a lawyer, Miss Iffy-genius, I wouldn't need the money to begin with. I need proof. You're a detective, go get me proof he was working for the company, and that the English whore wasn't in his truck. It's your fault she was there. Now you go make it up to me."

"Bron's behavior was not my fault, Sandra. And screaming about it won't solve any of your problems now. I've got way more to do than take abuse from you. If you can't calm down enough to talk sensibly, then I'm taking off."

Sandra wavered, torn between the anger that consumed her and the wish to know about Bron's death. In the end, the three of us sat at the kitchen table, drinking the weak tea, while I told them about Mitch leading me across the swamp to Bron and Marcena.

Sandra knew that Billy had lent his cell phone to Bron ("He told me he took it so he could stay in touch with April"), but she didn't know about the Miata. This led to a little skirmish between her and April ("Ma, I didn't tell you because you'd just do like you're doing now, yelling about him, and I can't take it.")

Their priest had warned them that Bron was so badly disfigured that Sandra shouldn't look at his body; did I think that was true?

"He looks terrible," I agreed. "But if it was me, my husband, I mean, I would want to see him. Otherwise, it would always haunt me that I hadn't said that last good-bye."

"If you'd been married to that prick, you wouldn't be so sappy, 'that last good-bye' and all that movie crap," Sandra snapped.

She stopped at an outcry from her daughter, but the two began quarreling again over whether Bron really had a plan to find the money they needed for April's health care.

"He called Mr. Grobian, and Mr. Grobian said he could come in and discuss it, Daddy told me that himself," April said to her mother, scarlet-faced.

"You never understood that your father told people what they wanted to hear, not what the truth was. How do you think I ended up marrying him, anyway?" She bit the words off angrily.

"When did your dad tell you about Grobian?" I asked April. "Monday morning?"

"He was making me lunch when we got back from the hospital." April blinked back tears. "Tuna fish sandwiches. He cut the crust off the bread like he used to when I was a baby. He wrapped me in a blanket and tucked me in his recliner and fed me, me and Big Bear. He said not to worry, he was going to talk to Mr. Grobian, it would be all right. Then Billy came, and he said if I could wait eight years until he got his trust fund he'd pay for the surgery, but Daddy said we couldn't take charity, even if we could wait so long, and he was going to see Mr. Grobian."

Sandra slapped the tabletop so hard her weak tea slopped out of the mug. "That is so damn typical! Him talking to you and not his own wife!"

April's lower lip quivered, and she hugged Big Bear tightly to herself. Patrick Grobian hadn't exactly struck me as the warmhearted Santa of the South Side. If Bron had been going to see him, it must have been to put the bite on him in some way, but when I suggested this April sat up again.

"No! Why are you taking her side against Daddy? He said he had a document from Mr. Grobian, it was all businesslike, shipshape."

"Why didn't you tell me before?" Sandra cried. "I could have asked Grobian when I saw him this morning."

"Because you kept saying like you're saying now, how his ideas were dumb and wouldn't work."

"So neither of you know whether he actually did talk to Grobian, or what this document might be? Sandra, when did you actually talk to Bron for the last time?"

Her response, stripped of all its emotional outbursts, boiled down to

Monday morning, when they brought April home from the hospital. They'd borrowed a car from a neighbor—their own car had been totaled in a hit-and-run last month and they hadn't had the money to get another yet (because, of course, Bron had let the insurance payments lapse, and the other driver hadn't been insured, either). Bron had dropped Sandra off at work in the borrowed car and then gone home to stay with April until he had to leave for work.

"He's on the four-to-midnight shift this week. I have to be at the store at eight-fifteen, so lots of weeks we don't see each other much. He gets up, has a cup of coffee with me in the morning. When April leaves for school, he goes back to bed and I catch the bus, and that's the story for the week. Only when we brought April home, we didn't want her climbing those stairs, they're so steep, the doctor said no major exertion right now, so she's sleeping with me down here in the big bed. Bron, he's upstairs, or he was, when he got off shift Monday night he was going to go up and sleep in her bed.

"Tuesday, I made April her breakfast, even if I don't cut the crust off the bread I make her breakfast every morning, but I had to go to work; you never know how long you have to wait for the bus, I couldn't hang around for Mr. High-and—" She broke off, remembering the object of her bitterness was dead. "I just thought he was sleeping late," she finished quietly. "I didn't think anything about it at all."

What document could Grobian possibly have signed that would make Bron think that By-Smart would ante up a hundred thousand dollars for April's medical care? Nothing made any sense to me, but when I tried to push April to see if she could remember anything else, any hint Bron might have dropped, Sandra erupted. Didn't I see April was tired? What was I trying to do, kill her daughter? The doctors said April couldn't have any stress and me barging in and harassing her was stress, stress, stress.

"Ma," April shrieked. "Don't talk to Coach like that. That's way more stress than I want."

I could see fertile new ground for mother and daughter to fight on here, but I left without trying to say anything else. Sandra stayed in the kitchen, staring at the kitchen table, but April followed me back to the living room where I'd left my parka. She was gray around the mouth, and I urged her to go to bed, but she lingered, nuzzling her head against Big Bear, until I asked her what she wanted.

"Coach, I'm sorry Ma is upset and everything, but—can I still come to practice, like you said earlier?"

I put my hands on her shoulders. "Your mom is mad at me, and maybe for good reason, but that has nothing to do with my relations with you. Of course you can still come to practice. Now let's get you to bed. Upstairs or down?"

"I'd like to go to my own bed," she said, "only Ma thinks stairs will kill me. Is that right?"

I made a helpless gesture. "I don't know, honey, but maybe if we took them superslow you'll be okay."

I helped her up the steps one at a time to her attic room. The stairs were in exactly the same place as they had been in my childhood home on Houston, and they were the same steep risers, decanting you through a square opening onto the attic floor. The little dormer room had been fixed up with the same care as my parents had put into my space. Where I had had Ron Santo and Maria Callas over my bed—a strange juxtaposition of my parents' unconnected passions—April had the same poster of the University of Illinois women's team that Josie did. I wondered how painful it would be for her to wake up every morning to the active life she no longer could take part in.

"Do you know who Marie Curie was?" I asked abruptly. "You don't? I'll bring you her biography. She was a Polish woman who became a really important scientist. A different life than basketball, but her work has lasted over a hundred years now."

I pulled the bedspread down for her and saw underneath the same red-white-and-blue sheets that Josie and Julia had on their bed. Was this solidarity with Team USA, or what?

"You and Josie buy your sheets together?" I asked as I tucked her bear into the bed.

"Oh, these flag sheets, you mean? We bought them at church. My church was selling them, and so was Josie's, and a bunch of the others.

Most of us girls on the team bought them—it was for something to do with the neighborhood, cleaning it up or something, I don't know, but even Celine bought a set; it was a team thing, we did it together as a team."

I looked for a label, but all it said was "Made with pride in the USA." I made sure she had everything she needed—water, a whistle to summon her mother if she needed her in the night, her CD player. Even her schoolbooks, if she felt like doing homework.

I was halfway down the steep stairs when I remembered Billy's phone. I'd taken it out of my peacoat when I left it at the cleaners and put it in my bag, wondering what to do with it.

I took it out and handed it over to April. "It's still pretty well charged up. I don't know if his family will disconnect the service, but he did give it to your dad to use, so I don't think he'll mind if you use it. I'll bring you over a charger." I handed her one of my cards. "And call me if you need me. This is a tough time for you to be going through."

Her face lit up with delight over the phone. "Josie was so lucky going around with Billy because he had all this stuff that we only can use at school. He went online from this phone, plus he let her use his laptop. He helped us find blogs to write on, and gave us nicknames. Like, he kept in touch with his sister through their private nicknames on this one blog, and Josie met his sister through the blog, even though his folks don't want them to be in touch with each other. So if Josie and me, like, get to college, we'll know how to do what the other kids do."

Before basketball practice, I'd have to talk to the assistant principal about April's academics. Surely with this much eagerness on April's part, the school could help her find a way.

Almost before I'd started back down the stairs, I heard April saying into the phone, "Yeah, Billy Bysen, he's like letting me use his phone until he needs it again. You going to practice?"

When I got back downstairs, I called out to Sandra that I'd put April to bed upstairs, and let myself out.

AND THE RICH
AIN'T HAPPY, EITHER

As I walked down the neatly planted walk into the wind, I wondered if Sandra was right. Had Bron died because he was with Marcena, or had Marcena been attacked because she was with Bron? The theft of Marcena's computer made it seem as though Marcena were the key player here. In which case, Bron would still be alive if not for me bringing the English reporter into his life. And if not for Marcena, who was always ready for new excitement, and if not for Bron himself, strutting his stuff for the exotic outsider.

I refused to feel responsible for those two falling into bed together, but I did want to know what they were doing in Billy's car when it ploughed into the Skyway Monday night.

I also wanted to know how Nicaragua and Fly the Flag were connected, since those were the only two things April could remember Billy talking about. Perhaps Frank Zamar had planned to move his plant to Nicaragua so he could meet By-Smart's price demands for the contract he'd just signed with them. That would certainly annoy Pastor Andrés, who was struggling to keep jobs in the neighborhood. But Rose was supervising a night shift at Zamar's second plant; if he'd opened a new plant for his By-Smart order, he couldn't have been planning a move to Central America.

The wind was blowing more steadily from the northeast as the sun went down, but the cold air felt cleansing after the heated emotions in the Czernin house. I held my head up so the air could blow right through me.

It was only a little after three when I got to my car. Pat Grobian should still be at his station at the warehouse. Maybe he'd tell me what document he'd given Bron that proved the company would pay April's medical bills. I drove across Lake Calumet and turned south to 103rd and the By-Smart warehouse.

When I'd come here the first time, I'd needed to prove to a guard that I had permission to be on the property. And when I'd reached the warehouse, another guard had catechized me. I didn't think Grobian would welcome me with open arms, so I bypassed the whole process, parking on Crandon and crossing to the back of the vast complex, my hard hat under my arm.

Razor wire enclosed the whole area. I stumbled around the perimeter: the leather half boots I was wearing were not ideal for cross-country hiking. Eventually, I came on a secondary drive, a narrow track that was probably used for service crews if they had to get to the power plant behind the warehouse. The gate was padlocked, but the rutted road left a gap plenty wide enough for me to slide under.

I was now behind both the warehouse and the employee parking lot. I put my hard hat on, and tried to remember the geography of the place from my first visit, but I still made a couple of wrong turns before I found the open door where smokers were huddling in the cold. They barely looked at me as I sidled past them and went up the corridor to Grobian's office.

A number of truckers were standing in the corridor waiting to see Grobian, whose door was shut. One had a handlebar mustache that seemed almost repulsive, so full and luxurious was the hair. Nolan, the man in the Harley jacket who'd been here on my previous visit was here; he clearly remembered me, too.

"Hope the other guy looks as bad as you do, sis," he said with a grin.

I answered in kind, but when I looked at my trousers I saw to my annoyance that I'd torn them sliding under the back gate. For a month that wasn't generating much income, I was sure racking up a lot of overhead.

"You knew Bron Czernin, didn't you?" I changed the subject, not very skillfully, but I wanted to get in a talk before Grobian came out. "I'm afraid I'm the person who found him yesterday morning."

"Hell of a thing," the handlebar mustache said, "although Bron shaved close to the skin. I'm kind of surprised no one went after him before."

"How so?" I asked.

"I heard that English woman was with him, the one he was driving around town with."

I nodded assent. I shouldn't have felt surprised that the men knew about Marcena—theirs was a small community in its own way. If Bron had been showing Marcena his routes and showing her off to his accounts, everyone who knew him would know about her. I could picture them alone in their cabs needing to pass the time, calling each other and spreading all the gossip.

"About fifteen husbands down here could a taken him out anytime the last ten years—the English broad wasn't the only piece of ta—well, you know, friend, he kept tucked in that cab of his. Against the law, of course, and against company policy, but—" He shrugged expressively.

"Was he seeing anyone else? Marcena doesn't have an angry husband who'd go after Romeo—Bron, I mean." I thought uneasily about Morrell, but that was ridiculous—even if I could picture him mad enough to beat up a man over a woman, even if I could picture him doing it over Marcena, I couldn't picture him doing it with his bad leg.

The men made a few suggestive comments about some of their acquaintances, but they agreed in the end that Marcena was Romeo's first fling in almost a year. "His girl was getting upset, all the harassing the kids in school gave her. Finally, he promised the missus he'd stop, but, what I hear, this English pus—English lady, she was so classy and so exotic, he couldn't resist."

I remembered young Mr. William's eagerness to find out who was squiring Marcena around the South Side. "Did Grobian know about her?"

"Probably not," put in the handlebar mustache. "Bron wouldn't've still been driving if Pat knew."

"Figured that was what that Mexican punk was talking to Bron about," the Harley jacket said.

My heart skipped a beat. "What Mexican punk?"

"Don't know his name. He's always hanging around jobsites down here, seeing what he can steal or get away with. My son, he goes to Bertha Palmer, he pointed them out to me, Bron and the Mexican. Last week, week before, I don't remember, I was picking my boy up after a game—see, he plays football at the high school—and there was this punk in the parking lot, and there was Bron and the English lady. Punk probably figured Bron would slip him a few bucks not to tell the company he had the lady in his cab with him."

One of the other guys guffawed and said, "Probably thought Bron would pay him not to tell his old lady. I'd be a hell of lot more scared of Sandra Czernin than Pat Grobian."

"Me, too." I grinned, although I was thinking about Freddy, the *chavo* who hung around jobsites looking for what he could finagle. Blackmail, that fit Freddy's unattractive profile. It made a certain kind of sense. But would Freddy have attacked Bron and Marcena? Maybe Romeo—Bron, I really should call him by his name—maybe Bron threatened to have him arrested for blackmail and Freddy lost his head?

"Can't see Bron paying blackmail to anyone," a third trucker drawled.

"So maybe the punk squealed," the mustache said. "Because Grobian and Czernin were sure going at it Monday afternoon."

"Fighting?" My eyebrows shot up.

"Arguing," he amplified. "I was waiting on my clearance, and Bron was in there, they were shouting at each other a good fifteen minutes."

I shook my head. "I don't know—Bron wanted help with his daughter's hospital bills."

"From Grobian?" Nolan in the Harley jacket snorted. "Billy is probably the only person in the world who could believe Grobian would give a rat's ass about someone's girl. Not that it wasn't a hell of a blow what happened to Czernin's kid, but sitting good with the Bysen family, that's what Grobian thinks about first, last, and foremost. And helping pay some guy's hospital bills, he knows the Bysens would never sit still for that—even though Czernin had twenty-plus years with the company!"

"They may have been fighting when Czernin went in, but they must've kissed and made up because Czernin was crowing like a rooster when he got into his rig," the third driver said.

"He didn't say anything?" I asked.

"Just that he might have a winning ticket."

"Winning ticket?" I repeated. "Lottery ticket, is that what he meant?"

"Oh, he was carrying on like a fool," the handlebar said. "I asked him the same thing, and he said, 'Yeah, the lottery of life.'"

"Lottery of death is what it turned out to be," Nolan said somberly.

Everyone was quiet for a moment, remembering that Bron had died. I waited for the silent tension in the men to ease before asking if they knew where Billy the Kid was.

"Not here. Ain't seen him all week, come to think of it. Maybe he went back to Rolling Meadows."

"No," I said. "He's disappeared. The family has a big detective agency out looking for him."

The trio looked at each other wide-eyed. This was clearly news to them, and welcome as a fresh source of gossip, although the Harley jacket said the Kid had just been there.

"Today?" I said.

"Nope. Last time I was in—that'd be Monday afternoon. Something was eating him, but I didn't know he'd have the guts to walk out on the family."

None of the three had any ideas, about what was eating Billy, or where he might have run to. In the middle of a lively discussion about the merits of Vegas over Miami if you were running away from home, Grobian's door opened. To my surprise, it was young Mr. William who emerged, with Aunt Jacqui at his elbow, businesslike today in a taupe military-style jacket, with a bias-cut silk skirt in the same shade twirling around her knees.

"Our lucky week," the Harley jacket muttered. "Grobian must be on the hot seat for that prick to come down here twice in a row."

None of the men spoke directly to William. Some of them might have known Mr. William when he was Billy's age, but he'd probably never inspired the kind of lively banter the men treated his son to.

"You men waiting on your dispatch clearances? You can go on in," William said curtly.

He passed me by without noticing me—I guess my hard hat and torn pants made me look like one of the men—but Aunt Jacqui wasn't so oblivious. "Are you hoping to get Patrick to take you on as a driver? We're down a man, with Romeo Czernin dead."

The trio of truckers paused outside Grobian's open door. The mustache frowned at her remark, but none of them risked a comment.

"You are the queen of tact, aren't you?" I said. "While we're all having a good time, you're down more than a driver. Aren't you short a supplier, too?"

William squinted at me, trying to place me. "Oh. The Polish detective. What are you doing here?"

"Detecting. What are you doing about your flag sheets and towels that Fly the Flag was producing for you?"

"What do you know about those?" William demanded.

"That he signed a contract and then realized he couldn't meet the price and came back to renegotiate."

Jacqui produced a dazzling smile. "We never, never renegotiate our contracts. It's Daddy Bysen's very first law of business. I did tell the man that—what was his name, William? Anyway, it doesn't matter—I told him that, and he finally agreed he would meet the price we'd all agreed on. We were supposed to take delivery of the first order last week, but, fortunately, we had a backup supplier, so we're only five days behind schedule."

"Backup supplier?" I echoed. "Is this the person who's been selling sheets through the churches in South Chicago?"

Jacqui laughed, the malicious laugh she gave whenever someone in the Bysen family was looking foolish. "Someone very, very different, Ms. Polish Detective; if you're investigating those sheets, I think you'll find yourself at a dead end."

Mr. William looked at her reprovingly, but said, "I always maintained Zamar was unreliable. Father keeps saying we should give South Side businesses priority just because he grew up down here. Nothing will convince him they can't meet the production schedules they agree to."

"It is pretty darn unreliable to die in the fire that destroys your plant," I said.

Mr. William glared at me. "Who talked to you, anyway, about his contract with us?"

"I'm a detective, Mr. Bysen. I ask questions and people answer them. Sometimes they even tell me the truth. Speaking of which, you were here Monday afternoon, and so was your son."

"Billy?"

"You have other sons? I don't know how you two missed each other. You really didn't see him?"

William pressed his lips together. "What time was he here?"

"About this same time. Four-thirty, five. I figure you said something to him that made him decide to take off."

"You figure wrong. If I'd known he was here—damn it, you'd think I was one of the stock clerks, not the CFO of this company. No one tells me one damn thing about what's going on."

He pushed open Grobian's door. "Grobian? Why in hell didn't you tell me Billy was here Monday afternoon?"

The truckers crowded in front of Grobian's desk backed away so that William could look directly at the warehouse manager. Grobian was startled, that much was clear from his expression.

"Didn't see him, chief. He cleared out his locker, but you already know that. He must have come in just to do that."

William frowned some more, but decided to let it go at that; he came back out to the hall to resume his attack on me. "Who hired you to look at Fly the Flag's business? Zamar didn't leave anything but debts."

"Now, how do you know that?" I said. "Busy man like you, CFO of America's fifth-biggest company, and you have time to look into one tiny supplier?"

"Attention to detail makes us successful," William said stiffly. "Is there any idea of foul play in that fire?"

"Arson always makes one suspect foul play," I said equally stiff.

"Arson?" Jacqui managed to widen her dark eyes without wrinkling her forehead. "I heard it was faulty wiring. Who told you arson?"

"Why does it matter to you?" I said. "I thought you had your new supplier hard at work and everything."

"If someone is setting fires in South Chicago companies, it affects us; we're the biggest company down here, we could be vulnerable, too." Mr. William tried to sound stern but only managed peevish. "So I need to know who told you it was arson."

"Word gets around in a small community," I said vaguely. "Everyone knows each other. I'd think your pit bulls from Carnifice would have picked up the story. After all, they're staking out Billy's pastor; they must have talked to the people he knows."

"They tried," Aunt Jacqui started to say at the same time William demanded how I knew Carnifice was watching Andrés.

"Now, that's easy. Strangers stand out down here. Too many vacant lots, so you know when someone is lurking, and too many people who don't have jobs, so they spend their days chilling on the streets. What did your guys find out about Billy's car?"

"By the time we got to it, it had been stripped," William said shortly. "Tires, radio, even the front seat. Why didn't you let me know right away you'd found it? I had to learn about that from that black policeman who acts like he's in charge down there."

"That would be *Commander* Rawlings, and he acts like he's in charge because he is. As for why I didn't call you, too much was going on for me to think about you—like hiking two miles across the marsh to find your dead driver. Events happened too fast for me to think of calling you."

"What did you find in the car?" Jacqui asked.

"You wondering if I ran off with Billy's stock portfolio?" I asked. "He left a couple of books in the trunk. *Violence of Love*, the one by the murdered archbishop, and"—I shut my eyes, conjuring the titles I'd seen in the dark—"*Rich Christians and Poverty*, something like that."

"Oh, yes." Jacqui rolled her eyes. "*Rich Christians in the Age of Hunger.* Billy read us so many passages at dinner I had to become anorexic—no decent person could keep eating, according to him, with children dying all over the place. Did you pick up any papers, thinking they might be a stock portfolio?"

I looked at her through narrowed eyes. "Rose Dorrado told me you'd gone through her books, even shaking her Bible so that all her page markers fell out. What did Billy run off with?"

"Nothing that I know of," William said, looking with annoyance at his sister-in-law. "We were hoping he might have left some kind of clue about his plans. He'd given away his cell phone and his car, which makes him hard to trace. If you know anything about him, Ms.—uh—you would do well to tell me."

"I know," I said, bored. "Or I'll never eat lunch in this town again."

"Don't treat it like a joke," he warned me. "My family has a lot of power in Chicago."

"And Congress and everywhere else," I agreed.

He glared at me, but strode down the corridor without answering. Jacqui clicked along next to him in her high heels, her bias-cut skirt swirling around her knees in a very feminine way. I felt acutely aware of my torn trousers and dirty parka.

35

WHY, FREDDY,
WHAT A SURPRISE!

The truckers didn't take long with Grobian. When they came back out, the Harley driver gave me a wink and a thumbs-up, which sent me in to see the manager with a lighter heart. Is it such a bad thing to depend on the kindness of strangers?

Grobian was talking on the phone while signing papers. His buzz cut was still at a military length—to keep it like that he had to get it mowed every couple of days, although it was hard to know how the manager of a domain like his found time to fit it in. He was in his shirtsleeves, and I couldn't help noticing how big his forearms were: a tattoo with the marine logo covered about four hairy inches.

He didn't really look at me, just waved me to a folding chair while he finished his conversation. My hard hat and torn trousers weren't as feminine as Jacqui's fluttering skirt, but they did help me blend in. As I sat, I noticed mud caked on my leather half boots. Not surprising, considering how I had crawled under the fence to get into the warehouse, but annoying all the same.

When Grobian hung up, it was clear I wasn't who he was expecting, but equally clear that he didn't remember me.

"V. I. Warshawski," I said heartily. "I was here two weeks ago, with young Billy."

His lips tightened: he would have shown me the door, not a chair, if he'd looked at me when I came in. "Oh. The do-gooder. Whatever Billy may tell you, the company doesn't care about your school day care program."

"Basketball."

"What?"

"It's basketball, not day care, which shows you haven't really studied the proposal. I'll send you a new set of numbers." I clasped my hands on his desk with the saintly smile of a confirmed do-gooder.

"Whatever it is, we're not supporting it." He looked at his watch. "You don't have an appointment. In fact, how did you get in? No one at the front gate phoned—"

"I know. It must be hard for you to stay on top of your schedule with Billy gone. Why did he run away, anyway? He came down here, after—" I suddenly remembered the conversation I'd had with Billy after church on Sunday.

"Oh, of course. You squealed on him to his dad—you reported seeing him with Josie Dorrado, and Billy came here to confront you. You said a few minutes ago that you didn't see Billy on Monday, so did he confront you on Sunday? You come into the office on Sunday afternoons? Have you told Mr. William about that?"

Grobian shifted in his chair. "I don't see what that has to do with you."

"Besides being a do-gooding basketball coach, I'm one of the detectives the family hired to look for Billy. If your conversation with him was the immediate cause of his disappearance, then the family will want to know about it."

He looked at me narrowly: I might have Mr. William's ear, or even Buffalo Bill's—or I might be a con artist. Before he could challenge me, I added, "Mr. William and I just had a little conversation in the hall right now. I'm the detective who found Billy's Miata the other night, where it had burrowed into the shrubbery underneath the Skyway."

"Yeah, but Billy wasn't at the wheel when it went off the road."

"Is that a fact, Mr. Grobian." I leaned back in the chair so I could see his face better. "Just how do you know that?"

"Cops told me."

I shook my head. "I don't think so. I'll call Commander Rawlings at the Fourth District to check, but when I saw him yesterday they didn't know who was driving it."

"Must have been chatter on the floor, then." His pale eyes shifted to the door and back. "The truckers all gossip about each other. Would have been better if they'd talked to me about Czernin before he died instead of after."

"Meaning?"

"Meaning, this English lady Czernin was balling." He watched to see if vulgarity would make a do-gooder detective wince, but I kept a look of polite interest on my face. "I hear she was in the car, not Billy, and no one knows how she got hold of it."

"I see," I said slowly. "So you didn't know about her until she showed up next to Bron on the golf course yesterday morning?"

"If I had, Bron would have been at the unemployment office on Monday. We don't tolerate rules violations, and having outsiders in the cab is a big By-Smart no-no."

"But if she was in Billy's Miata, she wasn't in the cab with Czernin."

"Czernin was—" He cut himself off. "He'd been driving her around the neighborhood the last two weeks, that's what I learned on the floor when I told the men what had happened to him."

"You tell me Marcena Love was in Billy's Miata and also that she was in Bron's cab," I said. "But the truck and the car weren't together, so Bron was driving for By-Smart that night, right?"

He looked at me, stone-faced. "He signed out a load at four twenty-two. He reached his first delivery in Hammond at five-seventeen. He was thirteen minutes late to his next delivery, in Merrill, and twenty-two minutes late to the third, in Crown Point. After that, which was ten-oh-eight, we didn't hear from him again. Now, if that's it—"

"That isn't 'it,' although it's interesting that you have those times down so exactly. What did you and Bron fight about Monday afternoon?"

"We didn't."

"Everyone heard you shouting," I said. "He thought you'd help with his kid's medical bills."

"If you knew that, why'd you ask?" His tone was belligerent, but his eyes were wary.

"I'd like your version."

He studied me for a long moment, then said, "I don't have a version. Truckers are a rough bunch. You can't manage them if you're not ready to go head-to-head with them, and Czernin was the worst in that regard. Everything was a fight with him, his hours, his routes, his overtime. He thought the world owed him a living, and fights were a regular part of life with him."

"I always saw Bron as a lover, not a fighter, and I've known him since high school," I objected. "If he was so obnoxious, why'd you keep him on for twenty-seven years?"

Grobian distorted his mouth into an ugly leer. "Yeah, you broads all saw his loving side, but in the shop we saw his fighting side. Behind the wheel, we didn't have a better driver—when he kept his mind on the job. Never had an accident in all those years."

"So going back to his pitch for By-Smart's help with his daughter's medical bills—"

"It didn't come up," he snapped.

"Hnnh. I have a witness who heard you promise Czernin you'd discuss—"

"Who's that?" Grobian demanded.

"Someone in the witness protection program." I smiled nastily. "This person said Bron had a document, businesslike, shipshape, that showed you promised to help with April's medical care."

He sat very still for a minute. The light reflected on his glasses, so I couldn't read his expression. Was he alarmed or just thinking things over?

"Your witness showed you the document, right?" he finally said. "So you know I never signed anything."

"So you agree that there was a document? Just not one you signed?"

"I agree with nothing! If you have it, I want to see it—I need to know who's making stuff up about me."

"No one's making anything up, Grobian. Unless you are, with your stories about how you knew Billy wasn't driving his car, or how you and Bron weren't really fighting. Bron died right after he had his fight with you. Is that a coincidence?"

A pulse jumped over his right eye. "You say that again and you'll say it in court in front of a judge. You have nothing on me, not one goddamn thing. You're fishing without worms."

His phone rang and he jumped on it. "Yeah?" He looked at his watch again. "Damn spic is twenty-six minutes late. He can cool his heels for another five . . . And you," he hung up and looked at me. "We're done here."

"No wonder you're the ideal manager for trucking routes—you're like a talking clock. Your so-called spic is twenty-six minutes late, not half an hour, Bron was twenty-two minutes behind schedule. The family will never promote you—you're the perfect clerk-manager for them."

He jumped up from his chair and stood over me, looking furious, but somehow also scared—I had put his worst fears into words. "The family trusts me," he cried. "I don't believe they ever even hired you. Prove it to me."

I laughed. "We'll call Mr. William, shall we? Or would you like to put some money on it first—say, a hundred dollars?"

He was so caught up in his swirl of emotion that he almost bit; I was picturing dinner at the Filigree or paying a third of my phone bill. At the last second, he recovered his poise enough to tell me he didn't have time for crap like this and that I needed to leave. At once.

I got up. "By the way, where did you find Bron's truck? It wasn't near the Miata at the Skyway, and it sure wasn't where I found Bron's body."

"What business is it of yours?"

"Bron was driving his truck; Marcena, according to you, was alone in the Miata. That means there is probably evidence in the truck showing who attacked him, or how he was attacked, or some darn thing or other. I think it's kind of hard to misplace a semi, although not really impossible."

"When we find it, Polack, you'll be the first to know—I don't think. Time for you to move on."

He thrust the arm with the bulging marine tattoo under my elbow and hoisted me to my feet. It was unsettling that he could shift me so easily, but I didn't try to fight him—I needed my strength for more important battles.

When we were facing the aisles of merchandise with the conveyor belts clacking overhead, he spoke into a lapel mike. "Jordan? I got a girl here who made it into the warehouse unannounced. She's heading for the front now—make sure she gets out of the shop, will you? Red parka, tan hard hat."

I decided telling him I was a woman, not a girl, would just get me into a tiresome exchange that wouldn't help any more than a physical fight. As he stood with his hands on his hips, snapping at me to get a move on, I started singing the old Jerry Williams song, "I'm a woman, not a girl—I want a real man," but I did get a move on.

I refused to turn my head to see if Grobian were still watching me and marched down the first aisle with my head held high. I wondered how he would know if I really left, but as I moved through aisles crammed with stuff, beneath the conveyor belts ferrying it around, past the crew in red smocks that read "Be Smart, By-Smart," stacking everything from crates of By-Smart's private-label wine to vast boxes of Christmas decorations, I saw the video cams at every corner. Woman in red parka and tan hard hat, visible to all and sundry. As I worked my way through the maze of aisles and forklifts and boxes, the loudspeakers kept booming—"Forklift needed at A42N"; "Bad spill at B33E"; "Runner to truck bay 213." If I turned back, I imagined they'd start booming, "Woman in red parka on the loose, search and destroy."

In between the wine and the Christmas decorations, I abruptly squatted behind a forklift laden ten feet high with cartons and took off my parka. I turned it inside out and folded it over my arm, hiding my hard hat underneath it. On the back of the forklift was a By-Smart hat that the driver had chosen not to wear, despite all the signs urging him to "Make the Workplace a Safe Place."

I put it on, left the parka tucked behind a crate of sunlamps, and doubled back to the hall where the offices were. Grobian was meeting with a Mexican and he didn't want me to know who it was. That meant—I was going to find out.

Grobian's door was shut, and someone with the By-Smart guard paraphernalia—stun gun, reflective vest, and all—was standing outside. I backed into the paper room, where the printers and fax machines were. I couldn't hear what was going on over the noise of the machines, so after a couple of minutes I looked outside again. Grobian's door was just opening. I ducked my head and moved down the hall to the canteen. In the shadow of the doorway, I watched Grobian summon a guard to escort his visitor back into the warehouse.

I didn't need to stand too close to recognize the *chavo* whom I'd seen at Fly the Flag two weeks ago. The same thick dark hair, the slim hips, the army camouflage jacket. Freddy. He'd been talking to Pastor Andrés, then to Bron, and now to Grobian. They kept talking while they waited for the guard. I could hear enough to tell that they were speaking Spanish, Grobian as fast and fluently as Freddy. Just what were they discussing?

36

SHOWN THE DOOR—AGAIN

Any hopes I had of intercepting Freddy were thwarted by the security staff. By the time I slipped back to the sunlamps to retrieve my parka and my own hard hat and got out the front door, the guards had put Freddy into a Dodge pickup and sent him on his way. I was just in time to see his taillights disappear as I jogged outside. I'd had to waste a minute talking to the woman standing guard at the entrance.

"You the detective? Can I see your ID? We lost track of you there for a few minutes—I'm going to have to search you."

"To see if I'm carrying out any soap dishes?" I said, but I let her pat me down and look inside my shoulder bag. Fortunately, I'd decided to abandon the By-Smart hard hat, although I'd been tempted to keep it—who knew when I might want to come back here.

I only got a glimpse of the Dodge's license plate—the starting letters "VBC"—but I thought it was the same truck that had been outside the Dorrado apartment the first time I visited Josie's family. Had it only been two weeks ago? It seemed more like two years, sometime in the remote past, anyway. The speakers in the flatbed whose bass had been rocking the neighborhood—Josie had hollered something at the guys in the truck, something important, it seemed to me now, but I couldn't think of it.

I trudged slowly down the drive to 103rd Street, dodging the trucks and cars that jolted through the deep ruts. Back in my own car, I took off my parka and turned the heater on. With David Schrader playing the *Goldberg Variations* on my CD player, I leaned back in my seat and tried to think through everything I'd been hearing this afternoon. The document April swore her father had, proving Grobian had promised to come through with money for her medical care. The Bysens wanted to find Billy because he had absconded with a document. Was it the same one? What was it? Had the fight over it between Bron Czernin and Patrick Grobian led to his death?

Then there was the explanation Pastor Andrés had given about his meetings with Frank Zamar at Fly the Flag. It had sounded convincing enough, that he had urged Zamar to go back to Jacqui Bysen and tell her he couldn't make sheets for that price. Zamar must have made some sheets for the neighborhood, because April and Josie both had bought them through their churches. Had this made the Bysens so angry that they blew up his factory? After all, "We never, never renegotiate; it's Daddy Bysen's first law."

Maybe Bron and Marcena, necking in a side street, had seen Jacqui and William, or Grobian, plant the device that torched Fly the Flag, and they had been assaulted to keep them from talking about it. But that didn't make sense: Marcena had met Conrad the day after the plant burned down. If she had seen someone committing arson, she would have told him. I think she would have told him—what could she gain by keeping such information to herself?

Jacqui's smirk when she said I'd find myself at a dead end if I was investigating those sheets, said that, at a minimum, she knew Zamar had been making them. But they still thought they'd had a deal with Zamar— she'd said they were five days behind schedule because he'd died.

And what about Freddy, Julia's—well, not her boyfriend, the person who had gotten her pregnant. I wanted to talk to that *chavo*, but I wasn't sure where I could run him to earth. He might be visiting Julia, or the pastor, or—I realized I didn't even know his last name, let alone where he lived. Anyway, it seemed critical, maybe urgent, to find Billy first, find him before Carnifice did.

I shut my eyes and listened to the music. The *Goldberg Variations* were so precise, so completely balanced, and yet so rich they made me shiver. Had Bach ever sat alone in the dark wondering if he were up to the job, or did his music flow from him so effortlessly that he never knew a moment's doubt?

Finally, I sat up and put the car into gear. Even though I was two blocks from the Dan Ryan, I didn't think I could face all that truck traffic this evening. I retraced my path across the Calumet and picked up Route 41. It's a winding road down here, lined with the ubiquitous vacant lots and fast-food joints of the South Side, but it hugs the Lake Michigan shoreline and is more restful than the expressway.

As I drove north, I tried to imagine a strategy for confronting the Bysens, but nothing came to me. I could picture wiping the smirk off Jacqui Bysen's face or somehow managing to lay Patrick Grobian flat, but I couldn't think of a way to get them all to confess the truth.

I passed the corner where I usually turned to see Mary Ann. It had been almost a week since I last stopped by and I felt guilty for driving past. "Tomorrow," I said aloud, tomorrow, after practice, after the pizza I'd promised the team.

I had a nagging feeling that there was something else I could have done while I was south, but I gave up trying to think about it, gave up on the whole South Side, indulging myself with a CD of old divas, singing along with Rosa Ponselle on "Tu che invoco," a favorite concert aria of my mother's.

Even with stopping at my own place to walk the dogs and collect some wine, I managed to make it to Morrell's by six o'clock. It felt luxurious to have a free evening ahead of me. Morrell had promised to make dinner. We'd lounge in front of a fire, not letting the break-in or Marcena's injuries worry us. Maybe we'd even toast marshmallows.

My romantic fantasies crashed to the ground when I got to Morrell's: his editor had flown in from New York to see Marcena. When Don

Strzepek and Morrell had met in the Peace Corps, Marcena had been there also, a university student traveling around the world, seeking out danger spots with the idea of doing a book. Morrell apparently had called Don yesterday to tell him about Marcena's injuries, and Don wanted to see her in person; he'd arrived ten minutes ago.

"I'm sorry I didn't let you know, darling." Morrell didn't sound very penitent.

Don kissed my cheek. "You know what they say—forgiveness is easier to get than permission."

I forced myself to laugh: Don and I had clashed a couple of years ago, and we still tread warily around each other.

He and Morrell were going to drive down to Cook County as soon as we'd eaten, although Morrell had been to the hospital this afternoon. Marcena still lay in a coma, but the doctors were encouraged by her vital signs and thought they might start waking her up over the weekend.

"Where are her parents?" Don asked.

"I've called," Morrell said. "They're in India, on vacation. Her father's secretary promised to track them down—I'm sure they'll be here as soon as they get the word."

I was glad to know Marcena's vital signs looked good. "No one bothered you while you were out?" I asked Morrell.

"Bothered you?" Don asked.

Morrell explained about the break-in and the theft of Marcena's computer. "So it's good you're staying here, Strzepek, because we need someone able-bodied around the house."

"Vic can fight twice her weight in charging rhinos," Don said.

"When she's fit—she's taken a few knocks of her own lately."

They joked about it some more—Don is a weedy guy, a heavy smoker, who doesn't look as though he could fight his weight in pillows—then Morrell said seriously, "I do think someone was following me this afternoon. I had to take a cab to the hospital, of course, and the driver actually mentioned that the same green LeSabre had been behind us since we left Evanston."

He gave a tight, unhappy smile. "Maybe I should have been paying attention myself, but when you're not driving you forget about things like looking in the rearview mirror. Going home, I did keep watching, and I think someone was there, different car—couldn't make out the model, maybe a Toyota, but once I went in my front door they took off."

"But that doesn't make sense," I objected. "Unless—they could have a remote listening device, I suppose, so they know when you're leaving, and what you're saying when you're here."

He looked startled, then angry. "How dare they? And who hell are 'they,' anyway?"

"I don't know. Police? Carnifice Security, seeing whether we know where Billy is?" I lowered my voice to a murmur just in case. "Did you find out anything from the neighbors?"

"Ms. Jamison saw a strange man letting himself into the building when she was out with Tosca. That was around six this morning." Tosca was Ms. Jamison's Sealyham. "Well-dressed white man around thirty-five or forty, she just assumed he was a friend of mine because he had a key that worked in the lock."

Morrell practically runs a B and B for his globe-trotting reporter friends—Marcena wasn't the first person I'd shared his time and space with. Another reason to wonder about living together. Aside from the sin, of course, I thought, remembering Pastor Andrés's stern warnings about Josie and Billy.

Morrell was still speculating on who could have gotten a front door key to his condo, but I interrupted to say it was too big a universe. "Your building manager, the Realtor, one of your old friends. Maybe even Don, here, if he has a pressed suit someplace in his wardrobe. Really, though, the guy probably had some kind of master device that Ms. Jamison didn't see him use, a sophisticated electronic tumbler pick. That kind of device is out of my price range, but an outfit like Carnifice probably gives them away as door prizes at the company picnic. The FBI has them, or—well, any big operation. The real question is why they're not doing anything except watching. Maybe they are waiting for us to find out what Marcena knew—maybe if we start acting, we'll prove to them we learned what she knew and then they'll move in for the kill."

"Victoria, I can't possibly follow that logic," Morrell said. "Why don't we forget about it while we eat."

He'd made a chicken stew he'd learned to cook in Afghanistan, with raisins, coriander, and yogurt, and we did a reasonably good job of putting all our conflicts and worries to one side during the meal. I tried not to mind that Don drank most of the Torgiano—it's a red wine from the Italian hill country where my mother grew up, and it's not easy to find in Chicago. If I'd known Don was going to be there guzzling, I would have brought something French that was easier to replace.

WHERE THE
BUFFALO ROAM

Don and Morrell left as soon as they'd done the dishes. I tried to interest myself in a novel, but residual fatigue, or worries about what was happening, maybe even jealousy, kept me from concentrating. I was even less successful with television.

I was pacing restlessly, thinking I'd be more comfortable in my own place, when my cell phone rang. It was Mr. William.

"Howdy," I said affably, pretending it was a social call.

"Did you tell Grobian that the family had hired you?" he demanded without preamble.

"I cannot tell a lie. And I didn't. You did hire me two weeks ago."

"And fired you!"

"Please, Mr. Bysen: I resigned. I sent you a certified letter, and you begged and pleaded with me to keep hunting Billy. When I said no, you hired my pals at Carnifice."

"Be that as it may—"

"Be that as it is!" I snapped, affability forgotten.

"Be that as it may," he repeated as if I hadn't spoken, "we need to talk to you. My wife and mother insist on being part of any conversation about Billy, so you need to come out to Barrington Hills at once."

"You guys are truly amazing," I said. "if you need to see me that badly, you can come down to my office in the morning. All ten of you. Bring your butler, too—I don't care."

"That's a stupid suggestion," he said coldly. "We have a company to run. Tonight is the one time—"

"You've been living with underemployed women too long, Bysen: I, too, have a company to run. And a life to live. I don't need to placate you to keep on going, so I don't need to jump every time you have a whim at a weird time of day or night."

I heard some kind of agitated consultation in the background and then a woman came on the line. "Ms. Warashki? This is Mrs. Bysen. We're all so worried about young Billy that we don't always remember to say things the right way, but I hope you'll disregard that and come out to talk to us. I would really, really appreciate it."

Seeing all the Bysens together versus pacing restlessly around Morrell's condo? At least in Barrington Hills, I'd get to see the floor show.

It was a long thirty miles from Morrell's place to the Bysen compound. No expressway cleaves through the North Shore and I had to make my way on side roads. The one good thing about routes like this is that it's easier to check for tails. At first, I thought I was clean, but when I'd gone about four miles I realized they were using a couple of different cars, changing places every few blocks. Unless they wanted to kill me, they were more an irritant than anything else, but I still tried to shake them, cutting off the main roads a couple of times into suburban cul-de-sacs. Each time, I'd be on my own for a half mile or so and then they'd be back. By the time I pulled off Dundee Road in Barrington Hills, I realized it didn't matter—if these were Carnifice people working for the Bysens, they'd just spent a lot of energy tailing me to home base.

Barrington Hills didn't run to streetlights—it was kind of like a large private nature preserve, with lakes and winding lanes. On a moonless night, it was especially hard to find my way since my trackers meant I couldn't get out of my car to check for street names. I pulled up to the gate of the compound in an edgy mood. The car that had been ahead of me drove on down the road, but the one behind me stayed on the verge, just out of sight of the guard station.

The estate had a high iron fence around it, sealed in the front with rolling gates. I went directly to the guard station, told the man I was a detective, and said old Mr. Bysen had talked to me about his missing grandson and wanted me to report to him in person. The man phoned into the compound, spoke to several different people, and finally said in amazement that Mr. Bysen actually wanted to see me. He explained how to find Buffalo Bill's house—not that he called the old man that—and slid the iron gates open for me.

Barrington Hills is dotted with lakes, real ones, not human creations, and the Bysen houses were spread around one big enough to boast a marina and several sailboats. Besides three of the four sons, one of the daughters, their families, and Buffalo Bill, my research had shown that Linus Rankin, the corporate counsel, and two other senior corporate officers also had houses on the estate.

The road had a few discreet lamps so that the families could find their way in the dark; even with such dim light, I could tell that the houses were monstrous, as if everyone needed enough space to house a cruise ship—should one crash on the lake.

Midway around the lake, more or less directly across from the guard station, stood Buffalo Bill's mansion. I pulled up a circular drive, lit by a row of carriage lamps. A Hummer and two sports cars were parked on the verge; I pulled in behind them, and walked up a shallow step to ring the front doorbell.

A butler in a tailcoat answered the door. "The family are drinking coffee in the lounge. I will announce you."

He led me down a long hall at a pace decorous enough for me to stare at the surroundings. The hall seemed to bisect the house, with salons, a conservatory, a music room, and who knows what all lying on either side. The same soft golds that I'd seen at the headquarter building dominated the decorating scheme here. We're rich, the embroidered silk wall coverings proclaimed, everything we touch turns to gold.

Mr. William strode up the hall to meet me. My efforts at small talk, admiring the music room, the Dutch masters on one wall, the time it must take him to commute from here to South Chicago, only made him tighten his lips so much they looked like little circular pickles.

"You should take up the trumpet," I said. "The way you purse up your lips all the time, those muscles will give you a really strong embouchure. Or maybe you already play, one of those nice twenty-dollar By-Smart trumpets, with lessons available on CD."

"Yes, all the reports we've had done on you say you think you're funny, and that it's a handicap in your business," Mr. William said coldly.

"Gosh, you've spent good By-Smart money having reports done on me? That makes me feel superimportant." I could hear my voice going up half a register, my cheerleader chirp.

Before our witty exchange could escalate, the Buffalo's personal assistant, Mildred, came clicking down the hall toward us on high alligator heels. So she really never left Buffalo Bill's side. What did Mrs. Bysen think about her husband's personal assistant living with him at home as well as at work?

"Mr. Bysen and Mr. William will talk to this person in Mr. Bysen's study, Sneedham," she said to the butler, avoiding my face.

Mrs. Bysen popped out of a side room to appear next to Mildred. Her gray curls were as tightly combed and groomed as they had been in church on Sunday, her green shantung dress as smooth as if invisible hands ironed it every time she sat down. But inside this formal attire, her face showed the benignity I'd observed on Sunday—except that in her home she had an assurance she'd lacked at the Mt. Ararat service.

"Thank you, Mildred, but if Bill is going to talk to a detective about my grandson I want to be there. Annie Lisa might like to hear her report, too." She sounded a little uncertain, as if Annie Lisa was either not sober enough, or perhaps not interested enough, to sit in on our meeting.

"Bill didn't tell me he was working with any lady detectives, but maybe a woman will have more understanding of my grandson than those corporate people who came through here yesterday. Do you have news of Billy?" She looked at me firmly—she might be benign, but she knew her own mind and how to express it.

"I'm afraid I don't have news, ma'am, or only of a negative kind: I know he's not with Pastor Andrés, or with Josie Dorrado's best friend, and I know Josie's family is racked with anguish—they have no idea where the two may be. Maybe you could help me understand why Billy ran away in the first place. If I could get a handle on that, it might help me find him."

She nodded. "Sneedham, I think we'll want Annie Lisa and Jacqui. I doubt if Gary and Roger have anything to contribute. Do you want coffee, Ms. War—I'm afraid I don't have your name firmly in mind—" She paused while I repeated it. "Yes, Ms. Warshawski. We don't serve alcohol in this house, but we can offer you a soft drink."

I said coffee would be fine, and Sneedham went off to herd the designated sheep into the fold. I followed Mrs. Bysen down the hall to where it ended in a room with a sunken floor, carpeted in a thick gold pile. Massive furniture, suitable to a medieval castle and upholstered in heavy brocades, weighted down the room. Stiff drapes, in a matching brocade, were pulled across the windows.

Mildred busied herself with moving a couple of chairs close together—no small job, considering their size, and the thickness of the carpet. William made no move to help her: she wasn't really a family member, just the most loyal of all the retainers.

While we waited on the rest of the family, Mrs. Bysen asked how well I knew Billy. I answered her honestly—her face seemed to demand honesty, at least from me—that I'd only met him several times, that he appeared to be a decent, fundamentally serious and idealistic young man, and that he often mentioned her as his most important teacher. She looked pleased but didn't add anything.

After a few minutes, Jacqui entered; she'd changed out of her fluttery taupe skirt into a floor-length, belted black dress. It wasn't a formal gown, just a tasteful cashmere at-home dress.

Another woman stumbled in behind Jacqui. She had Billy's freckles, or he had hers. The auburn curls he cropped close to his head stood out around hers, like the hair of an ungroomed poodle. So this was Annie Lisa, Billy's mom. An older woman, encased in magenta silk, kept an arm around Annie Lisa as they waded through the heavy pile. We were never introduced, but I assumed she was the wife of the corporate counsel, Linus Rankin, since he came in a few minutes later.

I knew from my database that Billy's mother was forty-eight, but she appeared more like a schoolgirl, with her uncertain, almost coltlike gait. She looked around with a puzzled face as if she didn't know why she was on the planet, let alone this particular bit of it. When I moved across the room to greet her, her husband immediately went to her side as if to forestall her talking to me. He took her elbow and almost pushed her to an armchair as remote as possible from middle of the room.

When everyone else was seated, and Sneedham had served weak coffee, Buffalo Bill stumped in, using his silver-topped walking stick like a ski pole to push himself through the high pile. He went to the heavier of the armchairs Mildred had moved; she took the one to his left. Mrs. Bysen sat on a couch and patted the cushion next to her for me.

"Well, young woman? Well? You've been trespassing on my warehouse, spying on me, so you'd better have a good explanation of what you're up to." Buffalo Bill glared at me and blew so heavily that his cheeks pouched out.

I leaned back against the thick cushions, although the couch was so deep it wasn't very comfortable. "We do have a lot to talk about. Let's start with Billy. Something happened at the company that upset him so badly he didn't think he could talk to anyone in the family about it. What was that?"

"It was the other way around, detective," Mr. William said. "You were present the day Billy brought that ridiculous preacher up to our offices. We spent days trying to smooth over—"

"Yes, yes, we know all that," Buffalo Bill cut his son off with his usual impatience. "Did you say something to him, William, to make him run away?"

"Oh, for heaven's sake, Father, you act as though Billy were as delicate as one of Mother's roses. He takes everything too hard, but he knows how we run our business; after five months in the warehouse, he'd seen everything. It's only been since he came under the thumb of this preacher that he started behaving so strangely."

"It's that Mexican girl, really," Aunt Jacqui said. She was sitting on an embroidered hassock, her legs crossed, the skirt of her long dress falling open just above her knees. "He's in love, or thinks he is, and it's making him imagine he understands the world from her perspective."

"He did get very upset when he found that Pat Grobian at the warehouse had been spying on him and reporting back to you, Mr. William," I said. "He went down to the warehouse on Sunday afternoon to confront Grobian. Grobian says he knows Billy cleared out his locker on Monday, but he didn't see him then. You also were there on Monday, Mr. William, but you say you never saw your son, either."

"What were you doing down at the warehouse?" Buffalo Bill demanded, lowering his bull's head at his son. "First I ever heard of it. Don't you have enough to do without shoving onto Gary's turf?"

I pictured the family chart I'd seen in my law enforcement database—it was hard to keep track of all the Bysens. Gary was Aunt Jacqui's husband; I guess he handled domestic operations.

"Billy has been behaving so strangely I wanted to check up on him in person. He is my son, Father, although you delight so much in undermining me that—"

"William, this isn't a good time for that," his mother said. "We all are devastated about Billy, and it doesn't help for us to attack each other. I want to know what we can do to help Ms. Warshawski find him, since your big agency hasn't succeeded. I know they tracked down his car and his cell phone, but he'd given those away. Do you know why he did that, Ms. Warshawski?"

"I can't be sure, but he knew they were easy to trace, and he seems to have been very determined to disappear."

"Do you think that Mexican girl has talked him into a runaway marriage?" she asked.

"Ma'am, Josie Dorrado is an American girl. And I don't know any state where it's legal for a fifteen-year-old to get married. Even a sixteen-year-old needs written permission from her guardian, and Josie's mother isn't eager for this relationship, either—she thinks Billy is a rich, irresponsible Anglo boy who will get her daughter pregnant and abandon her."

"Billy would never do that!" Mrs. Bysen was shocked.

"Maybe not, ma'am, but Ms. Dorrado doesn't know your grandson any better than you know her daughter." I watched her face change as she absorbed this idea, before turning to her husband. "Billy apparently has, or took, some documents that your son wants pretty badly. Mr. William tried to laugh it off when we spoke this afternoon, but he went to the Dorrado apartment Monday night and searched there. What's missing that—"

"What!" Buffalo Bill exploded at his son. "It's not enough the boy's gone, and now you're accusing him of stealing? Your own son? Just what have you misplaced that you're trying to blame on him?"

"No one thinks he's stealing, Papa Bill," Jacqui put in quickly. "But you know one of Billy's duties at the warehouse is to sort the faxes as they come in. He seemed to think some of the information from our Matagalpa plant down in Nicaragua meant more than it did, and he took it away with him two weeks ago. We thought he might have taken it to give to the Mexican minister, but no one down there seems to have it."

She sounded so sure of this that I supposed they'd had Carnifice search everyone's home to look for it—not just the careless once-over that William had given the Dorrado apartment Monday night. So it probably was Carnifice who'd come into Morrell's place this morning. Did they think Marcena had the Nicaragua faxes, or was there yet something else that they were really looking for?

"Mr. Bysen," I said to the Buffalo, "you know Bron Czernin was murdered Monday night while he was driving for—"

"It's not clear he was on the job when he was killed." Mr. William frowned.

"Now what?" I exclaimed. "Are you going to try to pretend he wasn't driving Monday night so you can deny his family's comp claim? Grobian himself has a log of where Bron took his truck!"

"That truck has disappeared. And we know now that he was—dallying with this Love woman, which means he was off the By-Smart clock as far as we're concerned. If the family wants to take it to court, they can try, but his widow will find it very unpleasant to have the details of her husband's life revealed in public."

"But her lawyer won't be offended at all," I said coldly. "Freeman Carter will be representing her." Freeman is my lawyer. If I guaranteed his fee, he might be willing to go up against By-Smart—you never know.

Linus Rankin, the corporate counsel, knew Freeman's name. He said if Sandra could afford Freeman, she didn't even need the insurance claim or her cashier's job.

I could feel anger rising in me, like a blood infection, starting at my toes and sweeping through my body. "Why do you begrudge Sandra Czernin her rightful settlement? A quarter of a million dollars would barely pay for the cars you have parked out front, let alone this massive estate here. She needs to look after her daughter who's seriously ill, and your company has denied her health insurance by keeping her hours just below forty a week. You claim to be Christians—"

"Enough!" Buffalo Bill roared. "I remember you, young woman, you tried to make some insane argument about fifty thousand dollars meaning nothing to the company, and now you think a quarter of a million means nothing to us. I worked for every dime I ever made, and this Czernin woman can do the same."

"Yes, Bill, of course," his wife said. "All of us getting angry about that tonight isn't going to help find Billy. Was there anything else, Ms. Warshawski?"

I swallowed some of the coffee, which was now cold as well as thin. I'm not a billionaire, but I would never serve a visitor such poor stuff.

"Thanks, Mrs. Bysen. Marcena Love, who was found with Bron Czernin yesterday morning, visited your husband several times. She was doing a series of reports on South Chicago for an English newspaper. I want to know what she and your husband discussed to see if she revealed anything unusual, even illegal, that she'd seen on the South Side. It might explain why she was attacked."

"What does that have to do with Billy?" Mrs. Bysen said.

"I don't know. But she was in his car when it was driven off the road under the Skyway. They're connected in some way."

Mrs. Bysen turned to her husband and demanded that he recount his meetings with Marcena. Even with Mildred's prodding, though, he seemed to think they had discussed only the Second World War and his illustrious career in the Army Air Forces.

I was tired, tired of the discussion, the Bysens, the heavy furniture, and when Mrs. Bysen announced that we had talked long enough I was as glad as her son to bring the evening to a close. William went over to collect his wife, announcing gruffly to his mother that it was time Annie Lisa was in bed. Jacqui followed them. While Mildred and Linus Rankin conferred with Buffalo Bill, I asked Mrs. Bysen if their detectives had searched Billy's room.

"His room, his computer, his books. Poor boy, he tries so hard to live a Christian life, and it's not always easy to do that, even in a Christian family. I am proud of him, but I have to confess it hurts me that he wouldn't turn to me. He must know I would help him."

"He's confused right now," I said. "Confused and angry. He feels betrayed in some fundamental way. He didn't say anything to me about this, but I wonder if he thinks you would tell Mr. Bysen anything he confided in you."

She started to protest, but then gave a watery smile. "Maybe I would, Ms. Warshawski, maybe I would at that. Bill and I have been married sixty years now—you don't turn off a lifetime of confiding. But Bill, for all his tough talk and tough business measures, is a fair and good man. I hope Billy hasn't forgotten that."

She took me to the hall, where her son Gary was standing with Jacqui. When she sent them to find Sneedham to take me to my car, I asked if there was a back way out of the compound.

"Your son's detectives are trailing me, and I would like to go home alone if I could."

She cocked her head, her curls stiff, but her face showed a faint trace of mischief. "They are somewhat heavy-handed, these men, aren't they? There's a service drive behind the house—it will take you out onto Silverwood Lane. I'll release the lock from the kitchen, but you must get out of the car to open the gate. Please close it behind you; it will relock itself."

As the butler came toward us, she suddenly clasped my hands between her own. "Ms. Warshawski, if you have any idea at all where my grandson is, I beg you to tell me. He is—very dear to me. I have a private telephone number for my children and husband to use; you may call me on that."

She watched me anxiously until I'd written the number down in my pocket diary, then turned me over to her butler.

38 PRIMITIVE ART

Mr. William and his wife were climbing into the Hummer when I got outside. The Porsche belonged to Jacqui and Gary, not surprisingly. The third car, a Jaguar sedan, probably belonged to Linus Rankin. The other children seemed to feel energetic enough, or safe enough, to come on foot.

I waited until Gary and William had driven off before leaving myself— I didn't want William to see me using the drive behind the house that led to the service road.

What a lot of friction builds up over the years in such close quarters. The conflict between William and his father was the most obvious, but William had told me the brothers fought with each other; Jacqui, who spent lavishly on her wardrobe and worked slavishly on her figure, inspired her own share of hostility in the family. No wonder Annie Lisa had checked into a dreamworld, and her daughter into sex and drugs. Poor thing, how was Candace dealing with life in Korea?

I made it through the back gate without anyone seeing me. Out on Silverwood Lane, I kept my lights off, moving slowly down the unlit road until it merged with a larger artery. When I got to a service station,

I pulled in to fill the Mustang and to check my maps. I was a couple of miles from a major expressway here that would ultimately take me into the city. It seemed easier to take a fast route home than to trek cross-country to Morrell's, especially since I'd be sharing the evening with Don. I took out my cell phone to call Morrell and then remembered my own advice to Billy: my phone, too, had a GPS tracking signal. That was how Carnifice, or whoever, was keeping track of me, of Morrell, of all of us.

I turned it off. I thought about finding a pay phone so I could call Morrell on a landline, but if they were bugging his phone they'd pick that up, anyway. I pulled out of the gas station, feeling oddly liberated by my anonymity, gliding through the night, no one knowing where I was. As I slid onto the expressway, I began belting out "Sempre libera," although I could tell I was woefully off-key.

There was so little traffic now that I pushed the needle up to eighty, coasting from expressway to Tollway, slowing only for the inevitable knot of traffic around O'Hare, and cruising to my exit in the city in twenty-seven minutes. Keeping time like that, I could replace Patrick Grobian, monitoring his truckers down to the second. I grinned to myself, picturing the family's reaction if I suggested it.

I wondered why they'd summoned me tonight—to prove they could? Of course, they'd drawn me away from Morrell's—maybe they wanted Carnifice to go back in for a more thorough search. Or maybe they had acted out of genuine concern about Billy. I supposed that could be true of his grandmother, but neither of his parents showed a tenth the distress that Rose Dorrado was feeling over Josie's disappearance.

I wished I had taken advantage of the opportunity to ask more questions of my own, such as what had happened to Billy's Miata—had they brought it home as a memento or sold it for scrap? I might stop by the underpass tomorrow afternoon to see if anything remained of it.

It had been stripped, William had said this afternoon; there was nothing left of it. And what was left had probably been explored pretty thoroughly by his high-powered Carnifice operatives. They could have carried the remains of the car to their private lab and examined every fiber of the floor to tell them when Billy had last driven it. Maybe it was among the ten acres of cars in the pound along 103rd Street, but, either way, the remains were most likely out of my reach.

I also hadn't brought up the document April mentioned, the one her father said he had—the one that proved the company had agreed to pay April's medical bills, or, at least, to give him money to cover them. I was crossing Belmont before it dawned on me that whatever document Bron had could be the piece of paper William was so desperate to find. Of course Bron hadn't had a signed paper that proved the company would take care of April's medical bills—he had something he was using for blackmail, and By-Smart had lost track of it and wanted it back.

Whatever it was would definitely have to wait until morning. I parked in the garage behind my building: there were only three spaces in it, and when one of them became vacant this summer my name had finally made it to the top of the waiting list. It would be pleasant in the winter to be able to go straight into my building from my car, and it was pleasant on a late night like tonight not to have to worry about leaving my car out on the street where anyone who was trailing me could find it.

On my way up from the basement, I saw that Mr. Contreras's light was still on. I stopped to tell him I was home. While we shared a glass of his homemade grappa, which smells like fuel oil and packs the kick of six mules, I called Morrell on my neighbor's landline to explain where I was. He and Don were still up, arguing over geopolitics, or reminiscing about adventures, but they were in good spirits, and definitely not missing me. No one had broken in, as far as they knew—or cared.

In the morning, I got up early to run the dogs before making my nine A.M. appointment with Amy Blount. I was still feeling stiff, but my fingers were down to their normal size, which cheered me greatly—it would make my driving day easier, and if I had to use my gun I wouldn't have to fret about getting my finger inside the trigger guard.

Amy got to my office right on time. It was a relief to have her there—not so much to take on a chunk of my outstanding workload as just to have someone to go over things with. Working alone is, frankly, a lonely business—I could see why Bron liked having Marcena, or other women, for that matter, in the cab of his truck with him—eight hours hopping around northwest Indiana and south Chicagoland would wear thin after twenty-some years.

Amy and I went over my outstanding caseload. I showed her how to log on to LifeStory, the database I use for doing background checks and getting personal information on people for my clients—or for myself, as I'd done yesterday in looking up the Bysen family.

I found myself telling Amy the whole story of the Bysens, and Bron Czernin, and Marcena; even my jealousy came seeping out. She made notes in her tiny, tidy handwriting. When I finished, she said she'd work the whole narrative up on a flowchart; if she had questions or suggestions, she'd call me.

It was eleven by the time I finished. I had to leave for an appointment in the Loop, a presentation to a law firm that is one of my bread-and-butter clients. I had hoped to get to South Chicago in time to search the underpass before basketball practice, but my clients were unusually demanding, or I was unusually unfocused, and I barely had time to grab a bowl of chicken noodle soup before heading to the South Side. I also made a side stop at a phone store to pick up a charger for Billy's phone; I could give that to April after practice. And I went to a grocery to buy food for Mary Ann—the day was cold enough that milk and cheese would keep in my trunk. In the end, I made it to Bertha Palmer High only a few minutes ahead of my team.

The practice wasn't as intense as Monday's, but the girls did a creditable job. Julia Dorrado came, with María Inés and Betto, who put the baby carrier in the stands and played with his Power Rangers during practice. Julia was out of shape, but I could see why Mary Ann McFarlane was enthusiastic about her game. It wasn't just the way she moved, but the fact that she could see the whole court, the way players like Larry Bird and M.J. had done. Celine, my gangbanger, was the only other person on the team who really had that gift. Not even Josie and April, both of whom we needed on the squad, had Julia's sense of timing.

When practice finished, I took them all to Zambrano's for pizza, even Betto and the baby, but I hustled them through the meal. It was already dark, and I wanted to get down to the underpass where Billy's Miata had crashed before the streets were completely deserted. I dropped Julia and María Inés at home, with her brother and the baby, but didn't take the time to see Rose, just sending up a message that Josie and Billy were still deeply hidden.

"I think they're safe," I said to Julia. "I think they're safe because the Bysens are spending a lot of money looking for Billy; if anything bad had happened to him and Josie, they'd have found them by now. Your mom can call me on my cell phone if she wants to talk about it, but I want to look myself in one place I don't think the detectives searched. Got that?"

"Yeah, okay . . . Do you think I can still play with the team?"

"You are definitely good enough to play with the team, but you've got to get yourself back in school before you can practice again. Can you do that between now and Monday?"

She nodded solemnly and got out of the car. It worried me that she left the baby carrier on the backseat for Betto to deal with, but I couldn't add a parenting skills class to my current load; I just watched until he and the baby were safely up the walk and inside the house, then turned south, to the underpass where I'd found Billy's Miata.

Carnifice might have searched this area for William, especially if my hunch was right that he was hot for whatever document Bron had used to threaten the company. Still, South Chicago was my briar patch. I refused to believe that Carnifice would think about it the way I did. The Bysen family was a job for them, not a complicated part of their roots.

The first part of the Skyway is built into an embankment that severs South Chicago—in fact, when it was built it put a lot of little shops and factories I'd grown up with out of business. But as it approaches the Indiana border, the highway rises up on stilts; homeless people build little shelters under them, but mostly commuters and locals use the road as a handy garbage bin. I pulled over to the verge, driving carefully—I didn't want to puncture a tire down here—and left my lights on, pointing into the thicket of dead branches and discarded appliances.

The bracken showed fresh scarring from where the Miata had plowed into it. It had been three days now, and the area saw a lot of movement, people hiding in the undergrowth or sorting through the debris for salvage, but because of the cold the car tracks were still visible. I was no forensic expert, but it looked to me as though the car had been driven deliberately into the thicket, as if someone wanted to hide it—I couldn't see any traces of swerving or other signs that the driver (was it Marcena? had it been Bron?) had lost control of the car.

I moved slowly, inspecting every inch of ground as I walked forward. When I got to the end of the broken branches, I got down on my knees—I'd put on old jeans after the basketball practice just for this search.

I was glad of my mittens, as I pushed the undergrowth aside and inspected the area for any trace of—anything. I found a small piece of the front fender, the paint still shiny, unlike the dull, rusted metal all around me. It didn't mean anything, but I still stuck it into my parka pocket.

Overhead, the traffic was crawling. It was the height of the evening rush, and everyone was creeping out of town to their tidy suburban homes. They were also eating and drinking—which I knew because they tossed out their empty cans and wrappers, which floated down into the garbage underneath. I was almost hit by an empty beer bottle when I started to explore the area to the left of the car's treadmarks.

I kept picking up stray pieces of paper, hoping that whatever document the Bysens were looking for might have fallen out of the car when it was being dismembered. I kept telling myself that this was futile, a sign of desperation, but I couldn't stop. Most of what I saw were discarded advertisements, oriental rugs for five dollars, palm readings for ten, which I guess showed we need guarantees about the future more than we need our floors covered, but all kinds of stuff got tossed over the side of the Skyway—bills, letters, even bank statements.

I'd been at it for about an hour when I found the two books that had been in Billy's trunk—Oscar Romero's *Violence of Love* and the book that Aunt Jacqui said made her anorexic—*Rich Christians in an Age of Hunger*. I put them into my parka pocket. I didn't know what I'd expected, but that seemed to be the net of what I was going to find. I looked disconsolately at the area I'd been searching. The daylight had gone completely, and my car headlights seemed to be getting dimmer as well. There was one last piece of paper near where I'd found the books. I tucked it into *Rich Christians*, and climbed back into my car on stiff legs.

I turned the car around to face north, but parked it while the engine warmed up again to look at my haul. I thumbed eagerly through Billy's books, hoping that some mysterious document would drop out, his will, for instance, revised to leave all his holdings to the Mt. Ararat church, or a proclamation to By-Smart's board of directors. Nothing emerged but Billy's round schoolboy hand making notes in the margins of Archbishop Romero's book. I squinted at his notes, but what I could make out in the dim light didn't seem very promising.

The paper I'd found by the books looked like a child's drawing. It was a crude sketch of a frog, done in Magic Marker, with a big black wart in the middle of its back, sitting on a dubious-looking log. I almost pitched it out the window, but the South Side was everyone's dumping ground—I, at least, could put it out with my home papers for recycling.

The car was finally warm; I could take off my mittens, which were cumbersome for driving, and head north. I needed to stop at Mary Ann's; I had groceries in my trunk for her, and I wanted to talk to her about Julia and April. I wondered, too, if she might have an inkling where Josie would choose to go to ground.

It was seven-thirty. Overhead, the traffic was moving fast, but the streets around me were deserted again—anyone who crossed them to get home was long gone. My route took me near the corner where the Czernins lived, but I couldn't see their bungalow. My heart ached for April, lying in bed with her bear, her daddy dead, her own heart doing something unknown and frightening inside her body.

My mother had died when I was only a year older, and it had been a terrible loss, one that still haunts me in difficult ways, but at least no one had killed Gabriella; she hadn't died in a pit next to a foreign lover. And the father who stayed behind had adored her, and adored me—an easier journey than April was going to make, with her mother's relentless anger scorching the house. I would have to talk to April's teachers, see what could be done to get her academics up to a standard where she'd have a chance at college—if there were even a way she could afford college.

Sandra's demand that I prove Bron had been on the job when he died was April's only hope, either for her heart or her education, and I wasn't optimistic. William had made it clear that the company would fight a comp claim to the bitterest possible limit. If I had Carnifice's resources, maybe I could track down just where Bron had been at those odd times Grobian had quoted to me, ten-oh-something in Crown Point, Indiana, prove that he died on the job, but I didn't even know where to look for his truck. For all I knew, it was in that pound over on 103rd Street, along with the Miata, or simply mingled with a lot of other By-Smart semis anywhere from South Chicago to South Carolina.

It made my head hurt, thinking about the number of things that needed to be done if I were going to figure anything out down here. And I still didn't know where Billy and Josie could have gone. I'd wasted an hour in a landfill, and all I had to show for it was two religious books and a child's drawing of a frog sitting on a—I slammed on the brakes and pulled over to the curb.

The child's drawing, of a frog sitting on a piece of rubber. Like the frayed piece of wiring Bron had in his workshop behind the kitchen. A drawing of how to make a nitric acid circuit breaker. Put a rubber plug in a froggy soap dish. Put it on top of the intake cable at Fly the Flag. Pour in some nitric acid. Eventually, the acid would eat through the plug, eat through the rubber casing around the intake line, the exposed wires would short out, spark, ignite the fabric nearby.

I tried to imagine why Billy would have had this sketch when it was Bron who'd been experimenting with the wire. I couldn't picture Billy committing sabotage at Fly the Flag—unless the pastor had told him to do it because it would somehow be good for the community. The pastor was the only person he could trust right now, Billy had said, but I still couldn't see his stubborn, earnest young face hovering over a wire with a dish of acid.

Bron, yes, Bron could do it, but if he was constructing the thing would he have carried a diagram around with him when he left the house? How had he gotten hold of the wretched frog, anyway? Julia, Josie, April. Julia had bought the frog, she'd said, as a Christmas present for Sancia. I'd thought at the time she said it she was lying; now I was sure of it. Josie could have taken it from Julia and given it to April, although that didn't quite make sense.

I drummed my fingers on the steering wheel. April, heartsore in every sense of the word, I didn't want to push hard on her, but I did have the charger for Billy's phone—I could question her while dropping it off, but I'd save that option for last. But Julia—Julia was another story. I turned the steering wheel hard to the left and made a U-turn back to South Chicago.

39 PAINFUL EXTRACTION

Rose Dorrado's face was even duller than when I'd been here two nights ago. Like Sandra Czernin, she hadn't washed, or even combed, her hair lately, and the red curls were matted and tangled, but she stepped aside to let me into the apartment. Betto and Samuel were on the couch, watching *Spiderman.* María Inés was propped up between them, cooing and clapping her hands aimlessly. She was wrapped in a little piece of red-and-white striped bunting. More of those flag remnants. I stared at it, wondering how many times I'd seen it without noticing it.

"Now what?" Rose was saying in a leaden voice. "You've found my Josie? She's dead?"

I shook my head. "Didn't Julia give you my message? The Bysens have a big team out looking for Billy; maybe they'll turn him up. The good news is that Josie is almost certainly with him. Have you talked to your sister in Waco?"

"It's good news that my girl is out sleeping with a boy? I don't need another baby in this house." Even the angry words came out in a listless tone. "Anyway, my sister, she never heard from them. Around the building, they say you found Bron Czernin and that English lady Monday night. They were using Billy's fancy car, and you found them next to it, lying in the landfill. So what's not to say that Billy and Josie are there, too, and you didn't find them."

The story had certainly gotten garbled as it raced around the neighborhood. "I can't guarantee that, of course," I said quietly. "But I know Billy gave his car to Bron because he didn't want his family finding him through his license plate, so I don't think he was with Bron. Anyway, when I found the car it was under the Skyway. No one knows how Bron and Marcena ended up by the landfill."

"So where did they go, Billy and Josie? Not to the pastor, not to you, I even went to see Josie's father—I thought, maybe you were right, maybe she did turn to him, but he could hardly remember which child she was."

We talked it over in as many ways as we could think of—which were pretty meager. I had a feeling Billy was staying in South Chicago—whatever was bothering him about his family was right here in this neighborhood, and he wouldn't be able to leave it alone.

"I'll call everyone on the team," I finally promised. "Monday night, I just scouted around their homes, looking for Billy's car or any sign the two of them were there. But before I go, Rose, I need to know a couple of things, from you, and from Julia."

I had come to ask Julia about the soap dish, but I wanted to know about that bunting. "Tell me about the sheets, the ones on Josie's and Julia's beds—and now this fabric you've wrapped María Inés in. Did Zamar make those at Fly the Flag?"

"Oh, those sheets." She half lifted an apathetic shoulder. "As if any of that matters now. He thought—the pastor thought, why not sell towels, sheets, pot holders, things like that, through the churches? Something good for the community, making sheets in the community, buying, selling, it was a dream of the pastor, that we have a buying cooperative—he was thinking maybe in time we could buy and sell everything, clothes, food, even drugs, and save money and make money. He started with Mr. Zamar, and Mr. Zamar, he tried, he really did, even though the pastor, he accused him, that Mr. Zamar didn't want the cooperative to work. But I was there, I was sewing, we made five hundred sheets, a thousand tow-els—and only seventeen people bought them, mostly the mothers of the girls who play basketball. Who can make a living when only seventeen people buy what you are selling?"

"So was that the second shop where you were working?" I asked, puzzled. "Making sheets for the cooperative?"

She gave a crack of hysterical laughter. "No and no and no. The second shop, it was right where the first shop is. Only we did it in the middle of the night, so the pastor wouldn't see. As if he doesn't hear everything going on in the neighborhood, he's like God, the pastor, what he doesn't see he knows anyway."

I squatted next to the boys, who'd been watching us nervously. "Betto, Samuel, your mama and I have to talk. Can you go into the dining room?"

They apparently still remembered me as the woman who could get you charred, because they scuttled off the couch into the back of the apartment with just one frightened look at their mother. If only I had that effect on Pat Grobian or the pastor. We sat down, the baby sleeping between us.

"Why didn't Zamar want Pastor Andrés to see the second shop?"

"Because we were using illegals!" she shouted. "People who are so des-perate for money they work for nothing. Now do you understand?"

"No." I was completely bewildered. "You need money; you can't af-ford to work in a sweatshop. What were you doing there?"

"Oh, if you are this stupid how did you ever go to a big university?" She waved her hands wildly. "How can I believe you can find my daugh-ter? I wasn't working, I mean, I was working, but I was supervising, he was paying me to supervise, to make sure people stay at the machines, don't steal nothing, don't take long breaks, everything that—that I hate!"

Maybe I was too stupid to find Josie, but not so stupid that I asked her why she did it, not a woman who'd been feeding six mouths on twenty-six thousand a year. Instead, I asked how long it had been going on.

"Only two days. We started two days before the fire. The day you came to the factory because of the sabotage, Mr. Zamar called me in, he was very angry because I was bringing a detective to the plant. 'But the sabotage, Mr. Zamar,' I said, 'those rats, the glue, and then some *chavo* around this morning trying to do something bad again,' and he said, like this—" She broke off to imitate Zamar sitting with his head buried in his hands, "He said, 'Rose, I know all about it, a detective, she will only get the plant closed down.' And then the next day, he came and offered me this job, this supervising job, and he said if I take it it's five hundred fifty dollars extra a week, if I don't want it he fires me for bringing you to the factory. Only the pastor, he can't know. Mr. Zamar knows I go to church, he knows how much my faith means to me, but he knows how much my children mean to me, and he catches me between these two sharp thorns, the thorn of my love for Jesus, the thorn of my family, what am I to do? God help me, I took the work, and then I am truly punished because two days later the plant burns; Mr. Zamar is killed. I only thank God that it happened early, before me and the workers arrived. I thank God for the warning, that He didn't kill me in the fire on the spot, that I have a chance to repent, but why must my children suffer as well?"

I stared at her in dawning horror. "You mean the pastor set fire to the building because Zamar was running a sweatshop?"

She clapped a hand over her mouth. "I didn't mean that. I didn't say that. But when he found out about the sweatshop, he was very, very angry."

Andrés had threatened Zamar that if he sent his business out of Chicago, the pastor would see he had no business left to protect. Was Andrés such a megalomaniac that he thought he really was God on the South Side? My head was reeling, and I couldn't even find the strength to sit up straight.

I finally went to a smaller question, something I could manage. "Where did the people come from, the ones in the midnight factory?"

"Everywhere, but mostly Guatemala and Mexico. Me, I speak Spanish; I grew up in Waco, but my family was from Mexico, so Mr. Zamar, he knew I could talk to them. But the worst thing, the worst thing is, they owe money to a *jefe*, and Zamar, he actually turned to a *jefe* to get workers in his factory. Never did I think I would be doing such a thing, translating for him with that kind of *mierda*."

Jefes, heads, they're go-betweens, fixers, who charge illegal immigrants exorbitant fees to smuggle them into the country. No poor immigrant can afford a thousand dollars for a trip across the border, complete with fake green card and social security number, so the *jefes* "lend" them the money. When they get here, the *jefes* sell people to companies looking for cheap labor. The *jefes* pocket most of the wages, doling out just enough for room and board. It's a system of slavery, really, because it's almost impossible ever to buy your way out of one of these contracts. I could imagine Pastor Andrés would be furious with any local business who bought people's work like that.

"This Freddy, he isn't a *jefe*, is he?" I blurted out.

"Freddy Pacheco? He is too lazy," she said scornfully. "A *jefe* may be evil, but he works hard; he has to."

Rose and I sat silent after that. She seemed relieved to have finally gotten her story off her mind: her face was brighter, more animated, than it had been since before the fire at the factory. I felt duller—as if I really were too stupid even to go to college, let alone find her daughter.

On the screen in front of me, Spiderman was easily tying up the villain who had been trying to rob the local bank, or maybe it was the local banker trying to rob his customers, but, either way, Spiderman hadn't even broken a sweat. Not only that, it had taken him less than half an hour to identify the villain and track him down. I desperately needed some superpowers, although even ordinary human powers would do right now.

The baby, which had slept through our talk, began to fuss. Rose sat up and said she was going to the kitchen to heat a bottle, she'd bring me a cup of coffee.

I took the baby from her. "Is Julia still here? I need to ask her some questions about the soap dish, that frog I showed you after church on Sunday."

Rose went to the back of the apartment; I began to pat the baby's little back. I sang her the Italian children's songs my mother used to sing to me, the song of the firefly, the song of the grandmother, with her bottomless kettle of soup. Singing steadies me, makes me feel closer to my mother. I don't know why I do it so seldom.

Rose returned with a bottle and a cup of bitter instant coffee just as

María Inés began to fuss in earnest. Julia trailed after her mother, looking at me suspiciously: Rose had told her we were going to discuss the soap dish, and any trust we had built up at practice this afternoon wasn't going to carry over to tonight.

I handed Rose the baby and stood so I could look Julia in the eye, more or less—she was a couple of inches taller than me. "Julia, I'm too tired for a night of lies or half-truths. Tell me about the soap dish. Did you or did you not give it to Freddy?"

She shot a glance at her mother, but Rose was frowning at her. "You tell the truth now, just like the coach said, Julia. Your sister is missing, we don't want to be a dentist taking the story out of you little bit by little bit with a drill."

"I did give it to him, all right? I didn't tell you a lie about that."

I smacked the couch arm. "The whole story, at once. This is more important than your hurt feelings. When was this?"

Julia's face turned as red and round as her baby's, but when she saw neither her mother nor I had any sympathy for her she said sulkily, "Christmas. Last year, already. And Freddy looked at it, he said, what did he want with some girly present like that? And then I found out he gave it to Diego, and Diego gave it to Sancia."

"And then?"

"What do you mean, 'And then?' "

I heaved a loud sigh. "Did Sancia keep it? Does she still have it?"

She hesitated, and her mother pounced on her before I could open my mouth. "You tell me this minute, Julia Miranda Isabella!"

"Sancia showed it to me," Julia yelled. "She bragged how Diego loved her, he gave her this beautiful thing, even with a little piece of soap in it shaped like a flower, and what did Freddy give me? I was furious. I said, how funny, I gave Freddy one just the same as this. Diego, he's Freddy's cousin, she asked Diego, did he steal Freddy's soap dish?, and Diego, he said, no, Freddy gave it to him. So she was all insulted, secondhand goods, she said, and she wouldn't keep it, she gave it back to me! Like I was trash who needed something like that, something I bought with my own money and my own boyfriend didn't want!"

The tears began to roll down her cheeks in earnest, but Rose and I just looked at her in exasperation. "Where is it now?" I asked.

"I threw it out. Only, Betto and Sammy, they wanted it. I said, fine, they could use it as a tank, they could break it, I didn't care."

"Do they still have it?" I asked.

Again she hesitated, and again it was her mother who forced her to speak. Freddy had come to her; he had changed his mind, he did want this soap dish after all. Diego had told him about it, about Sancia giving it to her, and could he have it back?

"He spoke to me so nice, like he did last year, before he made María Inés inside me, like I was beautiful, all those things. So I dug it out of Sammy's box and gave it to him, and then he left, not even a good-bye kiss, not even 'How is María Inés?' "

"Congratulations on a close escape," I said drily. "The farther you stay away from him, the better off you are. When was this?"

"Three weeks ago. In the morning, after Ma went to work and everyone else left for school."

"Did he say why he wanted it?"

"I told you! He said because he wanted something from me, after all, and he was sorry, all those things!"

"Where is Freddy now?" I demanded.

Julia looked at me nervously. "I don't know."

"Guess, then. Where does he hang out? What bar, where are his other babies? Anything."

"Are you going to hurt him?"

"Why do you protect him?" Rose burst out. "He's a bad man—he left you with a baby, he steals, he cares for no one but himself! His mother brought him to church every Sunday and what does he do but hang around outside in Diego's truck, insulting the service with their music. In five years, his pretty-boy looks will be gone and then he will have nothing."

Rose turned to me. "Sometimes he goes to Cocodrilo, it's a bar across from the church. The other girl who also has his baby, I don't think he sees her, either, but she's over on Buffalo. If you kill him yourself with your bare hands, I will swear to the police you never saw him, never touched him."

I couldn't help laughing. "I don't think I will come to that. But if it does—*muchas gracias!*"

40 AN ACID TOUCH

The lights were on in the church when I pulled up to the corner of Ninety-second and Houston. I went up the shallow step to the front door to see what was going on. Thursday night Bible study, six-thirty to eight, November topic, the book of Isaiah. It was just after six-thirty now, so the pastor was hard at it.

Directly across the street from the church was a vacant lot where a handful of cars and trucks were parked at skewed angles—including a Dodge with big speakers in the back and a license plate beginning "VBC." Next to the lot, three decrepit houses propped each other up. Cocodrilo, the bar where Freddy drank, was on their far side. The bar was really just the ground floor of a narrow two-flat, whose clapboard sides were sagging and peeling. The windows were covered with a thick mesh screen that didn't allow much light to seep out.

I had called Morrell from the car to let him know I would be a little late, just a little. He had sighed, the exaggerated sigh of a lover who is always being stood up, and said if I wasn't home by eight he and Don would eat without me.

The exchange sent me into Cocodrilo in a bristly mood. I let the door

bang shut behind me, like Clint Eastwood, and put on my Clint Eastwood face: I own this bar, don't mess with me. There were maybe fifteen
people inside, but it was a small place, and dark, just a narrow room with
a high counter and a couple of rickety tables jammed against the wall, so
it was hard to survey the crowd.

The television over the bar was tuned to a soccer match, Mexico versus some small Caribbean island. A few men were watching, but most
were talking or arguing in a mixture of Spanish and English.

Cocodrilo seemed to be a young man's bar, although there were a few
older faces—I recognized one of the men from this afternoon's construction site. And it was definitely a man's bar: when I walked in, conversation died down as they eyed me. A trio near the door thought they'd try a
smart remark, but my expression sent them back to their beer with a
surly remark in Spanish—whose meaning I could certainly guess, even
though it hadn't been in my high school text.

I finally spotted Diego, my center Sancia's boyfriend, in a small knot
at the far end of the room. The man next to him had his back to me,
which made him easy to recognize—he had the thick, dark hair and
camouflage jacket I'd trailed through the warehouse a couple of hours
earlier.

I pushed my way past the trio at the door and tapped him on the
shoulder. "Freddy! And Diego. What a wonderful coincidence. We're
going to talk, Freddy."

When he turned, I saw Rose was right: he did have sort of pretty-boy
good looks in his high cheekbones and full lips, but she was also right—
indolence and drugs were eating away at them.

Freddy looked at me blankly, but Diego said, "The coach, man, she's
the basketball coach."

Freddy stared at me in dawning alarm, then shoved me hard enough
to send me reeling. He barged down the narrow length of the room to
the front door, knocking over a bottle of beer as he went.

I righted myself and took off after him. No one tried to stop me, but
no one moved out of my way, either, so Freddy was out on the street before I caught up with him. I put on a burst of speed, forgetting my sore

thighs, my swollen hands, my shoulder. He was crossing the vacant lot to Diego's truck when I launched myself at him. I knocked him to the ground and fell heavily on top of him.

I heard applause and looked up to see three of the men from the bar, including the guy from the jobsite, laughing and clapping.

"Hey, missus, you go see Lovie Smith, you play for the Bears!"

"What this *chavo* done to you? Leave you with baby and no money? He got two babies already and no money for them!"

"She's not the kind, not the kind, Geraldo, mind your mouth."

Freddy shoved me aside and scrambled to his feet. I grabbed his right ankle. When he started to kick at me, an audience member moved in and pinned his arms. "Don't run, Freddy, the lady, she worked so hard to catch you, is very rude to run away."

The rest of the men trickled out of the bar and stood in a half circle around us, except for Diego, who moved uncertainly halfway between Freddy and the truck.

I got to my feet and pulled on my mittens. "Freddy Pacheco, you and I are long overdue for this talk."

"You a cop, missus?" the man holding his arms asked.

"Nope. I'm the basketball coach down at Bertha Palmer. Julia was a good student and a good ballplayer until this *chavo banda* ruined her life."

A murmur in Spanish rippled through the trio. *El coche.* Yes, but a detective, too, only private, not police; Celine, his *sobrina*, she was crazy about *el coche. Sobrina*, my tired brain fished in my high school Spanish. Niece. Celine, my gangbanger, was this man's niece; she was crazy about me? Maybe I was misunderstanding him, but the notion cheered me no end.

"So what you want to know from this piece of garbage, missus?"

"The soap dish Julia gave you for Christmas last year, Freddy."

"I don't know what you talking about." He was looking at the ground, which made it hard to understand his whining.

"Don't lie, Freddy. I sent the dish to a forensics lab. You know what

DNA is, don't you? They can find DNA even on a soap dish that's been through a fire. Isn't that wonderful?"

He balked some more, but after more prodding and a few threats, both from me and the men, admitted that he'd given it to Diego, who'd given it to Sancia Valdéz. "What Julia think I want with a girly present like that?"

"And Sancia was mad when she learned that Diego hadn't bought it for her. Secondhand goods, Sancia called it, and she didn't want it, so she gave it back to Julia. Isn't that right, Diego?"

Diego backed away from me in alarm, but another of the men caught his arm and dragged him back to the group, with a guttural command.

"So, Freddy," I picked up my narrative in a bright, schoolteacher voice, "recently you changed your mind. And you went to the Dorrado place and took it back from Julia. Why did you do that?"

There wasn't much light on the street, just what little was spilling out of the bar, and the one streetlamp across the road in front of the church, but I think Freddy was giving me a calculating look, as if to decide how big a story he could get me to swallow.

"I was sorry I treated her mean, man, she tried to do something nice for me, I shouldn't have been so mean to her."

"Yeah, Freddy, I believe in the Easter bunny and all those other warm cuddly stories, too. If you wanted it so bad, how did it end up at Fly the Flag?"

"I don't know. Maybe someone stole it from me."

"Yes, a three-dollar soap dish, that's worth breaking and entering for, isn't it? Here's the problem." I turned to the men from the bar, who were listening to me as closely as if I were telling their fortunes. "That soap dish was used to start the fire at Fly the Flag. Frank Zamar died in that fire, so the person who set it is guilty of murder. And it looks like that person was Freddy, here, maybe with Bron Czernin's help, maybe with Diego's."

Shocked comments in Spanish rippled through the group. Had this *gamberro* and his cousin killed Frank Zamar? Destroyed the plant?

"Why, Freddy? Why you do this?" Celine's uncle slapped him.

"I didn't do nothing. I don't know what she talking about!"

"How that soap dish start the fire?" one of the men asked.

I pulled the crude drawing of the frog from my pocket again. They crowded around to study it in the dim light.

"I don't know who made this drawing—maybe Bron Czernin, maybe Freddy. But here's how it worked."

Pointing at the drawing, I explained my theory, about the nitric acid and the wires, and there was another buzz of talk. I caught Andrés's name, and Diego, and *"carro,"* which at first I heard as the Italian *"caro,"* darling: Diego was somebody's darling? No, the pastor had done something to Diego's darling, no, to his—not his wagon, his truck, that's what it was.

The first time I visited Rose Dorrado, Diego was outside her apartment, playing his stereo at top volume, and Josie said if Pastor Andrés came around he'd totally fix Diego's truck like he had before.

"What did the pastor do to Diego's truck?" I asked.

"Not his truck, missus, his stereo."

"Diego, he starts parking his truck right here, in front of Mount Ararat, during the services," Celine's uncle explained. "He crank his stereo up real loud. No one even knows why, was he playing to Sancia, trying to get her to come join him, or bugging his ma, she's real religious, her and Freddy's ma, they're sisters, they both pray at Mount Ararat, but Pastor, he warn Diego two, three times, you turn that off during the sermon, and Diego, he just as much a *chavo* as Freddy, here, he jus' laugh. So Pastor, he fix up a metal dish with a rubber plug, put in some nitric, put it on the stereo, acid go through the plug, go through the wires, shut Diego down 'bout halfway through the worship."

In the poor light, I couldn't make out anyone's expressions, but I could tell the men were laughing.

Freddy was furious. "Yeah, everybody think, whatever the pastor do, thas cool, he cost Diego here three hundred dollars to fix his amp, his speakers, and you guys think it's all a joke because the pastor did it, but the pastor, he put glue in the locks at Fly the Flag, I saw him."

In the shocked silence that followed, the man holding Freddy must have loosened his grip, because Freddy broke free and bolted for the truck. Diego ran ahead of him and jumped into the driver's seat. I tried to follow but tripped on a piece of rubble and fell hard. As one of the men helped me back to my feet, Diego laid down rubber and the tail-lights of the truck disappeared down Houston.

I could hear the murmur in the group. Was this true? Could you possibly believe Freddy Pacheco? One man said, yes, he had heard the same thing before, but the man from the jobsite said he could not believe it of Roberto.

"He's at the church now with his Bible study. He has to tell us, tell this lady, here, did this *chavo* tell the truth or not? I work with him every day, he is the best man on the South Side, I cannot believe this."

Five of the men returned to the bar, but the rest of us crossed the street, an uneasy band, not talking, no one wanting to be the person who confronted Pastor Andrés. We pushed our way into the church, through the sanctuary to the big room in the back where they'd served coffee after the service on Sunday. In one corner, some toddlers were playing with plastic trucks and dolls, or just lying on cushions sucking on bottles. At a deal table near the door, Andrés was sitting with a group of some dozen parishioners, mostly women, hard at work on the Prophet Isaiah.

"What is this?" Andrés demanded. "If you have come for Bible study, Missus Detective, you are welcome, but if you are here to interrupt then you must wait until we are done. The Word of the Lord takes precedence over all human worries."

"Not all, Roberto," his coworker said. "Not when it is life and death."

He switched to Spanish, speaking so fast I could follow only in part. *El coche*, that was me, then something about Freddy, Diego, the fire, the factory, and *pegamento*, another word I didn't understand. Andrés fired something back at him, but the women at the table looked shocked and started speaking, too. Andrés realized he was losing control of his group and shut his Bible.

"We will take a five-minute break," he announced magisterially in English. "I will talk to this detective in my office. You may come, too, Tomás, doubting Tomás," he added to the man from the jobsite.

All of the men who had come with me from Cocodrilo followed us through the robing room to the pastor's study. There were only two chairs in it, besides the seat behind his desk, so the men, and many of the women from the study group, crowded around the doorway.

"Now, Missus Detective, what is all this? Why do you keep harassing me, especially in church?" Andrés said when he had seated himself behind his desk.

"Freddy says you put glue in the locks at Fly the Flag. Is that true?"

"Yes, Roberto, did you do this thing?" Tomás asked.

Andrés looked from Tomás to the group at the door, as if deciding whether to bluff it out, but no one gave him any encouragement. "Frank Zamar was a man who had to choose between what is right and what is easy, and he didn't always know how to choose wisely," he said heavily. "After 9/11, he was busy making flags for everyone in the world, and he got a big order from By-Smart. He added a second shift, he bought new machines."

"Then he lost the work," one of the men said. "We know all that. My old lady, she one of the people got laid off. Why you go put glue in his doors because he lost his contract?"

"It wasn't because of that; when he lost the contract, wasn't I the first one there to help your wife sign up for unemployment? Didn't I find housing for the Valdéz family?" Andrés burst out.

There were murmurs of acknowledgment, yes, he had done these things. "All the more reason to ask, why the glue, Roberto?"

Andrés looked directly at me for the first time. "It's what I told you this afternoon, that Zamar signed a new contract with By-Smart in a panic. And to warn him—I am sorry to confess it, I am ashamed to confess it—I did put the glue in his door to show him what could happen to him if he hurt the neighborhood. It was a child's trick, no, a punk's trick, now I am sorry I did it, but for me, as for many, repentance has come too late for amendment of life."

His voice was bitter, and he paused, as if swallowing his own bitter pill. "After the glue, first Zamar made threats, saying he will take me to court, but we talked, and he promised me, he will go back to By-Smart—like I told you already."

I nodded, trying to evaluate his tone, his eyes—his truthfulness. "Whoever destroyed Fly the Flag did it very carefully so as not to kill the illegal immigrants working the graveyard shift. Rose Dorrado said if you knew about the sweatshop Zamar was running, you would be furious—were you furious enough to burn down the plant?"

"I did not even know until this afternoon that he was running that sweatshop, and I swear"—Andrés put his hand on a big Bible lying open on his desk—"that I did not start that fire."

This brought some calls of support from the women crowding in at the door—and some dark glances in my direction—but Tomás looked at him soberly: Andrés was not just a coworker but a leader in the community. Tomás, at least, needed to know he could trust the pastor.

"The fire was set using the same method you used when you put Diego's stereo out of commission," I said. "Maybe you didn't start it yourself, but perhaps you showed Freddy how to do it."

Again, I took the drawing out of my pocket. I laid it on the desk in front of him. "Did you draw this for Freddy?"

To my astonishment, instead of rapping out a denial Andrés turned the color of putty and beads of sweat broke out on his forehead. "Oh my God. That is why—"

"Why what?" I demanded.

"Freddy came to me, he wanted some nitric acid, he said it was to clean the rubber that had melted into the truck bed when I ruined the stereo. He said I owed him, but now—oh, now, oh, Jesus, oh, what have I done in my pride? Shown him how to burn down a plant, and to kill a man?"

"But why would Freddy do such a thing?" Celine's uncle asked from the doorway. "Freddy, he's just a *chavo*, he would only make such a—a *esquema* for someone else, not because he thought of it himself. Who ordered him, who paid him if not you, Pastor Andrés?"

"I think Bron Czernin was making the plug in his kitchen workshop," I said, "and I found the drawing near where Billy the Kid's car was wrecked. Bron was seen with Freddy, but why would Czernin want to burn down the plant?"

Not everyone in the room knew who Bron was, but one of the women, announcing she was Sancia Valdéz's grandmother, explained to the others: April's father, the man who was killed last week. Yes, April, the girl who played basketball with Sancia and Josie, only now she was sick, her heart, she couldn't play anymore.

"What did you use to hold the acid when you put Diego's stereo out of commission?" I asked Andrés.

"Just a metal funnel, a small one; I clamped it to the back of the amplifier."

"So Josie knew how you'd damaged Diego's stereo," I said slowly, thinking through the network of connection in the neighborhood. "She and April were best friends; she told April. April probably thought it was a good joke and described it to Bron. Or maybe even Freddy suggested your scheme to Bron when he found out what Bron wanted to do."

Had Freddy gone to Bron, knowing—from Julia, I suppose, Julia who would have heard it from Josie—that Bron had a shop in his house? Or had Bron gone to Freddy to help plant the dish? Either April knew about the soap dish brouhaha and had mentioned it to her father, or when Bron explained what he needed Freddy remembered the soap dish. It all sort of made sense in a horrible way.

"What I don't understand is why they did it at all?" I continued out loud. "What would—"

I broke off, remembering Aunt Jacqui's dazzling smile: we never, never renegotiate contracts. And her malicious smirk when she announced I'd find the sheets being sold in the neighborhood were a dead end. Would she have hired Bron to burn down the factory?

"You have to tell me what was troubling Billy the Kid about his family," I said abruptly to the pastor. "It's too important now for you to keep it secret."

"It wasn't this," Andrés objected. "If Billy told me they were burning down Frank Zamar's plant, believe me, I would not have kept that a secret."

He gave a sad smile. "Billy knew I was working with Frank Zamar—

he knew our attempt to sell sheets through our churches here in South Chicago—he knew that failed. But Billy himself went back to his aunt, to his father and grandfather, to try to get them to renegotiate the contract with Fly the Flag. They were—like rocks, unmoving. This caused him great grief. And then he found in the records, the faxes that came from overseas, that they had already arranged with a shop in Nicaragua to make these towels and sheets, on a production schedule where the workers will be paid nine cents for every sheet or towel they make.

"Billy went to read a report on this factory and found a disturbing situation, that people must work seventy hours a week, with no overtime, no holidays, one short break for lunch. So he said it was time for Nicaraguan workers to have rights, to have a union, and he would go to the directors and tell them this if the family did not reconsider. His grandfather loves Billy greatly. When he saw how upset his grandchild was, he said, before they turned to Nicaragua they would wait a month and see how Frank Zamar did."

"And then Frank Zamar's plant burned down. How convenient. And Bron Czernin is dead." I laughed a little wildly.

I didn't see the whole picture but enough of it. Bron thought he could put the bite on the Bysens—he had done their dirty work, now they should pay for April's surgery. Only they had killed him instead. Or Grobian had killed him. All I needed was Billy and Freddy. And a little proof.

"You really don't know where Billy is?" I asked Andrés.

His dark eyes were worried. "I have no idea, Missus Detective."

He shut his eyes and started to pray, softly, under his breath. The women at the door eyed him with sympathy and a certain awe and began humming softly, a hymn to provide him support and company. After three or four minutes, Andrés sat up. His old authority sat on his shoulders again. He announced to the group that their most important task was to find Billy the Kid and Josie Dorrado.

"Maybe they are hiding in a building, a garage, renting an apartment under a false name. You need to ask everyone, talk to everyone, find these children. And when you do, you tell me at once. And if you cannot find me, then you tell this coach-detective."

41 PUNK, CORNERED LIKE A RAT

I walked slowly back to my car. One thing I had to do without delay was to call Conrad Rawlings at the Fourth District and report Freddy's role in the fire at Fly the Flag. I'd been keeping my cell phone off today. I'd checked in with Amy a couple of times, but I'd used the phone in the faculty lounge at Bertha Palmer when I'd had to call my clients. But now it didn't matter if someone was tracking me, and saw I was in South Chicago. In fact, if they were paying enough attention to me to listen in on my cell phone calls, me reporting what I knew to the police would keep them from bothering me further.

To my surprise, it was only seven-thirty. The emotions and exertions I'd just gone through made me think a whole evening had passed. I called down to the Fourth District, determined to hand Freddy over to the cops—Conrad would see what a good, cooperative PI I was. When I found I'd just missed him, I felt deflated.

The operator at the Fourth District didn't seem excited by my report of news about the arson at Fly the Flag. I finally got her to transfer me to a detective, a junior officer who went through the motions of taking my name and Freddy's name, but his assurance that they'd look into it sounded like one of those three common lies in the English language—he didn't even ask how to spell my name, which he couldn't pronounce, and he only took my phone number because I insisted on giving it to him.

When we'd finished, I hesitated a moment, then hit Conrad's home number—through all my changes and upgrades in mobile phones, I'd kept it on my speed dial, position four, following my office, my answering service, and Lotty. He wasn't in, but I left a detailed message on his machine. He might be annoyed with me for jumping ahead of him on the investigation, but I was sure he'd act on the information.

I flexed my shoulders, sore from the tensions of the afternoon. I was still tired, too, from Monday night's jaunt. So many of my brother and sister PIs seem to get beaten up, thrown in the slammer, or hungover, without needing to rest afterward. I looked at my face in the rearview mirror; true, the light was bad, but I looked pale.

I called Mary Ann, to tell her I would be there in about an hour if that wasn't too late for her. Someone answered the phone but didn't speak, which alarmed me, but eventually her deep, gruff voice came over the ether to me.

"It's all right, Victoria, I'm fine, just a little tired. Maybe you don't need to stop here tonight."

"Mary Ann, are you alone? Did someone answer the phone for you?"

"My neighbor's here, Victoria; she picked up the phone while I was in the bathroom, but I guess she didn't say anything. I'm going back to bed now."

There was something in her voice that was making me uneasy. "I need to stop to see April Czernin; I'll be heading north in about forty-five minutes. I'd like to drop in just for a minute, leave you some groceries and maybe see you if you're still up—I won't wake you if you're asleep. You did give me keys, you know."

"Oh, Victoria, you always were an obstinate, persistent pest. If you must come, I guess I can stand it, but if you're going to be later than forty-five minutes call so that I don't stay up for you."

"You guess you can stand it?" I repeated, hurt both by the words and her exasperated tone. "I thought—"

I broke off midsentence, remembering that she was ill, that pain made people react in uncharacteristic ways. My own mother, who had waited up nights for my father, occupying both herself and me with music, cooking, books—we read Giovanni Verga's plays aloud together in Italian—and she never complained about the wait, the worry. Then one night, in the hospital, she suddenly started screaming that he didn't love her, had never loved her, terrifying herself almost as much as she did me and my dad.

"Josie's still missing," I said to my coach. "How well do you know her? Can you think of anyone she'd imagine she'd feel safe staying with? She has an aunt in Waco who claims Josie isn't there, but maybe the aunt would lie for her."

"I don't know the Dorrado girls personally, Victoria, but I'll call some of the other teachers in the morning. Maybe one of them can suggest something. I'm in the kitchen and I need to lie down." She hung up abruptly.

Despite my admonitions to myself, Mary Ann's brusque manner hurt me. I sat in the dark, my sore joints aching. I had a new bruise on my thigh from where I'd landed on Freddy; I could feel the knot under my jeans.

I dozed off in the warm car, but after a few minutes a knock on my window made me jump out of my skin. When my heart stopped racing, I saw it was Celine's uncle. I rolled down the window.

"You okay, missus? You took a bad fall out there."

I forced a smile. "I'm fine. Just a little sore. Your niece—she's a very talented athlete. Do you think you could help her break away from the Pentas? They're going to slow her down, keep her from making the most of her gifts."

We chatted a bit about it, about the difficulty of raising children in South Chicago, and, sad to say, his brother had abandoned the family, and Celine's ma, she drank, not to mince words, but he'd try to make an effort with Celine: he appreciated what I was doing for her.

We finished our dance of thanks for each other's concern about Celine. He took off, and I phoned the Czernins. I might have hung up if Sandra had answered, but it was April, her voice sluggish.

"It's the drugs, coach," she said when I said I hoped I hadn't woken her. "They make me feel like I'm in this big tub of cotton balls, I can't see anything or feel anything. Do you think I can stop taking them?"

"Whoa, there, girl, you stay on those meds until your doctor tells you different. Better you feel a little dopey for a few weeks now than have to live your life on an oxygen tank, okay? I'm a few blocks from your house with a charger for your phone. Can I bring it in? There's something I want to ask you to look at, too."

She brightened at once: she clearly needed more company than her mother. I would have to talk to her teachers, find someone who could stop by with homework, and get some classmates to bring her gossip. When I got to the front door, April was there to open it, but her mother was standing behind her.

"What do you think we are, Tori, a public charity you have to stop by and look after? I can take care of my girl without your help. I didn't even know you'd given her a goddamn phone until this afternoon, and, if I'd known she was asking for one, I would have bought it for her myself."

"Take it easy, Sandra," I snapped. "It's Billy's phone; she's just using it until he comes back for it."

"And didn't Bron get killed on account of he had that phone on him?"

I stared at her. "Did he? Who told you that?"

"One of the women at work, she said they really wanted Billy, but they killed Bron because he was driving Billy's car and using Billy's phone, they thought he was Billy."

"It's the first I ever heard of this, Sandra." I wondered if there was any truth to the notion or if it was just one of those stories that circulate after a disaster. If I was the cops, or had Carnifice's resources, I guess I could go to the By-Smart store where Sandra worked to track it down. Maybe Amy Blount would be willing to go down there tomorrow.

"April, can you let me in for a minute? I want to show you and your mom a picture, see if it means anything to you."

"Oh, coach, sure, sorry." April backed out of the doorway to let me pass.

It hurt to see her move in such a slow and clumsy way, when just a short time earlier she'd been loping around like a colt with the other girls on the team. To cover my emotion, I spoke almost with Mary Ann's brusqueness, pulling out the drawing of the frog and handing it to them.

"Where'd you find that?" Sandra demanded.

"Over at 100th and Ewing. Bron showed it to you?"

She sniffed loudly. "He had it lying on the counter in that workshop of his. I asked him what it was, and he said it was a gimmick. He was making something for one of the guys he knew, and this was the drawing the guy gave him. He was always doing stuff like that."

"Good-hearted, helping out his pals?" I suggested.

"No!" Her face contorted. "Always imagining he had an idea that was going to make him rich. Frogs on insulating rubber, I ask you, who was ever going to buy that, and he laughed and said, oh, someone at By-Smart would fall for it."

"Stop it!" April cried out. "Stop making fun of him. He made good stuff, you know he did, he made that desk for you, only you were so stupid you sold it so you could go to Vegas with your girlfriends last Easter. If I'd known you were going to sell it, I would have bought it from you myself."

"With what money would that be, miss?" Sandra demanded. "Your trust—"

A loud crash, glass shattering in the rear of the house, interrupted her. I had my gun out and was running through the dining room to the kitchen before either of them could react. The kitchen was empty but I heard someone moving in the lean-to. I pulled the door open, crouching low, and hurled myself at the legs.

The space was too small for the intruder to fall over, but he crashed against the worktable, and I backed away just out of his reach to hold my gun on him.

"Freddy Pacheco!" I was panting heavily, and my words came out in short bursts. "We can't keep meeting like this. What the hell are you doing in here? If you've come for the picture you drew, you are way, way too late."

He straightened up and tried to come at me but backed off when he saw the gun. "You bitch, what you doing here? You following me? What you want from me?"

"So much I hardly know where to begin." I leaned over and smacked his mouth, too fast for him to react. "Respect, for beginners. You call me 'bitch' one more time and I'll put a bullet in your left foot. Second time, in your right foot."

"You wouldn't fire that, 'hos are too—"

I shot at the wall behind his head. The noise vibrated horribly in the closed space, but Freddy turned a greenish tint and collapsed against Bron's worktable. An unpleasant stench rose from him, and I felt ashamed once more for using my gun to terrify someone—but the shame didn't make me send him out into the alley with my blessing.

I heard Sandra tiptoe into the kitchen behind me. "You have a creep in your house, Sandra. Call 911. Right now."

She started to argue with me, her reflex, but when she looked past me and saw Freddy she scuttled away. The phone was by the stove; I heard her shrieking into the phone, and yelling at April to stay the hell out of the kitchen.

"So, Freddy, tell me about the frog. You drew this picture for Bron and he was going to make it for you, is that right?"

"It was his idea, man, he said his kid told him the pastor put out Diego's stereo. So Bron wanted to know how, man, and I told him, so he had me draw him a picture."

"So you drew the picture. And then you went and put the frog in the drying room at the factory."

"No, man, no way. I never killed nobody."

"Then what were you doing the morning I found you there, huh? Looking for work?"

He brightened. "Yeah, that's it, man, I wanted a job."

"And Bron found one for you: burning down the factory, killing Frank Zamar."

"It was an accident, man, the only thing supposed to happen was the electricity go out—" He shut up, suddenly realizing he was saying too much.

"You mean you killed a man because you didn't know you'd be start-ing a fire? You were surrounded by fabric and solvent and you didn't know they'd burn up?" I was so furious, it was hard not to shoot him on the spot.

"I didn't do nothing, man, I ain't saying one word more without my lawyer."

He eyed my gun uneasily, but I couldn't bring myself to brandish it again, even to get him to choke out a few more words. I was beside my-self, though, at the mayhem he'd caused, all out of his colossal stupidity.

"So what are you doing in here?" I demanded. "What did you break in for? To get the drawing?"

He shook his head but wouldn't speak.

I looked around the worktable. "The leftover tubing? Leftover acid?"

"Acid? What are you talking about?" Sandra said sharply behind me.

"A little trick Freddy learned from Pastor Andrés," I said without turning around. "How to use nitric acid to short out a wire. Bron made a device for Freddy and Freddy burned down Fly the Flag. Although he says he didn't mean to. Are the cops on the way?"

Sandra grasped only one part of my statement. "How—dare—you! How dare you come in here to my house of mourning and say Bron was setting fires? Get out of my house! Get out now!"

"Sandra, you want to be alone with Freddy, you and April?"

"If he's going to tell lies to the police about Bron, I don't want them arresting him." She started kicking at my calves.

"Sandra, stop! Stop! This guy broke in, he's dangerous, we need to give him to the police. Please! Do you want him to hurt April?"

She didn't hear me, just kept kicking me, pulling at my hair, her face red and swollen. All of her furies and griefs of the last week—the last thirty years—were spilling out of her onto me.

I moved into the corner of the workshop, trying to get away from her. She came after me, unaware of Freddy, of the broken glass, of everything but me, her old enemy. "You knew Boom-Boom slept with me," she spat. "You couldn't stand it. You thought he belonged to you, you—you man-woman!"

The insult pricked me in a remote way, a place that would be sore later, but not now, now when I had to focus my energy on Freddy. She was jumping around too much, and the space was too small for me to stay between her and Freddy. She whirled past me and he grabbed her, pinning her flailing arms. She suddenly went limp, sagging against him. A knife appeared in his right hand; he held it at Sandra's throat.

"You get out of here, now, bitch, or I'm killing this woman," he said to me.

If I shot at him, I had a good chance of hitting her. I backed out of the room. April was in the kitchen. Her swollen face was ashen, and she was having trouble breathing.

"Baby, you and I are going to go outside. You are going to take nice deep breaths. Come on." I put on my stern coach's voice. "Breathe in. Hold it for four. Now let it go, slowly, slowly, I'm going to count and you let it out a little bit on each count."

"But, Ma, is he—will he—"

"April, start breathing. He's not going to hurt her, and, anyway, the cops will be here soon."

I hustled April down the sidewalk and into my car. I got the passenger seat back as far as it would go, to ease the pressure on her lungs. I took the door key off my ring, turned on the engine, and set the heater going full blast.

"You lock the doors when I get out. You don't open them for anyone. I'm going around to the back to try to help your mom, okay?"

Her lips trembled and she was gasping for air, but she nodded a little.

"And keep breathing. It's the most important thing you can do right now. Breathe in, count four, breathe out, count four. Got it?"

"Y-yes, coach," she whispered.

I looked at my watch: it had been over ten minutes since Sandra called the cops. On my way around the house, I called 911 again on my cell, which didn't automatically register on the emergency room screen. I explained where I was and said we had called over ten minutes ago. The dispatcher spent several agonizing minutes looking for Sandra's call. She finally found it and said they were sending someone.

"When?" I said. "Now or with the Messiah? I have a kid going into cardiac arrest. Get an ambulance here on the double!"

"You don't have the only emergency in this city, ma'am."

"Look, you and I both know the story of the far South Side. I have a home invasion, I have the invader here and a very sick child. Pretend this is Lincoln Park and get me a team NOW!"

The dispatcher said huffily that every emergency was treated alike and she couldn't manufacture an ambulance for me.

"I probably could build one in the time I've been waiting. If this kid dies, it will be front-page news, and tapes of these calls will be played coast to coast. Your kids and grandkids will know them by heart." I snapped my phone shut and ran around to the back of the house.

Light streamed through the broken window leading into Bron's workshop, but the back door had been opened and slammed shut with a lot of violence—it hung unevenly in the frame now. I had my gun out, and grabbed a lid from a garbage can to use as a shield. At the door, I squatted down on my haunches, using the lid to pull the door all the way open. No sound. I duckwalked into the kitchen, caricature of a cop. My feet skidded on ball bearings that Freddy had dumped onto the floor, and I fell onto my knees. The noise brought a muffled scream from the room beyond.

I stood upright and hurried into the dining room. Sandra wasn't there or in the living room. I looked in the bedroom and saw the dresser had been knocked over to block the closet door. I yanked it out of the way. Sandra was lying on the floor, huddled in a little ball, whimpering.

I knelt next to her. "Are you hurt, Sandra? Did he cut you?"

She didn't say anything, just lay crying like a hurt dog, little squeaks of misery. I felt for her throat, but didn't find blood, and I couldn't see any on the floor under her. Freddy had dumped all the bedding onto the floor; I grabbed a blanket and wrapped her up.

In the few minutes I'd been outside with April, Freddy had gone through the house like locusts through Egypt. He'd dumped out the drawers in the bedroom and the medicine cabinet; he'd run upstairs to April's dormer, overturned her bureau, and pulled the mattress from her bed. And then he'd kicked open the back door and fled. Probably Diego had been waiting in the alley in the pickup.

I went slowly back downstairs to Sandra. "I have April safe outside in my car. If the ambulance doesn't get here soon, do you want me to drive her to the hospital?"

Her teeth were chattering, but she clenched them together and hissed, "You don't take my girl away from me, Tori."

"No, Sandra, I won't. You can ride along. What made that punk break your house up like that?"

"He s—s-said—he wanted the rec-c-c-cording," she burst out. "L-l-like I was—was—a radio st-st-station. Give me the rec-c-cording, he k-kept saying."

"The recording?" I echoed. "What recording?"

She was shaking and miserable; she didn't want to answer stupid questions from me. I got her to the couch, put on water for tea, and went out to my car. To my relief, when I unlocked the door April was still breathing. I was just explaining the situation to her when the blue-and-whites finally came screaming around the corner.

42 THE HIDING PLACE

Total confusion followed the arrival of the squad cars. Men ran through the alley and took up positions around the house, all the time squawking importantly through their walkie-talkies. I kept April in my car—it would be a tragic irony if she survived her heart failure and Freddy's assault only to get shot by one of these Lone Rangers. It took forever to get the men (and the one woman in the group) to understand that there had been a home invasion, that the perp had fled, and that Sandra and her mother needed medical help.

They finally got an ambulance to come. Even though April was breathing on her own, her pallor was bad, and I was relieved to have professionals take over her care. Sandra was still shaking too badly to make it down the walk on her own, but the crew carried her to the ambulance with a kind of impersonal briskness that seemed to brace her and make her function better.

"Can I call someone to go wait with you and bring you home?" I asked Sandra as they helped her into the back of the ambulance.

"Just leave me alone, Tori Warshawski. Every time you come near me, someone in my family gets hurt." She spat this out reflexively, because, a second later, she told me to call her folks, who lived over in Pullman. "They only have a pullout bed in the front room, but April and me, we can stay with them for a few days. My dad's old local, they'll send someone around to fix the house up for me."

It was a relief to know she wasn't completely on her own, but her departure left me to try to explain to the police what had been going on. I decided a bare-bones story would work best: I was the interim basketball coach; April was sick, her father had just died, I was dropping something off for her when a scumbag broke in through the back. He'd grabbed Sandra and threatened her; I took the kid out to my car to try to keep her out of danger. We waited for the posse—which, by the way, only arrived some thirty minutes after Sandra's first call.

The bare-bones story got bogged down when they saw my Smith & Wesson. I had a gun, yes, I had a license, yes, I was a private investigator, yes, but I wasn't here as a detective. I told them my history, my connection to the Czernins because April was on the Bertha Palmer basketball team and I was subbing for the coach, blah, blah. They didn't like it: I was here with a gun, the house was a wreck, they only had my word that Freddy had ever been on the premises.

I was trying hard not to lose my temper—that was a sure recipe for spending the night in a holding cell at the division—when Conrad called me on my cell phone: he'd gotten home, he'd gotten my message, and what the hell was I doing interrogating suspects?

"It took your damned squad twenty minutes by the clock to respond to a 911 call about a home invasion," I snarled. "Don't give me word one about staying out of your turf, leaving police business to the Fourth District, giving tea parties, or whatever it was you said last week."

"Home invasion? What are you talking about, Warshawski? You didn't say anything about that in the message you left."

"It hadn't happened then," I snapped, "but Freddy Pacheco, the guy I called you about, was breaking into the Czernin house less than an hour later. I did report my encounter with him to one of your detectives, but he wouldn't work up a sweat over it. Now your boys want to arrest me for saving Sandra and April Czernin."

"You're so wound up, I can't make head nor tail of what you're saying," Conrad complained. "Let me talk to the officer in charge."

I grinned savagely and handed the phone to my chief interrogator. "It's Conrad Rawlings, your Fourth District commander."

The officer frowned, thinking I was yanking his chain, but when he heard Conrad on the other end of the line he changed comically, sitting up at attention, giving an abbreviated account of their arrival. Judging from the officer's broken sentences, Conrad kept interrupting with demands to know why it had taken them so long to get to the Czernins, and what they had found when they searched the house. The officer got up to confer with another man, and reported that the house was empty.

I heard Conrad's voice scratchily through the mouthpiece; the officer said to me, "He wants to know what you know about the perp."

"Not much: he hangs out at a bar called Cocodrilo on Ninety-first Street, but I don't know where he lives. He rides with a cousin whose first name is Diego." I described Freddy's sullen, pretty-boy looks.

The officer relayed this information, listened some more to Conrad, then asked if I knew why Pacheco had broken in.

I shrugged elaborately. "He's a punk—the pastor at Mount Ararat calls him a *chavo banda* who does petty crime for a fee. In fact, the pastor may know where he lives."

I wasn't going to go through all the stuff about the frog, the fire at Fly the Flag, and Freddy's demand for a recording, not through an interpreter. Finally, Conrad and the officer finished, and the officer turned me back over to his commander.

"So take me through it, Ms. W. This *chavo* of yours, how do you know he set the fire?"

"He confessed it. In my hearing, while I had him cornered here—before Sandra Czernin acted like a horse's patootie and got between him and me. Whereupon he seized her and held her as a hostage. But I don't know what he wanted in her house. Bron Czernin made a device that Freddy used in setting the fire—Freddy had drawn a picture of it for him, and the picture was here in the house. He looked at the picture, but that wasn't what he wanted—it's still here." True, it was in my pocket, but Conrad didn't need to know that.

"While I was getting the kid out of the house, Freddy tore the house apart. I don't think he found what he was looking for. He drives around with his cousin in a Dodge pickup. The first letters on the plate are 'VBC'—I didn't catch the rest of it. That is my whole story. Can I go home now?"

"Yeah, and try to stay there. Even if we don't respond as fast as citizens want, we do get there—"

"In time to collect the corpses," I cut in nastily. "Which is what you'd have found if I hadn't been here. I coach a basketball team down here. April Czernin is one of my players, as is Josie Dorrado, who is still missing, despite the incredible energy your team is putting into looking for her, so I have to be down here whether you like it or not."

"All right!" he shouted. "Now you know my secret. I don't have enough money and enough bodies to do everything that has to happen to keep South Chicago safe. Send a note to the mayor, tell the super, but get off my back."

So his turf battle with me came partly out of pride: he didn't want me to know he couldn't look after the community. "Oh, Conrad, the mess down here is so big that seven cops with seven mops couldn't get it clear. I'm really, truly not trying to undercut you, but to give you some support."

"God save me from that, Ms. W.," he said, trying to recover his temper. "Go on home, go to bed—oh, hang on. I knew there was something else. That car, that Miata you found under the Skyway on Ewing, it was gone when we got there Tuesday afternoon. We called the Bysens, or their lawyers: the car belongs to Billy, they didn't want ugly cops pawing through it. They took it to a body shop, where it had been thoroughly dismantled and cleaned by yesterday morning. Thought you'd like to know. Try to stay out of trouble, Ms. W."

I was thankful to hang up while he was feeling more charitable and left the Czernin house while the going was possible. The officers searching the street and alley held me up while they checked to make sure I wasn't a fleeing suspect, but I finally was able to take off. When I was out of their range, I pulled over to the curb.

I reclined my seat until I could almost lie flat. I turned the CD of David Schrader and Bach back on and tried to think. I could go to Pastor Andrés to try to find out where Freddy lived, but I wasn't much interested in the *chavo* anymore. The police would track him down fast enough, and I didn't think he had anything helpful to tell me now. It was the recording I wanted to know about.

With my eyes shut, I let Bach float my mind away. Recordings. Sandra said Freddy had demanded recordings. When I was young, that meant 45s. That was why Sandra had said Freddy was talking to her as if she were a radio station. I had a brief memory of secretly listening to WVON when I was in high school—it was a black station, where the coolest music was played, and in those civil rights battle days, white girls who listened to WVON could get beaten up by their enlightened peers.

But a recording, that could also be a record of a conversation. I saw Marcena Love's wolfish smile as she held her fountain-pen recorder out to catch people's comments during the By-Smart prayer meeting we'd gone to. She recorded everything. Her little gizmo held up to eight hours of conversation; she could download its digital brain into her computer. So someone had taken her computer to destroy those records. But they didn't have the device, that red recording pen. If she had dropped it when she was in the Miata, it might still be back under the Skyway. Someone had searched the Miata pretty thoroughly, so if she'd dropped it in the car the people who searched it would have it—and they wouldn't have hired Freddy to look for it here. It could have fallen out when Marcena was dragged from the Miata—if that had happened under the Skyway, the pen might still be there.

I didn't relish a return to the underpass at this time of night. In the morning, I could bring Amy Blount down to help me look, if I didn't have any appointments. I pulled my Palm from my bag and saw the time: I'd told Mary Ann I'd call her at nine if I was going to be late and it was a quarter of ten now.

I tapped the screen with my pen. I should stop at her apartment on my way home—her manner had been so odd when we talked that I wanted to make sure she was really all right. I could leave the groceries in the kitchen for her, and maybe take the little dachshund out for a quick breath of air.

I looked at my Friday appointments. Nothing until one o'clock. I'd have the morning free, a welcome breather—I could sleep in, I could go to the Belmont Diner for corned beef hash and eggs. The thought almost made me drool, and I realized I hadn't eaten since grabbing that bowl of chicken noodle soup nine hours ago. I went to the trunk and broke off a piece of the goat feta I'd bought for Mary Ann. The tangy-sweet cheese was so delicious I ate another chunk. Before I knew it, I'd finished the whole piece. Oh, well—I'd get her some more next week.

As I started back up Route 41, I wondered if Marcena had left her pen at Morrell's. Carnifice, or whoever it was, had searched his place, but maybe they didn't know what device they were looking for. I called Morrell.

"Hippolyte! How's Your Majesty tonight?"

"Not very majestic, I'm afraid—I couldn't even slay an ordinary street punk, so I don't think I'm ready to take on a real warrior."

I told him about my encounters with Freddy. "He's looking for Marcena's recorder, and I think that's what they were hunting for up at your place, if that's any consolation. I know I'm too late for dinner, but I might still come back up tonight if you're going to be up for a while."

"I should drive down to South Chicago and carry you home on your shield after all you've been through. Since I can't, I think you should go to your own place—it's a shorter drive, and I don't like you on the roads when you're this beat. Don and I will have a look around—I'll call you if I find anything. And you call me when you get home." When I didn't answer, he said sharply, "Okay, Warshawski?"

My own untidy home with my dogs—I realized uneasily they sounded more comforting than Morrell's scrupulously clean condo. Maybe that was just because Don was visiting—I'd be filled with longing for Morrell as soon as I could see him alone.

It was only when I'd hung up that I remembered Carnifice or someone might be monitoring my phone, or Morrell's. I tried to remember the whole conversation. Not that I wanted strangers to hear my insecurities, but what I shouldn't have been talking about was the recorder. I called Morrell back, just to warn him. He was predictably annoyed at the idea that someone was listening in on his phone, but he agreed not to open the door without triple-checking a visitor's credentials.

"Anyway, Don is still smoking like a fiend. Anyone comes in, he can give them lung cancer while we wait for you and your gun."

I laughed more naturally. I'd been doing the irresponsible thing of talking while driving; I was at Mary Ann's now, so I told him I'd call him from home and hung up again.

It wasn't all that late: lights shone from most of the windows—I thought there was one on even in Mary Ann's—maybe she was reading in bed. I sat in the car, harvesting the remnants of my energy, before moving on stiff legs up the walk into her entryway. In case she was asleep, I didn't ring her bell but let myself into the building. I moved almost stealthily up the stairs, trying to disguise my tread so that Scurry wouldn't recognize it and start barking. With the same stealth, I undid the locks to her door and slipped inside.

The dog came skittering down the hall to meet me, but I put the groceries down and picked him up before he could make a noise. He licked my face with delight but wriggled free and ran back toward the kitchen. I picked up the bag and followed him. Mary Ann's bedroom door was shut, but a light was on in the back. I slipped past her room to the kitchen.

Fumbling with the locks to the back door, their faces tight with terror, were Josie Dorrado and Billy the Kid.

 THE FUGITIVES

I was so stunned that I stood for a moment, unable to speak or even think. Mary Ann's strange manner—her reluctance to see me, her insistence I be very precise in letting her know when I'd be coming—and the person who'd answered her phone without speaking—I'd never imagined she'd be harboring the fugitives.

Billy was shielding Josie from me as if I were going to wreak retribution on them. He swallowed nervously. "What are you going to do now?"

"Now? I'm going to unpack Mary Ann's groceries, make myself some coffee, and get you guys to tell me just what you're up to."

"You know what I mean," Billy said. "What are you going to do about—well, seeing us here?"

"That depends on what you tell me about why you're hiding out."

When I put the perishables into the refrigerator, I saw the kids had bought themselves Cokes and pizzas. I thought longingly of the bottle of Armagnac in my liquor closet, but I put on water for coffee and made myself toast.

"I don't have to tell you anything." In his truculence, Billy sounded much younger than his nineteen years.

"You don't have to," I agreed, "but you can't stay at Coach McFarlane's forever. If you tell me what you know, and who you're hiding from, I might be able to sort it out for you, or run interference, or, if you're in serious danger of your life, get you to a safe place."

"We're safe here," Josie said. "Coach doesn't let anyone see us."

"Josie, use your brain. If someone in your building had two strangers staying with them, how long would it be before you heard about it?"

She flushed and hung her head.

"People talk. They like to have news to report. Billy's family has hired the biggest detective agency in the world, certainly in Chicagoland, to find him. Eventually one of the investigators will talk to someone who knows Mary Ann, and they'll hear about the strange young couple who sometimes take her dog out for her, or pick up pizza and Coke at the Jewel, or hide in the kitchen when the visiting nurse comes. And if they come for Billy, they might hurt you, or Mary Ann."

"So we need to find another place," Billy said bleakly.

I poured out coffee for myself and offered the pot to them. Josie went to the refrigerator for a soda, but Billy accepted a cup. I watched, fascinated, as he stirred about a quarter of a cup of sugar into it.

"And what about your mother, Josie? She's sick with worry over you. She keeps thinking you're lying dead in the landfill where we found April's dad. Were you going to let her go on indefinitely imagining she'd lost you?"

Billy said, "They were in the landfill? Who put them in the landfill?" while Josie muttered something about her mother not liking her to be with Billy.

"How rotten of her. You're fifteen, smart and savvy enough for boys to be spending the night in your own bedroom, or to be sleeping together—where—on Coach McFarlane's pullout bed? You're going to have to go home sooner or later. Let's make it sooner."

"But, coach, it's quiet here, there's no baby, I don't have my sister taking my stuff, or the boys sleeping under the dining room table. There's no roaches in the kitchen—it's so peaceful here. I don't want to go back!" Her dark eyes blazed with passion, and a kind of longing. "And Coach

McFarlane likes having me here, she said so. She makes me work on my studies, and I help look after her, I do stuff like I did for my grandma when she was sick, I don't mind it."

"That's a separate matter," I said, calming down—I'd been in that apartment on Escanaba too many times not to respond to her yearning for quiet. "Let's sit down and figure out what to do about Billy's problems."

I pulled the chairs out from under Mary Ann's old enamel table. Billy's chin was still sticking out pugnaciously, but the fact that he sat down at my command meant he was ready to answer my questions.

"Billy, I just came from April's house. While I was there, Freddy Pacheco broke in. He tore the place apart. At first, I thought he was looking for the drawing he'd made for Bron—" I pulled out the paper, now very worn, with a tear along one crease.

"You have that?" Billy cried out. "How did you get it?"

"It was near where your car was wrecked Monday night. What do you know about it?"

"My car was wrecked? How did it happen? Where was it?"

I eyed him narrowly. "At 100th and Ewing. Who was driving it? Marcena?"

"No, because they'd put her—" He clapped a hand over his mouth.

In the silence that followed, I could hear the kitchen clock ticking and a drip from the bathroom sink. I thought irrelevantly that I'd have to remember to tighten the faucet before I left.

"Who put her where, Billy?"

He didn't speak, and I remembered Rose Dorrado, earlier tonight, telling Julia not to make telling the truth like a trip to the dentist. "All this decay will have to come out, Billy, before I can fix it and make it whole again. Start with your car. You gave it to Bron, right?"

He nodded. "I told Bron he could use it until I needed it again. I even wrote a slip out for him to carry, in case a cop or—or someone accused him of stealing it. But I wanted to go to the warehouse first and get my books, and a few things I'd left in the locker. I didn't want to work for Grobian anymore, because he had insulted Josie, and he had insulted me by spying on her. That was before I saw he—well, anyway, I told Bron I'd give him the car when I finished all that."

"You went to see Pat Grobian Sunday afternoon after church? He was at work, then?"

"No, but he lives down in Olympia Fields. I drove down after I talked to you. Pat was still in his underwear, watching football on TV, can you believe that? And he had the nerve to call Josie a—well, a name, I won't repeat it. We had a fight, an argument, I mean; I don't hit people. I was already worrying about stuff, and I told him I'd have to take some time off."

"The stuff you were worrying about—you'd seen it in a fax from Nicaragua? That's what your aunt Jacqui says."

"She told you about it? When?" His eyes were wide with disbelief.

"I was out at your grandmother's house last night. Jacqui didn't say much, just that you'd misinterpreted something about the Matagalpa plant, but she—"

"She said that?" Billy was almost shouting in anger. "She told that lie right in front of my grandmother? Do you know anything about what's going on down here?"

"Very little," I said meekly. "I know Pastor Andrés glued shut Fly the Flag to harass Frank Zamar over using sweatshop labor, but that Zamar went ahead and used it anyway. I know that Freddy—"

"You don't know about Matagalpa." Billy cut me off. "I found out—I saw this one fax to Aunt Jacqui, actually, it was the day you came to the warehouse to ask about money for the basketball program. They make jeans for By-Smart in Matagalpa, see, our house brand, Red River, and Aunt Jacqui, she wanted to see how fast they could set up to mass-produce sheets and linens and, you know, all that line. So I saw all the wage and hour figures and it was shocking, and I talked to her about it. She spends, like, two or three thousand dollars on every outfit she wears, I know because Uncle Gary keeps yelling about it.

"When I saw that Nicaragua fax, I did the arithmetic. The workers at the Red River plant work forty-four hundred hours a year, and they get not even eight hundred dollars, a *year*, I mean. So they'd have to work fourteen thousand *hours* to pay for one of her dresses, only, of course, they couldn't because they have to feed their children. I told her this, why can't she pay them something decent?, and she laughed, that way she has, and said their needs were simpler than hers. Simpler! Because she's depriving them!"

His face was red and he was panting. I could picture the scene, Billy flushed as he was now with righteous rage, Aunt Jacqui smiling maliciously as she always did when one of the Bysens was upset.

"So that's why you wanted to stay away from your family?"

"Sort of." He stirred the sugary sludge in his cup round and round. "I talked to them all, Grandpa, Grandma. Of course, Father is hopeless, but Grandpa, he just treated me like I was retarded, they all think I'm retarded, he said it would make sense to me when I knew the business better. So when Pastor Andrés went out to our headquarters, that day you were there, to lead the service, he tried to preach about it, and, well, you saw what happened then!"

Josie put a hand on his, with a sidelong look at me to see if I would try to stop her touching him. He patted her absently, but he was brooding over his family.

"You threatened to call the shareholders. What was that about?"

"Oh, that." He hunched an impatient shoulder. "That's so old now. I told my—my father, and Uncle Roger, I'd support a union bid in Nicaragua, that I'd go to the shareholders and tell them I was going to send money to the guys who the Red River manager is locking out in Matagalpa so they could afford to take their case to the World Court. Of course, that has Father and all my uncles freaked. I didn't really plan on hurting the family, not then, but now, oh, Jesus, now—!"

He broke off, real anguish in his face and voice, and dropped his head in his hands. This time, it was I who leaned over and patted him consolingly.

"What happened? Something about Zamar?"

"Everything was about Zamar." His hands muffled his voice. "They—Aunt Jacqui and Grobian, I mean—were threatening Zamar, see, threatening to destroy his plant, that was the business with the rats, because he was saying he'd have to break the contract. Pat, Pat Grobian, he and Father said no one could break a By-Smart contract. If Frank Zamar did, then everyone would think they could walk away if they didn't like the terms. Everyone wants to do business with us because we're so big, and then we make people agree to prices they can't afford . . ."

He stopped.

"So?" I prodded.

"I've gotten pretty good at Spanish," he said, looking up briefly. "I studied it in high school, but because of the warehouse, and worshiping at Mount Ararat, I understand it really well. So this fax came in from the Matagalpa manager, in Spanish. He was sending Pat the name of one of the local *jefes*, chiefs, you know, who get bad jobs for illegals and pocket half their pay, and, you know—"

I nodded.

"So the guy in Matagalpa, he was saying they should send Frank Zamar to this one guy, this local *jefe* here in South Chicago, and he'd see Frank got a stream of Central American illegals desperate for work. And Pat Grobian kind of told Frank, do it or else."

"But Frank started to run that sweatshop," I objected. "Rose's mother was working there. That was two days before the plant burned down."

"Yeah, but, see, Frank was so bitter and ashamed he didn't tell Aunt Jacqui or my father that he'd started making these things. He was taking the finished ones to his own home, waiting until he had a full load. Then he was going to deliver it, but he didn't want to talk about it." Billy looked at me with his wide, guileless eyes. "If he'd told them! But they thought he was still holding out, so they wanted more sabotage."

I remembered the cartons I'd seen being loaded into a panel truck the last time I was at the plant before the fire. That must have been the partial load Zamar was taking home.

"Your family sent in Freddy," I supplied. "How did Bron get involved?"

"Oh, you don't know anything!" he cried out. "Bron was the person doing it! Only he hired Freddy to do the actual dirty work. They'd just tell Bron, do something to the plant, they wouldn't spell it out, and he'd get Freddy Pacheco to collect all those dead rats, or—or take that frog dish and put it on the wires."

My phone rang. Morrell, saying they'd had a look around and hadn't found anything, meaning Marcena's recording pen, and he was going to bed.

"Mary Ann okay?"

"I think so," I said; I remembered in time not to blurt out the news that Billy and Josie were there, just said there were a few things that I needed to take care of since I hadn't been here for a week.

I turned back to Billy. "How long have you known about the frog? Why didn't you go to the cops?"

"I couldn't." The words came out in a whisper. He was staring fixedly at the tabletop, as if trying to fall into it and disappear, and I had to prod him for some minutes before the rest of the story emerged.

On Monday, he said he'd drive Bron to the warehouse in time for Bron to pick up his rig. Billy was planning to clean out his locker, and he'd leave the Miata in the employee parking area for Bron to drive home at the end of his shift. Bron, in turn, would drop Billy at the South Chicago commuter train station before going to his first delivery point.

On their way to the warehouse, Billy asked Bron what his plan was for getting the money for April's heart surgery, and Bron said he had an extra insurance policy that Grobian had signed up for, and he showed Billy the frog picture, the same one I'd been carrying around. Billy asked what it was, and Bron said part of his policy, Billy didn't have to know more than that, he was too nice a kid.

"I get tired of that, all the time being told I'm too innocent, or too nice, or too retarded, or whatever it is, to know what's going on," Billy flashed. "Like believing in Jesus, and wanting to do good in the world, automatically makes you an idiot. So—just to show you I'm not all that nice, I decided to find out what Bron was up to with Pat. There's a closet in Pat's room that connects to the next room—it used to be a big office suite or something, with a john or something in between the two rooms, but, anyway, I went in there, in the closet, and I heard the whole thing, Bron saying he needed a hundred grand for April, Pat laughing in this nasty way, 'You been hanging around the Kid too much if you think his family will part with one red cent for your brat.'

"Then I guess Bron showed him the frog picture, and Pat said, that proved jack shit—" Billy turned crimson as he repeated the phrase; he looked at me fleetingly to see whether I was shocked. "And Bron said, oh, he had a recording of it all, on account of Marcena Love had been with him when Pat asked him to do the dirty work, and she had everything on tape, she recorded everybody's conversations so she'd have an accurate record. So then Pat told him to wait outside for a minute. And he made a phone call and repeated the conversation, and then he called Bron back in and said, okay, he thought he could help him out after all. He said Bron should bring the truck over to Fly the Flag after he made his Crown Point drop-off—that he wanted to inspect that first load of sheets Zamar had made to see if they could be salvaged, and someone from the family would be there with a check, that it couldn't be, like, out in public, because the family didn't want to be involved. So I decided to go to Fly the Flag and see who showed up from the family."

"Where was Josie while all this was going on?" I asked.

"Oh, I was waiting in the Miata." It was the first time Josie had spoken—it was almost as though she hadn't been there.

"In the Miata? It's a tiny two-seater!"

"We had the top down." Josie's eyes were shining with pleasure at the memory. "I crouched behind the seats. It was so fun, I loved it."

On a cold November afternoon, yes, fifteen, close to death and to love at the same moment—that was fun.

"How did Marcena get into the car, then?" I asked, trying to figure out how all these people had ended up together.

"Bron picked her up in the truck. She was interviewing someone, or looking at something, I don't know what, but he told me he was going to get her, and he wanted to know was it okay if she drove my car. See, before I heard Grobian and Bron talking, we—Josie and I—were planning to run away to Mexico together, find Josie's great-aunt in Zacatecas. We were going to take the train downtown to the Greyhound station. Josie doesn't have an ID, so we couldn't fly, and, anyway, if we flew my dad's detectives would find us. We were going to take the Greyhound to El Paso and then hitchhike to Zacatecas.

"But then I decided I had to go back to Fly the Flag first—I had to see who from my family would be there, and I didn't want Bron to know I was doing that. If I had known what they were going to do, I'd never have brought Josie, you have to believe that, Ms. War-sha-sky, because it was the most awful—" His shoulders started shaking; he was trying not to sob out loud.

"Who came?" I asked in a matter-of-fact voice.

"It was Mr. William," Josie said softly after a minute, when Billy couldn't speak. "The English lady, she drove up in Billy's car. Mr. Czernin dropped us, see, over at the train station on Ninety-first Street. The factory is only, like, six blocks from the station. Billy carried my backpack, and we walked up, we picked up a pizza and stuff, and then we just went into the factory."

She kept talking in the same soft voice, as if she didn't want to startle Billy. "The big room where Ma used to sew, it smelled from the fire, but the front was still okay, you know, if you didn't know the back was gone, you'd think it was still okay. So we waited, it was, like, I don't know, three hours. It got kind of cold. And then suddenly I heard Mr. Grobian's voice, and he and Mr. William came in. We hid under one of the worktables—the electricity was off because of the fire, and they had this big, portable work light they turned on, but they couldn't see us.

"And then April's dad came in with the English reporter. They talked back and forth, about April's surgery, and what Mr. Czernin had done for Mrs. Jacqui and Mr. Grobian, and Mr. William, he said to the English lady, Mr. Czernin say you have—I mean, Mr. Czernin, he *says* you have a recording of all this?

"And the English lady, she said she had a tape recording, but she was just going to read them the—I can't remember the word, but she'd written it all down, copied it from the tape recording, I mean. Because she said they couldn't have her tape recorder, she knew what would happen to it if she let them at it.

"So she read this whole thing where Mr. Grobian was telling Mr.

Czernin to wreck up the factory, wreck up Fly the Flag, I mean. Billy's aunt, she was at the meeting, not in the factory, but the one where they told April's father to wreck up the factory. So the English lady read about what they all said, and how Mr. William himself said this would prove to the old man—he meant Billy's grandpa—that he knew how to take strong action.

"So when she finished, Mr. William, he gave this kind of phony laugh"—she darted a glance at Billy as if he might be offended—"and said, 'I see you were telling the truth, Czernin. I thought you were making empty threats. We'll work it out. You get the truck loaded up, we found the sheets okay, they're in these boxes here, and I'll write you out a check.'"

Josie gave a startling imitation of William's precise and fussy manner. Billy sat, glassy-eyed, as if he were in a drunken stupor. I didn't know if he was hearing Josie or just reliving the evening in his head.

"Then I don't know what really happened, because we were under a table, but Mr. Grobian and Mr. Czernin, they loaded up the forklift, and the English lady, she said, oh, she would adore to drive the forklift, she'd done tanks and the semi but never a forklift, and Mr. Grobian said, he would back the truck up to the loading bay and Czernin could show her how to handle the forklift. Only somehow the forklift went over and they fell off, the English lady and Mr. Czernin. She screamed, kind of, but Mr. Czernin never made any sound . . ." Her voice trailed off; suddenly it wasn't exciting anymore, it was frightening.

"What happened?" I was trying to picture the scene—the forklift driving up to the truck and then over the edge. Or Grobian and William dumping a load of cartons on Bron and Marcena.

"I didn't see it," Billy whispered. "But I heard Dad say, I think that's done it for them, Grobian. Load them into the truck. We'll take them over to the landfill, and their nearest and dearest can imagine they've run off to Acapulco together."

He started to cry, loud retching sobs that shook his whole body. The outburst terrified Josie, who looked from him to me with scared eyes.

"Get him a glass of water," I commanded her.

I went around the table to cradle his head against my breast. Poor guy, witnessing his own father commit murder. No wonder he was hiding. No wonder William wanted to find him.

I jumped as a voice spoke behind me. "Oh, it's you, Victoria. I might have guessed from all the racket that you'd shown up." Mary Ann Mc-Farlane was standing in the doorway.

44

THE RECORDING
ANGEL . . . OR DEVIL?

With her bald head atop her scarlet tartan dressing gown, Mary Ann made a startling sight, but all three of us responded at once to her authority. Billy's engrained good manners brought him to his feet; he drank the water that Josie had been holding out to him, and apologized to Mary Ann for waking her up. After we'd gone through the bustle of greetings, and how I'd happened on the fugitives, Billy finished the tale, by explaining how they'd ended up at Mary Ann's.

They'd spent the remainder of Monday night huddled under the worktable, too shocked and frightened to try to leave. They thought they'd heard more voices than just William's and Grobian's, but they weren't sure, and they didn't know if someone was watching the plant. But by morning, they were cold as well as hungry. They risked getting up to use the bathroom, which was in the intact part of the plant. When no one attacked them, they decided to leave but didn't know where to go.

"I wanted to call you, Coach Warshawski," Josie said, "but Billy was afraid you might still be working for Mr. William. So we came here, because Coach McFarlane was the person who helped Julia when she got pregnant."

I shadow-punched Mary Ann. "What was that you said to me this afternoon—about not knowing the Dorrado girls very well?"

She gave her grim smile. "I wanted them to go to you, Victoria, but I'd promised I'd keep their secret safe until they were ready to tell it. Trouble is, I thought Billy was hiding while he sorted out the ethics of his family's business—I didn't know 'til I heard him just now that they'd witnessed Bron's death. If I'd known that, please believe I'd have called you *quam primum famam audieram*."

Mary Ann breaks into Latin when she's agitated—it calms her down, but makes it hard for people like doctors and nurses to know what she's saying. I don't follow her easily myself, and, right now, I was too over-whelmed by Billy's narrative to make the effort.

"You said Marcena read from a transcript, that she didn't play the recording," I said to Billy. "But did you see her recorder at Fly the Flag?"

"We didn't see anything," Josie said.

"And Billy's dad didn't see you?"

"No one saw us."

I could see why William was looking so desperately for the recorder. They'd gotten her computer, but they didn't have the original. But why was he so desperate to find Billy if he didn't know his son had been there? I asked Billy who else he had told.

"No one, Ms. War-sha-sky, no one."

"You didn't instant-message anyone?"

He shook his head.

"What about the blog—April said there's one you and your sister use to stay in touch."

"Yeah, but we use nicknames, just in case. Candy's at a mission in Daegu, that's in South Korea, my folks—my dad, he sent her there after the—the abortion—to keep her out of temptation and make up for the life she'd taken. I'm not supposed to write her, but we post to this blog, it's devoted to Oscar Romero, on account of he's my—my spiritual hero. My dad doesn't know about it, and when I write her I use my blog name, Gruff, but—"

The hair prickled on my neck. "For 'Billy-the-Kid-Goat's Gruff,' no doubt. Did you tell her about Bron and your dad?"

He was looking at the linoleum, tracing a circle with his running shoe. "Sort of."

"Carnifice could track your blog postings through your laptop, even if you'd used the world's cleverest nicknames."

"But—I told her about Bron through Coach McFarlane's computer," he objected.

I yelped so loudly it sent Scurry running down the hall for cover. "They have your nickname, so they can look for any new postings you make! And now they can trace Mary Ann's machine. If you're trying to lay low, you absolutely cannot be in touch with the outside world. Now I need to figure out where to park you two—it's a question of hours before your dad's detectives track down Mary Ann's machine. We may need to move you, too," I added to my old coach.

Mary Ann said she wasn't budging from her home, tonight or any other time; she was staying here until they moved her to a cemetery.

I didn't waste time arguing with her or trying to persuade the kids to move; my most urgent task was to find Marcena's recorder before William's Dobermans did. Since she seemed to carry it everywhere, she must have had it on Monday. Maybe she'd only read from a transcript because she was recording the meeting, or she was wary enough not to let them see her device.

Her big Prada bag, which she also took everywhere, hadn't materialized after the assault, so William must have gotten that. He'd searched the remains of the Miata. If the pen wasn't there, or at Morrell's, or the Czernin house, then I was betting she'd lost it either at Fly the Flag or in the truck that took them to the landfill. Or at the landfill itself, I suppose. Since I didn't know where the truck was and couldn't look at the landfill until morning, I'd swing by the plant now, before William had the same idea.

I hoped Billy and Josie would continue to be safe if I left them behind. It was hard to live with so much uncertainty. I'd been trailed yesterday, but not today—as far as I knew. But I'd been using my phone this past hour, and Billy had been using Mary Ann's computer. I went to the living room and peered through a slit in the drapes. I didn't think anyone was watching, but you never know.

Josie had gotten them this far. She was four years younger than Billy, but a harder-headed urban survivor. It was she I coached to put the chain bolts on both doors and not to open them for anyone but me; if I didn't come back tonight, then tomorrow they had to tell a reliable adult what was going on.

"You two have been smart about not speaking on Coach McFarlane's phone, and you need to keep doing that, but you have to promise me that you will call Commander Rawlings in the Fourth District if you don't hear from me by morning. Don't talk to anyone but him."

"We can't go to the police," Billy objected. "Too many of them owe favors to my family, they do what my father or—or grandfather tell them."

I was about to say they could trust Conrad the way they trusted me, but how could I be sure of that? It might be true, but Conrad had superiors, he even had patrol officers who could be bribed or threatened. I gave them Morrell's number instead.

"When I do come back, I'm going to take you home with me. I don't like leaving you here with Coach McFarlane—you're too exposed, and it puts her in danger."

"Oh, Victoria, my life is too close to the end to worry about danger," Mary Ann protested. "I like having young people in the place. It keeps me from brooding over my body. They're looking after Scurry, and I'm teaching them Latin—we're having a grand old time."

I smiled weakly and said we could figure that part out later. I showed Josie the place in the curtains where she could see the street, and told her if she saw someone follow me she should call me. Otherwise, I'd see her in the morning.

I zipped up my parka, kissed Mary Ann on both cheeks, and let myself out the door. Billy came behind me and pulled briefly on my arm.

"I just wanted to say thank you for helping me out when I fell apart just now," he muttered.

"Oh, honey, you've been carrying way too big a load. You didn't fall apart—you just felt safe enough to let me know how hard it's been."

"Do you mean that?" His wide eyes studied me for mockery. "In my family, not even my grandma thinks it's all right to cry."

"In my family, we think you shouldn't wallow in your tears, we think you should act—but we believe that sometimes you can't act until you've cried your heart out." I put an arm around him and gave him a brief hug. "Look after Josie and Coach McFarlane. And yourself. I'll be back as soon as possible."

The skies had cleared. When I got to my car I could see the Big Dipper low in the northern sky; the moon was almost full. This was both good and bad; I wouldn't have to use a light to find the factory, but I'd be visible if anyone was watching Fly the Flag.

I checked my flashlight. The batteries were good, and I had a spare pair in the glove compartment. I put them in my pocket. Checked for my extra clip to the Smith & Wesson. I left my phone on until I was a couple of blocks from Mary Ann's, heading north, toward Lake Shore Drive and my home. At Seventy-first Street, I switched off my phone, then turned west and looped around the neighborhood until I was sure I was clean. I turned south again and made my way to Fly the Flag.

Once again, I parked on Yates and walked down to the factory. The Skyway embankment loomed in front of me, its sodium lights forming a halo above the street but not shedding much light below. Most of the streetlamps were out down here at ground level, but the cold silver moon lit the streets, turning the old factories along South Chicago Avenue into chiseled marble. The moonlight cast long narrow shadows; my own figure bobbed along the roadway, like a piece of stretched bubble gum, all skinny lines with little blobs where my joints were.

The avenue was empty. Not the quiet emptiness of the countryside, but one where urban scavengers moved under cover of the dark: rats, druggies, thugs, all looking for a fix. A South Chicago bus labored up the street. From a distance, it looked like *Mister Rogers' Neighborhood*—its windows were filled with light, and the headlights looked like a grin underneath the big front window. Get on board, ride home in warmth and comfort.

I crossed the road and went into the factory yard. It had been over a week since the fire, but a whiff of smoke still hovered faintly in the air, like an elusive perfume.

Even though the traffic on the Skyway was loud enough to muffle my sounds here, I walked along the edge of the gravel drive so that my running shoes wouldn't crunch in the loose stones. I went around to the side, to the loading bay.

I saw at once what had happened to Bron. Just as he had the heavy front load of the forklift suspended beyond the lip of the dock, ready to drop his load in the truck, Grobian had pulled away. The forklift had pitched headfirst off the dock, burying its forks in the ground. The cartons Bron had loaded on the front end were scattered in a wide circle around it. The fall itself must have broken Bron's neck; the wonder was that Marcena had survived it.

I shone my flashlight around the ground. Sherlock Holmes would have seen the telltale broken weed, or displaced piece of stone, to say whether Marcena had been in the truck when it went over. I could only guess that her war zone training had given her a sixth sense of the danger, so that she jumped clear of the forklift as it fell.

I climbed around the machine. I looked underneath it as best I could, but I couldn't see Marcena's red pen. Maybe it was buried under the front end, but I'd save that possibility for last—it would mean hiring a tow truck to raise the forklift.

I moved in a circle around through the weeds and the gravel. This side of the building faced away from the fire, so I didn't have to contend with the broken glass and charred remnants of fabric I'd found when I searched here last week, but there was still a tiresome amount of debris, jetsam from the Skyway, flotsam from the street. I'd read recently that Chicago's landfills were just about at capacity and we were starting to ship our garbage downstate. If all the bags and cans I'd seen on the streets today had been put into the garbage, maybe we'd have filled our landfills even sooner. Maybe litterers were saving taxpayers money.

After an hour, I was as sure as I could be in the dark that the pen wasn't out here. I put a foot onto the forklift and climbed up onto the loading dock. I sat on the lip and stared into the tangle of brush, trying to imagine Marcena.

Now that I wasn't moving around myself, the night noises started to sound loud. I strained to listen under the whoosh of the cars and grinding gears of the semis overhead. Were those rats and raccoons rustling in the brush, or humans?

Marcena wanted Grobian and William on tape, or chip. She saw she was onto a much bigger story than she'd thought; she knew the power the Bysens had—if she tried to publish the story, they could squash it, sue the paper, sue her. She needed their voices, saying what they were doing.

Maybe she'd had her recorder in her hip pocket, but maybe she'd put it where she thought it would pick up any private remarks the two men made. I pushed myself to my feet. Despite my parka, I was cold now, and I didn't want to go inside the dark, cold building alone.

Billy and Josie spent a night here, I scolded myself. Be your age, be a detective. I turned on my flashlight again and went into the loading room. Shelves ran along its high walls, filled with flat cartons ready to be made into flag boxes. There were still some bolts of fabric in their plastic sheathing, waiting to be carried to the cutting area. After two weeks, a thick layer of sooty dust covered them, and the edges had been eaten by rodents, charmed to have such soft nest-building material laid out for them. I heard them scuttle away as my light drove them from their work.

I gave a cursory look around the room, but the floors were bare; I think I would have seen the recorder if she'd dropped it here in the open. I did check walls, and under the shelves, to see if it might have rolled out of sight, but found only rat droppings. I shuddered and moved quickly into the workroom where William found, or claimed he'd found, a load of sheets.

Here was where the fire damage was obvious. There was a gash in the front wall where the firemen had axed through the entrance. Ash lay on the sewing machines and cutting tables, heavier toward the southwest corner, where the worst of the blaze had been, but sprinkled with a liberal hand where I stood, near the other end of the room. The big windows in the back had broken. Glass lay everywhere, even near the front of the room. How had it traveled so far? Pieces of window frames, chair legs, half-sewn U.S. flags—all these were strewn around, as if some giant playing dollhouse in here had a temper tantrum—she got tired of it, picked up all the pieces and dropped them any old how.

Marcena would have wanted as much material as she could get for her hot story; she would have tried recording Grobian and Mr. William while Bron loaded the forklift. So maybe she put her pen down near where they were standing.

And there it was, next to a sewing machine, lying against a pair of shears. I couldn't believe it, casually set out on a tabletop in plain sight. Of course, if you didn't know what it was you wouldn't imagine it was a recorder—it was really quite a clever gadget.

I picked it up and examined it under my flashlight. It was not much bigger than one of those fat, high-end pens you see in pricey stationery shops. There was a USB port for attaching it to a computer and down-loading it, and little buttons, with the universal squares and triangles of recorders—play, forward, reverse. There was also a screen about an inch long and a quarter inch wide; when I pressed the "on" switch, the screen asked if I wanted to play or record. I hit the play button.

"Her and me, we're the two best on the team, but Coach, she's always giving April the breaks."

The voice belonged to Celine, my gangbanger. The machine was starting from the beginning of the file, the day Marcena had come with me to basketball practice. I was tempted to eavesdrop more on how the team saw me, but I fast-forwarded. Next, I was startled by my own voice: I was talking to the woman next to me at the By-Smart prayer meeting, asking about William Bysen. I forwarded again.

This time, Marcena's clipped tones came tinnily into the room. "Look, put it in your jacket pocket, here. I've switched it on, but it won't record unless people are talking within about six feet of it, so hopefully you won't pick up a ton of useless background noise."

The next noises were smothered scrapings and gruntings, Marcena's laugh, a slap, mock outrage from Bron. An R-rated recording, oh, well. Then a few starts and stops with Bron maneuvering his truck and cursing at some other driver, and then he was telling Marcena to get behind the seats, to lie down on the mattress back there so the guard at the warehouse gate wouldn't see her. The guard checked him in; the two knew each other and kidded back and forth. There were similar exchanges all through the warehouse; he was talking to my friend in the Harley jacket about their routes and loads, bragging about April and her ball playing, joining in laments about the Bears and about company management, until Grobian summoned him.

Grobian went over his route and his load for the day, then said, "That supplier in your neck of the woods, Czernin, that flag maker, I don't know if it's his Serbian head, but it seems kind of thick, like he's not getting the message."

"Hey, Grobe, I did my best."

"And we showed our gratitude." That was Aunt Jacqui. "But we—the family—want you to give him another message."

"So what do you want me to do?"

"We want you to give him a message, shut his plant down for a day, but let him know we can put it out of business for good if he doesn't play ball. A hundred, like before, if you do the job by the end of the week. An extra hundred if you make the message strong enough to force him to come round," Grobian said.

"What did you have in mind?" Bron asked.

"You're creative, you're good with your hands," Aunt Jacqui used a provocative tone, implying that she wouldn't mind knowing what he did with his hands. "You'll think of something, I'm sure. I don't want to hear that kind of detail."

Her voice came through more clearly than Grobian's—she must have been sitting in the chair in front of the desk, while Grobian sat behind it. Was she wearing that black dress whose buttons only came down to her hips? Had she crossed her legs, casually, giving a suggestive flash up the thigh—this could be yours, Bron, if you do what I want?

All at once, I heard voices coming in through the loading area. I'd been so intent on the recording that I hadn't heard the truck pull into the yard. What kind of detective was I, sitting there like a turkey waiting to be shot for Thanksgiving dinner?

"Jacqui, if you wanted to come along you should have worn proper shoes. I don't care if your damn thousand-dollar boots have a scratch on them. I don't know why Gary tolerates your spending."

Jacqui laughed. "There's so little you know, William. Daddy Bysen will have six kinds of fits when he learns that you swear."

I stuffed the recorder into my hip pocket and ducked under the big cutting table. Red-and-white bunting hung over the sides like a heavy curtain—maybe I'd be safe under here.

"Maybe he'll choke on them, then. I am sick, *god*damn sick of him treating me like I don't have the wits to run my family, let alone this company."

"Willy, Willy, you should have taken your stand years ago, the way I did when Gary and I first married. If you didn't want Daddy Bysen running your life, you shouldn't have let him build your house for you out in—what was that?"

I had tripped on a chair leg and banged into the table as I went under it. I held myself completely still, squatting behind the bunting, barely daring to breathe.

"A rat, probably." Grobian spoke for the first time.

Light flicked around the floor.

"Someone's in here," William said. "There are footprints in the ash in here."

I had the Smith & Wesson in my hand, safety off. I slipped through the bunting on the far side of the cutting table, calculating the distance to the hole in the front wall.

"Neighborhood is heavy with junkies. They come in here to shoot up." Grobian's voice was indifferent, but he upended the cutting table so fast I barely had time to move out of the way.

"There!" Jacqui cried as I stood and started running toward the front. She shone her light on me. "Oh! It's that Polish detective, the one who's been lecturing us on charity."

I didn't turn to look, just kept going, skidding around the tables, trying to sidestep debris.

"Get her, Grobian," William shouted, his voice going up to a squeak.

I heard the heavy steps behind me but still didn't turn. I was two strides from the door when I heard the click, the hammer going back. I hit the floor just as he fired. I tried to keep hold of my own gun, but my fall sent it spinning out of my hand. He was on top of me before I could get to my feet.

I grabbed Grobian's left leg and jerked upward. He stumbled, and had to twist around to keep from falling. I sprang upright backing away from him. My head was wet. Blood was pouring down my hair and neck, into my shirt. It made me dizzy, but I tried to concentrate on him. Jacqui and William were helping him, shining their lights on me; Grobian was a shape in the dark, two shapes, two fists swinging at me. I ducked under the first one, but not the second.

45 DOWN IN THE DUMPS

My father was cutting the grass. He kept running the mower over me. My eyes were bandaged shut, so I couldn't see him, but I'd hear the wheels rumbling through the grass. They would hit me, go right over me, and then roll back again. It was so cold, why was he mowing the grass when it was so cold out, and why didn't he see me? The garden smelled terrible, like pee and vomit and blood.

I screamed at him to stop.

"Pepaiola, cara mia," his only words of Italian, used on my mother and me both, his two pepper pots, "Why are you lying in my path? Get up, get out of my way."

I tried to stand, but the long grass had wrapped itself around me and tied me, and then he was running the lawn mower over me again. He adored me, why was he tormenting me like this?

"Papa, stop!" I screamed again. He halted briefly, and I tried to sit up. My hands were tied behind me. I rubbed my face against my shoulder, trying to push up the bandages on my eyes. I couldn't budge them, and I kept rubbing, until I realized that I was rubbing my eyes. I wasn't bandaged; I was in a black space, so dark I couldn't even see the gleam of my parka.

I heard a roar, felt a horrible jerk, and then the mower rolled over me again, knocking the breath out of me, so I couldn't scream. My mind shrank to a pinprick in its retreat from pain. Another halt, and this time I forced myself to think.

I was in a truck. I was in the back of a semi, and something on wheels was rolling back and forth with the jolting of the truck. I remembered Marcena, with the skin missing from a quarter of her body, and tried to shift myself, but the motion of the truck and the assaults from the hand-cart, or conveyor belt, or whatever it was, made it impossible for me to move.

My hands were tied behind me and my legs were strapped together. I smelled, too, smelled the way Freddy Pacheco did when I attacked him. A hundred years ago, that had been. The vomit and blood and pee, they were all mine. My head ached, and blood had dried in my nose. I needed water desperately. I stuck my tongue up and licked the blood. AB negative, a good vintage, hard to find, don't lose too much of it.

I didn't want to be here, I wanted to be back in my other world, where my father was with me, even if he was hurting me. I wanted my mother on the other side of the door, making cocoa for me.

The detective who feels sorry for herself might as well write her own funeral oration. The next time the truck halted, I made a ferocious effort and sat up. I twisted so my feet were at right angles to where they'd been. Now I was leaning with my back against the back of the truck. The next time the wheeled thing came at me, it rammed into the soles of my boots. I felt the jolt all the way up my spine. No good, V.I., no good, a few more hits like that and you'll be paralyzed.

We stopped again. Wherever we were going, we were on city streets, I guessed, with a lot of stop signs, and my captors were obeying traffic laws—they weren't going to risk ticketing for running a red light.

I fell forward onto my knees and managed to move them, just a little, just enough to crawl forward until I ran into the wheeled thing. The top was about thigh high, and I flung myself onto it as the truck rocked forward again.

It felt like a victory, a triumph as big as scaling Everest. Yes, I was

Junko Tabel; what she'd done, scaling the big mountain, didn't compare with this scrabbling with bound hands and feet on top of something I couldn't see. I lay across the wheeled thing, my head throbbing, but the pleasure of getting away from the rollers kept me from losing consciousness again.

We made an abrupt hard turn and the truck bounced. The trailer went up and down on its eighteen wheels and then rocked from side to side. I rolled helplessly up and down with the cart, slamming crazily from one end of the truck to the other, trying to hold my head so it wouldn't bang up and down with the motion.

I knew where we were going. The knocked-over fence, the track through the marsh, I could picture our route, the gray sky and grass and the end, the end in a pit. I squeezed my eyes shut, not wanting to see the darkness, not wanting to see the end.

When we halted, I lay on my face panting shallowly, feeling the motor rumbling underneath me, too exhausted to brace myself against the next jolt forward. I heard a crash to my right and slowly moved my head to look. The doors to the truck swung open and I was dazzled by light. I thought it was daytime, thought it was the sun, thought I'd go blind.

Grobian strode along the back of the truck. Close your eyes, V.I.; blunk them up: you're unconscious, the eyes blunk up when you're unconscious. Grobian thrust a lid up with a rough thumb; he seemed satisfied. He grabbed me around the waist and slung me over his shoulder and thumped back out. I opened my eyes again. It was still night—being locked in total blackness had made even the night sky look bright at first.

"This time we're in the right spot," Grobian said. "Jeesh—suburban prick like you, dumping Czernin and the Love woman on the golf course instead of the landfill. This Polish cunt will be under ten feet of garbage by the time the sun comes up."

"You don't talk to me like that, Grobian," Mr. William said.

"Bysen, from now on I talk to you however I please. I want that job in Singapore, running the Asian operations for By-Smart, but I'd consider South America. One of those or I'm talking to the old man. If Buffalo Bill finds out what you've been up to with his precious company—"

"If the shock gives him a stroke and kills him, I'll be singing at his funeral," William said. "I'm not worried about anything you say to him."

"Big talk, big talk, Bysen. But if you acted as big as you talk—you'd never have gotten involved in crap like this. Men like your father, if they can't do their dirty work themselves they're smart enough to have friends of friends of friends figure it out so no finger ever points to them. You want to know why Buffalo Bill won't trust you with more of his company? Not because you're a lying, cheating SOB—he respects lying, cheating SOBs. It's because you're a lying, useless weasel, Bysen. If you hadn't been Buffalo Bill's son, you'd be lucky to have a job typing figures in your own warehouse."

Grobian swung me like a hammock and flung me from him. I landed facedown in muck. I heard him dust his hands and then heard him and William head back to the truck, bickering the whole way, not looking back at me, not even talking about me.

I lifted my head just as the truck jerked into gear again. The headlights flooded me for a moment, showing me where I was, the side of one of the giant mounds of earth where Chicago buries its trash. Beyond the By-Smart semi, I could see lights from other trucks, city trucks, a line of beetles moving toward me. Every day, another ten thousand tons comes in, gets emptied, and covered again with more dirt. The city trucks work round the clock, hauling away our refuse.

My stomach was frozen from fear. Grobian was backing the By-Smart semi, starting to turn it in a wide, clumsy circle. When he got out of the way, the line of beetles would crawl on up the hillside and dump their loads on me. I frantically pushed my left foot against my right, bending my toes inside my boot, bracing myself by putting my head into the sludge. I couldn't waste time watching the semi's progress. I pushed so hard I screamed from the pain shooting up my spine.

My right foot came out of my running shoe. I pulled my foot free of the fabric tying my legs together. Drew my knees under me and pushed myself standing. I was free, I could jump up and down, the drivers would see me. My thighs wobbled with fatigue, my arms were pinned behind me so that my shoulders felt they might burst in their sockets, but I wanted to sing and dance and turn cartwheels.

The garbage trucks weren't on me yet: the By-Smart semi was still blocking the track, lurching in a circle. I stopped jumping. Save your energy, Warshawski, save it for when you need it. The semi kept turning, not straightening out for the outbound road. The line of beetles had stopped and was honking at the semi. It seemed as though Grobian had forgotten how to drive. Or was William trying to prove he wasn't a completely useless weasel by taking the wheel himself? The tractor made too wide a turn and brought the trailer over the side of the hill. The trailer teetered for a minute on its inside wheels and toppled over. The tractor fell back on its hind wheels, hung for a second, and then collapsed on its side.

46

BEHOLD: THE PURLOINED PEN

The night ended for me as far too many had already this month: in a hospital emergency room, with Conrad Rawlings staring down at me.

"Whatever you have for breakfast, Ms. W., I want to start eating it, too: you should be dead."

I blinked at him hazily through the curtain of pain blockers shrouding my mind. "Conrad? How did you get here?"

"You made the ER nurse call me. Don't you remember? You apparently had ten kinds of fits when they tried to put you under, that I had to get here before you'd let them treat you."

I shook my head, trying to remember the shreds of the night behind me, but the movement hurt my head. I put a hand up to touch it and felt a sheet of adhesive.

"I don't remember. And what's wrong with me? What's on my head?"

He grinned, his gold tooth glinting in the overhead lights. "Ms. W., you look like the lead zombie from the *Night of the Living Dead*. Someone shot you in the head, which, if I thought it would pound any sense into it, I can only applaud."

"Oh. In the warehouse, right before he knocked me out. Grobian shot me. I didn't feel it, just the blood pouring down my face. Where is he? Where's William Bysen?"

"We sort of have them, although the Bysen legal machine is moving into action, so I don't know how long I'll get to keep them. When I got here, they were trying a story out on the cop on duty in the emergency room, that you had hijacked one of the By-Smart semis and they'd fought you for it, which is how the truck got knocked over. The fire department crew that brought the three of you in objected that your hands and feet were tied, and Grobian said they'd done that to keep you from overpowering them. Want to comment?"

I shut my eyes; the glare from the overhead light hurt too much. "We live in a world where people seem willing to believe almost any lie they're told, no matter how ludicrous, as long as someone with family values is telling it. The Bysens prattle so much about family values, I suppose they can get the state's attorney and a judge to believe this one."

"Hey, Ms. W., don't be so cynical: you've got me on the case now. And the city garbagemen have some evidence that the Bysen story doesn't exactly explain."

I smiled at him in a muzzy, dopey way. "That's nice, Conrad, thanks."

The pain blockers kept carrying me off on their tide, but on my rides to the surface I told him about Billy and Josie, and as much as I could remember of my night at the warehouse, and he told me about my rescue.

Apparently, when the semi toppled over at the landfill, the city crews had sprung from their trucks and raced to the accident scene—as much voyeurs as Good Samaritans. It was then that one of them had caught sight of me, feebly flopping about the hillside. They'd called for help, and gotten a fire truck but no ambulance, so after the firemen freed Grobian and William from the tractor the three of us rode a hook and ladder together to the hospital.

I sort of remembered that; the pain from bouncing up Stony Island Avenue at top speed in a fire truck had woken me, and I had a dream-dazed memory of Grobian and William shouting at each other, blaming each other for the mess they were in. I guess it was only when they got to the hospital, and had to give a story to the police, that they'd decided to join forces and blame me for their mess.

I tried to stay awake enough to follow Conrad's story, but behind the pain meds my shoulders throbbed from being pulled from their sockets. My kidneys ached, my whole body, from head to toe, was one pulsing sore; after a while, I just let go of it all and went to sleep.

When I woke again, Conrad had left, but Lotty was there, along with Morrell. The hospital wanted to discharge me, and Lotty was taking me home with her.

"It's criminal to move you now, and I said so to the director, but their managed care owners decree how much care a battered body gets, and yours gets twelve hours." Lotty's black eyes flashed—I realized that she was only partly indignant on my behalf—she was furious that a hospital could pay more attention to their owners than to an important surgeon.

After his own recent injuries, Morrell knew what to bring for the battered body to wear home. He'd stopped at a fancy Oak Street boutique and bought me a warm-up suit made of a cashmere so soft it felt like kitten fur. He'd bought fleece-lined boots so I wouldn't have to deal with shoes and socks. As I dressed in a wobbly, lethargic way, I saw that my skin looked like an eggplant harvest, more purple than olive. On our way out, the nurse gave me a bag with my slime-crusted clothes. I was even more grateful to Morrell for keeping me from having to look at them this morning.

Morrell helped me into a wheelchair, and laid his cane in my lap so he could push me down the hall. Lotty walked alongside like a terrier, her fur bristling when she had to speak to someone on the staff about my discharge.

Not even my injuries could keep Lotty from treating the city streets like the course of the Grand Prix, but I was too dopey to worry about her near miss with a truck at Seventy-first Street.

Morrell rode with us as far as her apartment: he would take a cab back to Evanston from there. In the elevator going up, he said that the British Foreign Office had finally located Marcena's parents in India; they were flying into Chicago tonight, and would be staying with him.

"That's nice," I said, trying to summon the energy to be interested. "What about Don?"

"He's moving to the living room couch, but he'll go back to New York on Sunday." He traced a finger along the line of my head bandage. "Can you stay out of the wars for a few days, Hippolyte? Marcena is having her first skin graft on Monday; it would be nice not to have to worry about you as well."

"Victoria is not going anywhere," Lotty pronounced. "I'm ordering the doorman to carry her back upstairs to bed if he sees her in the lobby."

I laughed weakly, but I was fretting about Billy and Josie. Morrell asked if I would feel better if they went to stay with Mr. Contreras. "He's aching to do something, and if he had them to fuss over, it would help him not mind so much that you're staying here with Lotty."

"I don't know if he can keep them safe," I worried.

"For this weekend, Grobian, at any rate, will still be in custody. By Monday, believe it or not, you'll feel a lot stronger, and you'll be able to figure out a better plan."

I had to agree: I didn't have the strength to do anything else right now. I even had to agree to let Morrell send Amy Blount down to Mary Ann's to collect the runaway pair; I hated not looking after them myself, hated Morrell for adding I couldn't manage the world all by myself, so to stop trying.

I slept the rest of the day away. When I woke in the evening, Lotty brought me a bowl of her homemade lentil soup. I lay in her guest room, luxuriating in the clean room, the clean clothes, the peace of her loving care.

It wasn't until the next morning that she showed me Marcena's red recording pen. "I took your foul clothes to the laundry, my dear, and found this inside. I assumed you want to keep it?"

I couldn't believe it had still been on my body after all I'd gone through—or that Bysen and Grobian hadn't found it when they had me unconscious and in their power. I snatched it from her. "My God, yes, I want this."

47 OFFICE PARTY

I f the shock gives him a stroke and kills him, I'll be singing at his funeral."

William's thin fussy voice hung like a smear of soot in my office. Buffalo Bill's full cheeks were sunken. His eyes under their heavy brows were pale, watery, the uncertain eyes of a feeble old man, not the fierce eagle stare of the corporate dictator.

"You hear that, May Irene? He wants me dead? My own son wants me dead?"

His wife leaned across my coffee table to pat his hand. "We were too hard on him, Bill. He never could be as tough as you wanted him to be."

"I was too hard on him, so that means it's all right that he wants me dead?" His astonishment brought some of the color back into his face. "Since when did you sign up for that liberal swill, spare the rod, spoil the child?"

"I don't think Mrs. Bysen meant that," Mildred murmured.

"Mildred, for once, you let me speak for myself. Don't go interpreting me to my own husband, for heaven's sake. We've all heard the tape that Ms. Warshawski played; I think we can agree it's a sad chapter in our family life, but we are a family, we are strong, we will move past this. Linus has kept it out of the papers, bless him"—she directed a grateful look at the corporate counsel, sitting in one of the side chairs— "and I'm sure he'll help us work out an arrangement with Ms. Warshawski here."

I leaned back in my armchair. I was still tired, still sore around the arm sockets from having my arms lashed behind me for two hours. I had a couple of broken ribs, and my body still looked like a field of ripe eggplants, but I felt wonderful—clean, newborn, that euphoric sense you get when you know you're truly alive.

By the time Lotty came on the little recording pen, its battery was dead. She wouldn't let me leave her place to get a charger, but when I explained why I was so desperate to listen to it she relented enough to let Amy Blount bring my laptop over. When I hooked it up to my iBook, it sprang obediently to life and spilled its digital guts for me.

Thursday night at the warehouse, there had actually still been enough juice in it that it had recorded William, Grobian, and Jacqui. Grobian's shot at me echoed horrifyingly through Lotty's living room, followed by a satisfied exclamation from William that I hadn't heard at the time. The pen had died on the way from the landfill to the hospital; it only gave me part of Grobian's and William's quarrel, but I got enough of Grobian's highly colored language that I could really grow my vocabulary if I replayed it a few times.

After we downloaded it to my Mac, I asked Amy to make about thirty copies: I wanted to ensure they were spread far and wide, so that even the best efforts of Linus Rankin, or the Carnifice detectives, couldn't eliminate them all. I sent a bunch to my own lawyer, Freeman Carter, put some in my office safe, sent one to Conrad and another to a senior police officer who was a friend of my dad's, and, after debating it up and down with Amy and Morrell, finally sent one to Murray Ryerson at the *Herald-Star*. Murray was madly trying to persuade his bosses to let him go up against the Bysen money and power; whether they'd ever let him dig into the story was still up in the air.

In the meantime, the recording so bolstered my story that it forced the state's attorney—nervous about going up against Bysen money and power—into motion. Grobian and William had been charged on Friday with assaulting me, but were released almost at once on I-Bonds. On Monday, though, Conrad's team arrested them again, this time for murdering Bron.

The cops tracked Freddy to earth at his new girlfriend's place and charged him with second-degree murder in Frank Zamar's death—since he hadn't intended to set a fire, just to short out the wires. They arrested Aunt Jacqui as an accessory—which somehow seemed really fitting: if charges stuck, if she ended up in Dwight doing time, she could run a class on how to accessorize your wardrobe with a murder charge. William and Grobian made bail within hours, as did Aunt Jacqui, but poor old Freddy was left to the mercy of the public defender, without money for bail—he would probably spend not just Thanksgiving in Cook County, but Christmas and maybe Easter, given the speed with which the state brings people to trial.

When Freddy realized he was being hung out to dry by Pat Grobian, he started to sing like one of Mt. Ararat's choristers. He told Conrad about his meeting with Grobian in the warehouse, the one I'd seen, where Grobian ordered him to break into Bron's house to look for Marcena's recorder. He told Conrad about planting the little frog full of nitric acid at Fly the Flag. He even told Conrad about driving the Miata into the undergrowth below the Skyway for Grobian: he was bitter about that, because he thought Grobian should have given him the car in thanks for all his, Freddy's, hard work, but all he'd gotten out of his night's labors had been fifty dollars.

Conrad didn't tell me all this at the hospital, but when he came by Lotty's to ask me more questions, he filled in gaps in the story. He added that it was a source of pure pleasure to him to listen to Grobian and William turn on each other. "That's how they got that big old semi over on its side—they were arguing over whether William was really a weasel or Grobian was a thug—I kid you not, Ms. W., the two reenacted their fight for my benefit—and William grabbed the steering wheel, saying he was a big enough man to drive the truck. They fought for control of the

wheel and the truck went over. I love it, I really do, when the rich and famous carry on with the same attitude that my street punks do.

"By the way, that truck you rode in was Czernin's rig, or the one he'd
been driving the night he was whacked. Why Grobian didn't scrap it is
beyond me: we found Czernin's and the Love woman's blood on that
conveyor belt do-hingus, along with your own AB negative. Trust you to
have the weirdest blood on the planet."

I ignored that crack. "What about Aunt Jacqui? She was at the factory
with them Thursday night; where was she when the truck went over?"

"She'd driven back to Barrington Hills. Now she's saying that she was
acting under Buffalo Bill's orders. She says when she told him that
Zamar was welching on Fly the Flag's deal with By-Smart, Buffalo Bill
told her she needed to teach Zamar a lesson, that he used to do it all the
time in his younger days, until word got out on the street that no one
messed with By-Smart. If they're forgetting their lessons, we need to
teach them again, she claims the old Buffalo said something like that."

Conrad said Jacqui insisted that Buffalo Bill told her dealing with
Zamar was supposed to prove she was ready to sit at By-Smart's management table. With that bunch, I could believe anything of any of them. I
could hear the old man say it, going "hnnh, hnnh, hnnh," but if Jacqui
thought she was any match for the old buffalo she was either gutsy or
delusional.

Tuesday, when Lotty was in surgery, Morrell came by her apartment
to visit me. He'd been over at County Hospital to see Marcena, who was
recovering from her first skin graft. She was in intensive care, but she was
finally conscious, and seemed to be recovering well—she was alert, with
no signs of brain damage from her own ordeal in the By-Smart semi.

Having gone through the same harrowing ride as she had, with the
semi's hand conveyor belt rolling over me, I felt a more personal relief at
her recovery than I might have before. She couldn't remember the moments leading up to her accident, let alone the accident itself, but now
that he knew where to look Conrad had sent a forensic team into Fly the
Flag. They figured that Marcena had jumped clear of the falling forklift,

but that Bron hadn't; the fall broke his neck. Marcena was probably knocked cold when she hit the ground, with the rest of her injuries coming during the ride to the marsh.

Another point that we could only speculate on was Marcena's scarf, the one Mitch had found that had led him to her. The forensics team guessed it was coming loose from her neck when Grobian tossed her into the trailer; perhaps it got caught in the doors and then was snagged on the fence when the truck left the road to go cross-country to the landfill.

These were just little points, the ones that I worried over. I had a private belief, or wish, that Marcena regained consciousness and left a deliberate trail: the scarf had been torn, with a big piece on the fence, and a smaller piece that Mitch found first. I liked to think she'd taken some kind of active steps to try to save herself, that she hadn't lain passively in the truck, waiting for death. The idea of anyone's helplessness terrifies me, my own most of all.

"It's possible, Victoria," Lotty said, when I talked it over with her. "The human body is an amazing instrument, the mind more so. I would never discount any possibility of remarkable strength and contriving."

That same Tuesday, I started picking up the reins of my business again. Among dozens of messages of good wishes from friends and reporters, and a van full of flowers from my most important client ("Delighted to know you're not dead yet, Darraugh," the card read), my answering service reported at least twenty calls from Buffalo Bill, demanding a meeting: he wanted to know "what fabrications I was filling his grandson's head with, and straighten out once and for all what I could and could not say about the family."

"Boy won't come home," the Buffalo said to me when I called him back Tuesday afternoon. "Says you've told him all kinds of lies about me, about the business."

"Careful with the words you toss around, Mr. Bysen. You accuse me of lying, and I could add a slander suit to your family's legal troubles. And I don't have any power over Billy—he's deciding for himself what he will and won't do. When I talk to him, I'll see if I can get him to agree to meet with you—and that's all I'll do."

Later that same afternoon, Morrell came by with Billy—and Mr. Contreras and the dogs. Josie had gone back to school—under protest, according to her mother. I myself had canceled basketball practice yesterday, telling the team I'd have to let them know when I was strong enough to return. They'd responded with a get-well card big enough to cover the wall in Lotty's spare room, filled with encouraging messages in English and Spanish.

Amy Blount had already filled me in on Billy and Josie, because she hadn't been able to persuade them to leave Mary Ann's place when she drove down there on Friday. Rose Dorrado had been more forceful, dragging Josie home and compelling her to return to school.

As Amy described it, the reunion between Rose and her daughter was a predictable combination of joy and fury ("You were here, not two miles from me, clean, well fed, safe, and me, I have not slept at night for worry!").

Billy, shell-shocked by his father's behavior, stayed on at Mary Ann's. He'd called his grandmother, and spoken briefly to his mother, but he wouldn't go home. He didn't even want to go back to Pastor Andrés: he thought the minister shared the blame in Frank Zamar's death because of the pressure he'd put on Zamar to back out of his contract with By-Smart.

The main reason Billy wouldn't leave Mary Ann's, though, was because he didn't have the energy to pack up and move one more time. He'd been at the pastor's, he'd been at Josie's, and then at Mary Ann's, all in the last ten days. He was too upset to organize himself mentally into another move—and my coach definitely liked having him living in the apartment with her. Now that he wasn't hiding, he walked the dog three or four times a day, and he brought all his intensity to studying Latin with her. Its rules, its complex grammar, seemed to be a haven for him right now, a place of purity, regularity.

On Tuesday, in Lotty's apartment, he tried to explain some of that to me, and some of his reluctance to see his family again. "I love them all, maybe not Dad, at least, I find it hard to forgive him for killing April's dad and Mr. Zamar—and even if Freddy and Bron made the plant burn down, I think it was really because of Aunt Jacqui, and—and Dad, that Mr. Zamar is dead. I even love Mom, and, of course, my grandparents, they're great people, they really are, but—but I think they're short-sighted."

He curled his hands in Peppy's fur and spoke to her, not to me. "It's funny, they have such a big vision for the company, how to make it an international giant, but the only people they really recognize as—as human—are themselves. They can't see that Josie is a person, and her family, and all the people who work in South Chicago. If someone wasn't born a Bysen, they don't count. If they are Bysens, it doesn't matter what they do, because they're part of the family. Like Grandma, she is truly against abortion in every way, she gives tons of money to antiabortion groups, but when Candy, when my sister, got pregnant, Grandma whisked her off to a clinic—they were mad at Candy, but Grandma got her an abortion that they'd never let Josie have, not that Josie's pregnant." He turned beet red. "We—we did listen to what you said, about—well, being careful—but it's just an example of what I mean about how my family sees the world."

"Your grandfather wants to talk to you. If we did it in my office, would you come?"

He worked furiously on Peppy's neck. "I guess. I guess."

So the day before Thanksgiving, much against Lotty's wishes, I went to my office for a meeting with Bysen and his retinue. For once, I had enough people in my office to make me glad of my huge space. Billy's mother was there with his grandparents, Uncle Roger, and Linus Rankin, the family lawyer. Jacqui's husband, Uncle Gary, had also shown up. Of course, Mildred was in attendance, gold portfolio in hand.

My team included Morrell and Amy Blount. Mr. Contreras insisted on being present, with the dogs—"just in case those Bysens try anything on you in broad daylight; I wouldn't put nothing past them." Marcena's parents also attended, curious to see the people who had nearly killed their daughter. I'd had to borrow five chairs from my warehouse mate's studio so everyone could sit down.

In the middle, stubbornly sitting next to Peppy after giving his grandmother a hug, was Billy. He wore an old flannel work shirt and blue jeans, setting himself apart deliberately from his family's gray business suits.

When Billy's grandmother said she was sure Linus could work something out with me, Mr. Contreras bristled at once. "Your son darn near killed my girl here. You think you can come in here and wave your big fat wallet around and 'work something out' with her? Like what? Give her back her health? Give the Loves back their daughter's skin? Give that poor sick girl on Cookie—Vicki—on Ms. Warshawski's basketball team her daddy back? What's going through your head?"

Mrs. Bysen frowned at him, sadly, as if at one of her grandchildren who was fighting at mealtime. "I've never involved myself in my husband's business, but I know he works with hundreds of small companies. We both admire Miss Warshawski's courage and her tenacity; we're sorry our son was so—well, did what he did. His behavior doesn't reflect our values, I assure you. I think if my husband started giving some of his investigative work to Miss Warshawski, she'd find herself amply rewarded as her business gained in importance."

"And in return?" I asked politely.

"Oh, in return you'd get rid of all those copies of that silly tape. We don't want that out in public, it doesn't help anyone."

"And I can probably get it suppressed as evidence, if William ever comes to trial at all," Linus Rankin added helpfully.

I rolled up my sweater sleeves and looked thoughtfully at my purple flesh. I had let Morrell photograph me, although I'd hated it, hated the sense of exposure. Now I didn't feel any embarrassment, didn't say anything, just let Grandma and Rankin look at my swollen, discolored skin.

"She doesn't need that kind of help," Billy said. "She isn't about money, she—Grandma, if you really knew her, you'd know, even though she's not a Christian, she lives her life by all the values you taught me: she's honest, she looks after her friends, she—she's so full of courage—"

"Billy." I laughed in embarrassment. "That's a beautiful testimonial. I hope I live long enough to deserve a quarter of it. Mrs. Bysen, here's the problem: that recording doesn't belong to me, it belongs to Marcena

Love. I can't speak for her. But I can make a little suggestion to you and your husband. You weren't involved in William's exploits. Stay away from them now. Even if Jacqui is right, that Buffalo Bill told her to bring Frank Zamar at Fly the Flag into line—that it was her test to see if she was worthy of the By-Smart management team—he didn't specifically order anyone to set the plant on fire and kill Mr. Zamar, or to kill Bron Czernin. At least, I don't think he did, did he?"

I gave Bysen and Linus Rankin my most brilliant smile. "So here's my modest proposal. Don't fight Sandra Czernin's workers' comp claim for Bron's death. It should be the full $250,000 payout: that would take care of April Czernin's medical bills, and maybe give her a nest egg for college. Second, get Rose Dorrado a job in your operation at the same wage she was making with Frank Zamar. She's an experienced supervisor. Hire her full-time, so she gets whatever measly health benefits your full-time workers get. And, finally, fund the basketball program down at Bertha Palmer High School, that $55,000 I came asking you for a month ago."

"Oh, yes, cut a dollar bill into forty thousand pieces, or whatever fool idea you had, hnnh?" Bysen said, some of his bluster returning. "And for that truck driver, even though he was stepping out on his marriage vows, I'm supposed to cut another bill into a quarter-million pieces. That's like saying I should give people money for sins—"

"Now, dear." May Irene put a reproving hand on her husband's knee. "And what would you do for us, Miss Warshawski, if we did that for you?"

"I'd support your statement that your son and daughter-in-law acted behind your back, that you weren't a party to all that bloodshed on the South Side."

"That's nothing, young woman!" Linus Rankin said. "That's ridiculous!"

I leaned back in my chair again. "It's the deal on the table. Take it or leave it, I don't care, but I'm not going to dicker over it."

"It doesn't matter, Miss War-sha-sky," Billy burst out, his cheeks flaming. "Because I'll pay April's bills if they fight Bron's work comp claim, and I'll put the money up for the basketball program. I'd have to sell some stock, and I need my trustees' permission to do that, but if they won't allow it, well, I guess a bank would lend me money, because they know I'll get my shares when I'm twenty-seven. I guess I can pay interest that long."

"That will make a wonderful headline." I smiled at him. " 'Bysen Heir Borrows Money to Meet Grandpa's Moral Obligations.' You all go home and think it over. Tomorrow is Thanksgiving—you can call me on Monday with your decision, after the long weekend."

Uncle Gary thought he would prove he was the tough son by arguing with me, but I said, "Good-bye, Gary. I need a rest. You go on now, all of you."

The Bysen party filed out, muttering to each other. I heard Buffalo Bill snap at Gary, "Jacqui was bad news from day one. Claimed to be a Christian, hnnh, I guess if you'd been in Eden, you'd have listened to the snake, too, because—"

May Irene cut him off. "We have enough worries now, dear, let's cherish what's left of our family."

My team stayed a little longer, hashing over the meeting, trying to guess which way the Bysens would jump. Finally, Morrell and the Loves left to visit Marcena. Amy was driving down to St. Louis to spend Thanksgiving with her family. I got up on my wobbly legs and hobbled out with Mr. Contreras and the dogs, heading to my own home for the first time in a week. We were going up to Evanston tomorrow, to have Thanksgiving with Lotty at Max Loewenthal's house, but this afternoon I was glad to fall into my own bed.

48 DANCING RHINO

Morrell and I joined a cast of thousands at Max's for Thanksgiving dinner. He always has a big crowd—his daughter flies in from New York with her husband and children, his and Lotty's musician friends show up early and stay late, and Lotty always invites stray interns from her service at Beth Israel. Mr. Contreras came this year, happy to escape his petulant daughter's house. As soon as Max heard about the Loves, he opened his doors to them, and even suggested I invite Billy and Mary Ann McFarlane—he hated to think of Billy, estranged from his family, spending Thanksgiving alone. But Billy was helping Pastor Andrés serve turkey dinners to the homeless, and Mary Ann said her neighbor was bringing dinner over and she'd be just fine without me.

Marcena was still in the hospital, of course, but she was recovering fast and her spirits were good. I'd gone to visit her before driving up to Max's. I'd run into her parents in the ICU. The Loves had been silent and anxious since their arrival, but Marcena's rapid improvement was making them almost effervescent.

We all had to put on protective masks and gowns before going into Marcena's room, so as to make sure we didn't spread germs into her vulnerable new skin. Her parents left me alone with her, since she couldn't have more than two visitors at a time.

I tiptoed into the room. Marcena's head was shaved and bandaged; she had a fading bruise on her left cheekbone, and her body was hidden in a kind of box with sheets draped over it, to protect her new skin, but her eyes held a hint of their usual spark.

Marcena pointed out that we were matching ghouls, with our shaved heads and bruises. "We should have done this for Halloween, not for your Thanksgiving Day dinner. What was that thing that skinned me?"

"A hand-operated conveyor belt," I said. "Didn't you ever see it in Bron's trailer? They use them for getting big loads on and off; it should have been tied up, but they were either careless or hoping it would do serious damage. Although they planned for you to be dumped at the landfill, as they did me—it was just Mr. William, ineffectual idiot, who took you to the golf course by mistake."

"And Mitch was my hero, leading you to the rescue, Morrell says. The hospital is rotten not to let dogs in. I'd like to give him a big, slurpy kiss. How come you got away with less damage than me?" Her eyes might sparkle, but her speech was labored; among the paraphernalia around her bed was a morphine pump.

I shrugged awkwardly. "Luck of the draw. You took a horrible knock on the head when the forklift went over; you couldn't maneuver the way I was able to."

I asked if she remembered anything about her time at the factory, such as how she got clear of the falling forklift, but she said her last coherent memory was driving up behind Fly the Flag in Billy's Miata—she couldn't even remember who all had been present—if Aunt Jacqui had been there, or Buffalo Bill himself.

I told her I had her recording pen, but wanted to hang onto it, at least until we saw how the endless legal battles were going to shape up. "The state may try to impound it. I've actually put it in a bank vault to keep the Bysen mafia from stealing it out of my office, but, of course, their legal team is trying to suppress the recordings altogether."

"You can keep it if you let me have a copy of the contents. Morrell says that William and Pat Grobian were arrested for Bron's death. Is there any chance they'll be found guilty?"

I made an impatient gesture. "The whole legal process is going to be a long and dreary battle; I'll be amazed if it even comes to trial before Billy is married with grown grandchildren of his own . . . Marcena, how much of this business did you know, before Bron's death. Did you know he was sabotaging the factory?"

Underneath her shroud of bandages she blushed faintly. "I got too caught up in it—it's why I always get the best in-depth stories wherever I go, because I do get caught up in my subjects' lives. Morrell says I manipulate the news I'm covering, but I don't. If I take part, I don't make suggestions or pass judgment, I just watch—it's no different than Morrell going on a raid with a tribal chief in Afghanistan."

She stopped to catch her breath, then continued in a more muted voice, "That factory owner—what was his name, Zabar? Oh, right, Zamar—he wasn't supposed to die. And when Bron decided to use that bloke, that gang member, Freddy, I did say Freddy wasn't the strongest filament in the bulb, but Bron said he couldn't go into the factory himself, because his kid's best friend's mum worked there, and she'd recognize him if she happened to see him. But I did help make the little gadget over at his house—his kid was at school, his wife was at work."

Her eyes sparkled again at memory; it didn't take much imagination to follow her mind down its track, to sex in Sandra's bed while the wife was standing in front of the By-Smart cash register. She'd helped construct a murder weapon, but what she remembered was the sexual excitement. Maybe she'd feel something else when she recovered: she faced two more major surgeries before she could go home.

She saw some of what I was thinking in my face. "You are a bit of a prude, aren't you, Vic? You take a lot of chances yourself—don't tell me you don't know that adrenaline kick from skating close to the edge."

I fingered my own head bandage reflexively. "Adrenaline thrills? Maybe that's my shortcoming: I take risks so I can get the job done—I don't take jobs so I can run risks."

She turned her head aside, impatient with me, or abashed—I'd never understand how she thought.

"What about those extra meetings with Buffalo Bill?" I asked. "He confess to all his dirty business practices?"

"Not in so many words. But a few admiring comments and he talked more than he realized. I'd say a streak of paranoia runs through the man, not enough to derail him, but the fact that he sees the world as his enemy means he's always on the attack, which I guess has fueled his success. We had a lot of 'hnnh, hnnhing' over the necessity to do things like pile garbage in the parking lots of smaller shops to get customers to agree that they'd be smart to 'By-Smart.'"

"So you've got yourself quite a nice story," I said politely.

She grinned weakly. "Even though I don't remember the climax, it didn't come out too badly. Except for poor Bron. He was so greedy he couldn't imagine there'd be a big fat stick of dynamite inside that carrot they were dangling in front of him."

"Greedy isn't the word I'd use," I objected. "He was desperate for a way to help his daughter, so he was going to shut a blind eye to the risk he might be running."

"Maybe, maybe." Her color was fading; she lowered the hospital bed and shut her eyes. "Sorry, I'm weak as a cat, I keep dropping off."

"You'll recover fast when you're out," I said. "You'll be back in Fallujah or Kigali, or whatever the next war zone is, in no time."

"Hnnh," she murmured. "Hnnh, hnnh."

Back in my car, I could hardly summon the energy to drive. Prude, she'd called me. Was that really me? Next to Marcena, I felt like some large slow object, maybe a rhinoceros, trying to do a pirouette around a greyhound. I had an impulse to go home and spend the day in bed, watching football and feeling seriously sorry for myself and my beat-up body, but when I got home the old man was packed up and ready to go to Max's. He had a large casserole filled with his wife's recipe for sweet-potato pudding. He had brushed the dogs until their coats shone, and tied orange bows around their necks—Max had said the dogs could come as long as they behaved and as long as I repaired any damage Mitch did to his garden.

In the evening, when we'd eaten the way one always does on these holidays, and I was in the garden with the dogs, Morrell limped out to join me. He didn't need his cane for short periods now, a hopeful sign.

With the crowd inside, and me watching the football game while Morrell talked politics with Marcena's father, we hadn't really spent any time together today. The sky was already dark, but the garden was protected by a high wall that kept the fiercest of the lake winds at bay. We sat under the trellis where a few late-blooming roses produced a feeble sweetness. I tossed sticks for the dogs to keep Mitch from digging.

"I've been jealous of Marcena." I was astonished to hear myself say that.

"Darling, not to be indelicate, but a Siberian tiger in the living room is less obvious than you are."

"She takes so many risks, she's done so much!"

Morrell was astounded. "Victoria, if you took any more risks, you'd have been dead before I ever met you. What do you want? Skydiving without a parachute? Climb Mount Everest without oxygen?"

"Insouciance," I said. "I do things because people need me, or I think they do—Billy, Mary Ann, the Dorrados. Marcena does things out of a spirit of adventure. It's the spirit, that's what's different between us."

He held me more tightly. "Yes, I can see that—she must look as though she's free, and you feel too tightly bound. I don't know what to say about that, but—I like knowing I can count on you."

"But I'm tired of people counting on me." I told him the image I'd had, the rhino and the greyhound.

He gave a loud shout of laughter but took my hand. "Vic, you're beautiful in motion, or even when you're lying still—not that that happens very often. I love your energy, and the grace you have when you run. For Christ's sake, stop being jealous of Marcena. I can't imagine you casually helping Bron Czernin rig a lethal device in his back kitchen and then not telling the cops because you didn't want to ruin your big story. And it's not because you're so damn conscientious, it's because you use your brain, okay?"

"Okay," I said, not really convinced, but ready to drop the subject.

"Speaking of jealousy, why does Sandra Czernin have it in for you?" Morrell asked.

I felt my face turning crimson in the dark garden. "When we were in high school, I helped play a very nasty practical joke on her. My cousin Boom-Boom invited her to the senior prom. My mom had just died, my dad was kind of clinging to me, didn't want me dating, and Boom-Boom had said I could go with him. But when I found out he was taking Sandra and I'd be like a fifth wheel, I really lost it. We'd already had some disagreements, she and I, so the prom felt like a total betrayal to me. She slept around, all us girls knew that, but I wouldn't acknowledge that Boom-Boom did, too. She used to be pretty, in a soft, Persian cat kind of way, and I suppose, well, never mind that. Anyway, I was furious, and—and my basketball team and I, we stole her underpants out of her locker when she was in the pool—we used to have a swim program at Bertha Palmer. The night before the prom, we broke into the gym and shinnied up the ropes and hung her pants from the ceiling, with a big red *S* drawn on them, next to Boom-Boom's letter jacket. When Boom-Boom found out it was me, he didn't speak to me for six months."

Morrell was roaring with laughter.

"It's not funny!" I shouted.

"Oh, it is, Warshawski, it is. You are such a pit dog. Maybe you don't have a spirit of insouciance, but whatever your spirit is—it keeps a lot of people on their toes."

I figured he meant it as a compliment, so I tried to take it as one. We sat in the garden until I was shivering in the chill air. After a while, we went back to his place with the dogs—a Loop-bound guest volunteered to drive Mr. Contreras home. We huddled in bed much of the weekend, two sore and fragile bodies, bringing each other such comfort as this mortal life affords.

On Monday, I had a call from Mildred, the Bysen family factotum, to say they had cut a check for Sandra Czernin and were messengering it down to her. "You might like to know that Rose Dorrado started work this morning as a supervisor in our Ninety-fifth Street store. And Mr.

Bysen feels he'd like to make a special gesture to Bertha Palmer High, since that's where he went to school. He's going to build a new gym this summer, and, next winter, he'll install coaches for both the girls' and the boys' basketball teams. We'll be holding a press conference on this down at the school this afternoon. We're creating a whole new program for teens called the 'Bysen Promise Program.' It will help teens keep a Christian focus through athletics."

"That's wonderful news," I said. "I know Mr. Bysen's Christian practices will be highly regarded on the South Side."

She started to ask me what I meant by that but decided to change the subject, just asking for my fax number so she could send me the complete details.

The press conference took place right before Monday's basketball practice. The girls were so excited that it proved impossible afterward to keep them focused on their workout. I finally sent them home early, but told them they'd have to have a double practice on Thursday to make up for it.

The Bysen Promise Program wouldn't start formally until next fall, which meant I was stuck with coaching the team for the rest of the season. To my surprise, I found I was glad to stay with them.

During the dreary winter months, Billy flew to Korea to see his sister. He brought her home with him, and they bought one of the little houses Pastor Andrés had been helping build. I had the feeling that Billy and Josie's passion might have run its course. He was such a scrupulous kid, he continued to look after her, to see that she worked hard on her academics, but his energy now was turned to a program he and his sister were running called "the Kid for Kids," to provide tutoring and job training for young people in the neighborhood.

Right after New Year's, April Czernin had her cardioverter defibrillator implanted. It would be several months before she could return to school, but she did show up for the Lady Tigers home games, where the other girls treated her as a kind of mascot. Celine and Sancia, the cocaptains, were very solemn about dedicating their games to her.

Sandra used part of the rest of Bron's indemnity check to build a small addition to her house, so her parents could move in and help look after April. She also bought a used Saturn, but the rest of the money she squirreled away for April. She knew she had me to thank for getting her the money so fast, and without any legal battles—or fees—but it didn't make her any less venomous when we ran into each other at the high school.

During the winter, I also kept having to make depositions to the various lawyers involved in the legal battles over By-Smart's operations. They were following a predictable course of discovery, investigation, motions, continuances—I didn't know if a judge would set a trial date in my lifetime.

I was outraged to learn that Grobian had actually gone back to work at the warehouse: Billy, flushing painfully, said his grandfather admired Grobian for his forcefulness. William, on the other hand, was taking an extended leave of absence: Buffalo Bill couldn't forgive his son's wish that he have a stroke and die. And Gary had begun divorce proceedings against Aunt Jacqui—another legal battle that was likely to go on for a few decades. She wasn't going to relinquish those Bysen billions at all easily.

The only good thing, really, to come out of the By-Smart carnage was a thaw in my relationship with Conrad. After basketball practice, we'd meet sometimes for a cup of coffee or a whiskey. I never told Morrell about it—Conrad and I were old friends—we could have a drink now and then. After all, it wasn't like he was staying with me the way Marcena was staying at Morrell's while she recovered her strength. Even if Morrell preferred my conscientious spirit to her insouciance, I didn't much like finding her propped up in the living room every time I went over.

If this were Disney, if this were that kind of fairy tale, I'd end by saying that the Lady Tigers went on to win the sectional and the state. I'd say they played their hearts out for me, their battered coach, and for Mary Ann, whose funeral we attended together late in February.

But in my world, things like that don't happen. My girls won five games during the whole season, where last year they had won two. That was all the victory I was going to get.

I had dinner with Lotty the day after the Lady Tigers' season ended, and told her how discouraged I felt. She frowned in disapproval, or disagreement.

"Victoria, you know my grandfather, my father's father, was a very observant Jew."

I nodded, surprised: she rarely talked about her dead family.

"During the terrible winter we spent together in 1938, the fifteen of us crowded into two rooms in the Vienna ghetto, he gathered all his grandchildren together and told us that the rabbis say when you die and present yourself before the Divine Justice, you will be asked four questions: Were you fair and honest in your business dealings? Did you spend loving time with your family? Did you study Torah? And last, but most important, did you live in hope for the coming of the Messiah? We were living then without food, let alone hope, but he refused to live hopelessly, my Zeyde Radbuka.

"Me, I don't believe in God, let alone the coming of the Messiah. But I did learn from my zeyde that you must live in hope, the hope that your work can make a difference in the world. Yours does, Victoria. You cannot wave a wand and clear away the rubble of the dead steel mills, or the broken lives in South Chicago. But you went back to your old home, you took three girls who never thought about the future and made them want to have a future, made them want to get a college education. You got Rose Dorrado a job so she can support her children. If a Messiah ever does come, it will only be because of people like you, doing these small, hard jobs, making small changes in this hard world."

It was a small comfort, and that night at dinner it felt like a cold one. But as the Chicago winter lingered, I found myself warmed by her grandfather's hope.